ETEKA

RISE OF THE IMAMBA

Ben Hinson

MUSINGS PRESS™

ETEKA: Rise of the Imamba
By Benjamin Hinson-Ekong
www.benhinson.com

Musings Press, LLC.
New York, NY. Houston, TX.

Character images and front cover ideation by Ben Hinson

Front cover and character illustration artwork executed by Deryl Braun
http://deryl-braun-worx.de/

The Musings Press tree logo is a trademark of Musings Press, LLC.

Eteka: Rise of the Imamba©
ISBN-10: 0-692-47012-3
ISBN-13: 978-0-692-47012-1

Library of Congress Control Number: 2015909611

Printed in the United States of America.

CONTENTS

In loving memory of my father, Mr. John "Eteka" Ekong

PROLOGUE

Her blood covered his arms and chest, his singlet drenched with her ebbing life. He carried her, running as fast as he could through the dark and abandoned warehouse somewhere in Abuja, Nigeria. His heart pounded, and the African heat gave him a headache that narrowed his field of vision to only the dying woman in his arms, and a portion of the dim warehouse. He had to stop the bleeding, but they were right behind him and he couldn't stop. He tore his eyes away from her and kept running. Blood bubbled from the hole in her neck, pulsing in time to her slowing heart. His powerful arms clutched her close as he desperately searched for a safe place to set her down and wrap a piece of his shirt around her neck, to slow the bleeding. They were both sticky from the heat, and he could feel her heart skipping beats, winding down the clock of her lifetime.

In the distance, he heard the BMW and the stolen motorcycles screech to a halt. Car doors opened, and footsteps began to approach the warehouse. The two of them were out of time. He was scared—not of the approaching thugs, but because he felt life leaving his lover's body, the woman he had just started to know. The only beautiful thing in his life now lay dying in his arms, her skin swiftly losing its usual golden glow. She choked on her own blood as she coughed, and looked up at him with terror in her eyes.

Climbing more stairs, he found a pillar in a concealed corner of the warehouse. The thugs were close. He heard them yelling insults and taunts in the local dialects of Yoruba, Igbo, and Nigerian pidgin English. From their footsteps, he guessed that there were at least four of them. He wanted to plan his defense, but—

Setting his lover against the pillar, he ripped off a piece of his sleeve and wrapped it around her neck. No cell phone on him to call for help. The clip in his Taurus PT-92 was only good for two more shots. Nowhere to run. Footsteps echoed up the stairs. His pursuers were only a few feet away.

"Please don't leave…" he whispered as he held her close. She was still beautiful. A tear rolled down his cheek, and with a heavy heart, he knew his time with her was about to end. She tried to respond but was unable to as her blood flowed from her mouth and neck onto his arms. Still, she managed a lopsided smile.

The thugs were in the room now. His adrenaline spiked—he had to move quickly. He took one last look at her, then spun around to face the men.

In his mind he told her he had always loved her, because there was no time to do it with his lips.

Things had not always been like this.

PEER PRESSURE

The Danakil Desert. Northeast Ethiopia, Africa. 1967.

On a hot August afternoon, a group of soldiers stood in a circle, deep within the Danakil desert. Within the circle, two dark-skinned men, drenched with sweat, faced each other over clenched fists. The desert heat had left all the men surrounding the two fighters with sweat stains blooming through their shirts. There was a blue-collar smell to the group, the smell of tough labor in harsh conditions. Some tents and two trucks could be seen in the distance, and a few yards away from the tents, other soldiers fired rifles at a target range. The soldiers were not uniformly attired or even of the same race. It was easily apparent that they were a collection from different units. One unit sported dark blue jerseys, khaki shorts, and red felt hats—they comprised the majority of the men there. The other unit wore grey camouflage fatigues and black berets, members of a brotherhood called the Imamba. Not much was known about the camouflage-clad unit, save their expertise with guerrilla warfare tactics and their well-earned reputation as brutal mercenaries. The other men in the group belonged to a rogue surviving regiment of the King's African Rifles.[1] Most of the KAR units in Ethiopia were of African or Indian descent, and the few whites among them were officers—in this case, numbering no more than three. These officers sat by a tent on a nearby dune with an imposing African man clad in the Imamba camouflage fatigues. Aviator glasses hid his eyes, and a full beard disguised the lower half of his face. The white officers, conscious of maintaining their superiority in front of their multiracial troops, still managed to treat their guest with an air of deference. The four men sat in relative comfort, watching the circle of soldiers cheer on the two fighters.

The words the soldiers shouted were indecipherable, each voice overlapping as the two men in the circle stared each other down. One of the men was gigantic, well over 6'5". A KAR soldier, his massive thighs stretched his khaki shorts. He had a round, pudgy face, a barrel chest, mottled, dark skin, and fists the size of melons. His short-sleeved shirt was unbuttoned, and he breathed heavily as he edged toward his opponent. His opponent, a clean-cut man with a trimmed moustache and ebony skin, was an Imamba fighter. He'd rolled his camouflage fatigues halfway up his arms, revealing sinewy biceps. The Imamba calmly waited as the giant approached, sweat dripping off his brow in the murderous heat. Only his eyes moved, darting from the large man's hands to his feet, calculating. The large man grunted, stepped to the left, and launched a powerful left hook at his opponent's face. The Imamba deftly evaded the

---

[1] The King's African Rifles (KAR) was a collection of battalions made up of native East Africans who fought for the British Empire in East Africa from 1902 until independence in the 1950s/'60s.

punch and delivered a lightning-quick two-hit combo: a sharp jab to the chin followed by a front kick, delivered with exacting precision to the same spot. The large man reeled back, dropping to one knee. The crowd let out a loud cheer as the Imamba circled his opponent before settling into another fighting stance.

"You're very fast," the large man growled in a thick East African accent as he stood up. "However, you cannot beat me."

The Imamba said nothing, his eyes following the large man. The giant moved slowly toward him, watching for sudden movements. The Imamba remained still, studying his prey. Suddenly, the large man feinted left and threw a right hook. The Imamba parried, but the impact from the blow knocked him into some soldiers. They shoved him back into the circle.

"You see, you cannot defeat a king. I am king of this place, and soon I will be king of everything, including my country and Britain. It is my destiny. Why do you think these white men are here?" the man said in his deep voice as he gestured to the officers sitting by the tent. "They know who I am, and they have heard of my power, and soon you will understand it as well. I will crush you like a cockroach."

The Imamba remained silent as the soldiers cheered. He watched the sweat on the large man's head glisten in the bright African sun. His arm still hurt where he had blocked his opponent's punch, and he knew he had to be careful of this giant's strength. Without warning—and with unnerving quickness—the large man

JUDAS

"I WILL CRUSH YOU
LIKE A COCKROACH."

ETEKA
RISE OF THE IMAMBA

attempted a tackle, which the Imamba sidestepped, eliciting a loud cheer from the crowd.

"I know you're scared, that's why you keep running," the large man taunted as he approached again. The Imamba remained still, waiting for the large man to give him an opening.

It came.

The large man tried to feint once more, stepping to the left before throwing a ferocious right hook at the Imamba's face. The Imamba ducked, throwing the large man off balance and giving him the opening he needed: the right side of the large man's face. In a split second, the Imamba centered himself, spun, and delivered a devastating roundhouse kick that snapped the large man's head back with sickening force.

The giant lost his balance as blood left his head. His eyelids fluttered and he hit the ground with a loud thump.

The soldiers cheered as he fell, and the Imamba calmly stepped back into another fighting stance, waiting. With blood gushing from his nose, the giant tried to regain his balance before giving up and rolling over onto his side. The soldiers let out another cheer and gathered around the Imamba, congratulating him as he made his way over to the other man to help him up.

"Strength is no match for speed and precision, just as power is no match for wisdom," the Imamba said with a grin. Medics walked over with water for both fighters.

"You just got lucky. And you didn't beat me," the giant replied groggily, pouring water over his head. The Imamba handed him a second bottle of water in grudging acknowledgment of his tenacity. A kick like that would have knocked most men unconscious.

"I didn't? Last time I checked, you were the one on the ground, not me."

The large man grinned.

"A man is not beaten 'til he is dead, and you did not kill me. If you want to beat me, you will have to kill me, and that is something no man can do," he replied.

"I wasn't trying to kill you."

"Well, you should have. As it is, I have won."

"How so?"

"Like I said, it is either you kill me or you lose. I told you that I am the boss around here, and those are the rules."

The Imamba chuckled as he drank some water and washed his face. The desert heat combined with the sparring had left both men sweating profusely, and the cool water felt good.

"Whatever you say, my large friend who makes the rules. What's your name?"

"Here, they call me Judas. What is your name?"

"I can't tell you," the Imamba replied as he took another swig of water.

"But I told you my name."

"You didn't have to," the Imamba replied as he walked toward the officers' tent and the bearded Imamba.

"My friend," Judas called after the Imamba. "You know, I could use a man like you when I return to my country."

"And which country is that?" the Imamba replied, pausing.

"Those details can come later, if you are interested. I could use a man with your skills. I could make you rich."

The Imamba grinned at Judas. The bright, hot sun made their dark skin glitter like chips of onyx strewn against the desert sand.

"After what you did to Jesus, I think I'm better off where I am. Thanks for the offer," he replied, resuming his walk toward the tent. Judas watched him leave, his jaw clenched. After a measure, he strode back to the firing range with his fellow KAR soldiers.

The British officers clapped in praise of the Imamba's performance as he approached the tent. The other Imamba just shook his head, chuckling.

"Good show. I've never seen anything like that. Those fighting moves were quite impressive," one of the officers said.

"Thank you."

"What's your name?" the second KAR officer asked. The Imamba glanced at his partner, who nodded imperceptibly.

"I am Yisa."

"Do you think it would be possible to teach our troops to fight like that, Yisa? We would be indebted," the first officer asked.

"He cannot," the bearded Imamba replied without looking at the men.

"And why not, Oga?" the second white officer asked.

"Because that's not what we came here for, and we are being paid less for our services than the rate we agreed to."

"Oh. Well, that's a shame. Anyhow, I must congratulate you and your men for a job well done in South Africa. Our superiors in England are quite pleased," the third KAR officer said.

"When do we get our money?" the Imamba leader asked.

"We've already made the appropriate arrangements with Omega. Your money should be in your accounts."

"Good."

"Who is that giant I was fighting?" Yisa asked, nodding in Judas's direction.

"Ah, Judas. He is the main reason we are here, but we cannot talk about him," the third KAR officer said with a smile as they all watched Judas bark orders at the other men in the distance.

"And why can't we talk about him?" asked Oga.

"Because, as you yourself said, Oga, that's not what you came here for," the officer replied.

The other KAR officers laughed at their comrade's wit while Oga remained silent. Even Yisa smiled slightly as he stared at Judas's huge silhouette in the distance. The British officer was right—it was none of their business. In their line of work, a big mouth could get you killed.

"Well, we have things to do," Oga said as he stood up. "Tomorrow we will go over the details of the mission. Good day, gentlemen."

"Good day," the KAR officers replied, and both Imamba officers headed to their tents.

The Danakil Desert was home to what the locals called the "fire wind"—a sweltering combination of deadly heat and swirling sand that felt like a blast from the open doors of a furnace. In this noxious environment of open lava rifts and salt pools, men grew as deadly as scorpions, unforgiving, and conscious of small slights.

The two Imamba walked in silence across a stone field to their tents, where four more Imamba sat basking in the setting sun. As Yisa and Oga approached, the other men saluted. The two Imamba officers returned their courtesy. The two men entered a nearby tent and sat down.

"Oga, what's the next mission about, and where will it be?" Yisa asked as he took off his boots. The fresh air felt good against his tired feet.

"I'm not sure if these Brits will be involved, but we received information from our Belgian and American friends regarding an opportunity in the Congo," Oga replied as he took off his sunglasses and reclined in a chair. His deep-set eyes were bloodshot, and he rubbed them.

"And?"

"We have to train some of the soldiers there, just like we are doing here. Nothing serious. The good part is that I heard the new military leader in the Congo is very generous with his country's money, so we can expect a nice bonus with our pay." Oga smiled as he lit a cigarette.

"I see," Yisa replied as he sat back up from rubbing his feet. He picked up a book that was lying on the floor and began to read.

Outside, the other Imamba were laughing and cracking jokes. Beyond the Imamba, far off in the distance, stood the Ertale Volcano,[1] majestic against the setting sun. A brief silence fell between the two men as an almost cool evening breeze blew through the tent.

"Does it ever bother you?" Yisa asked as he closed the book and looked at Oga.

"Does *what* ever bother me?"

"What we do. Does it ever bother you?"

"No. I rather enjoy it."

---

[1] The Ertale volcano is one of the few active volcanoes in Africa.

Yisa looked outside and sighed. His mind was troubled as he wrestled with both his conscience and his ego. For some time now, he had not been happy with his role in the brotherhood.

"I don't know, Oga. We have too much blood on our hands, and in most cases we get paid with money taken from the land—*our* land. That doesn't bother you?"

Oga sat up and studied his colleague. He flicked the ash from his cigarette onto the ground, where it disintegrated as it made contact with the sand. They had been having these sorts of conversations for the last few months, and he was getting frustrated.

"What did I tell you about making such talk, eh, Yisa? Stop being so pious, it gets you nowhere. If you're going to work with us, you can't think so much. You just act, make your money, and enjoy life."

"I did not start the Imamba with you and Omega to kill our own people for money."

"Your dreams are outdated, Yisa." Oga replied.

"All you think about is money. Omega is the same."

"We never said we had any other agenda. Why are you surprised?"

"I'm not surprised, I'm restating the obvious truth. And Omega, now he handles all the contracts, and I don't even know half the people he deals with."

"Omega knows what he's doing. He has the best connections, and we started this thing on trust, so you have to trust him."

Yisa sighed and scratched his head. "The longer I stay in, the dirtier I feel."

"You are the one who came up with the idea for our brotherhood in the first place. Do you mean you want out?"

"It's not going the way I thought it would."

They could see the lower-ranking Imamba standing around outside. They were tough young men, all wielding semi-automatic weapons and projecting menace in their camouflage fatigues.

"Take a good look, Yisa. We built that. We built those men into useful bodies that can restore the empires that once existed in Africa. We've created something that unites the best of our warriors under one banner. Nothing like this has ever been done, here or abroad. Take a good look."

"I see them. But our brotherhood is not in the business of making leaders of nations. We are in the business of killing and making money."

"Money makes the world go round, Yisa, and you have to kill to establish an efficient system. Why are you talking like this? Are you tired?"

"I don't know. Perhaps I'm not the man for this job," Yisa replied.

Outside, a new, young soldier joined the other men, a bottle of whiskey in his hand. The men laughed, exchanged words that were inaudible, and began to pass the bottle.

"Yisa, you need to stop talking like that," warned Oga, looking at him sharply.

"No, what we're doing is not right. Look at the Congolese affair: we helped kill an innocent man, and we both know that the Congo is not going to have peace, not after all that has happened."

"What do you care?" Oga answered as he took another drag from his cigarette. "What made you start acting like this? I find it strange that you of all people are uncomfortable with our system. You, the same person who suggested we join forces and start our venture."

"That has nothing to do with it."

"It has everything to do with it! Did you forget Algeria? Have you forgotten how passionate you were back then? What triggered all this doubt in you, Yisa? Why have you suddenly become so soft?" he sneered.

"I've just been reading, that's all."

"Ah, a book. A book is a soldier's worst enemy," Oga replied as he looked at the closed book in Yisa's hand, titled *Leadership in the Motherland*, by Oluko.

"Or it can be his best friend." Yisa said. "I've also been thinking of my son. I don't know what legacy I will leave him. There has to be more to life than what we do. I'm worried that he might follow in my footsteps."

"That may not be such a bad thing, especially with your blood. We could use someone like him in our brotherhood when he's old enough," Oga replied with a grin.

"My son will not join us, brother. When he's old enough I will send him to Ghana for school, and then abroad for a proper education."

Oga leaned back in his chair and laughed, blowing cigarette smoke into the air.

"Ghana… I always thought the name 'Gold Coast' sounded more lucrative. Sounding smart will not put money in your pocket, and sending your son to fancy schools does not guarantee that he will be a great man. Stop dreaming, Yisa. When your son is old enough, he should join us."

Yisa shook his head, got up, and walked over to a cot.

"As long as I'm alive, my son will never join the Imamba."

"Perhaps I should kill you then," Oga replied with a laugh, holding up his hands as Yisa turned sharply. "I'm only joking."

"My family's involvement with the Imamba ends with me." Yisa yawned as he reclined.

Oga smiled, put out his cigarette, and unlaced his boots.

"Never say never, Yisa," he said as he got up and sat down on the other cot. The desert heat drained whatever energy was left in both men, and they soon fell asleep.

It was around 6 p.m. the following day when a cargo jet filled with weapons and Imamba fighters, including Oga and Yisa, touched down on the runway at the Moanda airport in the town of Muanda, Congo. The landscape here was a stark contrast to the desert: dense grasslands surrounded them, and they were being pelted with fat drops of rain. Yisa enjoyed watching the raindrops beat against the airplane's windows as it taxied across the runway. Upon exiting the plane, they were met on the airstrip by a heavy blanket of humidity and a white man sporting a brown suit and a safari hat.

He was elderly, with a greying beard and balding hair, but his hands were big and scarred—capable hands. He wore a smile and an air of relaxed confidence. From his blasé indifference, it was clear that he was no stranger to war and dangerous surroundings. A burst of distant shots made him glance swiftly toward the direction of the sound, but his stance was unflinching. His name was Bernard Cole. The Imamba had first met him in Algeria a few years earlier, developing a business relationship when his credentials checked out. Bernard presented himself to the Imamba as an influential businessman from the United States, but Yisa suspected otherwise. Yisa could not bring himself to trust Bernard Cole, believing him to be a foreign agent of some sort. There was something a little too smooth about the man, a little too practiced for an ordinary businessman who liked to meddle in foreign affairs. The comfort with violence and military bearing all suggested "spy" to him.

The rest of the Imamba saw Bernard as their ticket to America, and as such they paid him well. To date, they had provided him with the resources he needed to carry out his operations in the Congo, all in exchange for information and access to key individuals in the States.

"Ah, Oga, so nice to see you again," Bernard greeted, offering a warm handshake.

"Nice to see you as well, Bernard," Oga replied as they watched the Imamba troops unload weapons from the plane.

"And Yisa, so nice of you to come," the American continued as he turned to shake Yisa's hand. Yisa smiled, but the warmth didn't quite reach his eyes.

"Thanks. So, what are we doing here?" Yisa asked.

"Well, there's been a lot of civil unrest since the Prime Minister was killed, but we've been enjoying good economic relations with the Congolese and, more importantly, we're not worried about Congo aligning itself with those damned Communists," Bernard replied, wiping sweat off his brow.

"You're referring to the Russians?"

"And the Chinese."

"I see," Yisa said, "but, you still haven't answered my question about what we are doing here."

"Patience, my boy. The soldier we placed in power is proving to be very effective, but he lacks experience. He's been indulging himself by publicly executing a lot of his opposition—very ugly—and we anticipate a rebellion soon. We were thinking of enlisting your services to guide his budding military strategy," Bernard said as the three of them walked toward a waiting Jeep.

"Why don't you train him and his men yourselves?" Yisa asked.

"Well, in all honesty, I would if I had the capability," he smiled. "But, I'm just a businessman," Bernard said, shrugging benignly. "Boardroom battles are more my forte."

"Sure you are, Mr. Cole. A simple American businessman with an interest in Congolese internal affairs."

"There are diamonds here, as I'm sure you know. If helping my government facilitate deals in this region gives me access to those resources..." He smiled and gave an innocent shrug.

"Your hands are dirty," Yisa's mouth twisted in disgust.

"My hands seem pretty clean to me," Bernard Cole replied with a chuckle as he examined his hands. The American's comment made Yisa uneasy.

"I think you Americans should be the ones training him and his men, not us," Yisa replied as they approached the Jeep. A few Congolese soldiers stood around the vehicle, each toting a loaded AK-47. Before they stepped in, Bernard turned around and faced Yisa.

"Listen, if you want my opinion on why America is not involved, my guess would be that this damn Cold War business is going to end any time now. So, I don't think 'my fellow Americans' have a vested interest in the internal affairs of the Congo. But, I'm just a businessman, so what do I know?"

"I think you want to have a hand in Congolese affairs, and are using us to mask your involvement," Yisa accused.

"Don't mind Yisa," Oga cut in, stepping between the two men. "We would be more than happy to lend our services," he assured Bernard, gesturing angrily for Yisa to keep his mouth shut.

"Good. You and your men will be well taken care of, and you should know that there is a lot of money with this assignment. I already spoke to Omega, and he will make sure the funds are deposited in your Swiss accounts once this deal goes through. Let's hope Kato cooperates."

"Is Kato your puppet ruler?" Oga asked.

"Yes, and he's expecting you. Just so you know, he's very generous to those who help him," the American said with a wink as they entered the Jeep. Yisa and Oga exchanged looks as they climbed in after him.

Driving through town, Yisa noticed that people freely roamed the streets—evidence that this community had fared far better than the rest of the country. They drove on newly tarred roads—an uncommon feature in any war-torn nation—and new buildings and building sites surrounded them. Men in suits walked in and out of what appeared to be a lavish hospital, and as they crossed an intersection, a toddler standing beside her mother smiled and waved. Yisa smiled back as Oga and Bernard made small talk.

They soon arrived at the ruler's palace, where four soldiers and two young maids greeted them and escorted them from the Jeep. The entrance was adorned with polished marble floors and four marble lions, a theme of opulent excess that extended throughout the palace. Palm trees, and exotic imported flowers were everywhere, in sharp contrast to the many hardened soldiers patrolling the palace grounds. They were escorted to a massive outdoor swimming pool where beautiful women lounged in seductive swimsuits, giggling with men who could only be high-ranking soldiers. They were led to the far end of the pool, where the ruler, Kato, sat waiting, an elegant woman on either side of him.

"Ah, Bernard, you have come. Quick, bring our guests some refreshments," Kato ordered a nearby waiter in a thick French accent. The waiter bowed, then rushed off into the palace.

"Hello, Your Excellency. These are our friends from the Imamba, Yisa and Oga. I gave them a short briefing on what they will be doing," Bernard said with a smile.

"You Americans, always trying to tell me how to rule my country—you and your imperialist friends. You're a bunch of greedy bastards, I tell you. All you want are the diamonds and minerals here, and you try to cover it up by telling me you are helping. I do not need help training my soldiers."

Kato paused and glanced at the two mercenaries. A smile materialized on his face. "Regardless, we are brothers," he continued, looking at the two Imamba. "How are you gentlemen doing?"

"We are fine, thank you, sir," Oga replied.

Yisa studied the ruler. Kato was a lean man in his thirties with skin as dark as charcoal. His speech sounded educated, and he wore expensive, custom-tailored clothes. Judging from his surroundings (even the women wore high-fashion, imported swimwear and negligees), Yisa could tell that Kato had very expensive tastes. Soon, a waiter arrived with a selection of refreshments, and they all sat down.

"What will you gentlemen have?" Kato asked. "I have juice and beer. Or would you like champagne instead?"

"I will try your champagne," Oga replied as a waiter filled his glass.

"Me too," Bernard chimed in.

"Water is fine," Yisa said.

"Water?" Kato scoffed. "I had this champagne flown in from France—Orléans, to be exact. You really should try some."

"Water will be fine," Yisa replied as he looked Kato in the eye. There was a brief silence as both men stared at each other. It was rare that anyone said no to Kato, and he sized up the mercenary with an evil grin as a waiter poured him a glass of champagne.

"I have heard of you Imamba. I know that a lot of countries line your pockets, like our American friends," Kato said as he glanced at Bernard, who was stuffing his mouth with shrimp. Bernard tipped his glass and smiled.

"You requested our services to discuss history?" Yisa asked.

"I did not request your services, he did," Kato replied as he looked at Bernard again. "My soldiers are very competent, and I already have tactics in place to secure my power." He paused, eyeing the two black men closely. "Someone once told me that the Imamba was created to unite us as Africans. Is that what the Imamba

Brotherhood stands for today?" Kato asked, taking a sip of his champagne.

"Of course it is what we stand for, and that's why we are here," Oga replied with a sly smile. Yisa said nothing.

"Is this true? Do you feel the same way?" Kato asked Yisa.

The question angered Yisa to some degree. He got the feeling that Kato was trying to get under his skin. Not to mention, it seemed he was about to do business with the exact thing he despised.

With whatever dignity he could muster, Yisa fired back, "Yes, that's what I stand for."

"How ironic it is that the ones you are against in principle are the same ones who feed you. The hero's irony," Kato said in a cool tone as he sipped his champagne. "Well, you've come to the right place, because I am always looking for ways to improve my forces. You are more than welcome to stay here and offer your services. But, I do not need them."

"I have expertise in strategic and guerrilla warfare. I would love to share some of my ideas with you, if you are interested," Oga said to Kato, trying to change his focus.

"I would be interested in that, yes. Do not worry about money, I have more than enough. How about you? Do you have any expertise you want to offer?" Kato asked Yisa.

"Pretty much the same thing my partner just said," Yisa replied without making eye contact.

The ruler grinned at Yisa.

"We are finished here, then. You and your men can stay in my country for as long as you like. Relax and be merry."

"Actually, we cannot stay if we are not needed. We never stay in one place for too long unless it's for business," Yisa replied as he abruptly stood up.

"We can always make exceptions," Oga cut in, looking at Yisa with a raised eyebrow.

"No, we can't. We have to report back for new orders. Kato said he does not need us."

Oga stepped up to Yisa as Kato and Bernard looked on. "Can I have a word with you?" Oga hissed in Yisa's ear. The two Imamba walked out of hearing distance of Kato and Bernard.

"What are you doing?" Oga asked with a serious look.

"What do you mean? The man said he doesn't need us, so we must go. Those are the rules."

"Fuck the rules," Oga replied. "This guy's loaded. We have to convince him he needs us. We don't just walk away from millions. He's new in power, and this is the time to establish solid connections."

"Oga, I told you already that I'm losing interest in causing harm. We both know what Kato is all about. It has nothing to do with what we represent."

"Forget that nonsense! Don't start with your philosophical, noble bullshit. Please, not here. We've come too far. Are you trying to be a martyr or something? Omega set up this connection for us, so let's not blow it for all of us, eh? All we are doing is training his men. We're not killing anyone."

"We are training them to kill innocent people. When does it end, Oga?"

"We are mercenaries, Yisa. This is what we do. This Kato most likely will become another dictator, and yes, people will die. But that means more money for us. If he brings order to this country, why not help him? Doesn't that fall under what our objectives are? Think about the money, Yisa—let's focus here."

As the two Imamba spoke over in the corner of the courtyard, Kato looked over at Bernard, who was still stuffing his face with ngai ngai and fried fish.[1] A slim young girl approached and began massaging Bernard's shoulders.

"How do you know these men?" Kato asked.

"Who? Those two? Oh, they've been around for a while. Mercenaries, assassins—call them whatever you want. They served with a few South African private military firms, and were involved with some covert operations in Zambia and Equatorial Guinea. In fact, I'm quite certain they were involved with containing the Mau Mau rebels.[2] I believe they were training soldiers in that region."

"And how do you know?"

"Respectfully, I think you ask too many questions, Your Excellency. I'm not sure why you're giving them the impression that you don't need them, especially since you asked me to bring them here."

---

[1] Ngai ngai with fried fish is a dish native to Congo. Ngai ngai is Congolese for "Rosella leaves."
[2] The Mau Mau movement in the 1950s was a rebellion by Kenyan peasants against British colonial rule.

"I wanted to see their true colors first."

Bernard smiled as he savored the taste of the fried fish and the girl's strong hands massaging away the tension in his shoulders. He placed his hand on her inner thigh and grinned at her discomfiture.

"You have a funny way of figuring people out. Just know that they lend their services to anyone with enough cash to pay. And they'll kill anything for money. Typical African stuff, you should know," Bernard said with a chuckle as he chewed on more succulent shrimp, his hand moving up the young girl's leg.

Kato did not respond to Bernard's sarcasm. He had worked with his local fighters, the majority of whom had been trained by the Belgian forces that reigned before him. The Imamba represented an opportunity to enhance his army's skill sets. He knew he needed them, but he wanted to be assured of their loyalty. He had to let them know who was in control. Kato was not accustomed to Yisa's defiant behavior—his own underlings had seen enough public executions to give alacrity to their absolute obedience.

"If what you say is true, we shall need them to prove the extent of their loyalty to any business relationship we may have."

"What do you have in mind?" Bernard Cole asked between chews. The young girl was now on her knees, her head buried between Bernard's sweaty thighs.

"You shall see," Kato replied as he resumed looking at the two arguing Imamba.

✝

"Yisa, you're acting strange—and dangerously foolish. I'll do the negotiating from now on. You don't have to say a word. All we're doing is a little training, and we'll leave. Deal?" Oga insisted in aggravation.

"Fine."

They walked back to Kato and the American.

"Sorry about that," Oga said with a diplomatic smile as they sat down.

"Do you gentlemen normally have this much trouble making decisions?" Kato asked, enjoying the tension between the Imamba.

"No, we don't. My partner is not feeling well, that's all. We've not really had much rest recently," Oga replied, lighting a new cigarette.

"I am perfectly fine," Yisa cut in, glaring at Oga.

"What is your decision?" Kato asked.

"Our services will be available to you. We can share some of our knowledge with your men," Oga replied.

"Good. But we shall have to put your sincerity to the test. Follow me."

Kato stood up and walked toward stairs leading down away from the pool, the guards snapping to attention as he passed. Yisa and Oga looked at each other, then glanced at Bernard Cole, who shrugged in return with a smile on his face as the young girl finished her work. They followed the ruler, nonplussed at the sudden change in events. Kato led them to two Jeeps in a rear parking lot, both waiting with drivers.

"Get in the other vehicle and follow me. I wish to show you both something," Kato said as he got in the first Jeep and drove out of the parking lot. The mercenaries and the American jumped into the second Jeep, and the driver followed Kato's car.

They left the palace grounds and drove into a more rural environment. The thick Congo bush began to surround them on all sides, and the tarred roads faded into rutted dirt paths. Two more Jeeps joined their convoy along the way, and as they drove, Yisa could spot people lining the paths and roadways, obviously aware that their ruler was passing by. They watched with curious, unsuspecting faces, unaware of the forces at play in their land.

An hour later, the convoy arrived at an encampment deep in the bush. It was evening, and campfires were the only source of light aside from the headlights of the Jeeps as they pulled in. A group of soldiers sat in a circle by a bungalow, quickly standing as Kato's envoy arrived. One soldier approached as Kato stepped out of the Jeep.

"Bonsoir, Majeste. Nous ne vous attendions pas,[1]" the soldier said respectfully as he eyed the mercenaries behind Kato.

"Je sais, ce voyage n'était pas prévu. Sont-ils encore là?[2]"

"Oui."

"Ont-ils parlé?[3]" Kato asked.

---

[1] "Hello, supreme ruler. We were not expecting you."
[2] "I know, this trip was not planned. Are they still here?"
[3] "Did they talk?"

"Oui. Nous avons l'information dont nous avons besoin. Ils sont à l'intérieur.[1]"

"Bon. Vous avez bien fait. Je vais le prendre d'ici,[2]" Kato said as he patted the soldier on the back and turned to face the mercenaries, who were now standing behind him. "Follow me."

Yisa and Oga followed him past the soldiers into the bungalow. It was dimly lit, and a foul stench filled the air. Sitting in chairs were two men drenched with blood, their arms tied behind them. They had been severely beaten, and sat with swollen faces and cuts all over their necks and arms. One of them had had two of his fingers cut off, and Yisa could see them lying in a nearby bucket. The other's visage was so swollen that his eyes were not visible. On a table next to them rested a bloodstained Marakov pistol. Three guards sat in the background, pleased smiles on their faces as Kato and the mercenaries walked in. They stood and saluted Kato, then eyed the mercenaries.

"So, here we are. If you are going to train my men, you have to lead by example. These men sitting before you are traitors—spies sent by my enemies to gain information on my activities. We plucked them from a village nearby," Kato said as he picked up the Marakov and handed it to Oga. He kept his eyes on Yisa.

"Nous n'avons pas vous trahir la majesté, nous… nous sommes des paysans simples. S'il vous plaît, nous ne tuez pas![3]" one

---

[1] "Yes. We have the information we need. They are inside."
[2] "Good, you've done well. I will take it from here."
[3] "We did not betray you, supreme ruler, we… we are simple peasants. Please, do not kill us!"

of the captives said in slurred, panicked French that Yisa understood. He knew that the men were protesting their innocence.

"Ce n'est pas que vous dites à mes hommes, imbecile,[1]" Kato replied, his eyes still on Yisa.

"Nous avons dit à vos hommes ce qu'ils voulaient entendre. La douleur était trop forte,[2]" the man replied. One of the guards walked up behind him and slapped the back of the peasant's head without warning, causing him to yelp in pain.

"Kill him," Kato said to Oga. Oga glanced at Yisa and shrugged. Without hesitation, he cocked the weapon and shot the pleading peasant in the head. The gunshot sent a resounding echo through the bush, and the peasant slumped over in his chair, a messy hole in his head. Yisa knew his fate had already been decided, regardless of Oga's decision. Kato smiled, took the gun from Oga, and handed it to Yisa.

"Your turn. Prove your loyalty," he said as he placed the weapon in Yisa's hands.

Yisa looked at the gun, looked at Kato, and then looked at the second battered peasant sitting before him. The farmer's eyes were swollen shut, but he could hear everything that had happened—his friend had been shot and his captors were now speaking English, which he probably didn't understand. Yisa pitied the man as he squirmed in his chair and began to plead:

---

[1] "That is not what you told my men, fool."
[2] "We told your men what they wanted to hear. The pain was too much."

"Je vous en prie, je n'ai rien fait de mal! Je vous prie de me croire! S'il vous plaît, laissez-moi partir! J'ai une famille. S'il vous plaît! Je n'ai rien fait de mal![1]" the peasant wailed.

"God, this is boring. I can't watch this; I need a cigarette," Bernard Cole said as he walked out of the bungalow. "Call me if you need me to hold your hand, Yisa."

All eyes focused on Yisa, whose face twisted at Bernard's taunt. The mercenary looked at the gun in his hand. This was terribly wrong. He suspected that the peasant was innocent, but the pressure around him was building to a fever pitch. Kato smiled triumphantly as Yisa struggled with his dilemma. He had asserted his dominance over the mouthy Imamba.

"S'il vous plaît, laissez-moi partir! Ce n'est pas juste![2]" the blinded peasant continued to plead.

Yisa raised the weapon.

---

[1] "I beg you, I have done nothing wrong! I beg you to believe me! Please, let me go! I have a family. Please! I have done nothing wrong!"

[2] "Please, let me go! This is not fair (just)!"

GANG-RELATED

Mack Pool. Ann Arbor, Michigan. 1990.

The water in the swimming pool felt cool against Eteka's body as he swam up and down its length. It was about 7 p.m. and, save for a solitary lifeguard sitting at the opposite end flipping through a magazine, he was alone in the public pool. He finished a few laps of freestyle and switched his stroke, gracefully powering through the water as he used the butterfly stroke. The water splashed on his face as he kept his eyes on the lane ahead through his goggles. It was his 20th lap and he did not feel fatigued. Tomorrow, he and his associates would be responsible for another murder. That's how it went. The orders came; they went to work; they got paid. No questions asked. He had been doing this for as long as he could remember. He flipped in the water and kicked off the wall for a return lap. The atmosphere in Michigan was not as festive or as warm as other places he had been. To him, Michigan was cold, dark, and gloomy. He loved it.

After his 30th lap, the young black man stepped out of the pool and grabbed a towel. Eteka's athletic frame was rippled with muscle, and scars were mapped across the dark skin of his back, chest, and arms. He had a light scar that ran across the bridge of his nose and another that sat on his left cheek—trophies from past knife battles. A tattoo of a black mamba snake was coiled prominently on his left pectoral muscle. Eteka still sported the beaded necklace his father had made him many years ago, though it was beginning to wear. He assumed a serious look and wiped his goatee dry, spotting a man walking in his direction. The man was also tall and dark-skinned, with a powerful build clad in a black tracksuit. A menacing scar ran across his left eye and a similar tattoo of a black snake sat on the back of his right hand. He ate from a bag of chips, a sly smile on his face as he sat on a nearby bench.

"Hello, brother."

"Hello, Cyrus."

"Did you get enough laps in?" Cyrus asked in a thick Liberian accent.

"Yes."

Cyrus glanced at the lone lifeguard at the end of the pool and smiled, his mouth half full of chips.

"Eteka, swimming is not for hard guys like us," Cyrus said with a grin, swallowing the mouthful of chips.

"You don't honestly believe that, do you?" Eteka asked, slipping on a white tracksuit and a pair of Puma running shoes.

"I do."

"On the contrary, swimming laps is one of the best conditioning exercises," Eteka replied as they left the pool. Outside, a sharp, icy blast of wind that complemented the snowstorm raging outside rushed to greet them. They put on masks, jackets, and goggles to shield their eyes from the snow, and headed toward a nearby hill.

"You heard from Oga yet?" Eteka asked loudly, the wind furious as they trudged forward.

"Yes. We have a green light on our assignment in Detroit."

"Good. Just the two of us?"

"No. Another one of our guys just arrived. He's at the safe house downtown. He'll be coming with us," Cyrus replied between breaths.

"Do I know him?"

"You might. His name is Pacman. Jamaican guy, always smiling…"

"Oh, him. Crazy guy."

"Yeah. He knows these gang members in Detroit. They will carry out the hit, and we'll tag along just to make sure it happens," Cyrus said.

The men jogged slowly uphill, trudging against the wind and snow.

"It's about time we left," Cyrus said "I'm getting tired of the weather."

"I agree. But it's good for our training," Eteka replied as they both panted.

"When we finish this assignment, I say we find some women. I know some good strip clubs in Detroit."

"We could do that, although I'd prefer that we leave right away."

"What's the rush, Eteka? Our next assignment after this won't be for a couple of weeks. There'll definitely be women we can grab in Detroit when we're done."

"That's the difference between you and me, Cyrus: I prefer to stay disciplined. Our orders were to report to Morocco for our next assignment when we're done here, not have fun chasing women."

Cyrus laughed as they pressed through the thick snow.

"You always play by the book, Eteka. They did not tell us to report right away. We'll have a couple of days to spare before they start looking for us. C'mon, you know you want to."

Eteka shook his head as they reached the top of the hill, turned, and started running back down.

"Let's get this assignment out of the way, then we can deal with your cravings."

Cyrus grinned at his response, and the two men ran for another thirty minutes before catching a local bus back to the safe house in downtown Ann Arbor.

They walked into the safe house at around 10 p.m. It was a spacious second-floor apartment situated in the main business district of the city. Two chairs and a table were the primary furnishings in the apartment's living room. A television hooked up to a Nintendo game console and a VCR sat on the table. In a corner of the room was a fridge; in another corner stood a closet. Doors to two separate bedrooms stood at adjacent ends of the living room. The men walked in on Pacman, an athletic, dark-skinned man sporting a soul patch and long dreadlocks, smoking a blunt and watching the television.

"Wa yuh deal mi bredah?" Pacman greeted them in thick Jamaican patois. He wore a big smile and jeans. Strange inscriptions and tattoos were carved into his heavily inked upper body. He too bore a tattoo of a black snake, this one strewn across his chest.

"What's up, man? No introductions needed, right?" Cyrus asked as he sat down and accepted the blunt from Pacman.

"Nah," Eteka replied, shaking hands with Pacman. As Eteka sat down, Pacman got up to use the bathroom.

"So, how're we handling this thing tomorrow?" Eteka asked.

"We'll leave at 5 a.m. sharp. Pacman rented a car for us, so we'll use that to get to Detroit."

"How long's the drive?"

"Forty-five minutes. His friends should be waiting for us as planned. We're to catch the target as he heads out for work and have the gang members take him down," Cyrus replied.

"Who is the target, anyway?" Eteka asked as Pacman returned from the bathroom and sat down on the floor.

"Some diplomat. We're not supposed to ask questions. We have his home and office addresses, and we have his picture. Pacman's friends will take care of the rest."

Eteka looked at Pacman, who still had a big smile on his face.

"Your friends, they're reliable?" Eteka asked.

"Yes," Pacman replied with a hazy nod, a little blurry from the pot.

"And what are we giving these guys in exchange? Money?" Eteka asked.

"They think they're getting money, but we're not giving them anything," Cyrus answered as he opened the fridge and grabbed a beer.

"Okay, then I'm going to get cleaned up and get some rest. You guys should do the same," Eteka said as he got up and headed toward the bathroom.

It was a dark, chilly, pre-dawn morning when the men left for Detroit. Pacman was at the wheel of a rented Honda Civic as they made their way through the icy roads toward the city. They reached the outskirts at sunrise and headed downtown, parking in a commercial lot next to a bank. Another car was parked nearby, its two occupants wearing sagging jeans, matching shirts, and bandanas. Both men stepped out of the car and waved.

"Okay, bredren, dat's dem. Let's go talk," Pacman said as they exited the vehicle.

Eteka and Cyrus followed Pacman across the parking lot. The air was icy-cold, and Eteka's fingers began to numb.

"Wha gwaan, mi bredah?" Pacman greeted as he shook hands with both thugs. Air, normally invisible, took on a ghost-like tangibility as the men breathed.

"What's good, homie? You got our money?" the first thug asked in a raspy tone.

"You'll get your money when you do your job. You know what to do?" Cyrus cut in, receiving glares from both thugs.

"Who's this fool?" the second thug asked, looking at Cyrus.

"You don't need to know who this 'fool' is. All you need to worry about is being ready," Cyrus replied, returning the thug's stare. "The money isn't yours yet, so don't get cocky, my friend. I'll ask again: You know what to do?"

The thugs looked at each other and snickered unpleasantly.

"This dude's tryina' punk me," the first thug laughed.

"Fo' sure," the second thug said, still looking at Cyrus.

The first thug turned and faced Cyrus.

"I ain't no bitch, nigga, st—"

"Shut up, both of you. We're wasting time here," Cyrus said sternly, cutting the man off. "We need to know if you two clowns are capable of handling the assignment that's in front of you. Do you know what to do?"

The first thug clenched his jaw. "Yeah, we good."

"What do you mean, 'we good?' That's not an answer."

"Yeah, man. Damn. We know what to do: take him out as he drives to his office, at least two shots to the domepiece. We got it," the first thug replied.

"Good. We'll be right behind you to make sure you do the job right. No mistakes. We leave in fifteen minutes," Cyrus replied.

"And our money?" the second thug asked.

"We'll meet up at the spot my associate here gave when he first contacted you," Cyrus replied, patting Pacman's back. "Then you'll get your money."

"Better not play any friggin' games wid us, homie. The deal was two grand each. Don't mess with us, Kunta Kinte," the second thug said in an angry, mocking tone.

Cyrus smiled. "You're a true knucklehead, but I have to say that you both seem perfect for the job," he replied.

The gang members headed back to their car, the first thug muttering something under his breath as they walked off. Not a word was said as the mercenaries watched them leave. A crisp breeze blew past them, and Eteka's nose began to run. Across the street, he spotted a deli.

"You guys want anything? I'm going to get some coffee and a bagel," Eteka said as he started across the street.

"Just get me a coffee," Cyrus replied, "I'll wait in the car. And don't take too long, we leave in fifteen."

By 7 a.m., they were waiting in cars parked on the street of their target's residence in the middle-class Grandmont Rosedale neighborhood. The street thugs sat in a car in behind the Imamba while the mercenaries monitored the proceedings from their car, enjoying an impromptu breakfast of bagels and coffee. After a few minutes, an elderly man emerged from the house, holding the hand of a little girl who looked to be about five or six. He paused on the front stoop to fuss with one of her hair ornaments, straightening it as she beamed up at him. He leaned down to kiss her forehead and then ushered her over to the car, helping her into her seat and closing the door behind her. They pulled into the street past the mercenaries. As they drove by, the little girl spontaneously waved at Eteka.

"She likes you," Cyrus grinned as Pacman started the car.

Eteka did not reply as he stared out of the window, his breath fogging the frosted glass. The gang members pulled up next to their car, gave them a nod, and began to follow the target at a slow cruise.

"Are we taking out the girl as well?" Eteka asked as they tailed the thugs.

"No, just the man," Cyrus replied.

"And what if these guys hurt her?" Eteka asked.

"Then that'll be too bad. You don't have feelings for her, do you?" Cyrus asked. He and Pacman both chortled. "Shit, man, we need to get you to the strip club if you're starting to get hard-ons for little girls."

Eteka bit his cheek, frowning out the window, ignoring the taunt.

"The girl wasn't in the contract. We should stick to protocol."

"Hey, it's out of our hands now. I can't guarantee anything, especially when it has to do with Pacman's friends," Cyrus said, laughing. "You know he likes to improvise."

They continued following their target until he came to a red light. The thugs pulled their car up alongside the diplomat's.

"Here we go," Cyrus said, taking a sip of coffee.

In an instant, multiple shots rang out from the thug's car in quick succession, shattering the silence. The thugs sped off, running the red light before disappearing onto a side street. Screams could be heard as a few Good Samaritans rushed toward the bullet-riddled car and others fled the scene.

"Shall we, gentlemen?" Cyrus asked with an evil chuckle. Pacman pulled the car over and stepped out. Eteka and Cyrus followed. A black man in scrubs was in the car, doing his best to stop the blood gushing from the diplomat's head.

"What happened?" Cyrus asked the man, bending over to look into the car.

"Goddam punks," the man said, tears in his eyes as he tried desperately to save the diplomat's life. "They have no regard for human life. How could anyone do such a thing?"

"Will he make it?" Eteka asked the man.

"I don't think so," the man replied.

Sirens were approaching. Eteka felt someone looking at him and turned around. Across the street, he spotted the little girl in a woman's arms. She had tears in her eyes, but she was not crying. She stared at Eteka with a blank expression even as the police arrived and took her from the woman. It was a piercing stare, and he couldn't stand it. He felt a lump form in his throat and looked away.

At that moment, two policemen came up to the crime scene.

"Sir, can you step away from the vehicle?" one of the policemen said to the man in scrubs as he got out of the car.

"It's okay, I'm a doctor. You might want to call in your homicide unit. He didn't make it," the doctor said with a sigh as he stood up, tears streaming down his face.

"Don't sweat it, Doc, you did all you could," one of the policemen said as he patted the doctor on the back.

"This just made no sense. What did that poor old man do to anybody? And he even had a little girl in the car with him…" the man continued to sob.

"People are messed up these days, y'know? We'll take it from here. We just need a statement from you," the policeman said as he led the doctor away. Eteka watched the doctor recede, feeling neither pleasure nor remorse. Another cop stepped up to the mercenaries.

"You guys see anything?"

"We were a few cars behind. We heard the shots and saw the shooters drive off that way," Cyrus said, playing his part. "So terrible."

"Okay, we'll need statements from you gentlemen as well. Just sit tight," the cop said as he walked off.

"Well, it seems that we're done here. When we finish with these cops we'll go deal with our thug friends. Then later we can have some fun," Cyrus said, rubbing his hands together.

Eteka said nothing as he spotted the little girl in the back of a police car. She was still looking at him.

Around 3 p.m. that same day, Eteka, Pacman, and Cyrus drove into a secluded alley, where the thugs were already waiting for them.

"Good job, guys," Cyrus said as he and Eteka stepped out of the car. They approached the gang members. Pacman was nowhere in sight. "You made quite a scene."

"Aight, nigga, cut the bullshit. Where's the loot?" the first gang member asked.

"Yeah, where's our money?" the second chimed in.

"The only reason we came by here is to clean up the mess, leave no trace," Cyrus replied with a chuckle.

"Clean up what mess? What the fuck you talkin' 'bout, homie?" the first thug demanded.

Cyrus smiled and stepped to his left just before a faint "phut" was heard. The first thug dropped to the floor, a bullet in his head.

"What the—?" the second man began, drawing a gun from his jeans.

Another shot and he too slumped to the ground, a bullet in his chest.

47

"Pacman is not a bad shot. I'm impressed," Cyrus said as Pacman emerged from a vacant building to their left holding a sniper rifle. Eteka retrieved a gallon of gas from their car and walked over to the bodies.

"I think I'll take a raincheck on partying with you guys," Eteka said while he poured the gasoline, taking care not to spill any on himself.

"C'mon, brother, it's well deserved," Cyrus replied.

"I'm just not in the mood. Something doesn't feel right."

"Ah, don't worry. It's probably the weather. I guarantee we'll have a great time tonight when we get our private sessions at the strip club. You'll see," Cyrus said with a grin as the men headed back to their car. As they pulled out of the alley, Pacman flung a prepared Molotov cocktail at the dead bodies. Flames erupted, lighting up the rearview mirror as they sped away.

HOME

Ibadan, Nigeria. 1967.

Yisa was tired. His eyes were bloodshot, and fatigue from traveling weighed down his body. He had left the Congo yesterday after staying a week longer than he had planned. Now, seeking a break from seeing death, he headed home for some rejuvenation from the two people dearest to his heart: his wife and son.

He caught a flight from Brazzaville in the Congo to Lagos, Nigeria, haunted by the many terrible things he had seen—images that fueled his conscience. From Lagos, he caught a helicopter to the city of Ibadan[1] in southern Nigeria, his home. When he finally landed, he was driven through the city in a hired Danfo.[2]

Yisa made his way through the city's commercial center, and soon his ride was weaving through a quiet residential area with large, gated mansions. Soldiers and large blockades were on every street, stopping cars frequently and conducting searches. These were the ripple effects of the recent tensions between the secessionist state

---

[1] Ibadan is the capital of Oyo State in Nigeria and is the third largest city in Nigeria by population.
[2] A Danfo is a term for a taxi-van in Nigeria. They often carry as many passengers as can squeeze into the vehicle.

of Biafra and the rest of Nigeria. Hoping to surprise his family, Yisa was dropped off a block away from his home. It was quiet, and he enjoyed the sunshine and the breeze that cooled his body as he walked down the street. He spotted a few neighbors who waved at him from behind their front gates, and he waved back. Around these parts, Yisa was a rare sight, staying only for a day or two before leaving again. To most of the neighbors, he appeared to be a rich international businessman, because sometimes he was dropped at his gate in an air-conditioned Mercedes-Benz. Only rich men rode in luxury in Nigeria.

Yisa rang the bell at the front gate. He couldn't wait to see his little boy's face and feel his wife's embrace. He knew that his son usually wrapped up his English lessons with Oladele—Yisa's best friend from university—in about three hours. It was just enough time to catch up with his wife and make love to her. He had spent many days dreaming of her beautiful smile, her radiant skin, her slender curves, and her full, plum-purple lips that spoke to her African heritage. He had first seen her when he started university, before he dropped out to begin his life as a contract killer. He had seen other women prior to her, but Amina… Amina was different. She was the first woman who understood him, who took care of him, who gave him good advice, who prayed with him, who listened to him, who had seen him at his best. Shamefully, she had not seen him at his worst: the many times he had killed people he did not know. All she knew of him was that he was a military contractor. She knew nothing of his associates or the Imamba. And he did not want her to know. Those demons would live and die with him. His wife and his son were the light of his life. He would have to make good use of his time with them, because in a few days he would have to travel north to Morocco to meet up with Oga and Omega.

Yisa was buzzed in through the gate and walked into his two-acre compound, on which sat his white two-story home. A 1967 Corvette L89, a 1967 Jaguar E-Type, and a 1967 Peugeot Scooter sat in the driveway—cars that even many elites in Nigeria did not possess. As he strolled up the driveway with a wide smile on his face, two male servants tending the grounds smiled and bowed their heads. He waved at them and at two middle-aged housemaids who quickly dashed inside his home, giggling. No doubt they were off to inform his wife of his arrival.

Yisa took his time, savoring the peaceful scenery. His lawn was trimmed to an even, healthy-looking green. A small, beautiful garden sat to the right of the house. All around him were smiles. Warm, genuine smiles. He stepped through the front door and into the living room. A delicious scent wafted from the kitchen: the smell of his favorite dish, Ogbono soup. He dropped his knapsack and plopped down on a nearby couch, the cool air from an overhead fan relaxing his tired body.

"Not so fast."

That voice. There she was, standing like a goddess at the bottom of the stairs that led to the upstairs bedrooms. At 5'8", Amina stood out in any environment, partly due to her height, partly due to her posture. She had stunning features, and her magnificent body was kept fit from her hands-on work around the house. She had spoken in clear, fluent English, although she also knew Yoruba, Efik, and French. When Yisa had first met Amina, she had been a medical student, having studied for two years in the United Kingdom before returning to Nigeria out of a passion for contributing to the country's development. She had had aspirations of becoming a doctor, while he had planned on becoming a teacher. But in the end, life had different plans for the both of them.

"Hello, my queen."

"Hello, my king."

Amina's ebony skin stood in perfect contrast to the white wall behind her. She wore a traditional wrap around her body, revealing her bare shoulders and sexy legs, and her hair was held up in a traditional silk wrap. She smiled at him, winking her eye and revealing her perfect white teeth. Yisa stood up and slowly walked over to her. He held her in his arms and ran his nose up and down her soft neck. She had just bathed. Her fresh scent was nothing but pleasure to Yisa's nose. Amina put an arm around him and gave him a passionate kiss. Her lips felt good, even better than in his dreams.

"I've missed you," she said, "but you've been traveling, and you're filthy. I've prepared a bath upstairs for you. Let me wash you down."

"Mmm, that would be nice," Yisa replied, and they shared another kiss. She guided him upstairs, took off his dirty clothes, and led him to the bathtub where a cool bubble bath waited. They laughed and flirted as she washed him, and when she was done they made unforgettable love.

✝

Yisa was surrounded by a ring of flames. Oga stood just outside the ring, regarding Yisa blankly. On Oga's right, Amina sat in a chair wearing the same blank look. They neither blinked nor spoke. Tosin, Yisa's son, stood to Oga's left, but his face was transfixed with terror. The fear on his son's face sent chills down Yisa's spine. He couldn't reach them through the ring of fire…

Yisa woke with a start, waking Amina. He had had a nightmare. Or a premonition. The dream had felt so real.

"Bad dream?" Amina asked, sleepily sitting up and caressing his back.

"Yes, very strange. How long have I been sleeping?"

"For about one and a half hours. It's almost five now," she replied.

Yisa reclined his head and Amina rested her head on his chest, looking up at him. She began to trace invisible shapes on his chest with her finger as he ran his hand across her back.

"It's good to have you home," she said softly.

"Thanks, Amina. How have you been?"

"Financially? The money you send is more than enough. And thankfully this Biafra trouble hasn't affected us. But, we miss you."

"I know. I miss you, too."

"Then come home. You've been away for far too long."

"We have this conversation every time I come back. I told you, it's not that simple," Yisa replied without heat. It was an old argument.

"What makes it so hard? Just quit. You always wanted to be a teacher, yet you decided to run off and join your soldier friends."

"Being a teacher doesn't pay anything. We needed the money, that's why I left."

"You left because you're an idealist and you wanted to make our people great, not because we needed money," she replied, narrowing her eyes.

"Times were different back then. We were winning back our lands from foreign occupation. I didn't think we would be at war, as we are today with this whole Biafran thing."
She kissed his cheek and smiled.

"You have such a good heart, and you've always been a dreamer. It's part of what made me fall in love with you. But you have to be realistic sometimes. We need you at home. You can always come back and work with Oladele. He's doing great things here."

"I'll give it some serious thought," he replied in a tone meant to end the conversation. She scratched his chest softly.

"He looks more and more like you each day."

"Who? Tosin?" he asked.

"Yes, your son. It's a shame you're missing out on a lot of his growth and development because you want to keep doing whatever you're doing. You're missing out on the very thing life is about."

Her words hit home, rattling his already tender conscience.

"I'm working on coming home for good, Amina. It's something that has been on my mind for some time now. Just give me some time to sort things out."

"Don't wait too long, my dear. You were not even here for his birth."

She was right. He was away on a mission when his son came into the world, and he knew he would never forgive himself for it.

"I am sorry, Amina. You always bring that up. You know I would have given anything in the world to have been here when Tosin was born."

"I cannot tell you how to be a father, Yisa. Tosin is already four and will be grown up before either of us can blink. It would mean a lot to both of us if his father was a part of his childhood," she said as she climbed out of bed. Her naked body glided across the room in search of clothes. She slipped into a robe and Yisa sat up.

"Where are you going?"

"To prepare dinner. Your son and Oladele will be here soon. It would be nice for us all to have dinner together."

"Was that Ogbono soup I smelled earlier?"

"Yes. I made it just the way you like, with stockfish and lamb."

"I love you."

"Do you love me because I made your favorite Ogbono soup, or because I am your wife?" she asked playfully from the doorway.

"Because you made the Ogbono soup," he replied, deadpan.

"Silly man," she giggled. "Hurry up and put some clothes on, then come downstairs." With that, she blew him a kiss and glided out of the bedroom.

Yisa stood up, revitalized. This was the way life should be. He picked up a loose-fitting, casual agbada[1] that Amina had laid out for him and walked over to a mirror. Scars from various battles lined his naked body.

I'm not even sure what I'm fighting for anymore. Yet I've been fighting—the scars prove it, he thought to himself as he ran his finger along a particularly long scar on his chest. *Amina is right. I have to stop this so I can be around my son. I have to be in his life. Perhaps I will do just one more mission. The rules are that you are an Imamba for life, but I started this thing…I'm sure if I talked to Omega and Oga they would understand.*

He smiled at his reflection in the mirror, put on the agbada, and headed downstairs.

---

[1] An agbada is a flowing robe with large sleeves worn by men in much of West Africa. It is known by different names depending on the ethnic group (e.g., "agbada" – Yoruba/Dagomba; "babban riga" – Hausa; "k'sa" – Tuareg).

BODYGUARD

Above the Atlantic. En route to Morocco. 1990.

The little girl looked at him, a sad smile on her face. Tears of blood streamed from her eyes, and she held her hands out to him…

"AAARGGH!!!" Eteka screamed, as he woke up with a start.

"Bad dreams, brother?" Cyrus asked with a chuckle.

They were on a plane, seated in first class. Eteka rubbed his eyes and sat up.

"Weird dream, nothing crazy," he replied, as much to reassure himself as anything else.

"It's probably the aftereffects of those hookers in Detroit," Cyrus said, flipping through a magazine.

"I have to admit, American women really know how to move in bed," Eteka replied as he stretched in his seat.

"I told you it would be unforgettable."

Cyrus was seated next to Eteka, dressed in a jet-black suit and sporting an expensive pair of sunglasses. Pacman sat in the adjacent aisle in an unbuttoned, long-sleeved cotton shirt. Eteka wore a white suit with no tie, exposing a beaded necklace strung on a thick, weathered piece of string. Eteka signaled a flight attendant over and ordered a soda, then looked out the window at the Atlantic Ocean below.

"You know, we make a lot of money. You should upgrade your jewelry," Cyrus commented, his eyes following the attendant's curvy body as she left their cabin.

"Huh?"

"Your jewelry. Why do you wear that piece of string on your neck? You've had it on for as long as I've known you. It makes me depressed," Cyrus said with a grin as he glanced at Eteka's necklace, an elaborate collection of beads and a gold ring on a piece of string.

"Oh, my father gave it to me when I was little. It's all I remember of him."

"I see. Is it a Juju charm or something?"

"Juju? I'm not superstitious; I don't believe in that stuff…"

"You should, I use it. See this?" Cyrus asked as he held up his pinky finger and flashed a gold ring in front of Eteka.

"Yeah, what about it?"

"As long as I have this on, no man can kill me. I got it from this priest in Benin."

"That's rubbish, those things don't work."

"Yah mon, fi mi chain ave magic tu, [1]" Pacman cut in with Jamaican patois as he held up a gold chain dangling from his neck. Attached to the chain was a piece of animal hair.

"Oh, you have a charm as well, Pacman? Interesting. I think you Caribbean people call it voodoo. Almost the same, but ours is stronger," Cyrus said with a grin, licking his lips at another flight attendant walking by. Eteka shook his head, not understanding why his Imamba brothers felt the need to trust in charms.

"A gun is the only thing I trust," Eteka said. "A gun and my instincts. You can keep your magic bullshit."

"There are a lot of forces at play that we men can't see with natural eyes, my brother. Don't assume that what you see in front of you is all there is. But seriously, you should upgrade your jewelry. Women won't talk to you with that cheap piece of string on your neck," Cyrus said, turning his amused gaze back to Eteka.

"I'm fine with women, as you saw when we were in Detroit."

"We paid for those women's services, my brother. The money won them over, not your charm," Cyrus replied as he leaned back in his chair and drifted off to sleep. Eteka shrugged dismissively and turned his attention to the plane's window.

They arrived in Morocco in the late afternoon, first stopping at Marrakech and then making the three-hour trip by car up to the coastal village of Oualidia. The drive was uneventful in the air-

---

[1] "Yeah, man, my chain has magic as well."

conditioned Jeep, but their destination was worth the tedious trip. The village was a rustic, serene paradise, boasting a beautiful tidal lagoon and villas housing wealthy Moroccans, tourists, and French expats. They arrived at a quiet beach resort, and after walking into the venue and checking in, they headed across the sand toward some men on the beach.

"Ah, the boys are here," a man with a large, uneven scar on his face said as the Imamba approached. He was an older man in impeccable shape, with a tall, lean, muscular frame. The scar on his face was by far his most distinguishing feature, as it covered half of his head with scar tissue, preventing hair growth. It resembled the remnants of a nasty burn. Dressed in all black, he stood with a larger man who wore a sinister smile on his face. The larger man had an authoritative presence, and he sported a linen shirt and trousers, two gold necklaces, and a diamond ring on his pinky finger. Three other men stood with them, a tough-looking bunch with the whipcord-esque sinews and high cheekbones of Slavic mercenaries.

"Hello, Oga," Eteka greeted the scarred man with a half-smile.

"It's good to see you," Oga replied as they exchanged a hug.

"How did it go?" the larger man asked in a raspy Nigerian accent. His potbelly moved as he talked, as if it had a rebellious life of its own.

"It went well, Omega," Eteka replied.

"Good. That man you disposed of in Detroit was causing a lot of trouble. Your money has been deposited in your accounts,"

Omega said with a smile. A cool breeze blew off the ocean, bringing the sounds of children playing in the waves as sunset approached.

"Thanks. Who are these guys?" Cyrus asked as he scrutinized the three men behind them.

"They are our Russian friends. Specialists, like you," Oga replied.

"And what are they doing here?" Eteka asked.

"What we're doing here is not your business," one of the men replied in a thick accent.

Eteka looked at Omega, who smiled reassuringly and patted him on the back.

"He's right, it's none of your business," Omega said. "Why don't you boys go inside, get some drinks, and relax? I'll finish up with these men and join you in a few minutes."

"C'mon, let's go. I need a drink myself," Oga said as he led the mercenaries away. As they walked off, Eteka exchanged one last look with the three Russians, who all watched him suspiciously.

Leaving the Russians and Omega behind, Oga, Eteka, and Cyrus walked into the resort and found seating in a lounge area. Oga then signaled a waitress over.

"I'll have a Guinness. What are you boys drinking?" Oga asked. His scar made a few passing guests stare with curiosity.

"I'll have a beer as well. Any kind," Cyrus said.

"Glass of water," Eteka said.

"Glass a' rum," Pacman requested.

"Who are those men and what are they doing here?" Cyrus asked as the men watched the waitress walk away.

"They are contract fighters from Russia. There is business in Sierra Leone they are attending to, and they need our assistance," Oga answered.

"Since when did we start helping people?" Eteka asked.

"Everything has its price," Oga replied elusively as the waitress returned with their drinks.

"And the Russians pay well?" Cyrus asked.

"We would not be dealing with them if they didn't. The Imamba Brotherhood does not deal with small pockets, remember that. You boys are a part of something great."

"How great are we, Oga? Great to you might not be great to me," Cyrus said with a chuckle.

"Great for me is definitely great for you. We've grown a lot since we first started, and we now have clients all over the world. There is a lot of money coming in for what we do, remember that," Oga replied as he took an appreciative sip of his beer, a layer of thick foam coating his upper lip until he licked it off.

"Then I guess great for you is great for me," Cyrus said.

"How about you, Eteka? Is what's great for me also great for you?" Oga asked as he faced Eteka.

"I don't care about money. I am an Imamba. Whatever is good for the brotherhood is good for me," Eteka replied.

Oga smiled and stroked his beard. "Good answer."

Omega walked into the lounge area and joined them, taking a seat next to Oga. There was a brief silence before he spoke.

"So the diplomat you handled in America—you're sure he's dead?" Omega asked as he lit a cigar.

"Yes, sir. We even stayed behind to make sure," Cyrus replied.

"Good. Well, I have two new projects for you guys, both to do with protection. Cyrus, there's an open bid for some diamond business in the Congo that I thought would be a good fit for you. Pacman can go with you. $75,000 each, cash. The details are all here," Omega said as he handed Cyrus a folder.

"And what about me?" Eteka asked.

"Ah, the mighty Eteka. I saved a good one just for you," Omega replied as he handed another folder to Eteka. In it was a picture of a black man wearing an agbada surrounded by a few white men in suits.

"Who's he?"

"He is your client, Omoniyi Adeboyo. He is linked with the past government of Nigeria, and he'll be making a large deposit in a bank in London. You'll be protecting him while he makes that deposit. $50,000 job; details are in the folder."

"He needs protection to make a deposit? I don't understand," Eteka remarked, glancing through the folder.

"His planned deposit is public information, and there'll be a lot of protesters in London. They believe the money belongs to their country and not to our client. You'll be there to ensure his safety for the duration of the transaction. He has bodyguards, but they're not trained like you. Do a good job and we could have repeat business."

"How much is he depositing?"

"A lot of money, that's all you need to know," Oga cut in sharply, giving the younger man a quelling look.

"Yes," Omega continued as he puffed on his cigar. "You'll all leave in one week for your destinations. When you return—if you return, that is—I'll introduce you to a new project in Liberia, another short one."

"How much will that one pay?" Cyrus asked.

"I'm still negotiating, but I'm guessing around $150,000 each. I'll try for more."

"Sounds good," Cyrus said as he stood up. "You boys want to go find the women around here?"

"I've already arranged for a handful of fine local ladies to give you guys special treatment tonight in your rooms," Omega replied with a grin. "Why don't you go for a swim in the ocean or the pool? I will send for you when it's time."

"Sounds like a plan. See you gentlemen later," Cyrus replied as he stood up with Eteka. The mercenaries walked off, leaving Omega and Oga at the table.

"He asks a lot of questions," Omega said as he watched them head toward their rooms.

"Who?"

"Eteka."

"Yes, he does," Oga replied as he took another sip of his beer.

"Will he be trouble?"

"No."

"I still don't know why you picked him up," Omega replied. There was a brief silence as they listened to the waves crashing against the shore. Oga thought about Omega's words and clenched his jaw.

"Although I must admit, Eteka has turned out to be one of our finest fighters, so I cannot say that your decision was a completely foolish one. I just hope for his sake that he does not give us problems," Omega continued as he glanced at Oga.

"Don't worry. It will never come to that," snapped Oga.

"I hope not."

They watched a pair of beautiful Moroccan women walk by, their café au lait skin reflecting the setting rays of the sun, hips swaying against the backdrop of the ocean. Omega licked his lips and took another puff of his cigar.

"Eteka will have to be tested to prove his loyalty to us. There must be no doubt as to his allegiance to the Imamba."

"And what sort of test do you propose? I've been training him his whole life," Oga replied.

Omega grinned as he played with the cigar in his mouth.

"When the time comes, you will know. The test I will give will erase any doubts," Omega replied, standing. His large frame commanded the attention of everyone in the vicinity.

"Where are you going?"

"I, my friend, am off to get a Swedish massage from a very beautiful lady in the spa. Care to join me?" Omega asked with a grin.

"No."

"Suit yourself," Omega replied, walking away.

Oga leaned back in his chair as he put out his cigarette and gazed out the window, his expression serious.

✝

It was a sunny Wednesday morning when Eteka arrived at London's Heathrow airport, fresh from a week of luxury at the Moroccan resort. He was picked up by a waiting driver and driven across the city to Hampstead in North London. After about thirty minutes, the car pulled into a large estate and Eteka was escorted into the mansion by two guards.

"Good afternoon, sir," a freckled butler greeted Eteka, who simply nodded in return.

"I trust you had a good flight, sir?" the man continued as he led Eteka down a long hallway.

"Do you honestly care about how my flight went? I'm not very good at small talk," Eteka replied, scrutinizing the paintings on the wall as they passed.

"Very well, sir. Mr. Adeboyo is expecting you," the man said politely, showing Eteka into a room on his right near the end of the hall.

There were a few men and one woman in the room. All but one of the men stood while the one sitting continued talking with the woman. A messy pile of papers sat on a desk next to the woman as she read a document, and on the man's lap sat a Toshiba laptop with a large floppy disk resting on its keyboard. Eteka recognized him as the man in the picture, Mr. Adeboyo. They stopped their conversation when Eteka was shown in.

"You must be Omega's man," Mr. Adeboyo said as he looked Eteka up and down.

"I am."

The man was dressed smartly in a long-sleeved shirt, top two buttons undone, and crisply ironed trousers. He was clean-shaven save for a perfectly lined moustache, and he spoke with a heavy Nigerian accent. Slight wrinkles edged his eyes, hinting that he was either in his late forties or early fifties.

"You must know who I am, then," Mr. Adeboyo said as he got up and walked over to Eteka.

"I know who you are."

Mr. Adeboyo looked at Eteka narrowly. They stood at the same height, and were almost of the same build.

"What's your name?"

"Eteka."

"You have an intense stare, Eteka. I like that, means you're all about business." He paused. "Care for anything to drink?"

"I'll take a glass of water."

"Arewa, would you bring our guest a glass of water?" Mr. Adeboyo asked the woman, keeping his eyes on Eteka.

"Yes, sir," the woman replied as she got to her feet. She was beautiful, with smooth chocolate skin, slanted brown eyes, and a seductive stare. She exchanged glances with Eteka as she walked by, and his eyes followed her as she passed.

"Pretty girl, isn't she?" Mr. Adeboyo remarked, watching her leave the room. "Clever, too. She's my accountant, and she will be coming with us today."

"You're referring to your bank visit, I presume?"

"Yes. We will leave in about an hour. I hope that's not too soon for you?"

"Not at all. I'm ready."

"Good. It should go well, but these people do get rowdy sometimes and I have many enemies, so we must take extra precautions—hence your presence."

Eteka said nothing, briefly exchanging glances with one of the men in the room. The man stared back defiantly.

"These are my bodyguards. They will be with us in the car and will secure the premises when we get there, even though the London police should also be there. You will escort me and my accountant in and out of the building. You must protect her as well."

"There will be an extra charge for that. I'm here just for you, and guarding an extra person is more complicated," Eteka replied.

Mr. Adeboyo grinned and looked at his men as Arewa reentered the room with a glass of water and handed it to Eteka. She smiled as she handed it to him, and he looked away shyly. She seemed intrigued, looking over her shoulder as she returned to her seat.

"I wasn't wrong about you being all about business. I will sort out the financial details with your superiors and work out the additional charge," Mr. Adeboyo said.

"Good."

"We'll leave in about an hour. We're taking two cars and you'll be riding with me. As soon as we're done, you'll escort us back here. I'll be throwing a little party to celebrate the occasion later on this evening, and you're welcome to join us. If not, I'll have a driver take you back to the airport. In the meantime, feel free to relax in any of the rooms in the building. My butler can get you settled. You'll be notified when it's time; right now I have to finish looking over my accounts."

"Okay. Thanks for the water," Eteka replied, glancing at Arewa, who threw him a quick smile before he turned and left the room.

†

It was around 11:30 a.m. when Mr. Adeboyo's two-car convoy left the estate and headed toward London's financial district. Eteka found himself in the back seat of a Rolls-Royce Silver Spur with Mr. Adeboyo. Arewa sat in the passenger seat, and one of the bodyguards was driving. In front of them, the other car was filled with more of Mr. Adeboyo's bodyguards.

"Beautiful day, isn't it?" Mr. Adeboyo commented benignly as they drove through London's streets.

No one replied, and he looked over at Eteka.

"You don't talk much, do you?"

"No, sir," Eteka replied without looking at him.

Mr. Adeboyo laughed and shook his head. Arewa was watching Eteka through the rearview mirror, and he had to admit, she was quite distracting.

"Are most of your assignments like this?" Mr. Adeboyo asked.

"No, sir. My assignments vary."

"If I wanted someone dead, could you take care of that for me?"

Eteka glanced ahead—Arewa was still watching him, waiting to hear his answer. "For the right amount, the Imamba can kill anyone for you."

"I see. Well, I might be calling on your services in the near future," Mr. Adeboyo said with a raised eyebrow. "I have quite a few enemies I need disposed of."

Eteka said nothing.

Mr. Adeboyo grinned and looked out the window.

"I've always found men like you intriguing. So focused on your mission you cannot even smile."

"What's there to smile about?"

"Well, for one thing, I'm about to deposit enough money to buy a small country into my bank account. That's enough to make me smile!" Mr. Adeboyo laughed, hitting Eteka's face with his spittle. "But you wouldn't know anything about that, now, would you?" Mr. Adeboyo continued with an evil chuckle.

Eteka did not respond, choosing instead to take in London's scenery. Mr. Adeboyo continued to laugh, and although he forced himself not to look, Eteka could feel Arewa's scrutinizing gaze upon him.

Their car arrived at the bank around noon. A large crowd had gathered outside, mostly made up of angry Nigerians carrying placards and shouting obscenities at the convoy. The car pulled up in front of the bank, and two bodyguards from the first car walked up and flanked it on either side.

"Let me get out first, then we can all walk in together," Eteka said, stepping out of the car. It was a chaotic scene outside as the crowd grew wild and swarmed against uniformed police officers, who shoved them back. A few threw rotten fruit and eggs, and everyone shouted insults and threats at them. Eteka scanned the crowd, signaling one of the bodyguards to escort Arewa from the passenger seat into the building. He then opened the rear door, and Mr. Adeboyo emerged from the car. As he did so, the crowd began chanting, "OLE! OLE! OLE!"[1] while pelting Eteka and his client. They hurried into the bank, Eteka's eyes scanning the crowd for someone with a more sinister intent.

"See how much my people love me?" Mr. Adeboyo laughed as the bank doors closed behind them. Arewa had already exchanged

---

[1] "Ole" in Yoruba means "thief."

greetings with the bank manager, a short, balding white man dressed in a grey suit. The manager smiled as Mr. Adeboyo entered and walked up to shake his hand.

"Hello, sir, and welcome to Dalant Bank. My name is John Waddle, and I am the general manager. We have been anticipating your arrival. Quite a scene outside," Mr. Waddle said in an upper-crust British accent as he glanced outside at the mob.

"Yes, they are my fans," Mr. Adeboyo replied with a wink. "Let's get down to business, shall we?"

"Of course, sir. This way," Mr. Waddle said, ushering them toward a large conference room.

"I'll be out here," Eteka said to Mr. Adeboyo, who simply nodded and entered the conference room with Arewa.

Eteka stood outside the conference room door with two bank security guards and one of Mr. Adeboyo's bodyguards. The commotion outside seemed to escalate, and Eteka watched a policeman with a baton subdue a few people in the angry crowd.

"Must be a busy day for you," one of the security guards said to Eteka. Eteka ignored him and glanced down the hall. Some movement had caught his attention.

"Are there other people working today?" Eteka asked, keeping his eyes on the hallway.

"No, the office is supposed to be empty," the security guard replied. "Why do you ask?"

"Watch this door for me; I'll be right back," Eteka said to the guard as he started down the hall.

"Do you need assistance?" the security guard asked.

"No. Stay here. I'll be right back."

Eteka walked down the hall and came to a corridor lined with offices. Dead silence. He looked to his left, then to his right and spotted a door that was slightly ajar. He approached silently and opened it. It turned out to be the entrance to the men's room, and once inside he spotted a pair of feet under one of the stall doors. He walked up to a urinal and pretended to relieve himself. After a few moments, the stall door opened and an elderly black man emerged. The man had a calm face and sported a messy beard and ragged clothes. His hair was grey with dark patches that had not been combed. Despite his appearance, there was an air of dignity about him, and he moved with youthful energy. He seemed a bit startled when he saw Eteka.

"Oh, you scared me," the old man said in a Nigerian accent. Eteka smiled slightly as he watched the man. He had a bulge in his trousers around his pocket, and Eteka guessed that it was either a gun or a knife.

The man stepped beside Eteka and began to relieve himself, a move that Eteka found odd for a man who had just exited a toilet stall. He seemed to be a nice man, with a hint of nervousness about him, as if he were about to do something he had no business doing.

"Do you work here?" the man asked.

"No, but I am working," Eteka replied, flushing the urinal and heading toward a sink.

"Oh, that's nice," the man said. There was a slight tremble in his voice.

"How about you? Do you work here?" Eteka asked as he washed his hands. His eyes were still on the man through the bathroom mirror.

"Er, no, but I am working, I guess, just like you," the man answered, zipping up his trousers and heading over to the sink, next to Eteka. "What do you do?"

"Many things. Today I'm watching over someone."

"I see," the man replied, the nervousness still in his voice.

"And yourself? What work are you doing around here today?" Eteka asked as he started to dry his hands.

The man was quiet for a second, then he faced Eteka.

"I am helping my people. There is something very important that I have to do."

"Can you say what it is?" Eteka asked as he started to move toward the man.

The old man smiled. "No, I can't. I have to dry my hands, if you don't mind."

Eteka stepped aside as the man moved in the direction of the paper towel dispenser. Eteka's adrenaline spiked as he felt the tension in the air. The old man retrieved some tissues, his back to Eteka. Then, suddenly, he spun around and lunged at Eteka, a large knife in his hand. But Eteka was ready. He threw the man off balance, tripping him with his foot. As the old man went down, he fell on the hand holding the knife.

Eteka walked over to the man, now lying face-down on the floor. He turned him over with his foot and the man groaned, the knife protruding from his chest.

"Who are you?" Eteka asked the dying man.

"D-d-does it matter?" the old man replied with a cough. He twitched, and blood oozed from his chest and mouth.

"I guess it doesn't. It did not have to end like this."

"It had to end, one way or another."

"But not like this. You knew you did not stand a chance against all the guards posted out front, much less against me."

The old man smiled.

"What's your name, boy?"

Eteka bent down and got close to the man. He could feel the man's breathing slowing down, and his old frame beginning to tremble with shock.

"Why do you want my name?"

"I'm curious. It's the least you could do for killing me," the man replied, managing a slight grin.

"I can't give you my name."

"Fair enough. You're not as ruthless as most of Adeboyo's men."

"What gives you that impression?"

"Because if you were, we wouldn't be having this lovely conversation," the man replied, clutching his chest. "Something tells me you don't know anything about the man you serve," the man said between coughs.

"I know enough."

"Did you know he's a thief, and has stolen much money that belongs to my people?"

"What makes you think I care?" Eteka asked.

"You have a good heart, I can sense it…" the old man said, his breathing getting fainter.

"You're wrong," Eteka said, standing up.

"People are poor and suffering while the man you protect squanders their money. I came here to try and fix the situation…" the old man said, his eyes becoming glassy.

"I foiled your plans, old man."

"You certainly did. But I'm a free man. I wonder if you can say the same," the old man replied, and with one last shuddering breath, life left his body.

Eteka studied the old man's lifeless form for a few minutes, trying to make sense of the man's last words. Then, he quietly walked out of the bathroom.

After an hour, Mr. Adeboyo emerged from the conference room, a big smile on his face. Arewa and the bank manager were not far behind.

"Always a pleasure doing business with you," Mr. Adeboyo said heartily as he shook hands with the manager. "I trust everything will run smoothly from here on out?"

"Yes, sir. You will have our utmost cooperation, and we look forward to doing business with you in the future. Your selected accounts will accrue interest as discussed," the official replied.

"Good. Arewa?"

"Yes, sir?" Arewa asked as she stepped up to Mr. Adeboyo.

"Please make a note to follow up with our friends here at the bank to make sure our—excuse me, *my* interest grows as discussed."

"Yes, sir."

"Good," Mr. Adeboyo said as he turned around to face Eteka. "How did it go out here?"

"Everything went well, sir."

"Excellent. Well, let's head out, then," Mr. Adeboyo said as he started to walk toward the main entrance.

As they left, Eteka whispered casually into the bank security guard's ear, who shot him a surprised look. They stepped outside the bank into the hail of objects and curses being thrown by the angry crowd. "OLE! OLE! OLE!" was all that could be heard as the bodyguards rushed to bring the cars up front.

"We'll travel in different cars, just to play it safe," Mr. Adeboyo said to Eteka. "You ride with Arewa, and I'll go with my men. We'll rendezvous at my estate."

"My job is to protect you, sir. I cannot leave you."

"I have to discuss private business over the phone."

"You can sit with us and have your discussion. We will give you your privacy," Eteka replied.

Mr. Adeboyo smiled and nodded. "Very well, I'll ride with you."

Eteka escorted Arewa and Mr. Adeboyo into the first car as the second car zoomed off. Soon, they pulled out of the bank's parking lot, leaving the pandemonium behind. As they set off, Mr. Adeboyo whipped out a phone and started a business conversation, while Eteka and Arewa sat in silence.

"Phew! That was a bit frightening," Arewa said as she looked through the back window at the fading crowd.

Eteka said nothing as he studied her. She was a pretty woman with a petite, curvy frame, a heart-shaped face, short natural hair, chocolate skin, and large, slanted, almond-shaped eyes with thick lashes. She spoke with a strong British accent and wore her navy skirt suit as though she'd grown up wearing Western clothing.

She turned around and met Eteka's gaze.

"Hi. I'm Arewa," she said as she extended her hand.

"I know," Eteka replied as they shook hands. Her French-manicured hand felt soft in his.

"Oh…your name is Eteka, right? And you're with Mr. Omega and the brotherhood?"

"How do you know about the brotherhood?"

"It was on your file. As Mr. Adeboyo's accountant, I have to make sure you and your associates get paid."

"Of course."

Nothing was said between them for a couple of minutes, and Arewa continued to study Eteka. He kept his eyes on the passing scenery while Mr. Adeboyo droned on about percentages on the phone to someone in another country.

Arewa shook her head as she giggled softly. "Will you be staying for the party?"

"Huh?" Eteka asked, facing her again.

"Mr. Adeboyo will be throwing a party in a few hours. Will you be attending?"

"Yes, I might. Will you be there?"

"I don't have a choice."

"Why don't you have a choice?"

"Let's not get into that," she replied pleasantly, but shot a quick look at her employer.

"Okay."

She continued to watch Eteka as he pretended to look at the cars passing by. A soft rain began to fall, the tiny drops of water on the windows indicating that the heavens had begun their work of cleansing London's streets.

That evening, Eteka stood in a grand ballroom at Mr. Adeboyo's residence. A few guests were already present, some wearing flowing agbadas and most speaking with thick Nigerian accents. There were also a few white men in suits, and beautiful women in elegant cocktail dresses and evening gowns. Eteka was dressed in a dark blue suit with no tie. He stood in a corner of the room, watching people converse and move about the room. His thoughts kept returning to the old man he had encountered at the bank in London.

What did that man mean when he asked if I was a free man? Eteka wondered. He was deep in thought when he felt a tap on his shoulder. He turned around to face Arewa.

"Hope I'm not disturbing you," she said. She looked exquisite in the outfit she wore, a black silk halter dress that hugged her slender curves and dipped low in the back. They eyed each other without saying a word, and Eteka shyly shifted his gaze when she smiled.

"No, not at all," he replied.

They were both quiet for a few seconds as they surveyed the room.

"So, how did it go today?" she asked, breaking the silence. She moved a little closer to Eteka, curiosity written on her face.

Eteka kept his expression neutral. "It went well, I guess. How did it go with you?"

"Okay. I just deal with balance sheets and ledgers, so there's really not much excitement in my world."

"You work for a very influential man, seems pretty exciting to me," Eteka replied, his eyes tracking Mr. Adeboyo from across the room as he mingled with his laughing guests.

Arewa followed his gaze and smiled. "Yes. He is well known within certain elite circles. Money gives a person many friends."

"You don't sound too happy about that."

She met his eyes and smiled again. "Money isn't everything."

"It isn't? So why are you here?"

"Long story," she replied.

"I see."

There was another brief silence. Eteka shifted uncomfortably, looking through the crowd of people he didn't know. Part of him wished he could find an excuse to get away, but a much more influential part of him wanted to stay near Arewa, hear her voice again, and look into her soft brown eyes, so full of curiosity and light. He wondered if he even remembered how to talk to a woman that wasn't a paid escort.

"Eteka is a Nigerian name. Are you Nigerian?" she asked, breaking his train of thought.

"Yes."

"Do you ever visit?"

"If I'm needed there for work, I go."

"Oh. And work entails protecting other people, I take it?"

Eteka eyed her narrowly. He'd never had anyone question him like this before—hookers were not a curious group, as a rule. "Why are you asking all these questions?"

"Just trying to make conversation, that's all. I'm not really fond of talking to Mr. Adeboyo's colleagues," she replied, "but you seem nice."

"Why does everyone think I'm such a nice guy?" he asked, his mind going back to his brief conversation with the old man in the bathroom.

"You don't think you're nice?" she teased, widening her eyes playfully.

"You don't know me."

"It's your energy. You don't feel bad, even though you're wearing that frown on your face. Open-minded people can sense these things, you know."

"And you're open-minded?"

"I would like to think so, yes."

Eteka looked at her. He enjoyed her attention—attention he was not accustomed to getting.

"Do you ever go to Nigeria?"

She smiled at his question.

"Yes, actually I go there quite often. I own an apartment in Abuja. Have you been there?"

"I know Abuja. Nice city."

"Where do you live?" she asked.

"You're a nosy one, aren't you?" Eteka responded with a grin.

"Yes, I tend to talk a lot, especially when I see someone I like. Anyway, my questions made you smile."

She brushed her elbow against him and it sent a nice tingle through his body. She continued to smile as she looked into his eyes.

"So, you like talking to me?"

"I already told you that I do. But let's not change the subject. Where do you live?" she asked.

"I move around."

"I'm enjoying your one-line answers, man of mystery! Well, next time you're in Nigeria, you should give me a ring, or come visit me. Here, take my card," she said, producing a business card from somewhere in her dress. On it was her contact information for both London and Abuja. He glanced at it briefly, then smiled. It carried the faint essence of her perfume.

"So, where do you spend most of your time, in Nigeria or here in England?" he asked.

"I go back and forth. But I'll be in Nigeria for the next couple of months. Just look me up the next time you're there. I would love to have you over," she replied with a wink.

"I'll do that."

They said no more as Mr. Adeboyo, dressed in a lavish agbada, walked over to them with a glass of champagne in his hand. He had two white men with him.

"Arewa, how is everything?" Mr. Adeboyo asked.

"Fine, thank you, sir."

"Good. These two gentlemen have a business offer for us regarding land right here in London. Take notes on their offer and get their contact details, please."

"Yes, sir. Gentlemen, please follow me," Arewa replied as she led the men away to a secluded part of the ballroom. As she did so, she gave Eteka one last look. Mr. Adeboyo caught the exchange and grinned.

"Pretty girl, don't you think? You like her? Don't worry, a lot of men do," Mr. Adeboyo said as both men watched Arewa walk away.

"You must be happy to have her working for you, then."

"One mark of a powerful man is the quality of the women he keeps around him. Arewa is my property, but I think I can arrange something between you and her for a few 'favors,' if you know what I mean," Mr. Adeboyo said with a wink as he nudged Eteka. Eteka repressed the urge to slug the man.

"I'll think about it," he replied, barely managing to be gracious. "How soon can I leave?"

"We have arranged a flight for you from Heathrow tomorrow morning around eight, first class," Mr. Adeboyo said.

"Thank you."

Mr. Adeboyo looked at Eteka for a long moment, then turned his attention to the crowd.

"I've enjoyed your services. I heard you took care of a possible threat back at the bank."

"Yes."

"Did you get a name, by any chance?"

"No."

"Were any words exchanged?"

"He called you a thief," Eteka replied without looking at him. Mr. Adeboyo burst out laughing.

"My money is well earned. A lot of people think just because you're Nigerian and rich that you are a thief. There are a lot of wealthy, honest people in Nigeria. Don't mind these speculators. All they do is cause trouble. Here, come and meet a few of my friends."

"I'm fine, sir. I will take my leave now, if you don't mind," Eteka declined.

"Leaving so soon?"

"Yes. I want to get some rest," Eteka replied.

"You're definitely all about business. Follow my butler," he said, signaling the same freckled man Eteka had met earlier. "He'll show you to the quarters we've prepared. I'll be sure to tell Omega what a professional you are," Mr. Adeboyo said with a laugh as he turned and headed back to the crowd.

Eteka nodded and followed the butler out of the ballroom. As they stepped out, he looked back and caught Arewa's eyes on him, looking away swiftly as she continued her work.

DEADLY ALLIANCE

Géryville. Northern Algeria. 1955.

The Algerian Revolution[1] was in full swing. Yisa limped as fast as he could on this particularly hot afternoon, the bullet wound in his right leg leaving spots of blood on the sandy ground. Not too far behind him and in hot pursuit was a menacing man, standing at about 6'4", in brown camouflage overalls. The man was French, an assassin from the French Legion, known within select circles as Démon. Démon had been sent to assist the French government with the French occupation in Algeria by eradicating some key Algerian targets. Démon chased Yisa, firing off repeat rounds from a black MAT-49 submachine gun, the bullets barely missing him as they bounced off the walls of the buildings around them.

The French hitman had been hired to assassinate a prominent member of the Algerian Revolution here in Géryville.[2] Yisa was part of a two-man team sent to stop him. The private military company Yisa had signed up with in South Africa had

---

[1] The Algerian Revolution/War of Independence lasted from 1954 to 1962 and ended with Algeria securing its independence from France.
[2] Géryville was the former name given by the French occupation for the city now known as El Bayadh.

offered him this contract, which at the time hadn't seemed particularly difficult or dangerous in the grand scheme of things. Now his partner was dead—killed by the very same man pursuing Yisa—and he was on the run. What had he been thinking? Only a few months ago he had wed the love of his life, Amina, in a quiet ceremony in Nigeria, and they planned on having children. What in the world was he doing here? Sure, the money was good—if he lived—but the odds were against him: he was running for his life from a professional killer, and there was also the small matter of the bullet wound in his leg.

Yisa did his best to apply pressure to the wound as he limped between buildings in a remote part of the city. At least the air in this part of Algeria was merely arid, unlike the intense humidity he had experienced in some of the West African regions. There was something about wet heat that sapped the strength out of a man.

A hail of bullets whisked past Yisa, their sound ricocheting off the walls and drumming into his ears. Yisa swore he could feel the heat coming off them as a few came perilously close to his face. His pursuer was closing the distance, and this was not good. He had told that idiot partner of his to wait as they stalked Démon at a local café in the city, but the fool had drawn his gun and fired prematurely. And to add insult to injury, he had missed. He'd had a wide-open shot of the assassin sitting and eating breakfast and missed.

Démon, obviously no stranger to street exchanges, had quickly whipped out his shiny black MAT-49—the weapon itself

looking like death incarnate—and let both Yisa and his partner taste
a few rounds. Yisa had seen it coming and jumped for cover behind
a parked car, but not before taking a bullet to the leg. His partner,
who was decidedly not as smart, nor blessed with good reflexes,
took the brunt of the return fire, the 900-rpm weapon tearing his
body to shreds and leaving a big red mess on the ground where he
had stood. At least Yisa had had the good sense to turn and run. He
was perhaps the first West African man in history to get shot at by a
French assassin while being chased through a remote part of Algeria.
Not a record to be proud of—or perhaps one he'd live to celebrate.

Yisa limped around a corner. He could see the few residents
in the area quickly darting into their homes and shops and shuttering
their windows. Limping like this in the open only made him a target,
and he knew it. He had his back to his pursuer, which diminished the
accuracy of returning fire with his pistol. Démon had the advantage
with his longer-range weapon. The only thing saving Yisa was the
closeness of the buildings between which he darted, offering him at
least some cover.

Yisa knew that sooner or later Démon would catch up to
him, but would rather it be on his terms. He had to close the
distance. He made it around another corner—dead end. His injured
leg was becoming a burden now, as the bullet wound had begun to
swell. He could hear Démon's footsteps approaching quickly behind
him. Looking around, Yisa spotted a closed door and, with all the
strength he could muster, rammed through it and crashed to the

ground on the other side just as another round of gunfire erupted and tore through the spot where he had just been standing.

Yisa looked up. A family was sitting on the floor in a circle, enjoying an early lunch of chorba beida[1]. They looked at him with terror in their eyes.

"GET OUT! WE DON'T WANT TROUBLE!" a woman in the family screamed at the fallen Yisa in Arabic. Covered in dust, he frantically scurried into an adjoining room, took cover behind a wall, and withdrew his pistol from its holster. The woman continued to scream, her large family fleeing the home like ants from a flooded anthill. Then it was quiet. Yisa could hear his own heart beating, his weapon's handle dripping with the sweat from his palms.

Suddenly, the wall next to Yisa's face exploded as Démon's foot crashed through the aging brick and smashed the Nigerian mercenary in the face. Yisa was thrown across the room, his head snapping back violently. He crashed into a decorative table nearby and Démon emerged from around the wall, the MAT-49 in his hands now looking like a coiled black snake. Yisa's vision was blurry, and as it came into focus he could see Démon walking toward him. Where was his pistol?

The damn thing was now across the room. He hoped they'd break the news gently to Amina.

Démon stood on top of Yisa, placing a foot on his neck. The hard sole of his dusty boot cut off Yisa's breathing, but more troubling was the fact that the French assassin's weapon was now

---

[1] Chorba beida (Algerian white soup) is a common dish in that region.

pointed directly at his face. Oddly enough, Yisa found himself studying the man's face. He seemed to be in his thirties, Caucasian, with brown hair and rough stubble. He had cold green eyes and a cleft in his upper lip. Yisa studied the barrel of the gun as it gaped back at him. Perhaps this is what people thought of right before they died.

"Qui êtes-vous?"[1] Démon asked in a deep voice, slightly decreasing the pressure on Yisa's neck with his foot.

"Ce n'est pas votre affaires. Tuez-moi et finissez-le,"[2] Yisa gasped in response.

Démon paused for a moment, his eyes searching Yisa's. It was an intimate moment they shared, the last few seconds of a man's life. Yisa would spend it as prey. He would never get to see his lovely Amina again. Perhaps this was the end of the line. Démon nodded, as if agreeing with Yisa's thoughts, then squeezed the trigger.

Click.

Out of ammo—a second chance. As Démon sighed with frustration and reached for a new clip, Yisa shifted his position on the floor and, using his good leg, hooked his assailant at the knees and threw him to the ground. Démon fell and a struggle ensued. Yisa reached for the man's gun and they both rolled on the ground, panting as they struggled over the weapon. Démon was thrown onto his back, the weapon almost within Yisa's reach. Using his right hand, Démon tried to poke Yisa in the eyes, and then violently

---

[1] "Who are you?"
[2] "That's none of your business. Kill me and get it over with."

yanked on Yisa's ears. The move was so painful that it made Yisa's temples ring, and the mercenary howled in pain, releasing his grip on the gun. A powerful elbow to the face followed, knocking out two of Yisa's teeth and sending him sprawling to the ground.

As Yisa toppled over, he flailed his good leg, knocking the weapon away from Démon and across the room. Démon tried to dive for the gun, but Yisa held onto his leg, crawled onto his back, and punched him in the ribs. With Yisa still on his back, Démon stood up slowly and performed a judo throw, using his hips to fling Yisa over his shoulder and onto the ground. As Yisa fell, Démon raised his foot to crush Yisa's face into the hard floor, but the mercenary rolled upon landing and evaded the attack. Both men stood upright, Yisa favoring his uninjured leg. The gun lay a few feet away from them. They looked into each other's eyes and glanced at the gun, then back at each other.

"Je n'ai pas besoin d'un revolver pour vous tuer,[1]" Démon grunted as he lunged at Yisa. Yisa responded with a sudden front kick that landed squarely on his opponent's chest, sending Démon flying into the wall behind him. Démon charged again, this time parrying a right hook thrown by Yisa, and tackled him to the ground. Punches followed, rained down by Démon as Yisa covered his face. He couldn't take this punishment much longer... he just needed an opening... and soon he found one. Démon placed a hand on Yisa's chest, intending to hold him down while he used his other hand to strike.

---

[1] "I don't need a gun to kill you."

DÉMON

"JE N'AI PAS BESOIN
D'UN REVOLVER POUR
VOUS TUER."

ETEKA
RISE OF THE IMAMBA

Yisa quickly lifted his hips, secured Démon's outstretched arm and locked his legs around the man's exposed shoulder and neck, performing the triangle submission.[1] He had him. Démon struggled to free himself, blood rushing to his head, his face turning red. Urgency was clearly written in his expression as he struggled in Yisa's grasp. If Yisa could only hold on for a few moments, the French hitman would pass out.

But the leg doing the locking was the same one that had been shot. Its strength had diminished, and Yisa could feel it starting to shake and give way. Bit by bit, Démon moved Yisa's leg until finally he freed himself. Grabbing Yisa's collar, he then picked Yisa's entire body up and ferociously slammed him into the ground.

---

[1] The triangle choke is a four-figured chokehold that constricts the blood flow from the carotid arteries to the brain. It is commonly used in judo, jiu-jitsu, grappling and mixed martial arts.

The impact knocked the wind out of Yisa and the French assassin pounced, locking him into a position in which he could not move.

"Assez de jeux, maintenant vous meurez,"[1] Démon said, retrieving a large knife from his belt that Yisa hadn't noticed before. The blade glistened in the sunlight that shone through a broken window. No chance of a blade jamming, or Démon's gun running out of ammunition—fixed-blade knives were sadly very reliable. And he couldn't move—Démon had pinned him down. Maybe this was it. Here in Algeria, in the middle of nowhere, he would be butchered like a pig. He closed his eyes and thought of his wife...

BANG! BANG! BANG! BANG! BANG!

Five shots rang out in quick succession, and just like that, Démon's body fell, his large frame crumbling on top of Yisa. Yisa rolled him off with difficulty and looked up. Where had those shots come from? They were unmistakably rounds from a Colt M1911, a weapon traditionally used by American personnel at the time and not native to French or Algerian forces. The new visitor was not a local.

A dark-skinned man stepped into the room, tall and athletically built. He sported aviator sunglasses, green army fatigues, and an unkempt, scruffy beard. He was holding a pistol, no doubt the one that had killed the French assassin. A camera on a strap was slung around his shoulder. He stood in the doorway and grinned at Yisa.

"Good thing I was around or your insides would probably be all over the floor by now," the man said with a grin, holstering his

---

[1] "Enough games, now you die."

weapon. He had a strange accent with hints of French and Portuguese.

"Who are you?"

"My name is Oga."

"Thanks for helping me. What are you doing here?" Yisa asked.

"I work for a private military company, like you," Oga replied as he began taking pictures of Démon's body.

"How do you know who I work for?"

"Because we are both mercenaries, as they say in English. I was also on contract to track and kill this man," Oga said, prodding Démon's body with his boot. "It seems you got to him first."

"Yes. Well, you killed him," Yisa replied as he slowly stood up.

"After you softened him up. But I did save your life," Oga replied as he finished taking pictures.

"So what do you want?"

"Maybe you can give me a little cut from your earnings."

"And if I refuse?" Yisa asked sternly.

"Then I guess I'll finish the job your friend here started," Oga said, placing his hand on his weapon.

"I guess the odds are against me, for now."

"They are. Ten percent of your earnings," said Oga as he put his camera away.

"Only if you help me get to Batna."[1]

---

[1] The Algerian Revolution began in the city of Batna.

"Deal. I'm headed there myself."

Oga placed an arm around the injured Yisa, supporting his weight on the side with his injured leg, and together they walked out to the desolate street, where an army Jeep awaited them.

After a few hours of driving across various checkpoints manned by French troops, Yisa and Oga arrived in the city of Batna. Heavy rains greeted them in the Algerian stronghold for the resistance movement. It was evening, and heavy artillery and shell explosions echoed in the distance. They drove on narrow streets, resistance fighters darting between buildings and eyeing the mercenaries with curiosity. Five security checkpoints later, they parked their ride next to a large structure that could have passed for a former army barracks. Three Algerian natives, two of whom were engaged in an argument, escorted Yisa and Oga from their Jeep. Yisa, leaning on Oga for support, studied his surroundings.

Smaller white buildings badly in need of fresh paint surrounded the large structure. Behind the old barracks were train tracks, upon which sat an old freight train. They were led to one of the boxcars on the train. The third Algerian man banged on the boxcar while his comrades continued yelling at each other. Some movement could be heard inside the boxcar, and its door slid open, the bare metal frame grinding against the base of the train itself. A short man dressed in a white shirt, slacks, and a fez stood before them holding a rifle nearly as large as he was. He smiled warmly at their escort and they spoke with a familiarity that hinted at friendship.

After their exchange, mostly in Arabic, Yisa and Oga were guided into the boxcar. Its interior was furnished with soft woven rugs, cushions to sit on, and a wooden table with a tray of assorted dry meats, a teapot, and four cups, one of which was filled with tea. Leaning in a corner were three rifles. Two lanterns sat at opposite ends of the space, making the shadows of the men inside dance on the walls.

The most interesting fixture was a large man who sat quietly on one of the cushions with his legs crossed and his back against a wall, puffing smoke out of a thick cigar. He had dark skin with Sub-Saharan features—a strong jaw and a wide forehead—and wore long white robes, a gold ring on his right pinky finger, and a shiny gold necklace around his neck. He stared briefly at both mercenaries as they entered the boxcar, then switched his focus back to his cigar. Yisa and Oga sat down on some cushions across from him while their guides stepped outside.

"You need treatment for your leg," Oga said to Yisa.

"Yes."

The door slid open again and a clean-shaven Algerian man with a headpiece and long robes stepped in. The newcomer paused and smiled, taking the time to study each occupant. He spoke to the quiet large man smoking the cigar, "Nous sommes charger votre argent dans les camions maintenant. Merci encore pour les armes que vous avez apporté. Ils semblent haut de gamme."[1]

"De rien. Je fournis seulement les meilleurs produits pour mes clients. Vous serez sûr d'avoir votre hommes donnez-moi passage à Alger, oui?"[2] the large man replied in a deep, raspy voice.

"Oui, bien sûr,"[3] the Algerian man replied, a wide smile still on his face as he turned to the two mercenaries.

"Ah, Monsieur Oga. Assalamu Alaikum."

"Wa alaikum assalam,"[4] Oga replied with a grin.

"The job is finished, yes?" the Algerian continued in English.

"Yes, I have the proof here," Oga replied, patting his camera. "I'll send it over when I get a chance to develop the film.

"Good, and when you do, you will get your money," the Algerian said as his eyes shifted to Yisa. "Who is your friend?"

"I am Yisa."

"What are you doing here, Yisa?"

"I helped your friend here do his job," Yisa replied, receiving a glare from Oga. The Algerian man looked confusedly between the two men.

"I thought you said you worked alone, Oga."

"I thought I did as well. Yisa turned out to be an unexpected source of help, despite nearly getting himself killed," Oga grinned.

---

[1] "We are loading your money into the trucks now. Thanks again for the weapons you brought. They seem top-of-the-line."
[2] "You're welcome. I only supply the best products for my clients. You will be sure to have your men give me safe passage to Algiers, yes?"
[3] "Yes, of course."
[4] "Assalamu Alaikum": "Peace be unto you." "Wa alaikum assalam": "And upon you be peace."

The Algerian smiled and shrugged. "What matters is that you did your job. Send the proof and you will get your money. You both can stay here 'til the storm passes," the Algerian said, heading for the sliding door.

"I need a medic, I'm injured," Yisa said out loud, causing the Algerian to pause and turn around. He studied Yisa again, his eyes resting on Yisa's bloodstained trousers.

"I will send one of my men to take a look," he said. And with that, the Algerian walked out of the boxcar.

Faint smoke from the lanterns wafted in the dim light as thunder crackled and raindrops pattered softly on the roof. A cool, wet breeze blowing through a crack in the wall brushed against Yisa's face. It was so soothing after the stifling heat of the day. He began to doze off, his eyes fluttering as he thought of his wife. What he wouldn't give to be in her arms at this moment...

"So, who are you?" Oga's question snapped Yisa out of his slumber. The large man, to whom the question was posed, looked up at Oga and took the cigar out of his mouth.

"None of your business."

"I will decide what business is mine or not. Again, who are you?" Oga asked.

The large man smiled and shook his head. There was an air of authority about him, and Oga felt distinctly uneasy. The mercenary shifted closer to the large man, positioning his body so his sidearm could be seen.

"Are you threatening me with your little toy?" the large man asked with a chuckle.

"Maybe I am," blustered Oga.

The large man placed his cigar on the table and calmly grabbed a piece of meat. He took a huge bite, his large jaw clicking as he chewed. Yisa became hungry watching him eat.

"There are three kinds of people in this game: idealists, businessmen, and the grunts that we both control, like you," the large man said, fixing his eyes on Oga's. "Your trying to intimidate me is like an ant trying to intimidate the sole of a man's boot. You should have some meat and rethink your foolish words," he concluded, turning away from Oga to recline back against the wall.

Oga paused a moment, considering, then scooted back to his original position, retrieved a cigarette from his back pocket, and began to smoke. Yisa sat back and observed everything. He found the large man interesting.

"I am Yisa. What is your name?" Yisa asked out loud, deciding to take a different approach. The large man sat up and smiled.

"Hello, Yisa. You can call me Omega."

"That's an unusual name."

"It was given to me by some unusual people," Omega replied, his gaze settling on Oga. Oga returned the stare as he took a drag from his cigarette.

"What is your friend's name?"

"He calls himself Oga."

"Oga? Ha, now *that* is an interesting name to have. What are you two doing here? You don't look Algerian or French to me."

"Neither do you."

"Good observation," Omega responded, his features obscured by the small cloud of cigar smoke around his head. "So, what are you doing here?"

"We just finished a contract. Now, just trying to go home with our money."

"You were both on the same contract?"

"No, but our target was the same," Yisa replied.

"My, what a coincidence. Will you two work together in the future?" Omega asked, grabbing another piece of meat.

"You ask too many questions," Oga cut in.

"I'm a businessman: I question everything. So, how are you both going to split your reward? 50/50?" Omega continued, a sly grin on his face.

"Mind your own business," Oga snapped angrily.

Omega's smile broadened at the rebuke. He took his time chewing the piece of meat, licking his fingers when he was done and maintaining eye contact with Oga.

"Well, if you two need help deciding how to split your reward, I would be more than happy to assist. You should both try this lamb, by the way. They seasoned it very well. I would hate to eat it all," Omega said.

"We will be fine. What are you doing here?" Yisa asked.

"Me? Oh, just business. I specialize in moving things around."

"What kinds of things?"

"You know, ammunition, materials, things like that," Omega replied.

"You're an arms dealer?"

Omega smiled expansively. "I prefer the word businessman. I'm into whatever makes a profit. Here, take my business card. You can tell whomever you report to that I have the most modern and relevant inventory this side of the world. I'd be more than happy to do business with your group," Omega said, reaching under his robe for two business cards. The first he handed to Yisa.

"Here. I promise not to ask any more questions you don't like," Omega said with a grin as he handed the second card to Oga.

Oga studied the card, placed it in a pocket, poured himself some tea, and leaned back in his seat, studying the contents of his teacup. Omega reclined on the cushions and puffed on his cigar.

A young medic came into the boxcar for Yisa. He wordlessly extracted the bullet with a wicked set of surgical tweezers, then cleaned and bandaged Yisa's wound. The bullet had missed the bone, and though the wound was painful, it was not terribly serious. The medic gave him a shot of antibiotics to guard against infection. After his treatment, Yisa reclined as his mind drifted into a sea of abstract concepts. He thought of his homeland, all the fighting he had done up to this point, and the reason for it all. What was really being achieved?

The emergence of nationalist movements in resistance to colonial control was common these days. But there was no unity. The groups operated in individual units, sometimes different nations or even multiple groups fighting in small territories. What would the future hold? Sure, nations might win independence, but without a solid ideology—a unified vision for all the fighters involved—and an honor system that required accountability and consistency, there would be chaos. If only all the fighters in Africa could unite under one banner, one code, one creed... a loud crack of thunder sounded, stirring Yisa out of his dreamy state. Omega was watching him.

"You seem deep in thought."

"Yes, I am."

"What are you thinking of?" Omega asked.

"Ah, it's nothing."

"Please, share. We might as well entertain each other 'til this storm ends."

Yisa sat up and poured himself a cup of tea under Oga and Omega's watchful gazes. The few years Yisa had spent in school helped him formulate his thoughts, and then he spoke.

"Where are you from, Omega?" Yisa asked. Omega chuckled at the question.

"My mother was Nigerian. I am not sure where my father was from, although I know he was not African."

"And you, Oga," Yisa continued as he turned to Oga, "where are you from?"

"My mother was from the Congo, my father from Guinea-Bissau," Oga replied after a long pause.

"And I am Nigerian," Yisa said, "just like Omega. Funny we should be having tea together in Algeria."

"I have broken bread with many different types of people. This is nothing new," Omega commented.

"Forgive me, I am not the best at articulating my thoughts," Yisa replied. "What I am trying to say is, we all have unique skill sets, yet we are divided. Can you imagine if we came together for a common cause?"

Omega tapped his chin, a thoughtful look on his face. "An enterprise of sorts," Omega said. "A partnership could be an interesting business model worth exploring. I've always been keen on adding human assets to my inventory," he finished as he lit up another cigar.

"But this would not just be for personal profit, Omega. Africa is changing as we speak. There are many revolutions and nationalist movements on the rise, and thousands of fighters are bred from different armies and guerrilla groups. More and more foreign countries are supporting our cause. When these movements and wars end, we need a place for our fighters to come together as one. A place where they can get educated, learn about honor, follow a common creed."

"And get paid," Oga cut in. His interruption made both Yisa and Omega smile.

"Yes, and get paid," Yisa finished. "There is no reason why we cannot work together and organize the fighters we know. There is much we can accomplish."

"So, tell me—after you organize these fighters as you say, what do you plan on doing with them?" Omega asked.

"We can use them to defend our people as we build ourselves up."

"Defend our people? And who are our people?"

"Our people—you know, our brothers and sisters across Africa."

"All of them?"

"Yes."

"And why do you think they are *all* your people, or mine? Do you know how many ethnic groups there are in Africa? Thousands. What makes you think they all want your help, or will buy into this vision of yours?"

"I haven't figured that part out yet, but my heart tells me gathering all our top fighters under one banner would be a great and powerful thing," Yisa replied.

Omega leaned back, cigar in mouth, and shook his head. "I respect your passion and ideals, my friend, but I've heard this sort of talk many times before, and I do not share your sentiment. I am a businessman, not an idealist. Any partnership should first and foremost have the goal of making money by increasing the return on investments," Omega said.

"Speak English, please," Oga said, now tuned in to the conversation.

"I forgot that I am speaking with illiterate grunts," Omega said playfully. "Like I said, I am not an idealistic human being. The business I'm in requires conflict. But, the idea you propose presents the possibility of a profitable business model. I have the right connections to gain weapons, contracts, and foreign training. You two are experienced in the field. You can recruit, manage, and train members for this organization. I like the idea."

Another round of thunder crackled across the skies. The rain seemed to increase in its intensity, but the outside elements had no effect on their conversation. Yisa was excited. Something unique was happening.

"So, what are we saying? Are we agreeing to do business together?" Yisa asked.

"Yes, at least you and I are. And I name myself as CEO. Oga, are you in?" Omega asked in his deep, raspy voice.

"How come you get to be the leader?" Oga asked.

"Because I am smarter than both of you combined, and all this talk is just an idea until I provide some capital. Are you in or not?"

Oga clenched his jaw, studying Omega, and after a long pause he responded.

"I'm in."

"Good!" Yisa exclaimed.

Omega scratched his chin as he puffed on his cigar.

"It will need many hours of careful planning. A thing like this should not be rushed. We will have to plan every step involved and begin to build our reputation. This thing has the potential to make a lot of money."

"Yes, but let's just remember that money is not our only motivation," Yisa said, "We are trying to unite fighters under one banner."

"Yes, we'll unite the best warriors across Africa, that is the plan," Omega replied. "I also think that calling it an organization makes it feel wrong. We have to make whomever we recruit feel as though they are a part of something special, something unique."

"Like a brotherhood," Yisa said.

"Yes, like a brotherhood," Omega replied.

"What shall we call this brotherhood?" Yisa asked.

"I don't know. But having the right name is key," Omega said with a smile. "To come up with a name, we must come up with traits that represent who we are."

"We will be the most powerful force in Africa," Yisa said.

"Forget Africa. We have to think big. We will be the most organized private military force in the world," Omega said.

"And our fighters will be efficient, stealthy, and deadly," Oga added, brightening.

Yisa searched his memory for a symbolic name. "I've got it," Yisa said out loud. "We shall call ourselves the Imamba."

"The Imamba? I like the sound of that. What does it mean?" Omega asked.

"It is what some groups in South Africa call the Black Mamba snake," Oga answered, raising his sleeve to reveal two scars. "I was bitten by one once—a rare dry bite without venom. Had I been poisoned, it would have killed me before an hour had passed. It is the only opponent to have nearly killed me."

"I like it. Imamba it is. Let us drink to that," Omega suggested, topping their cups off with hot tea.

Thunderous rain poured from the sky as the three men toasted their new partnership. And at that moment, on a stormy Algerian night in 1955, the Imamba Brotherhood was born.

SUGAR DADDY

London, England. 1990.

Arewa was worn out from her boss's party, and had just taken a long bath using new rose and lavender soap that she had bought the day before at Harrods, lining the tub's edge with pillar spa candles. The warm water relaxed her tense muscles and the scented beeswax candles appealed to her love of elegant beauty.

The bath was the ideal place for her to ponder her powerful reaction to that man who had come to her boss's office earlier—Eteka. He really turned her on in a visceral way that she hadn't experienced since being a young teenager, freshly discovering love. There was just something about him… something innocent, yet dangerous. Sure, she had dated all sorts of bad boys here in London and around the world. Her ex-boyfriend was a professional football player in the Barclays Premier League and had a notorious affinity for wild parties. Before that, she had dated an American rapper on tour in Europe—she'd once shared a decadent bath with him, filled with champagne instead of water! She'd had her fair share of one-night stands with men here and there on her travels. But she found that most—if not all—of them put up quite the façade. They weren't *really* bad boys—they were spoiled more than anything else. The worst they did was spend a night or two in jail for "disorderly conduct" (her footballer had spent many a night sleeping it off in a jail cell); for that matter, her rapper had had to fabricate his so-called thug life previous to music fame. The poor dear lived in fear of his audience finding out about his upper-middle class upbringing, happily married parents, and art history degree.

But this Eteka—he seemed to be the real deal; nothing about him rang false. Especially if he was dealing with a character like her boss, Mr. Adeboyo, who was known for his foul play and dangerous associations. Arewa felt attracted to the innocence Eteka exuded in her presence. The way he couldn't look in her eyes, and how shy he became, really piqued her interest.

She walked naked into her bedroom, lit up a scented candle, and slipped between the sea foam green silk sheets on her bed—another little present to herself. Tomorrow, her younger brother, Fallal, would be coming to visit her. Fallal was a musician who was now making a name for himself in the jazz scene, chiefly due to Mr. Adeboyo's financial support. Fallal had asked her to accompany him to Mr. Adeboyo's place tomorrow to discuss his contract. But tonight, she would fall asleep to the fantasy of the new man in her life, this Eteka. Her hands slowly moved south as a smile materialized on her face. In her life, she'd learned that while boys were nice to have around, sometimes you just had to rely on yourself.

✝

The next morning, Arewa was awakened by her doorbell. Fallal! She snatched up a robe she'd left hanging over a chair, cinched it, and headed to the door, knocking over a glass of water she had left sitting by her nightstand. She looked through the peephole, confirming, and then let her brother in, shaking her head.

Fallal was Arewa's twin, younger than her by 44 seconds. He had the same large, slanted brown eyes as she had, and the same lean physique. He stood at an even 6' and wore his hair in a large afro. Today, he sported a thin moustache, numerous beaded bracelets and necklaces, green-rimmed glasses, and a loud green/purple/yellow plaid print button-down over fitted dark-wash jeans. Fallal smiled as he saw his sister and gave her a big hug.

"Today is the day, sis."

"What's so special about today? Is there something you're not telling me that you want to discuss with Mr. Adeboyo?" she asked sharply.

"I said today is the day, you'll see," Fallal repeated with a smile in his soft, melodic voice.

"Whatever you say," Arewa replied as she ushered him inside and up to her bedroom. "I'll hop in the shower and then we'll head out."

Fallal took a seat as she headed to the bathroom. He glanced at the partially melted candle by her bed and grinned.

"Steamy night for you?"

"Huh?" she called out from the bathroom.

"I know you and your girly scented candles. You had sex last night?"

"No!"

"C'mon, tell me, who is the guy? Is he still here, hiding? In the closet or under the bed? Bathtub? Don't drown the poor sucker!"

"I can't see any man hiding from you," Arewa retorted. Fallal grinned and continued to look around. Her bedroom was an unholy mess, with expensive clothes and fashion magazines all over the floor. A particular magazine, an issue of *Vogue*, caught his attention. He picked it up and began to flip through it.

"So there is a man, right?" Fallal asked when she finally came out of the shower.

"Maybe."

"C'mon, stop beating around the bush. Who is he?" he asked.

Arewa walked out of the bathroom with a smile on her face and a towel wrapped around her body. She took a seat by her dresser and began to put on her makeup and lotion.

"His name is Eteka."

"Eteka? Where is he from?" Fallal asked.

"I think he's Nigerian. He's really cute. I like his chin."

"I'll bet you like more than that," he replied, winking. "Have you slept with him?"

"No. Well, not yet."

"So. . ." he paused. "Last night was a solo mission, eh?" Fallal asked with a laugh. She threw a Kleenex box at him, but he ducked.

"None of your business."

"So what does this guy do? Is he a footballer? You seem to like the big dumb ones," he teased, hoping to get a rise out of her.

"No. He works for a security company, I think," she replied, distracted by the need to even out her eyeliner.

"How did you meet him?"

"He was on a contract working as a bodyguard for Mr. Adeboyo."

"Interesting. Must be a tough guy. What's with you and dating bad boys? You're getting awfully close to spinsterhood—you need to find a good guy to settle down with."

Arewa smiled at her reflection in the mirror as she put on some lipstick. Then she got up to throw some clothes on.

"I wouldn't say I go for bad boys per se, more like guys with an edge. There's a difference. I know it sounds strange, especially since our parents were so religious."

Arewa's thoughts drifted to her parents, who had died in a fatal car accident back in Nigeria as they traveled to a church conference. Life had been hard on her and her brother since then, until she'd met Mr. Adeboyo and fallen into the proverbial tub of butter.

"If only Mother and Father could see us now," Arewa said with a sigh. Her mother would throw up her hands and give her the lecture of her life.

"They see us all the time, sis. From Heaven. C'mon, let's go," Fallal said, placing an arm around his sister and walking her out of the apartment. Arewa blushed, hoping that her parents had missed a good portion of last night's fantasy about the intriguing Eteka.

They arrived at Mr. Adeboyo's mansion an hour later. It was a sunny day in London and scores of pedestrians lined the streets, taking in the good weather as they went about their business or toured the sights. Arewa and Fallal were met by Mr. Adeboyo's butler, who escorted them down a long hall to a large office at the rear of the mansion. A tall bodyguard dressed in a black suit let them in the office door. Mr. Adeboyo sat behind a large oak desk with his glasses on, leafing through a stack of papers as Arewa and Fallal sat in the chairs on the other side of the desk.

"How are you both doing?" Mr. Adeboyo asked without looking at them.

"Fine. We came to discuss Fallal's contract with you," Arewa said.

"What's there to discuss? Is there a problem?" Mr. Adeboyo asked as he looked up at them. Arewa turned to Fallal. She had no idea what her younger brother wanted to discuss today and she hoped he wouldn't waste Mr. Adeboyo's time.

"Well?"

"I, er, wanted to discuss our contract, Mr. Adeboyo," Fallal began.

"No shit. Spit it out, boy. What do you want? You looking to make more money? Don't I do enough for you and your sister?" Mr. Adeboyo demanded, glaring at him over his glasses.

"Yes, you do a lot for us, sir."

"I do more than a lot for you. You both have places to live— nice places, I might add. I helped you release your first album, and you've been featured with some top acts here in London. Let's not even begin to talk about the following I've built for you back home in Nigeria. What more could you possibly want?"

Arewa looked at her brother, curious about what Fallal had to say. Whatever it was, she would be behind him.

Fallal cleared his throat and sat up in his seat. "I want out of this contract, Mr. Adeboyo. I want our contract to end at the end of this year."

A long silence followed. Arewa had been blindsided. What was Fallal doing? He was on the rise and doing well for himself with Mr. Adeboyo's help—why would he want out of the contract now?

Mr. Adeboyo nodded and stood up. He walked over to Fallal and placed a fatherly hand on his shoulder. "Why do you want out of our agreement, Fallal? We have a good thing going here. What brought you to this decision?"

"Well, sir, I… um, I'm not really happy with the way things are," Fallal responded, squirming.

FALLAL

"I WANT CREATIVE
FREEDOM, SIR."

ETEKA
RISE OF THE IMAMBA

"What are you unhappy about? You want more money? Women? A better band?"

"I want creative freedom, sir," he replied softly, looking directly at the older man.

Mr. Adeboyo nodded again and walked back to his seat. Arewa blinked stupidly at Fallal. What was he talking about? His demands could not only affect him, but her as well—angering Mr. Adeboyo could have serious consequences!

"Creative freedom… what exactly do you mean by that?" Mr. Adeboyo asked, steepling his fingers.

"I want to be able to say what I want to say and have complete control of my music."

"You have a lot of control over your music."

"No, I have control over what you allow me to do. There are certain topics I cannot talk about."

Mr. Adeboyo smiled pacifyingly, tapping his index finger on the table as he did so. "We've had this conversation before, Fallal. What topics do you think are off-limits to you?"

"Corruption and greed, especially in Nigeria," Fallal said with conviction.

"Ah, that. We've talked about this before, and I told you that there are some dangerous people you could offend if you started singing about such things in your music. It's best not to make enemies. It's for your own protection," Mr. Adeboyo replied, a faint note of threat in his voice.

"Then what is the point of being an ethical musician? You want me to sell my soul?"

"That's a good way of looking at it. But it will fetch you a fine price!"

"I'm serious, sir. I want out of our agreement," Fallal said again, looking nervously at the older man and his sister.

Mr. Adeboyo looked at Fallal, the edges of his eyes crinkling. Then, he turned to Arewa.

"Where is all this coming from?" Mr. Adeboyo asked Arewa.

"I don't really know, sir. I'm just as in the dark as you are."

"And do you support his decision?"

"He's my brother, and he has my support on anything he decides to do," she replied as confidently as she could. She certainly didn't feel very confident.

Mr. Adeboyo smiled and shifted his gaze back to Fallal.

"You know you're like a son to me, right? When I discovered you in Nigeria, you were only a small boy, orphaned and alone, and now look at you. You think you're ready to go out on your own? I have sheltered you and your sister from many of the harsh realities out there. The world is not a pretty place. There are all kinds of people out there, people who will smile but mean you harm, manipulative people... you have no experience dealing with these sorts of things, Fallal. But I do. I didn't get to where I am overnight. I can guide you and your career, as I have been doing. Let's rethink this decision of yours."

"No, I've made up my mind, sir. I need to have my creative freedom," Fallal replied.

Mr. Adeboyo quietly nodded and turned his attention to Arewa.

"And what about your sister? Hmm? If you go, she cannot have the things she has anymore. Her comfortable lifestyle will vanish, thanks to you. You sure you want to put her in that position?" Mr. Adeboyo asked, keeping his eyes on Arewa, whose eyes widened.

"My sister works for you for free. You need her more than she needs you," Fallal defiantly shot back.

"I don't need anyone, young man. I have money, which means I can replace things. And your sister is replaceable," Mr. Adeboyo replied calmly. "Although, I am quite fond of her."

Arewa shifted in her seat, confused. Why was Fallal doing this? They had comfortable lives, no financial needs and were doing well. She surely wasn't ready to give up her lifestyle. And she wasn't sure why Fallal wanted to risk giving up his.

"What are your thoughts on all this, Arewa?" Mr. Adeboyo asked. "You looked shocked at your brother's decision."

"I, emm... I, uh, I don't know what to make of all this, to be honest," she said, looking at Fallal. "Do you really want to part ways with Mr. Adeboyo?"

"Yes."

"What will we do?" she asked.

"I will take care of you," he assured her.

"You can barely take care of yourself," Mr. Adeboyo cut in with a laugh. "How are you going to take care of your sister?"

"I found a new distributor and a new producer," Fallal replied with a smug smile. "A rep approached me after a show I did in Leicester Square and linked me up with them. And I have a lawyer friend who's going to help me set up my own label. We will be fine."

Mr. Adeboyo's smile quickly turned into a frown. "You went and made deals behind my back?" Mr. Adeboyo asked in an angry tone. Fallal said nothing in response, simply bowing his head. Mr. Adeboyo shook his head for a moment, then stood up and leaned against his desk.

"You are a foolish boy, and I will let you learn the hard way, as you want. You have your wish. At the end of this year, you'll be on your own."

A smile materialized on Fallal's face, while Arewa's heart caught in her chest. What would happen to her? She looked at Mr. Adeboyo with wide doe eyes and a worried expression.

"Mr. Adeboyo, sir, does this mean I'm not working for you anymore?"

Mr. Adeboyo smiled at her and shook his head. *What did Fallal just do?* she wondered to herself.

"You don't have to worry about anything, my dear. You clearly did not know anything about your brother's decision. Now, if you'll both excuse me, I have work to do. Arewa, stop by tomorrow, we have some catching up to do."

"Yes, sir," Arewa responded as she stood up.

"Thank you, sir," Fallal said as he stood up and extended his hand for a handshake.

"I asked you to leave." Mr. Adeboyo said coldly, pointedly denying Fallal his handshake.

Fallal nodded and they both left Mr. Adeboyo's office. Fallal grinned broadly as the butler escorted them outside. The fresh air was a refreshing change from the tension in Mr. Adeboyo's office. Arewa breathed a sigh of relief. Now she could get some answers.

"Okay, what's going on? I knew you wanted to discuss business with Mr. Adeboyo, but all this is a bit much. You have to consider me and my position as well, you know," Arewa said.

"Don't worry, sis, I've been planning this for some months now."

"And you didn't tell me?"

"I wanted everything to be set before I did. I thought you'd be happy, sis."

"I am, well… more surprised than anything," she replied as they arrived at her car. "What about Mr. Adeboyo? He's not going to let you off that easily."

"He gave me his word. I'm done with him when the year ends."

"And you believe him?"

"He has no choice. He can't force me to perform."

"Have you really thought this through, Fallal? I mean, he has done a lot for you—aren't you grateful?"

"C'mon, sis, we've been working for free for many years now. It's about time we worked for ourselves. And you! Aren't you the one who's been telling me that you always dreamed of being a teacher in Nigeria? This is the chance for us to do what we're really meant to do. You don't have to work for Mr. Adeboyo anymore. We can live our dreams!"

"I don't know," Arewa sighed, "I kind of like the way things are now. Mr. Adeboyo takes care of me."

"But you're not happy."

"Says who?"

"Says me," Fallal replied. "I'm your brother. I know you. You were never comfortable with the idea of working for Mr. Adeboyo. You only did it for me."

Arewa sighed. She knew he was right, but she'd gotten used to Mr. Adeboyo and her fancy lifestyle. Teachers didn't sleep on silk sheets and spends hundreds of pounds shopping for haute couture.

"C'mon, sis! You could become a teacher like you've always wanted, and I can express myself freely with my music and collect everything I've earned. What d'you say?"

Putting her hands on her hips, Arewa turned to face Fallal. Deep down she had always dreamed of being a teacher, but until this point they had not achieved much without the help of Mr. Adeboyo. This would be a chance for them to strike out on their own and make something for themselves.

"What about my apartments? And my cars? And all the pocket money he gives me? You expect me to just give all that up?" she demanded.

"He said you don't have to worry about your job. And if he takes anything away, I'll take care of you, don't worry. You may have to sacrifice a few things, but I promise that everything you give up will be indulgences that you don't need. It'll be nothing compared to the ultimate satisfaction of working together and building our family legacy. We don't need Mr. Adeboyo. If anything, he needs us."

Arewa smiled at her brother's reassuring words. No man in this world, Mr. Adeboyo included, could make her feel safe and secure the way her brother could. The sincerity in his voice was as soothing as his passion was motivating. She had to be there for him. Maybe starting over wasn't such a bad idea.

"Okay, Fallal, I'm in."

"Great! Oh, I'm so happy to hear you say that!"

"What do you want me to do?"

"Don't do anything, just be yourself and don't let Mr. Adeboyo think you want to move on. We'll be just fine," Fallal assured her.

"Okay. This is really exciting!" Arewa exclaimed.

"Yeah. Let's get out of here, I'm hungry."

As she trailed after her brother, she glanced up. Mr. Adeboyo was watching them through his office window. He did not smile.

CABRAL

Bissau, Portuguese Guinea. Africa. 1964.

Oga looked at the glistening, naked body of the prostitute in his bed. She lay in the moonlight streaming from an open window and he noticed that she was young, no older than sixteen. The sex had been good, but she had done what she came to do. He shoved her awake, made her grab her things, and kicked her out.

Yisa was in another room down the hall in a rundown motel. Almost ten years had passed since they had founded the Imamba Brotherhood in Algeria, and now they were in Portuguese Guinea, in the capital city of Bissau to be exact, on a mission to find new recruits. Omega had informed them of a secret conference organized by a revolutionary known as Cabral. The conference was supposed to happen in Cassaca, about 100 kilometers west of Bissau. Cabral and his group, the PAIGC,[1] had been pressing the Portuguese colonial forces in Portuguese Guinea for independence, and he was holding this conference to reorganize his war effort. Omega got word of it from one of his "secret" contacts, and had suggested that

---

[1] A political and military force in Guinea-Bissau during the fight for independence from Portugal, the PAIGC eventually became the ruling political party after independence was gained.

Oga and Yisa attend to try and recruit some fighters for the Imamba Brotherhood. So here they were, a few hours away from the scheduled conference location.

It was a little past midnight. Oga sat looking out the window as he lit up a cigarette, watching the prostitute he had kicked out walk barefoot down a dirt path. Dense vegetation and sparse housing surrounded them, filled with the sounds of the night. He couldn't sleep, partly because this place brought back bad memories for him. There were people in Portuguese Guinea that Oga had hoped he would never see again. It seemed life had other plans.

The next day, Oga and Yisa set off for Cassaca. Omega had managed to gain contacts through bribery within the black sections of the Portuguese forces in the region, but unfriendly Portuguese patrols were rampant. A direct trip was impossible. As a result, Oga and Yisa were transported by air to the southern town of Cufar and then took a bus through dense forests to their destination.

It was nearing evening when both mercenaries arrived. It seemed the meetings for the day had just ended, and they were escorted through the throngs of hardened men milling about. At least one out of every three men brandished an AK-47; all wore assorted machetes and other wicked knives. It was hot and humid, and all the men were swatting at mosquitoes on the prowl for human blood. The town itself seemed very rural, kerosene lamps and torches illuminating a few single-story houses, shacks, and huts dispersed here and there. Most of the area was filled with thick bush, the few clear areas made for footpaths and meeting spaces.

In a large clear area, the mercenaries spotted some young guerrillas that looked like promising recruits for the Imamba. The men seemed to be in their early 20s, or possibly their late teens, and Oga deduced that they were here because someone had convinced them they had to be. Young men were so impressionable. Oga prepared his pitch as he headed in their direction. His Portuguese was a little rusty, but he remembered enough to have a basic conversation.

"Bao tarde,"[1] Oga greeted as he walked up to the men, Yisa not far behind.

The men stopped their conversation and turned around to size them up, examining their weapons.

"Olá. Você fala português?"[2] one of the men asked. The others smiled benignly while a young man in their group rested his hand on a pistol tucked in his pocket.

"Um pouquinho. Tu falas inglês?"[3]

The men unanimously shook their heads, looking at him distrustfully. Oga surveyed them, realizing it would be a long night if he couldn't meet anyone that spoke English. He couldn't convey his full message in Portuguese alone.

"I speak English," a voice called out from behind them.

---

[1] "Good evening."
[2] "Hello. You speak Portuguese?"
[3] "A little. Do you speak English?"

Oga turned to face a lean man wearing military fatigues and a soul patch. There was a giant black star on the man's cap and a pistol at his side. He had the hands of someone accustomed to hard labor, and he had a tough, scarred face, even though he was smiling.

"You're not one of us," the man said as he walked up to Oga. He paused, taking some time to observe Yisa as well.

"No, we're not."

"Are you spies?"

"No."

"So what do you want with the PAIGC?"

"I have a business proposition for some of your men."

"A business proposition? What sort of business proposition?" the man asked as a small circle of fighters began to gather around them.

"The chance to join my organization and implement some real change here in Africa. We can also assist you and your group with your missions here in Portuguese Guinea. But, I cannot discuss the details out here in the open," Oga replied.

As more guerrillas continued to gather around both men, obviously curious and interested in the strange newcomer, Oga realized that speaking to the lower-ranking guerrillas would get them nowhere. They would have to speak with someone who had power. Someone like Cabral.

"What is your name?" Oga asked the man.

"Adão."

"Nice to meet you, Adão. Are you in charge here?" Oga asked the man.

"I am a commander, yes."

"But you're not in charge. Where is your leader, Cabral?"

A soft murmur drifted through the small gathering. Even if they didn't understand the conversation, they certainly recognized Cabral's name.

Adão surveyed the men in the group, then seemed to come to a decision. "Follow me," he said to Oga, and he led both Imamba away from the group.

They walked past some small shacks and parked Jeeps. The mosquitoes were still at it, and Oga hoped that he would not catch malaria as a result of this trip. They were led past a large white building that seemed to have been a church or mosque in a past life and toward a cluster of benches covered with straw umbrellas. Beyond it was a large open area containing a large circle of benches that looked like a meeting place. Five hardened men carrying AK-47s stood on guard, and drew their weapons as Oga, Yisa, and Adão approached.

Adão nodded, and they lowered their weapons and stepped aside. Alone in the space on one of the benches, a man who could only be Cabral was writing on a piece of paper by the light of a kerosene lamp. Cabral was a short, slim man with a handsome face hidden behind glasses and a receding hairline. A funny-looking bowl hat hung off the back of his head. He had a neatly lined chinstrap beard and a toothpick in his mouth. Cabral had a commanding presence, an air of authority that Oga could sense as they approached.

Cabral looked up at the mercenaries. Adão said a few words to him in French-based Creole, then stepped aside. Cabral turned to regard Oga, sizing him up from behind his glasses. It appeared that he had been writing notes on the paper he had lain on the bench, and Oga caught the title the man had scribbled on the document: "Palavras de Ordem."[1] Cabral, seeing Oga's wandering eyes, neatly folded the paper and shoved it in his pocket.

"Como é seu nome?" Cabral asked.

"Oga."

"De onde você é?"

"Here."

The man gave a surprised look at Oga's last answer and sat up, extending his hand for a handshake.

"Meu nome é Amílcar Lopes Cabral."

"Muito prazer," Oga replied as the two shook hands.

"My English is not perfect, so bear with me," Cabral said in English with a smile.

---

[1] This was a document written by Cabral after the Cassaca congress re-emphasizing the principles underlying the PAIGC's political strategy.

"Neither is my Portuguese, or my Creole" Oga replied with a grin.

"Then we speak Inglês. Please, sit down. Who is your friend?"

"He's my brother in arms, and his name is Yisa."

Yisa nodded at Cabral as they sat on the benches. The flickering light from the lamp left their faces in shadow and made Cabral's eyes look like reflectors through his glasses. Cabral nodded at Adão, and he took a few steps back.

"Who told you about our meeting here in Cassaca?" Cabral asked.

"My group keeps tabs on everything regarding our motherland, including you."

"Is that so?"

"Yes."

"So do you know what we are doing here?" Cabral asked.

"I know you are reorganizing your war effort."

"Such a general answer for a specific question," Cabral replied with a grin.

"So, what are you doing here?"

Cabral hesitated, regarding Oga closely.

"You are partly right when you say we are reorganizing our war effort. Our fight is going well, but some of our commanders are acting foolishly and independently, outside of the goals of our organization. We need to reorganize our military structure so that we're all on the same page," Cabral replied.

"And how will you deal with these commanders of yours who are causing trouble?" Oga asked.

"They will be liquidated. Why do you care?"

"We could use those men. Or any men you don't need. Rather than dispose of them, let them come with us and join the Imamba Brotherhood."

"The Imamba Brotherhood? I've never heard of you before," Cabral remarked.

"We are a brotherhood of fighters. We have troops from all over Africa in our ranks, and we get stronger every day."

"I see. And what exactly is the goal of this Imamba Brotherhood?"

"We fight together for Africa against the invaders. We seek to unite our African brothers as one," Yisa cut in.

Cabral exchanged glances with Adão, scratching the hairline under his bowl hat. At that moment, another man joined their group.

He was a tall man with a lean build and a surprisingly thick, bristling moustache. The newcomer gave Oga a disapproving look and Oga stood up, toe to toe with the new visitor. The air spiked with tension and Yisa sensed trouble.

"François," Cabral said to the man. "What's going on? Do you know this man?"

"Yes," François replied gruffly in Portuguese. "I know him all too well." Cabral, a confused look on his face, looked over at Yisa, asking for an explanation. But Yisa was just as confused.

"They told me someone matching your description had walked into our camp," the man continued in English, staring daggers at Oga. "After all the damage you caused, what makes you think you can just walk in here unnoticed?"

Yisa stood up and placed a hand on his holster. Things could get ugly.

"What's going on, François? How do you know this man?" Cabral repeated.

"He's a coward. I would kill him now, but that would be doing him a favor."

"What do you mean? Explain yourself!" Cabral demanded.

"Some years ago I called this man my brother. I was leading a small battalion against the invaders on Orango Island, and we were surrounded. We made some ground against the enemy, and I led most of my troops into the fight as we pushed back their lines. I left this man with simple instructions to protect the women and children in the village, our stronghold on the island in case the enemy made it through our lines. But you," the man said, poking Oga in the chest with his finger. "You deserted us. The enemy flanked us and you ran, you coward," the man said, suddenly grabbing Oga by his collar. Yisa moved to separate them, but Adão stood in his way.

"All those women and children were slaughtered because of you. Good people that took care of us, that gave us food and shelter, and you let them all die."

François suddenly gave Oga a vicious backhand slap, knocking his head to the side. Oga kept his eyes fixed in the middle distance, off in a private world of his own. Blood trickled from his split lip.

"This man is a deserter. You cannot trust him," François said to Cabral as he let Oga go. "He has no honor."

Cabral and Yisa looked at Oga, who looked at the ground in silence.

"Is this true?" Cabral asked Oga. Oga did not respond.

"Oga is no deserter. He has fought by my side on many occasions and I know he would die for me. I trust him with my life," Yisa said, stepping in.

François looked at Yisa. "Who are you?"

"I'm Yisa. I've fought with Oga for many years, and he's always been by my side. I can vouch for him."

"Your claim is very different from what François says, and François is my chief strategic officer in our fight for freedom. If what he says is true, I cannot give you any men, as I do not do business with cowards," Cabral replied with a hint of a sneer.

"It's not true, and I'm no coward," Oga cut in, looking François dead in the eye. The other man stared at him.

"One man's word against the other's," Cabral said, tapping his chin. "There's only one way to resolve this matter. Both men will have to fight till one submits."

"Are you serious?" Yisa asked in disbelief.

"Yes. François challenged your friend's honor, so he must defend it. If François loses, I will consider your request for some of my men. But if your friend loses, you'll have to leave and never come back."

Whispers flew through the group, and a few men began to circle the clearing where Cabral and the Imamba were talking. Word traveled fast, and these men were bored—ready for entertainment of any sort.

Yisa looked over at Oga.

"Can you handle this guy?" he asked in a low tone.

"He shouldn't be a problem," Oga replied, stepping up to François.

✝

Without warning, François threw a punch, which Oga just barely blocked with both hands. He had expected a little more fanfare before the fight started, and only his reflexes saved him. François's hands felt heavy to Oga—heavy and hard with calluses that would prevent the small bones in his hands from breaking. Oga knew he would have to be careful, as this meant his opponent had knockout power. François swung again, but this time Oga chose to evade the blow. François followed with another round of combination punches to the head and body. Oga blocked all but one, a ferocious straight that found its mark on his forehead. He reeled back from the blow, his vision blurry for a few seconds. He shook his head to clear it, but François kept coming, throwing another set of combinations and finishing with a roundhouse kick to Oga's chest. The Imamba fell to the ground, quickly getting back up. The two men circled each other four times, feinting here and there to draw reactions. François shouted in anger as he threw a vicious overhand right, and followed by grabbing Oga by the throat.

His grip was strong, and his fingers dug into Oga's neck, hanging on like a vise around his throat. Oga struggled to remove his opponent's hand, and after staggering around for a brief moment he kicked François in his shin. The move made François release his grip, and as he did so, Oga poked him directly in his eyes, momentarily blinding him. The blinded François shouted and swiped around like an enraged animal, and with his eyes closed lunged at Oga, but Oga stopped him in his tracks with an overhand elbow to his temple. The move dropped François to one knee, and Oga followed it up with a front kick that sent François crashing to the ground. As François stumbled and tried to stand, Oga quickly got behind him and placed his head in a rear chokehold.

"I'm no coward, you piece of shit," Oga whispered into François's ear as he began to appy pressure. François clawed at Oga's grip, but it was futile. Within a few seconds, his body went limp, and Oga threw him to the ground. The Imamba wiped a trickle of blood from his nose as he stepped over François's body and walked up to Yisa and Cabral. All the soldiers standing around watched in silence as two of their own dragged François's unconscious body away.

✝

"Congratulations. François was a strong man, and you beat him quickly," Cabral said, watching the men drag François away.

"Long fights don't agree with me," Oga replied.

"We held up our end of the bargain. Now, you must hold up yours," Yisa chimed in.

"Indeed. So you want some of our men?"

"Yes."

"Quantos?" Cabral asked.

"No less than four."

"Four is a high number when it comes to war. What can you offer me in exchange for your request?"

"You told us that the condition would be to beat your man, and Oga did just that."

"I told you that I would consider your request, not that I would give you men," Cabral replied. "So, what can your Imamba friends offer me in exchange?"

Both Imamba looked at each other, then back at Cabral in obvious anger. In response, several of the men in the clearing drew their weapons and stepped up.

"Pick your next words carefully. Again I ask: What can your Imamba friends offer me in exchange for my men?"

"We know the Portuguese are going to start using airstrikes against you. We can even tell you ahead of time when and where they will strike. It is in your best interest to work with us," Yisa said.

"We're not worried about anything the Portuguese have for us. Our Russian and Cuban friends have already promised us support in those matters," Cabral replied calmly. "So again, what do you have to offer us?"

"I offer you an alliance with us. We can move in many areas, and do many things that your group cannot."

"The PAIGC can do many things, including winning independence for the people of Cape Verde and Portuguese Guinea. So far you have not offered us anything substantial. Besides, my friend, we need all our men here with us. That is part of the reason we are holding our conference here in the bush."

Cabral bit the top off the mango in his hand and began to eat its pulp. "Yet," Cabral continued. "I like you. Our fight is based on principles, not selfish gain. If your Imamba are fighting the same fight we are, why not join us?" Cabral asked.

"We will work together, and help you on your missions, of course. But we serve other interests as well. All we need are a few men," Yisa replied.

"And if I give you men, will you treat them well? Will you pay them?" Cabral asked.

"Money is not a problem. If they join us, they will do things they never imagined possible," Yisa replied. He waited pensively as Cabral worked on his mango.

"You can have one man from my camp who I think is better suited for your purposes than ours," Cabral said as he turned to Adão. "Bring Maximus here."

"Maximus? Respectfully, sir, do you think that is a good idea? Maximus is our best fighter!" Adão said to Cabral in a mixture of Portuguese and English.

"I know he is our best, but he is also a specialist that we do not know how to use," Cabral replied patiently. "He may become a liability to us if we keep him here, bored. I have a feeling these Imamba will have a better use for him. Bring him to me," Cabral said sternly.

Adão barked an order at a nearby soldier. The soldier ran off, reappearing a few minutes later with a hulking giant behind him—nearly seven feet tall—with a powerful, wrestler's build and exceptionally large forearms. A joker's smirk peeped out of Maximus's disheveled beard as he towered over the other soldiers.

"Maximus, these men want you to join their outfit," Cabral informed him. "They are willing to pay you good money for your services."

Maximus turned his smirk on the Imamba. Yisa was taken aback by his size; he had never seen a man that large before.

"Who are you, and what makes you think you can contain me?" Maximus asked in a booming voice.

"We are the Imamba, a brotherhood of the best fighters from all over Africa. And we want you to join us," Yisa said, nodding at Maximus. "You'll be paid better than anything you've ever made."

"I love to fight. Will I have the chance to fight people that will give me competition?" Maximus asked.

"Yes, yes you will. You will do many things with us."

"Then I accept your offer," Maximus said.

"You have what you came here for. Just remember your promise of allegiance to me," Cabral said.

"Yes. You can reach me at this number when you need us," Yisa replied, reaching into his pocket and handing Cabral a card.

Pleasantries were exchanged, and soon Yisa, Oga and Maximus walked through the camp and back into the bush toward the town of Cufar. As they trudged along, Yisa looked over at Oga, who seemed deep in thought.

"What was that all about?" Yisa asked.

"It's nothing. Just some demons from my past," Oga said. "Thanks for stepping in and speaking for me."

"We are brothers—that's what brothers do," Yisa replied as he placed an arm around Oga, and gave him a reassuring squeeze. Oga nodded in agreement as he lit up a cigarette, the orange glare standing out in the darkness around them.

BLOOD DIAMONDS

Tubmanburg, Liberia. Africa. 1990.

The sun was setting as Eteka and Cyrus made their way through the war-torn streets in the back of an old pickup truck. They were on their way to a rebel base in the forest to meet General Morning Coffee,[1] the commander of the IFW[2] rebel group, for the first time. Both men were dressed in their customary grey camouflage fatigues, and were accompanied by other young men (some still just children) in the pickup truck with hardened faces, all wielding AK-47s. A cool evening breeze made the smells of war and of men who hadn't bathed in a long time a little more bearable.

Cyrus had dozed off while Eteka sat contemplating Omega's instructions for the mission—to retrieve two briefcases full of diamonds and transport them to one of their safe houses in South Africa. It sounded easy enough.

---

[1] While this character is fictional, during both Liberian civil wars, outlandish nicknames were par for the course.
[2] Fictional group.

He watched the sun set as he daydreamed about Arewa.
Something about her arrested his attention, left him speechless and
shy in her presence. He'd never talked to a woman for more than a
couple of minutes, and most if not all of the women he'd been with
had been prostitutes. But Arewa…she was different. She flirted with
him and looked in his eyes like no other woman had before. He
pulled out her card from a side pocket and studied it. If she was in
Nigeria when this was done, he could stop by her place after he
finished delivering the diamonds to Omega in South Africa. Eteka
looked up at the empty houses lining the street and the few women
walking with babies on their backs. Yes, he would go see Arewa
after this mission.

Swatting a mosquito off his neck, Eteka noticed a boy
staring at him from the other end of the truck. No older than ten, the
child carried a bloodstained machete. The boy regarded Eteka
without a hint of fear for a minute before he got up, stepped over a
few of his comrades, and sat next to Eteka, hardly breaking his gaze.

"What are you looking at?" Eteka asked the little boy.

"Wha' you think I lookin' at?" the boy replied without
smiling in a thick Liberian accent.

Eteka, a little surprised by the boy's response, studied him
for a few moments. The kid had an innocent face, with big brown
eyes, big cheeks, and a thin mat of coarse, messy hair. He was also
missing a few teeth. The machete was half his size and he wielded it
like a toy—clearly he'd used it before. He regarded Eteka seriously,
his eyes heavy and glazed. Eteka presumed the boy was high on

something. Eteka adjusted himself in his seat to better return the boy's stare.

"What's your name?"

"Ma men, I won know if you will pay my money."

"Pay you for what?" Eteka asked.

"For my name."

"No, I'm not going to pay you for your name."

"Den I will not tell you," the little boy replied belligerently.

Eteka smiled, feeling a genuine liking for his new little companion. He handed the boy one Liberian dollar, and the boy smiled.

"So, what's your name?" Eteka asked.

"Bisi."

The truck shook as it hit a few potholes and made a sharp right off the road, heading up a dirt road into some dense vegetation. As the sun set, the truck's headlights flickered on. There was total darkness on all sides as the truck jerked violently from the bumpy ride.

"How old are you?"

"Old enough."

"I see. Do you know how to use that thing?" Eteka asked, pointing at the machete.

The little boy looked at the dirty blade, and then back at Eteka.

"I na able to use it that well. I na use it plenty times now."

"To cut grass?" Eteka laughed.

"No. To cut people."

Cyrus woke up as the truck jolted violently.

"Ah! I was sleeping…" he said as he stretched and met Bisi's intense stare. Cyrus couldn't help but be amused.

"Small boy, why are you looking at me like that?" Cyrus asked with a laugh.

"Becos I can."

Cyrus laughed and leaned toward Bisi.

"Shouldn't you be at home with your mother and father? What are you doing here with men like us?" Cyrus asked.

"My ma and pa will not save Liberia. Ma commander say I can fight with anyone da I want. So I will fight, and kill all of them," the boy replied with the same hard look.

"Kill who? Who is 'them'?"

"The bad man."

Cyrus laughed and shook his head, as Eteka turned his attention to the passing Liberian terrain.

They finally came to a stop at the rebel base deep in the forest later that evening. It was dark now, as electricity did not run into these parts. The air was moist and hot, and the ground was wet. There were a few fires going around the base, and Eteka caught a whiff of roasting meat. Sentries were posted everywhere, and some of the young men at one post had a small radio that was playing a track by reggae musician Lucky Dube. The rest of the light was provided by kerosene lamps, which lit the three houses in which the majority of the rebels stayed. The men climbed out of the truck, walking off in different directions. Eteka and Cyrus climbed out as well, stretching, and noticed Bisi walking off alone.

"Hey, boy, don't you know how to say goodbye?" Cyrus called after the kid in a teasing tone.

Bisi waved his machete at them as he smiled, disappearing into the night like a wraith.

"I like that kid. He has a bright future," Cyrus said as he made sure the clip in his sidearm was full.

"Yaw excuse me yah, yaw here for the rocks?" a voice with a thick Liberian accent asked from behind them. They both turned around to face a young man wearing a bandana and a sleeveless shirt. He was toting a rusty AK-47.

"Yes, what is it to you?" Eteka asked.

"Ma boss man want to see yaw now. Please, follow me," the young man replied politely. He led them up a hill through thick brush to a group of men sitting around a fire. Most of the men in this group were slightly older, though there were also a few young boys, and they all held AK-47s. The pungent aroma of cheap marijuana permeated the air as the men passed a thick blunt around the circle. They laughed, enjoying spirited conversation as the mercenaries approached.

"Sah, the men na come," the young guide said to his commander, the oldest-looking man in the group.

General Morning Coffee stopped laughing and looked up. He was a tough-looking old man, with years of hard experience written all over him. The light from the fire illuminated his face, his grey beard, and the wrinkles in the corners of his eyes. He wore camouflage army fatigues and had a very messy afro. General Morning Coffee studied the mercenaries for a few seconds, then smiled.

"Ma man, yaw come join us oh. We've been expecting you," he said as some of the men made some space for them to sit next to him in the circle. "What yaw want drink?"

"Maybe later. Let's get to business," Eteka replied.

"Yeah, of course," the General said as the blunt was passed to him. He took a few puffs and inhaled deeply as he looked up at the stars. He then handed the blunt to Eteka.

"No thanks, I like to have a clear head when I'm doing business," Eteka said as he passed the blunt along to Cyrus. "So, when do we get the diamonds?"

"Time will tell. A na get too late for yaw to travel tonight. In fact, we have something to ask you," the commander said.

Eteka looked at Cyrus, who shrugged as he took a hit from the blunt.

"Our business here is to get the diamonds and leave. Nothing more," Eteka said.

General Morning Coffee grinned at Eteka.

"Tomorrow in the morning we be advancing on Kle, and we know some government soldiers will give us hard time. They are very hard, hey. You know they give us hard time before. We want you to fight for us, so we can win. They are protecting that dissident who space on us about our area. I want yaw to catch him alive or dead. I hear plenty good things about you Imamba, and I told my boss men that I will catch the dissident if you agree to fight for us."

Eteka frowned. He knew it would be bad for the traitor if he were captured alive. Better to die in battle than be at the mercy of those you betrayed.

Tapping Eteka on the shoulder, Cyrus whispered, "Let's go with them. You and I both know they won't give us the cases if we don't."

Eteka nodded and faced the General. "Okay, but you will have to pay us for our time."

General Morning Coffee smiled as the blunt came back to him. He took a few drags and blew some smoke in the air.

"I didn't even catch yaw names."

"I'm Eteka."

"And I'm Cyrus."

"You sound like one of us. Are you Liberian?" the General asked Cyrus, passing him the blunt.

"Yes, I am Gio.[1]"

"I thought so. So am I. You should be here, fighting with us," General Morning Coffee said with a wink.

Cyrus grinned as he took another long drag from the blunt.

"I used to fight with you guys, a very long time ago. I just found a job that pays me better."

---

[1] The Gio are a tribe in Liberia and in Côte d'Ivoire.

"So, did you space on us, too?" the General asked, sparks from the crackling fire settling to fizzle in his beard. The other rebels in the circle looked at Cyrus, awaiting his response.

"If I had, I wouldn't have agreed to help you," Cyrus replied. "Tomorrow we'll get your traitor for you, and then we'll leave with the cases. As an extra bonus for our support, you can throw in two extra rocks for the both of us. Deal?"

Some of the men whispered to General Morning Coffee. After a moment, he faced the mercenaries, nodding his head.

"Okay, good. We leave tomorrow at dawn, and should get there around eight. This is the man we're looking for," the General said, handing Eteka a photograph of a lean man with a chiseled face and a bald head. "When we're done fighting, you'll get yaw cases, with more rocks."

"What's this traitor's name, anyway?" Eteka asked.

"We are calling him Kali Po Po," General Morning Coffee replied.

"Do you have any weapons for us? We have only our side arms," said Cyrus.

"We have weapons you can use—mostly AKs and a few grenade launchers. You can have your pick. Tonight you can rest with the men; we will make some beds available for you. Tomorrow we will hang, hey. Stay with us for a while, so we can show you our battle plans for tomorrow," the General replied.

One of the men pulled out a well-marked map and a compass. The mercenaries listened closely as the General went over the plans and prepared them for their upcoming side mission.

The IFW rebels arrived at the village of Kle by 8:00 a.m. the next morning. It was a small village, with only a handful of abandoned houses and empty streets—the locals had obviously known that they were coming, and had fled to hide in the bush or other nearby villages. They parked their vehicles on the outskirts of the village and proceeded on foot under the cover of some brush. Cyrus and Eteka, each wielding an AK-47, followed the rebels to the first building.

General Morning Coffee faced his troops, gesturing with his hand. The rebels split into three groups, with about 15 of them moving to the right and circling the village as the other 15 moved to the left and did the same. The remaining force of 20 consisted of young men and boys, the mercenaries, and General Morning Coffee. The General turned to address the mercenaries.

"We will go down to the bone,"[1] General Morning Coffee whispered in Liberian slang.

"Okay, you go ahead. We'll find your traitor for you," Cyrus whispered back.

The commander nodded and moved to the edge of an abandoned building, his troops following behind. Suddenly, a

---

[1] "We are going to go down the center."

gunshot rang out, followed by a loud explosion and lots of shouting—the battle had begun.

"Let's sweep around the left side and stay low, in the grass. I'm sure our target is in one of those houses on the left," Cyrus said as gunfire roared all around them.

Eteka nodded. He could see movement from what he figured were government troops in the nearby houses. The mercenaries got low and snuck around to their left as the fighting intensified. Bullets ricocheted off the buildings as they moved behind the first house they came to. Looking back, Eteka could see a few of the rebels getting shot and falling to the ground. The General was still behind them, urging his troops—most of them young boys not yet in their teens—to fight. Cyrus peeked through a window and spotted two government soldiers shooting out opposite windows at the rebels. He got ready to shoot them from behind, but Eteka stopped him.

"Let's get the target first, don't attract unnecessary attention. Those rebels are giving us cover."

Cyrus nodded in agreement and they moved on, crawling through the grass toward the next house. All kinds of sounds blended together: gunshots, mortars, and screaming—the symphony of war. A stray bullet hit a tree a few yards away from the mercenaries, and a piece of tree bark grazed Eteka's face. He kept moving. As they approached the second house, they were spotted by a young soldier.

"OVER HERE!! OVE—"

Cyrus silenced him with two well-placed shots, and the young soldier's body slumped to the ground. They got behind the second house, and Cyrus peered through an open window. There was a commotion inside with some men running around, some firing shots out of another window at the rebels and some huddled in one corner of the room, stacking reams of paper into boxes. Cyrus spotted their target behind a group of men in the corner.

"Got him," Cyrus whispered to Eteka.

Eteka peeked in, spotting their target as well.

"They are too close; let's retreat to Monrovia," one of the government soldiers said in his thick Liberian accent as the others looked worriedly at the fighting outside.

"Then let's lay now, before they ambush and catch us here," replied a second soldier, nervously shifting his gun from hand to hand.

Kali Po Po stood up nervously. "Wha aba me?" he asked.

The soldiers didn't say a word, exchanging glances with each other.

"Wha aba you?" asked the soldier in command.

"You told me da your men will protect me once I help you. You sey you were going to help me lay from this country. I can come with you, yes?"

The soldiers gathered their weapons while the ranking officer shook his head at Kali Po Po.

"I having a feeling that the rebels came for you. You can come with us, but only because you've still got some information we need. Get your things."

Outside, Cyrus and Eteka exchanged looks, lowering themselves below the open window.

"You open fire from here and I'll support from the front when they turn their attention to you," Cyrus whispered, readying his weapon. Eteka nodded in agreement.

Cyrus started making his way around the house, and Eteka readied his weapon. Eteka set his sights on two government soldiers guarding the front door—eliminating them would open the way for Cyrus to come in the front.

Eteka opened fire, quick bursts of bullets hitting both guards square in their chests.

"What the—" an officer let out as the fallen soldiers slumped to the floor. The remaining soldiers in the room opened fire in Eteka's direction. He ducked just in time, the open window shattering above his head as pieces of the window frame flew everywhere.

"Hurry! Withdraw!" their leader yelled as the soldiers rushed for the front door.

Cyrus opened fire through the front door, taking out the rest of the soldiers in a hail of bullets. The government officer dropped to the ground, clutching his stomach in pain, and drew his revolver. Behind him, Kali Po Po cowered behind a table, having hidden just in time to avoid the gunfire. Outside, shouting could be heard as the gunfire let up. The government officer pointed his gun at the front door.

"Foolish people! I na scare of you!" the commander of the government officers yelled, blood oozing from his wound onto the floor. The officer's eyes moved rapidly between Cyrus at the front door and Eteka, who had moved into the room.

Cyrus calmly stepped into the room, pointing his gun at the soldier's head. As the soldier laboriously brought his gun to bear on Cyrus, Cyrus squeezed his trigger, shooting the officer in the arm. The officer screamed in pain, dropping his blood-stained revolver on the floor. Cyrus approached him slowly and cocked his gun.

"What you waitin' for?" the officer panted, clutching his arm in pain. "Finish it."

Cyrus smiled and pointed his weapon at the officer's head.

"As you wish."

"Cyrus, wait," Eteka said.

"What?"

"We didn't come here for him. Let him go."

Cyrus lowered his weapon. "I don't get you, my brother. If he had the chance he would kill me."

"The rebels are not paying us for his head. Being an Imamba means being disciplined, or else we're just brutes like those guys out there. Let's stick with the plan," Eteka replied.

Cyrus shook his head. "You just take the fun out of everything, don't you?"

"I'm just saying that we have to stick to the plan and do what we're getting paid for. And we have our target," Eteka replied as he glanced at Kali Po Po cowering behind a table.

Cyrus grinned and looked at the wounded officer. "Seems today is your lucky day. Get up."

The government commander watched both mercenaries warily and slowly got to his feet, hunched over his gut wound. Gore from his arm littered the floor, and blood lined the walls of the room. He clutched his arm and stomach as his eyes remained trained on Cyrus's gun.

"Leave. Now," Eteka commanded. The officer hesitated for a moment, then nodded at Eteka. He limped to the door, keeping his eyes on Cyrus, and disappeared.

Both Cyrus and Eteka turned to face Kali Po Po. He shook visibly as Eteka grabbed his collar and stood him up.

"Please, let me go. I have some money. I also have some land. Please," the traitor begged.

"Sorry, friend, this is just business. You can offer your land to your old friends," Cyrus replied, tying the man's hands behind his back.

Cyrus shoved Kali Po Po outside just in time to catch sight of the last government troops fleeing, the rebels in close pursuit. The remaining rebels emerged victoriously from their cover, jumping and shouting as they celebrated their victory. Some fired shots into the air, and one teenage rebel holding a battered boom box on his shoulder put in a cassette, turned up the volume, and began to play Kool G Rap's "Death Wish."

"Ma men Kali Po Po," General Morning Coffee said, addressing the traitor, "it's good to see you."

"Please, sah, I have some money I can give you, and land. Please, I beg you. I did not do anything to lead them to you," Kali Po Po implored. He was so frightened that he pissed in his trousers. A group of young rebel soldiers surrounded him, several rubbing the sharp blades of their machetes together. Eteka knew Kali Po Po would suffer a fate worse than death.

General Morning Coffee fixed Kali Po Po with an expression of disgust. He motioned toward two of his men, who dragged the sobbing Kali Po Po away.

"We'll take the cases now, plus our additional payment," Eteka said, watching as Kali Po Po was led behind a bullet-riddled house.

General Morning Coffee smiled and signaled for two boys with a wave of his hand. They ran off, returning moments later with two medium-sized briefcases which they dropped at the mercenaries' feet.

"And here's your extra payment," General Morning Coffee added, handing Eteka a little bag containing two uncut diamonds the size of marbles.

"Good. We'll need transportation to Monrovia," Eteka said.

"I organize that for you, ma men. Government soldiers are plenty in that area, so we will put you down five miles from the city. You will try and find your way from there," the General replied.

"We have connections in the government, we should be fine," Cyrus replied.

Eteka watched as rebels led the remaining government troops away at gunpoint. He knew that, just like Kali Po Po, they were about to meet their fate. Shrugging away his doubts, Eteka returned his attention to the General.

"Ma men have a car waiting in front. They will put you down," General Morning Coffee said, grasping Cyrus's arm. "Liberia needs you, ma men. Somebody like you can help our fight."

"You're not my brother, and what Liberia needs is peace, not me," Cyrus replied, disengaging his arm. He and Eteka picked up the cases and followed a boy toward a waiting car.

"What Liberia needs is peace? Funny—I never thought that you, of all people, would say something like that," Eteka remarked.

"I guess you don't know me that well," he replied, winking. "We should hurry, the government is sure to shell this area soon."

As they walked, Eteka noticed a familiar figure lying motionless on the ground in their path. It was his surly little friend, Bisi, with a large bullet hole in his head. Other boys—likely his comrades—would eventually pick up his little body and dump it in some nearby bushes, and it would be as if he never existed.

FATHER FIGURE

Chefchaouen, Morocco. 1974.

A light mist covered the air this late morning in the beautiful city of
Chefchaouen, the "Blue Pearl" of Morocco. Young children ran
through the city's trademark blue-washed streets and houses,
laughing as they threw water balloons at each other. On the streets,
women and men walked to and fro, most with their heads covered. A
few women sat along the blue city's small, windy Moroccan
corridors, selling their wares while trading neighborhood gossip.
Tourists filled the area, many sitting for local delicacies like atai
(Moroccan green tea with mint), saffron, citrus fruit, and goat cheese
at cafés, while other tourists could be seen walking in and out of the
shops in the city's medina. In the background immediately behind
the blue city stood the Rif Mountains, hosting numerous marijuana
fields across its hills and valleys.

Oga smoked some local kif[1] as he sat by a café. A fly landed
on the large scar that covered part of his face, and he brushed it off

---

[1] Hashish/Marijuana

as he fixed his aviator sunglasses and continued to stare at her. She was the only local woman he had seen walking around without her head covered—most of the population was Muslim. She was young, and her long hair fell down past her shoulders to her waist. Elaborate henna designs covered much of her hands, and the silk dress she wore flowed around her like a cloud. She was fair in complexion, with large, round brown eyes and dimples in her cheeks. Oga did not know why he was so transfixed by her appearance, nor why he had spent every afternoon since he arrived here in Chefchaouen three days ago sitting at this café to watch her buy food across the street. The concept of being in love was foreign to his hardened mind—he couldn't understand this simple fascination.

He sat quietly, smoking his kif as he watched her smile, carry off her goods in a basket, and disappear down the street. Playing on a television set in the same café was coverage of the Nixon Watergate trial in the United States. Oga stood up, stretched, said goodbye to a few other men he had been smoking with, and walked off.

He had come to this city in Northeast Morocco to rest and clear his head. He had also come here to spend some alone time with a boy he had adopted from Nigeria, a child called Eteka. Oga had come across a very young Eteka as he was leaving Nigeria a few years ago on a mission for the Imamba. Oga himself had been abandoned by his parents when he was only a child, so he felt sympathy for Eteka when he first laid eyes upon him. He picked Eteka up and raised him as his own, teaching him the arts of warfare, one-on-one combat, and his perspective on life. Eteka was 11 years old now and already showing signs of maturity well beyond his years.

Oga walked into the room he had rented in a hotel on the outskirts of the city. He plopped down on a bed and lit up a cigarette just as Eteka walked into the room from an adjacent bathroom. He had just taken a shower.

"Hello, Uncle Oga."

"Hello, Eteka. Did the phone ring?"

"No."

Oga sat up and looked out of a window, which offered a grand view of the nearby Rif Mountains.

"Tomorrow we'll hike up the mountain trail. Are you hungry?"

"Yes," Eteka replied.

"Okay, get dressed so we can find something to eat. I'm hungry, too."

As Eteka put on some clothes, a black rotary phone sitting in a corner of the room rang. Oga walked over.

"Hello?"

"We got another assignment," Omega's voice said over the phone.

"What kind of assignment?"

"Sabotage. Overseas."

"Where exactly?"

"In Brazil. When can you get to Oualidia so we plan? The client is offering a good chunk of money for this one."

"It depends," Oga said, looking at Eteka. "I'm on vacation. What's the timeframe?"

"We have a month to get it done, not that much time, so we have to start planning," Omega answered. "Is the boy with you?"

"Yes."

"Refresh my memory, but where did you pick him up from again?"

"Nigeria. I adopted him."

"I see. We are hitmen, Oga. We're not in the daycare business. Why did you of all people think it okay to pick up a random child when you know what we do?"

"He's my responsibility, and not your concern," Oga shot back. "I'll be in Oualidia in two days."

"Two days it is," Omega replied, before hanging up. Oga shook his head and stood up just as Eteka finished getting dressed. The young boy looked up at him, wide brown eyes crinkling as he smiled at his adoptive uncle.

"C'mon, let's get you some of that chicken tagine[1] you liked so much last night," Oga blustered, patting him awkwardly on the shoulder. The boy beamed at him, trotting along at his heel like the most naïve of puppies.

---

[1] Tagines are Berber dishes that are named after the native 'Tagine' pots in which they are usually cooked and served.

✝

Early the next day, Oga and Eteka set off toward the mountains for their trek. The air was fresh as they trudged uphill, past quiet homes, a few people saying their morning prayers, and vast, leafy marijuana fields. They continued past beautiful grasslands, and up a trail that led to a mountain pass. They kept on walking, stopping briefly at a house on the trail to have mint tea with a family. Then they continued on. Four hours passed, and overhead, heavy storm clouds began to form. They reached a small village on the trail, and after offering some money to a kind family, they sat down in a cottage and enjoyed some more mint tea just as heavy rains began to fall. They sat next to each other on a balcony that offered a great view of the mountains and the city below, as the heavy rains quenched the land of thirst. As they sat, another hiking party made up of two white men, a woman, and a girl that appeared to be her daughter walked in. The young girl appeared to be around Eteka's age. They sat across the room from Oga and Eteka, and were also treated to mint tea by their hosts. The woman and daughter began to laugh with each other, and one of the men kissed both females on their foreheads.

"Uncle?"

"Yes?"

"Why did my mother and father give me away?" Eteka asked, his eyes on the group across the room.

"Your real parents died in a car accident. Your foster parents could not afford to take care of you, so I adopted you. We spoke about this already."

"Did my foster parents love me?"

"I don't know if they loved you or not," Oga replied, sipping on his tea. "But they asked me to watch you. You'll have to accept that."

"Will I ever see them again?"

"That's up to them. They are in Nigeria. I'm sure we could arrange something in the future."

Eteka took a few sips of his tea, pausing every now and then to look at the family across the room. Oga noticed Eteka's interest.

"That life was not meant for you, so stop looking at them and tormenting yourself."

Oga watched Eteka take one last look at the family, then turn to look at the falling rain.

"I just don't understand... did they have to give me away? There must be something wrong with me."

"There is nothing wrong with you," Oga said. "Don't ever think that way. You were meant to be strong, to be a warrior. A warrior's path is different from the average person's. He has to experience things most people cannot handle. But those things make him strong. They make his mind sharp. You are going to be a great warrior, Eteka. One day you will be a leader in the Imamba Brotherhood. So you must learn to deal with all the challenges life will throw your way, and be both mentally and physically strong."

"Did you grow up with your family, Uncle Oga?"

"No, I did not," Oga replied, sitting up in his chair. "Like you, my family offered me up, abandoned me. But unlike you, I had no one to go to. I had to fend for myself from a very young age, learn a lot of hard lessons the hard way."

"Our families did not treat us well, Uncle Oga. I wish they would have treated us better," Eteka said, taking another wistful glance at the family as he did so.

"Stop being so emotional and listen carefully to what I'm about to tell you, young man. Very few people in this life give a shit about you. At the end of the day, it's you against the world," Oga said, lighting up a cigarette. Oga took a long drag, then pulled out a shiny black Browning 9mm pistol from a hidden gun holster. He studied the pistol with a smile for a moment, as if admiring a valuable piece of art, then handed it to Eteka.

"That, young man, is the only thing you can trust in this world. Not people, because people are full of shit and are not reliable. But a gun—a gun always tells the truth. And a gun will make a man show you his most honest self. The gun is your best friend, and the only thing you need in this life, remember that."

Oga watched as Eteka studied the weapon, a look of awe on the young boy's face. The heavy rains had stopped, and a thick fog covered the mountainous area. Oga grabbed his gun from Eteka and put it back in his holster.

"The rains have stopped. Let's head back."

That evening, Oga and Eteka decided to take a walk around the main plaza[1] in Chefchaouen to get some fresh air. It was a cool evening, and the plaza was filled with a mixture of tourists and locals. Restaurants, food stalls, and cafés lined one side of the plaza, with tourists seated on cushioned outdoor chairs soaking in the view over mint tea. Overlooking the square stood the Rif Mountains, its peaks covered in thick fog. Oga and Eteka walked in silence, simply enjoying the serenity of their surroundings. They passed a few cafés, stopping to buy a kebab at one, while making small talk with a few locals. And then Oga saw her. Standing, by herself, was the same woman that had earlier transfixed him. There she was, with the same smile that had captivated him, standing by an ancient pine tree at the center of the square. She was laughing with a few men sitting by the pine tree.

Oga walked over to her, his eyes outlining the shape of her body underneath her clothes.

"Buenas noches,[2]" Oga greeted in Spanish, as Eteka watched. The woman turned around and smiled, as the men sitting by the tree looked on.

"Hola,[3]" she responded.

"¿Cómo estás?[4]"

"Estoy bien, gracias.[5]"

---

[1] The "Plaza Uta el-Hammam" is the main square in the medina of Chefchaouen.
[2] "Good evening."
[3] "Hello"
[4] "How are you?"
[5] "I'm fine, thank you."

"¿Cuál es tu nombre?[1]"

"Salma. What is your name?" she asked in English. He found her voice soothing.

"Oga. You speak English?"

"Yes, I do," Salma replied. "I speak Spanish[2], French, English, and Arabic."

"Smart girl."

"Gracias. You're not from here. I've never seen you before."

"No. We're just visiting."

"I see. Is that your son?" she asked, nodding at Eteka.

"You could say that. You're very beautiful," commented Oga, which made the woman blush and look away. "I was going to get some tea at one of these cafés here. Will your husband object?" Oga asked. "

"I have no husband."

Oga scratched the scar that ran across his face and smiled. He turned to Eteka.

"Go wait for me at the hotel."

"What?" Eteka said, taking some time to look at the woman. "Is this about her?"

"Just go back and wait for me. I'll be back before it gets too late," Oga answered as he locked arms with the woman and walked off, leaving Eteka standing alone in the middle of the square. This was not uncommon, as Eteka was used to Oga walking off with strange women whenever they spent time together. Eteka embraced

---

[1] "What is your name?"
[2] In the 15th and 17th centuries, Chefchaouen took in exiles from Spain. Despite it being a Moroccan city, Spanish is widely spoken amongst the locals.

his solitude, and decided to explore Chefchaouen before heading back to the hotel room. His 11-year-old legs walked through the blue city, past the medina, and into the city's labyrinth of narrow streets and blue-tinted homes. The aromas of spices, fresh bread, and olives caught his nose as he walked past different homes, in which he could hear families gathering for dinner and speaking Arabic amongst themselves. As he made a turn down a dimly lit street, he passed by four old men who were playing cards. All the men had long hooded robes on, each in a different color: red, blue, black, and white. They all smoked kif from long wooden pipes, and stopped playing their cards as Eteka walked by.

"¿A dónde vas?[1]" the old man wearing the blue robe asked. Eteka stopped in his tracks and turned around.

"Huh?" Eteka reacted, finding it hard to see the men's faces under the dim street lighting.

"Él quiere saber a dónde vas,[2]" the old man wearing the red robe said.

"Mi español no es muy bueno,[3]" Eteka replied. "Hablas inglés?[4]"

"Yes, we speak English," the old man wearing the white robe answered. "So, where are you going?"

"I was just taking a walk."

"It's a little late for you to be out by yourself, no?" the old man in the blue robe asked.

---

[1] "Where are you going?"
[2] "He wants to know where you are going."
[3] "My Spanish is not very good."
[4] "Do you speak English?"

"My uncle is busy and could not walk with me, so I'm just walking around."

"Your uncle is busy, here in Chaouen[1]?" the old man in the white robe laughed. "Busy doing what?"

"He's with a woman."

"Ah. Women can have that effect. Was she easy on the eyes?" the old man in the red robe asked.

"Yes. Very."

"Then it means he'll be with her for a long time. Come, sit with us," the old man in the blue robe suggested, and they made some space for Eteka. The old man in the black robe still had not spoken.

"Have some, it will put things in perspective," the old man in white said as he offered Eteka a pipe. Eteka took a puff, the cannabis filling his lungs and make him cough in spurts. The old men all laughed, save for the man in black.

"What is your name?" the old man in red asked.

"Eteka. What are your names?" Eteka asked. At that, none of the men responded and they went back to playing cards, behavior that Eteka found very strange. Only the man in black remained still, with his head turned toward Eteka.

"Don't mind them. You can call me Anansi. How long have you been in Chaouen?" Anansi asked. His voice was raspy, and he had alcohol on his breath.

---

[1] Chefchaouen is referred to as Chaouen by the locals/Moroccans.

"A few days. We tried to climb the mountain today, but it started raining," Eteka answered as he took another drag from the pipe.

"And now you are here, smoking kif with four strange old men. You think being here is by chance? Or do you think certain events were put in place to lead you here?"

The question was one that Eteka found strange, yet was willing to answer, in part due to the kif now in his system. The world had taken on a warm, hazy glow.

"I don't know, sir. I just decided to take a walk, and now I'm here."

"What if I told you that the girl your uncle is with now was placed there intentionally?" Anansi asked.

"She was?" Eteka asked, blinking.

"Maybe she was, maybe she wasn't. It's all a matter of perspective."

Eteka looked at Anansi with a raised eyebrow. The old man's face was mostly hidden due to the large hood covering his face.

"Are you high, sir?" Eteka's question made all the men laugh, including Anansi.

"No. The question I asked you is a reflection of your life now, and your life to come, my child. It will all come down to your perspective."

ANANSI

"IT'S ALL A MATTER OF
PERSPECTIVE."

ETEKA
RISE OF THE IMAMBA

"Nevertheless, we cannot use you. It is your kinsman to whom we shall make our offer."

Eteka again looked at Anansi, feeling very confused. What the heck was this strange man talking about? He became uneasy and stood up.

"I have to go now. Thanks for letting me smoke with you." And with that, Eteka walked off, deciding to head back to the hotel. At the end of the street, Eteka turned around. He saw all the old men sitting quietly, staring right back at him.

OLD FRIENDS

Ibadan, Nigeria. Africa. 1967.

Yisa sat on a cushioned bamboo chair on his front porch, sipping on a chilled glass of palm wine and chewing on some bitter kola nuts. Sunset was approaching, and the signature outdoor scents of roasted yams, suya,[1] and corn from Ibadan's street vendors whetted his appetite. Perhaps later he would take a stroll through the streets and buy a snack—maybe some suya. Yisa would ask Oladele to join him after he finished tutoring his wife in philosophy. Despite the busyness that came with having a child, Amina had maintained her love for academia, and for the past three years she had arranged for Oladele to teach her philosophy in the evenings three times a week. She and Oladele mulled over the books and writings of Augustine, Aristotle, Lao Tzu, and many others before ending their session with a prayer. Both were inside the house now—Yisa could hear their soft murmurs through the walls. Tosin was probably playing with one of the servants in the house somewhere. Yisa

---

[1]Suya is a type of kebab seasoned with tankora that is popular in West Africa.

swatted a mosquito off his neck and waved at a neighbor walking by. This was the way life should be lived: peacefully.

Yisa had been home for five days, but in two more he would have to fly out to the small coastal village of Oualidia in Morocco to meet with Oga and Omega. Omega had chosen Oualidia as the Imamba leadership's meeting place because of its remote, beautiful nature. Yisa had to admit, he did enjoy going there and receiving first-class treatment. There were some new contracts on the table to be resolved, some of which he was sure would involve hits on key figures in the Biafran conflict currently underway.

The past 12 years had gone by so quickly. Much had changed since Yisa had first met Oga and Omega in Algeria in 1955. The Algerian conflict had ended in 1962 with Algeria finally gaining its independence from France. During the conflict, both sides had benefitted from Omega's weapons and the profits had helped build the infrastructure of the Imamba Brotherhood. The Portuguese colonial wars, specifically in Angola and Portuguese Guinea, had provided the Imamba with a significant number of young, able-bodied men formerly linked with guerrilla nationalist movements. The Imamba's clients now included guerrilla movements, foreign governments, powerful drug dealers, and foreign corporations. Omega was a smart businessman—he had taken Yisa's ideological thesis and transformed it into a money-making machine.

And how could Yisa complain? Here he was, sitting in a gated two-story home, the latest sports cars parked on his front lawn. His son, Tosin, was well-protected and his wife, Amina, was without a financial need in the world—free to pursue her studies and mother their child. Yet he seldom saw them, and the dark side of his occupation made him a walking moral contradiction. He did business with evil men—ruthless killers who would do anything for a fat paycheck. This was not what he'd envisioned all those years ago. Nonetheless, here he was, destroying his own people. He had become the virus he so desperately wanted to cure.

Americans, Europeans, the Chinese—nations and cultures like these dominated the world with their economies and ideologies. The wealthiest of the Imamba's clients came from these places. Perhaps the idea of getting the most skilled warriors across the continent and uniting them under one banner was a foolish idea, partly because, even after all these years, he still wasn't sure what he wanted to unite them for. What would be their goal? To fight against their former foreign oppressors? It was 1967, and save for Portuguese Guinea and a few southern territories, most African nations had gained their independence. Those days of supposed heroism and nationalist movements were fast becoming memories. It seemed Yisa's vision was surprisingly short-sighted.

Omega, on the other hand, had goals. Real, tangible goals— the most important of which was to make lots of money. The Imamba's activities brought in about eight million U.S. dollars a year from hits alone. The men under their leadership enjoyed the financial security that the brotherhood offered. How could Yisa convince any of them to drop their weapons or fight for more noble causes?

"Daddy?"

Yisa looked down at his son. Tosin was four now, and had grown into a handsome little boy, his curious brown eyes looking intently at Yisa. He carried a board game and his shirt had a food stain on it.

"Yes?" Yisa said with a big smile.

"Do you want to play Ludo?"

"Ludo? Who taught you how to play?"

"Uncle Oladele taught me."

"I see," Yisa replied, feeling a bit disappointed that he hadn't been the one to teach his son the game. "I would love to play with you."

Tosin sat next to his father near a table and set up the game board, grinning from ear to ear. Father and son played, Yisa outsmarting Tosin each time yet allowing him to win. After about 30 minutes Tosin stood up.

"Daddy, how did you become so strong?" little Tosin asked as he poked at Yisa's arms. Yisa laughed and flexed his arm, making Tosin's eyes widen.

"I make sure I eat all my vegetables," Yisa replied. "So if you want to be strong like me, you have to eat all your vegetables when your mother gives them to you. She told me sometimes you do not like eating them."

"I eat my vegetables. I just don't like cucumbers. And spinach. And tomantoes. And…"

"Wait. It's not tomantoes. It's *tomatoes*."

"Tomantoes."

"No, *tomatoes*. To-ma-toes. Say it properly," Yisa said.

"To-ma-toes," Tosin parroted.

"Good boy. It sounds like you don't like any of your vegetables. You have to eat your vegetables. That is the only way you can become strong."

"Okay, Daddy, I will eat my vegetables. I like it when Mummy makes spaghetti. I like eating that. I like eating that and jollof rice."

Yisa shook his head and smiled.

"You are a spoiled little boy. When I was your age we hardly ate rice. And spaghetti? Now that was only for special occasions."

"Really? So what did you eat?" the boy asked.

"Lots of gari. Many nights we slept on just gari, water, and some sugar if we were lucky."

"Daddy, I think you are lying. How can you have never eaten spaghetti when you were my age?"

Yisa laughed loudly and settled in for an evening of storytelling.

While Yisa and Tosin enjoyed their time together outside on the veranda, Oladele and Amina sat next to each other in the kitchen. *The Tragedy of Othello* by William Shakespeare lay on the table before them. Amina was reading a chapter as Oladele listened, his eyes glued to her lush lips.

"I miss you," Oladele whispered, eyes intense.

"Oladele, please. Not here, not now," Amina replied, darting a glance at the veranda where her husband and child were playing together.

"I love hearing you read. I dream about your voice at night."

"Shhhh! He might hear you! He's right outside!" Amina hissed.

"I don't care. He's never here to take care of you, and I might as well be your husband. Do I not take care of you and Tosin?"

"Yes, you do," Amina replied, placing a hand on Oladele's face. "But he is my husband, and you are his best friend."

Oladele placed a hand on her leg and leaned in to kiss her. She returned the kiss briefly, then suddenly pushed him away.

"Please, Oladele, this has to end. This thing we've been doing, it has to end."

"You cannot possibly believe your own words," he replied. "You spend more time in my arms than his, and I treat Tosin like my own son. Yisa was not even here when Tosin was born."

"I was the one who was by your side through your whole pregnancy. How can a man and a woman with an attraction like ours spend so much time together and not fall in love?" Oladele asked, sliding his hand up her leg. "We should tell him."

"Are you crazy?" she asked, pushing his hand off. "He would kill us both!"

She closed the book, turning to face Oladele.

AMINA

"SHHHH! HE MIGHT HEAR YOU!
HE'S RIGHT OUTSIDE!"

ETEKA
RISE OF THE IMAMBA

"You are a good man, Oladele, and we both fell for our passions. But my husband, your best friend, is home. He works so hard—let's forget about ourselves for some time and make him happy. Okay?"

Oladele looked at her briefly, then smiled.

"Okay. I'm sorry for making you uncomfortable. Let's head outside and see what they are doing. We can pick up where we left off with Othello when Yisa leaves."

Amina breathed a sigh of relief as they got up and headed outside together.

"Ah, there they are," Yisa said with a smile as Amina and Oladele joined him outside. "I've been trying to tell this young boy how tough life was for us when we were his age, and he doesn't believe me."

"Daddy said he used to eat just gari and water for dinner when he was my age. Did you do the same thing when you were my age, Uncle Oladele?" Tosin asked.

"At least he had gari. I used to settle for only water to put me to sleep on many nights," Oladele replied, and they all laughed, glad that for this child, the thought of going to bed hungry was only a story. The sun had set, and it was dark now, the only light coming from homes and kerosene lamps in each street vendor's station. It was time for dinner.

"And what are you people teaching my son? He can't even speak English. He can't even say tomatoes properly," Yisa said as he stood up.

"Well, maybe you should come home more often and teach him yourself, then, since we are doing such a poor job," Amina said tartly. Yisa nodded, kissed her, and turned to his boy.

"Go off now with your mother, it's time to eat."

"Will you come and eat with us?" little Tosin asked.

"No, I have to talk to Uncle Oladele. Go on."

"Don't stay out too late," Amina said as she whisked an excited Tosin into the house. Her slender, curvy hips stood out in the tight-fitting skirt she wore, swaying from side to side as she walked indoors, entrancing Yisa and Oladele.

"Stop staring at my wife's ass," Yisa said, nudging Oladele.

"I'm sorry, my brother, but it was staring at me first," Oladele replied cheerfully, and they both laughed.

"Come on, make we go chop some suya,"[1] Yisa said in pidgin, and they both headed for the street.

In many respects, Oladele was Yisa's opposite. Standing at a mere 5'6", Oladele's small frame did not command as much authority as Yisa's did, and he was neither athletic nor particularly handsome. Always clean-shaven, he wore large bifocal glasses and a perfectly ironed shirt, tucked into equally perfectly ironed trousers. His default stance was with his hands behind his back even when he walked, and he would nod his head every now and then as if he debated and agreed with himself on a continual basis. Commonly dismissed as socially awkward, Oladele had a very engaging personality, provided he was in a comfortable environment.

The son of an Igbo farmer, Oladele had spent his childhood helping his father at his farm before studying English and philosophy at the University of Ibadan, where he was currently a professor. An avid thinker and a prolific writer, Oladele had begun to make a name for himself with some of his publications. His most recent work, *Leadership in the Motherland,* was written under his pen name of Oluko, which meant "teacher" in Yoruba. Oladele and Yisa had been roommates at the University of Ibadan, and maintained their relationship as best friends even when Yisa dropped out of school to pursue a full-time career as a mercenary.

---

[1] "Come on, let's go grab some suya."

They walked in silence for the first few minutes as street vendors and pedestrians continued their usual evening routine around them. It was a nice, cool evening after the heat of the day.

"Times have changed since we were young, Oladele."

"I'm still young, I don't know what you're talking about," Oladele replied, adjusting his glasses.

"You don't look that young to me."

"I'm young. It's all in my mind. And I'm also better-looking."

Yisa chuckled. They walked by vendors selling fried yams, roasted peanuts, pof-pof pastries, and roasted corn. No suya was to be found, even though its unmistakable aroma hung tantalizingly in the air.

"How have things been with you?" Yisa asked.

"Things are good. Thankfully this Biafra business has not affected us that much, at least not yet. I love teaching and my job at the university is fulfilling, even though at times I wish I was paid more. But, that's what I get for teaching something like philosophy in Africa. It doesn't interest many people so it doesn't get much funding. One day, perhaps, things will change."

"I see. And your writing? I've been reading the book you gave me. I take it with me on my travels. It's very informative."

"Thank you. I put a lot of research into it. The book has received a lot of praise here as well, but it's also made me a few enemies. The truth always seems to have that effect," Oladele replied.

"So then, the question is, is the truth always worth telling?"

"Yes, or else there would be no balance. Evil needs to be balanced out with good. Without balance, the world cannot exist. The question is not *if* the truth should be told, but rather when and how."

They continued down the street. Rusty taxicabs drove by, whistling for customers. Two policemen with outdated assault rifles stood at a corner, questioning a bus driver. A toothless old man sat listening to a small handheld radio that was playing some Fuji music. Three men gathered around the old man and started dancing to the tunes coming from the device. Yisa and Oladele passed all these things, but still no suya.

"How did you know this was what you wanted to do, Oladele? I mean, we both went to school and all."

"You dropped out," recalled Oladele, with a hint of smugness.

"Yes, thanks for reminding me," Yisa said with a chuckle. "But seriously, what made you certain that the path you're on is what was meant for you?"

Oladele rubbed his chin, deep in thought.

"Why do you ask?"

"Just answer the question."

They continued to walk down the street. The pleasing aroma of suya was getting stronger now, and Yisa knew they were close.

"I guess the catalyst of change began when I made my trip, my pilgrimage to Bandung in 1955," Oladele said thoughtfully.

"Bandung, Indonesia? I never knew you went there."

"You weren't around for me to tell you," Oladele replied. "I was there for the Bandung Conference.[1] It changed my life."

That was the same year in which Yisa, Omega, and Oga had formed the Imamba Brotherhood. He had been a world away and on an entirely different path from his lifelong friend.

"So, this conference made you want to become a teacher?" Yisa asked.

"No. This conference inspired me to make a difference, a positive difference for our people. The writing, teaching, and everything else I do supports this goal."

"I see. You'll have to give me full details on this pilgrimage you made, my friend."

"It would make for good conversation," Oladele responded, "maybe on the way back, I'll share some details. Enough about me, what about you?"

"What about me?"

"Why do you do what you do?"

"What do I do, my friend?" Yisa asked vaguely.

"You are a killer, this I know," Oladele curled his lip in disgust.

"Have you seen me kill? You're just making assumptions." Yisa bristled, a little offended at Oladele's snide comment.

"I have seen many things, my brother, including a murderer's eyes. You have such eyes now," Oladele responded.

---

[1] The Bandung Conference in April of 1955 in Bandung, Indonesia included 29 countries from Africa and Asia. Its main goal was to promote the independence of these regions from their former colonial masters, both economically and politically.

Does my wife notice the change in my eyes as well? My son?

"You know me well. I started on this path for what I thought were noble reasons. But it seems that times have changed, and my reasons no longer seem applicable."

"Tell me, what were your noble reasons?"

"Maybe I will tell you," Yisa replied slyly, "after you fill me in on your pilgrimage. Just know that I tried to mobilize forces to bring our people together."

"Using an army to promote unity is not the most ideal of formulas, Yisa."

"Yes, I know," Yisa replied, glancing at a pretty woman walking by. "I know now."

"Why don't you walk away from whatever it is you're doing? Your wife needs you. Your *son* needs you. You could come home and work with me at the university," Oladele said, guiltily reflecting that if Yisa stayed at home, Amina would never agree to continue her affair with her philosophy teacher. Nevertheless, he knew that Yisa was who she really wanted—Oladele was a clear second choice.

"It's not that simple, my brother. There is a lot of money floating around and a lot of dangerous people involved. It's not something I can just walk away from."

YISA

"It's not something I can just walk away from."

ETEKA
RISE OF THE IMAMBA

"It sounds like something you *should* walk away from, especially for your son. This is a very important time for you to be in his life, to aid in his development," Oladele replied, scratching his chin. Two firebugs made a trail behind them and Yisa admired their lighted dance.

"These people you deal with, where are they based?" Oladele asked.

"I cannot tell you."

"Why not? What if something happens to you, or we need to find you? You leave without us ever knowing where you're going," Oladele replied with heat. When Amina worried, he was the one who had to helplessly bear with her concerns.

"It's too dangerous for you to know. I'm not telling you for your own good."

"At least give me a name. Who do you work for?" Oladele pressed on.

Yisa sighed. He could understand his friend's concern for him. What harm could come from giving Oladele a name? Surely he'd never be able to connect it to anything else.

They finally located the suya vendor. The seasoned meat grilling over the burning charcoal made their mouths water. Yisa bought two kebab sticks, and turned to his friend.

"We are called the Imamba," he said softly, handing Oladele a kebab.

"The Imamba? What does it mean?"

"That's all you're getting out of me on that subject. Let it go."

They bit into the tasty skewered meat, taking a moment to savor the spices and perfect roasted texture of the suya. Then they headed back, and as they walked in silence, Yisa caught Oladele staring at him.

"What are you looking at?"

"Do you plan on seeing your daughter while you're here?" Oladele asked abruptly. The question made Yisa uncomfortable.

"I told you to never bring her up to me again."

"Yes, I know, but she's your daughter, and I'm raising her."

"With my money."

"Money is not the only thing involved with raising a child. Can't you at least stop by and see her before you go?"

"That child was a mistake, a product of random sex with a random woman. She's a bastard child, and not a part of my family."

"That's a very harsh thing to say," Oladele replied as they trudged along.

"Maybe. But I love my wife and my son, and cannot let anything come between us, including her. Let's change subjects—I want to hear about your pilgrimage to Indonesia."

Oladele sighed with disappointment and began to tell his friend about long sea voyages, plane trips, and the adventure that was his trip to Indonesia 12 years prior.

BANDUNG

University of Ibadan. Ibadan, Nigeria. Africa. 1955.

Hot, dry Harmattan winds blew from the north, keeping everyone indoors except for a few agama lizards sunning themselves in protected nooks. Oladele was standing outside his dormitory room at the University of Ibadan, transfixed on the paper in his hands, which described a major conference set to take place in Bandung, Indonesia, a world away from where he stood. These were interesting times in the world, especially in Africa, the Americas, and some Asian nations. The Cold War was in full swing, and the world's most powerful nations sought to extend their influence and ideologies on their one-time subjects and prospects. Proxy wars were being fought all over the globe, with opposing factions often receiving funding and support from competing world powers. Gone were the days of physical dominance, mass movements, and large colonial settlements. Political and economic control over dependent territories was the new trend.

Oladele had only a few months left before graduation. All that remained was to complete his thesis for his final graduate class, Political Science. He had been searching for a topic when one of his college professors mentioned the conference taking place in Bandung. The conference's purpose was to host talks between specific Asian and African nations freed from their former colonial yokes, with the hope of promoting collaboration. Oladele felt that the conference presented the perfect opportunity for developing his thesis.

It was the perfect opportunity—in theory. But in reality, getting to Indonesia seemed like an impossible feat. Oladele was a poor college student in Nigeria. He could barely even afford to buy himself food some days. Who would fund his trip? How would he get traveling documents? Where would he stay once he got to Indonesia? What and how would he eat once he got there? As a non-native, how would he get around? And how would he get a pass to attend the conference itself? These questions dampened his excitement like a bucket of cold water. He folded the paper and placed it in his pocket, dreaming of Bandung as he set off toward a lecture hall.

That evening, on his way back to his dorm after classes, he walked past a woman who seemed to be lost. She was an albino, wearing large glasses with her pale hair in a natural afro. An African print dress complimented her round figure, and she wore thick multicolored beads around her wrists and neck. Her smile was warm and gentle.

"Excuse me, are you okay?" Oladele asked, a little startled.

"Oh, hello. I'm trying to find this building. I'm supposed to meet my guardian there," she said as she pointed to a name on the piece of paper she was holding. It was a female hostel not too far from Oladele's dormitory. He smiled at her.

"I'm actually headed that way. Come, I'll escort you there."

"Thank you very much." She had an accent he had never heard before.

"Where are you from, if you don't mind me asking?" Oladele asked as they walked along a dirt path.

"I come from East Africa. I came here for a few classes. My name is Bayinna, but my friends call me Kiki," Kiki replied with a smile as she extended her hand.

"Very nice to meet you, Kiki," Oladele replied. "My name is Oladele Akinjide.

"Nice to meet you, Oladele."

"What classes are you taking, Kiki?"

"Just a few on religious studies. And you?" she asked.

"I am a political science major, and I'm actually working on my thesis."

"Oh. You're a graduate student?"

"Yes."

"Well, congratulations on making it so far with your studies."

"Thank you."

They came to the end of the dirt path and began walking across a small grass knoll past some students playing football.

"So, what's your thesis about?" Kiki asked, watching the men as they ran around.

"Well, I've decided that I want to attend this upcoming conference in Indonesia in a few weeks. Some countries from Africa and Asia are meeting there to see how they can collaborate in this new world."

"That sounds interesting. So, are you going to go to Indonesia?"

"That's the problem I'm facing right now, Kiki. I have absolutely no idea how I'm going to get there. I have no money. I don't even have a passport."

Kiki smiled as they approached the dormitories. "Have faith, Oladele. It can happen."

"Thanks, Kiki. Unfortunately I don't know if faith alone can help me. I have aspirations that are beyond my means. Maybe I'll just pick another subject to do my thesis on."

"They say adversity introduces a man to himself. I have a strong feeling you will make it out there, and that the trip will change your life," Kiki replied, smiling at him.

Oladele breathed deeply. Why did Kiki's words feel soothing to his soul? He found himself believing her, though he did not know why.

"Thanks, Kiki. I'll have faith as you suggest. How long will you be in Nigeria?" Oladele asked.

"As long as it takes. Don't worry, I'll be here when you get back from your trip. I have a feeling we are meant to talk some more."

They reached the female hostel. Sitting on a bench near the main entrance was a tall man dressed in long robes and a Fulani hat that covered the upper half of his face. He stood up as Kiki approached, gracefully balancing the long stick he carried.

"Well, thanks for escorting me here. Let me know how your trip goes," Kiki said as she and Oladele shook hands.

"Ha! Okay, Kiki. Thanks for having faith in me. I'll hopefully see you later."

They both waved goodbye and Oladele walked off, feeling good about himself and his new friend.

Kiki watched him leave, smiling.

The following day, Oladele walked to the home of Professor Ulli Beier[1] and his wife. The German professor had taken a special liking to Oladele and offered him a job cleaning his home every few days in exchange for pocket money. He had also told Oladele about the upcoming Bandung Conference. Professor Beier was a rugged-looking, bearded man standing a few inches taller than Oladele. As

---

[1] Ulli Beier was a German scholar and former professor at the University of Ibadan in Nigeria. He was a pioneer of the arts and literature in both Nigeria and Papua New Guinea.

Oladele walked in, Beier was sitting in his living room reading a newspaper. Oladele greeted him and began his cleaning routine.

"How are things, Oladele?"

"Things are fine, sir," Oladele replied as he began to sweep the floor.

"That's good to know. How is your writing coming? Have you written any new poetry or essays?"

"I have some ideas, sir, and I'm sure I'll put them to paper soon. My mind has been preoccupied with my thesis. I wanted to write about the Bandung Conference coming up, but I don't think I will be able to."

"And why won't you be able to?" Professor Beier asked.

"Well, how will I get there? I have no money, no papers, nothing."

Professor Beier smiled and stood up, leaving the room. After a few minutes he returned with some papers in his hand.

"What's this?" Oladele asked.

"This, my young friend, is your ticket and passport to Indonesia."

"My what?" Oladele asked in shock.

"I used one of your pictures to get an international passport for you. And I got you a ticket. You didn't think I would get you excited about some event you could not attend, did you?" Professor Beier asked with a laugh. "Here, take it. I was looking forward to surprising you with it."

Oladele held the plane ticket in his hand. He had never held one before, and his hand trembled slightly. But after studying it carefully, he noticed that it was a ticket leaving from Accra, Gold Coast and not Nigeria. The flight had one stopover in Egypt before heading to Indonesia.

"This ticket says the flight will leave from the Gold Coast… but we are in Nigeria. I don't understand."

"It's the best I could do," Professor Beier said, "And this new exchange student from East Africa agreed to link you up with a friend of hers over there, who she said can get you into the conference."

Kiki, Oladele thought to himself.

"I also spoke to some friends of mine who know some of the workers at the docks in Lagos. You'll have to sneak on board a cargo ship heading toward Accra and find the airport."

"Sneak on a ship? Professor Beier, are you serious?" Oladele asked in disbelief.

"Yes. Do you want to go to the conference or not?"

"Of course I want to go!"

"Then you have to do what you have to do. The best things in life don't always come easily. Remember that, Oladele."

"Okay, sir. Thank you!" Oladele said, giving the Professor a bear hug. They both laughed, and Oladele looked at the ticket, speechless.

"Well, don't just stand there—you have cleaning to do!" Professor Beier said as he sat back down to resume reading his newspaper. Oladele smiled and went back to sweeping the floor, his mind racing in anticipation of the adventure to come.

A week passed, and after getting as much money as he could through donations and sponsorships from a few kindly professors, including Ulli Beier, Oladele set out for Indonesia. He first journeyed to Lagos aboard a local bus that stopped every few minutes at checkpoints manned by local troops loyal to the colonial regime before arriving in Lagos at nightfall. Tired and hungry, Oladele bought some groundnuts and bananas that dulled his hunger before falling asleep in an empty marketplace, surrounded by the homeless and street vendors. He hid his valuables inside his shirt and dozed lightly, terrified of losing his few belongings. It was a long night, and Oladele was often awoken by people arguing in Yoruba, cars driving by, and mosquitoes humming loudly in his ears.

The next morning, after washing his face with water supplied by a friendly old woman and cleaning his teeth with a chewing stick he had handy, he hopped on another bus and made his way to the docks. Following Professor Beier's directions, he found the docks and met the Professor's contact: a short, sturdy Igbo sailor named Temi. As other young men carried cargo to and from various vessels, Temi led him toward a medium-sized ship, evading the vessel's security officers and hiding Oladele behind some large crates containing live goats, fertilizer, and sheetrock in a storage area below. Temi told him he would be down every now and then to bring him food, and after shaking hands, he was gone.

Oladele sat in an uncomfortably tight position between the crates as the ship's horn went off and the anchor was retracted. It would be a lengthy trip, a good couple of days in which Oladele would be in that uncomfortable position, but he knew it would all be worth it. Going to this Bandung conference would allow him to meet people just like him from across the world who shared similar experiences. Finally, his thesis would come out the way he had envisioned. His mind soared so high, he almost couldn't smell the goats.

After his ship landed in Ghana, Oladele treated himself to a meal of kenkey,[1] pepper sauce, and fresh salted tilapia from the sea. Afterward, he traveled by bus and met up with a pilot friend of Professor Beier's, who flew him to Cairo (on the condition that he serve refreshments to the rest of the plane's passengers). Oladele arrived in Cairo after a five-hour flight. He then caught another flight to Indonesia, the plane full of North Africans who spoke fluent French amongst themselves. Thankfully, a few of them spoke English, and Oladele enjoyed a heartfelt conversation with one man in particular named Yusuf who spent most of the flight confessing his infatuation with plus-sized women. The plane made a few more stops in Calcutta, India and Bangkok, Thailand. It was here that Oladele met some interesting personalities on the flight, including a very pleasant man called Abdul.[2] Together, they spoke about

---

[1] Kenkey (fermented maize dumplings) is a very common dish in Ghana.
[2] Abdul Rahman Pazhwak was a poet and diplomat from Afghanistan. In the 1950s, he served as an ambassador to the United Nations.

philosophy, writing, and poetry, subjects dear to Oladele's heart. Oladele told him about his world back home in Nigeria, and Abdul told him about his native Afghanistan. They talked for hours until Oladele, worn out, fell asleep.

Oladele was awoken by a rough shove from an Asian man in a pin-striped suit. Tired and with heavy eyes, he looked outside the plane window as it landed and was amazed. The runway had been decorated with the flags of all the attending nations. Large crowds of Indonesian people stood by the airport, waiting to catch a glimpse of the international spectacle that was happening on their land. Oladele stumbled out of the plane, looking around in awe. Everyone was smiling, and even before he got into the airport people pulled at his clothes, excited to see a black man in their midst. Clearly they thought he was one of the delegates or someone important—if only they knew he was just a student who had hustled his way across the world to get there. After a couple of hours of fighting through a rowdy Customs service, Oladele found himself standing outside the airport, suitcase in hand. Not far off, a queue had formed around a local street vendor selling Mie Goreng.[1] The scent from the cooking food made his stomach rumble. Professor Beier had told him that a contact had been arranged to meet him here, but he saw no one looking for him. The people in this new land stared at him curiously, and some even ran up to him to shake his hand, but they all spoke in their local tongue and he did not understand them. The weather was

---

[1]Indonesian fried noodles

hot and humid, and he sat down under a canopy to catch his breath
when he had a moment to himself.

"Are you Oladele?" a voice with a heavy Sundanese accent
asked in English from behind him.

"Huh?"

Oladele turned around to face a tall, dark man with distinctly
Asian features holding a briefcase. The man had a thin moustache
and chemically relaxed hair that had been tied into a small ponytail.
His clothes were neatly pressed and his sunglasses looked like less
of a fashion statement and more of a necessity in this bright climate.

"Are you Oladele?"

"Uh, yes. Yes, I am, sir."

"No need to call me sir. My name is Rashid, and I was asked
to escort you to the conference. What do you prefer to be called?"

"Oladele."

"Fine. Let's head to my flat here in Jakarta. We'll head up to
Bandung for the conference after you've had a chance to rest.
C'mon, my car is over there."

"Okay, sir. Thank you very much."

"No problem. And stop calling me sir."

Rashid helped Oladele load his luggage into a red VW
Beetle before they sped off toward the city.

"We'll have to get you a special pass to the conference. You can't get into the conference without a pass of some sort, you know."

"How do I get a pass, then? I was hoping I could pay for one once I got here."

"Leave that to me."

The weather was hot and humid, and even the breeze did not stop Oladele from sweating profusely. The city of Jakarta was very busy, just like Lagos or Accra. Many of the people on the streets were either walking, shouting, or involved in some sort of lively commercial activity. They passed by some canals, which Rashid said were built by the Dutch when they colonized the region. The canals no longer served their original purpose, and had collected filthy, stagnant water that many of the city's people used for all kinds of purposes—such as an open sewage system, as well as for bathing.

"You must be tired and hungry. I'll fix you something when we get to my place."

"Thank you very much."

Rashid turned on the car radio, and after flipping through a few local stations, he settled on a station playing some jazz by Charlie Parker and Dizzy Gillespie.

"So, Kiki seems very fond of you," Rashid said.

"Kiki? Oh, yes, your friend. I don't know why, I barely know her."

"You will in good time, I'm sure. You must be excited about being here."

"I am. I'm really looking forward to attending the conference. Do you have any interest in the conference, Mr. Rashid?" Oladele asked.

"Yes. I wish to hear Nehru, India's first Prime Minister—one of the major players at this conference," Rashid emphatically replied.

"Yes, I know of him," Oladele replied. "I heard he's the reason Chou-En-Lai, the Chinese Premier, will be attending the conference."

"Good. You've done your research. Do you understand why India needs China to participate in order for this conference to be a success?" Rashid asked.

"I, uh, I have no idea."

"You see, Nehru understands that a unified Asia cannot be strong without China's attendance. But China is allied with the USSR and is Communist. It should be interesting to see how this all plays out."

"Yes, that's right," Oladele replied, nodding.

After driving for another hour they pulled up to Rashid's flat. It was a large space with high ceilings and limited furniture.

"You can spend the night here," Rashid said as he showed Oladele to a room. "Tomorrow we'll get you sorted out with credentials and all that stuff. Make yourself at home; the bathroom is down the hall on the left."

Oladele got settled, glad to finally relax after his long journey. After a long bath and a tasty meal prepared by Rashid, the young Nigerian fell fast asleep.

✝

The next day, Rashid drove Oladele to the Ministry of Information, and after using a hookup from a friend of his within the Ministry, he presented Oladele with a press card full of fake credentials.

They spent the rest of the day driving around Jakarta, with Rashid showing Oladele all the famous landmarks and treating him to local delicacies such as Bakwan Malang soup[1] and sickly sweet Selendang Mayang[2]. That evening, they returned to Rashid's flat and had dinner. Oladele spoke over dinner about his studies, his aspirations for the future, his friends Yisa and Amina, Professor Beier, and the difficulty of being shy. Rashid quietly listened, smiling slightly here and there as he sipped on a glass of scotch. Before they knew it, it was midnight.

"We should get some rest. We'll be leaving here early to get to Bandung," Rashid suggested as he stood up. "Good night."

Oladele thanked him for the meal and went to his room. He lay smiling as he looked through an open window at the clear night sky.

---

[1] Bakwan Malang is a meatball noodle soup with fried wontons, a common street delicacy in Jakarta, Indonesia.
[2] Selendang Mayang is an Indonesian delicacy that is usually served as dessert. It is made from coconut milk, crushed ice, syrup, and striped jelly.

Kiki. I have to find her as soon as I get back, Oladele thought to himself. He lay there for ten more minutes before getting up to use the bathroom. As he tiptoed down the hallway, Oladele walked past Rashid's room. The light was on and the door was slightly ajar. Oladele was about to apologize for any disturbance, but held his tongue when he saw that inside, Rashid was putting together and cleaning a gun.

They left Jakarta early in the morning and headed up the mountains toward Bandung. The trip was a four-hour drive, time Oladele spent admiring the scenery when he wasn't drifting off into a catnap. Rashid educated him on the history of Indonesia and its people: the former Dutch occupation, the origins of the different local dialects and languages, the various ethnic groups, island politics, and the local economy. Oladele in turn spoke of his university in Ibadan, and the effects of colonialism in Nigeria. To his surprise, he learned that Rashid had visited Nigeria before.

"Really? Where did you go to in Nigeria?" Oladele asked.

"Many different parts. I had to learn Yoruba and Igbo to get by."

"You can speak Yoruba, and Igbo?"

"Well, not fluently, but I know a few words."

"Go ahead, say something in Yoruba," Oladele said with a laugh.

"Ibereyi ti poju, [1]" said Rashid, after thinking for a moment.

Oladele smiled and nodded in response, then reclined in his seat. It was a beautiful sunny day, and Oladele took in the passing landscape as they sped along, noting that, in many ways, the scenery was similar to that of the Nigerian countryside, or the Gold Coast for that matter, especially in the way the locals lived. Women carried loads on their heads as their men carried burdens on their backs. Others walked around barefoot or sat under trees, escaping the sun. In the distance he saw volcanic craters, with low-hanging clouds enveloping them like soft wool. It was a serene scene that made him happy he had decided to undertake this adventure, dangerous though it had been.

It was mid-afternoon when they arrived in Bandung, and the city had been decorated with the flags of all the attending nations. The locals in the vicinity were all smiles, proud that their city had been chosen to be the conference venue. Military troops lined the city streets, staring down the newcomers with intimidatingly blank faces and precise, martial order. It was clear that the Indonesian government had placed a high priority on security for the conference, and the two men both had their credentials verified at a checkpoint before being allowed to continue into the city.

"That's where the conference will be held," Rashid said as he pointed at the Gedung Merdeka, a large white building decorated

---

[1] "You ask a lot of questions."

with flags and surrounded by more stern soldiers. Large crowds had already begun to gather, mesmerized by a diplomatic motorcade navigating the city streets like a giant caterpillar. Two blocks from the conference center, Rashid and Oladele turned off and pulled into an elegant hotel called The Grand Preanger. Oladele knew that what little money he had on him would not be enough to cover the cost of paying for a room here, and he glanced at Rashid in embarrassment.

"Don't worry, I'm not inconsiderate enough to bring you here and expect you to pay for it," Rashid said with an understanding smile. "It's on me."

"There is no way I can repay you for your kindness, Rashid," Oladele said, blushing.

"Don't worry, you're entertaining me and I could use the distraction," Rashid replied. "Why don't you grab our luggage and go inside while I pay for our rooms."

The hotel room was more luxurious than anything Oladele had ever experienced: original art on the walls, plush carpeting, and a huge bed—all completed by a spectacular view of the city. He jumped up and down on the springy bed in excitement before kneeling down to thank God. A soft knock on his door interrupted his prayers before Rashid entered the room, grinning at Oladele's apparent excitement and gratitude.

"The conference begins in a few days," Rashid said, "which will give us enough time to do some sightseeing around Bandung. There are beautiful craters and hot springs around here that you would love. We could also pick up extra clothes for you. Sound good?"

"Why, yes, Rashid!"

"Excellent. Let's grab a few drinks at the bar later on."

Rashid left and Oladele jumped back on the bed, a big smile on his face. He'd never in his wildest dreams imagined that his trip would have played out in this way—even if he'd been able to imagine going in the first place. Truly, he was blessed.

On the morning of April 18, Oladele and Rashid made their way to the Gedung Merdeka. The building was heavily guarded by troops in white military hats, and a large crowd had already gathered. Oladele was shown to the press gallery and, after taking a seat, he surveyed his surroundings.

The press gallery was in a grand conference hall, with many side rooms and endless rows of seats. Unlike Jakarta and the Bandung countryside, everyone here seemed to speak fluent English. It wasn't long before the delegates from the different member nations began streaming in to loud chants of "MEDERKA! MEDERKA!" from the crowd. Oladele had never witnessed such a spectacle in all his life. There were so many different nationalities present, each of them proudly dressed in the traditional attire of their particular nation.

As the delegates filed in, the reporters snapped away with their cameras, while other spectators leaned in to get the best view they could. Then the stars of the show walked in. First through the doors was an Indian man, sporting a white cap not dissimilar to those worn by low-ranking army officers. He was elderly, probably in his sixties, and he had a calm yet authoritative presence that seemed to command silence from the audience as he walked to his seat.

"Who is that?" a wide-eyed Oladele asked Rashid.

"That is Nehru, my young friend. I told you about him before."

A uniformed man with a black hat and a well-groomed goatee followed Nehru. He, too, had a commanding presence, which he hid behind a pleasant smile.

"That is Ali Sastroamidjojo, Indonesia's Prime Minister. I'm pretty sure they will elect him to be the chairman of the conference," Rashid whispered.

Last through the doors was Mohammed Ali, Prime Minister of Pakistan. The delegates took their seats and a short man dressed in formal military attire stepped up to the podium to speak. He also had a black hat on, and sported medals and military decorations on his uniform.

"That is Sukarno. He is our President," Rashid said.

"Your Excellencies, ladies and gentlemen, sisters and brothers, it is my great honor on this historic day to bid you welcome to Indonesia. As I survey this hall and the distinguished guests gathered here, my heart is filled with emotion! This is the first international conference of colored people in the history of mankind!" Sukarno said to resounding applause.

"Wait here. There is something I have to take care of," Rashid said to Oladele.

"Where are you going?"

"I'll be back, relax. I'm not going far."

Oladele watched Rashid squeeze his way through the packed audience and then disappear. He turned his attention back to President Sukarno's speech, quickly jotting down notes in a notepad he'd bought earlier that day. He didn't want to miss a thing.

Rashid walked away from the conference hall, away from the crowds and the press. Three men with strong Sundanese features had been standing across from him and Oladele as the delegates walked in, and Rashid had watched them walk off and disappear down an empty side corridor. He carefully followed them from a distance, and stopped when he heard some light chatter coming from a side room.

Rashid drew his gun from inside his sport coat and took a deep breath as he screwed a silencer onto the gun's muzzle. He then walked up to the room with his weapon drawn, and after making sure the bottom of the door was low enough to hide his feet, he placed his ear on the door. Three men were talking in a mixture of

Arabic and Cantonese, and he heard the familiar clicking sounds of semi-automatic guns being put together. Rashid waited patiently by the door and listened to their movements. After a few minutes, when he felt their conversation was relaxed and they were close to each other, he barged into the room, staying low.

Two men were sitting smoking cigarettes by a table while a third stood directly in front of Rashid, an Uzi held loosely in his hand. On the table sat three pistols, a knife, and two grenades. Rashid raised his gun and shot the closest man, the only armed one. As the first man fell, the other two lunged for the guns on the table. Rashid unleashed a precise hail of gunfire, killing one man as the other leaped for cover behind a chair, the rounds shredding the soft back covering.

He stopped when he ran out of ammo, quickly ejecting the used bullet casings and reaching for a fresh clip from his side pocket. The remaining man took this opportunity to grab the knife from the table and lunge at Rashid. The man swiped violently, preventing Rashid from reloading his weapon. Rashid parried the man's attack, drew him in, and performed a standing armlock, forcing the man to drop the knife. The man dropped to one knee, performed a front roll on the ground and escaped Rashid's hold. He kicked Rashid in the stomach, forcing him back, and reached for the knife again. Rashid stopped him by kicking the table, knocking it into the other man's head and throwing him momentarily off balance.

The man spotted his dead friend's Uzi lying nearby, and he dove for it as Rashid picked up his revolver and resumed reloading it. The man grabbed the Uzi and pointed it at Rashid just as Rashid finished loading his gun and swung it toward his enemy. Only one shot was fired…

Oladele sat in the conference hall, his notepad now filled with notes. Different delegates went up to the podium to speak, while others talked amongst themselves. A few even said hello to him, smiling at the earnest young man. About 45 minutes had passed, and Rashid had not returned. Oladele glanced through the people in the conference hall for what must have been the fiftieth time, but saw no sign of Rashid. The conference had finally reached a brief intermission, and many of the delegates were taking the opportunity to stand up and stretch. Oladele decided to walk out to the main hallway and stretch his legs as well, while keeping an eye out for Rashid.

In the hallway, Oladele noticed a handsome black man, clean-shaven and a few inches taller than himself (he inwardly sighed—everyone was taller than him). He had philosophical eyes, thoughtful and farseeing. Oladele had seen a few blacks walk in, but none with the businesslike air and composure of this man. He was dressed in a striking blue and green pin-striped three-piece suit that looked expensive—definitely not off the rack. The man smiled as he noticed Oladele's interest and walked over, a cigarette in his mouth.

"Hi, there. Which delegation are you with?" the man asked with the drawl of the American South.

"I am not with any delegation, sir. I am sitting with the press."

"So am I. What is that remarkable accent?" he asked with interest.

"Oh, I'm from Nigeria," replied Oladele, ducking his head in embarrassment.

"My, my, my, Nigeria. Would you look at that," the man said with a look of surprise as he looked intently at Oladele. "You've come a long way from home. What's your name?"

"My name is Oladele, sir."

"My name is Richard, Richard Wright.[1] Pleased to meet you," Wright said with a smile and an outstretched hand. Oladele shook hands with the author. The man had a firm handshake.

"What brings you all the way from Nigeria to here, Oladele?"

"I am a student; I came here to learn."

"We are all students here, my friend."

"No, I really am a student, literally," Oladele replied awkwardly. "I will be finishing school soon, and I'm writing my thesis on my experience here. I also want to learn what I can to help my people move in the right direction."

"You can learn a lot here, then," Wright replied. "Just take as many notes as you can and try to get to know everyone you meet. I'm sure your thesis will come out great."

---

[1] Richard Wright was a pioneer in African-American literature and at one time was the wealthiest and most respected black writer in America, in large part due to his revolutionary novel, *Native Son*. He was also heavily involved in international politics and affairs, and his book *The Color Curtain* gives a detailed account of his experience at the Bandung Conference in 1955.

"Thank you, sir!"

"Did you come here alone?" Richard Wright asked.

"No, sir. My friend Rashid was with me, but he ran off somewhere. He should come back soon."

"RICHARD! THERE YOU ARE!"

Both Oladele and Richard Wright turned around to face a smiling, middle-aged Filipino in a sharp white suit. He was a short man with a warm smile and an air of authority. Two guards walked with him as he made his way over to both black men, a skip in his step.

"I enjoyed our previous chat. I wanted to see if you cared to join me back at my hotel after the conference so I can learn more about your projects. Who is your young friend?"

"This," Richard Wright said as he placed a heavy hand on Oladele's shoulder, "this is my new friend. His name is Oladele, and he is a student visiting all the way from Nigeria. Oladele, meet Carlos Romulo,[1] chairman of the Philippine delegation to this conference."

"A student? You must be an important man to have found your way into this gathering between leaders of the underdogs of the human race. I often wonder how it is that we came to be in this position, how it is that our peoples became the dominated and not the other way around," Romulo said, his kind eyes searching Oladele's.

---

[1] Carlos Romulo was a central figure in Filipino politics, an army general and journalist. He also served as chairman of the United Nations Security Council and was President of the United Nations General Assembly between 1949 and 1950.

"And what answer do you come up with?" Richard Wright asked.

"I am neither a scientist nor a historian, but I imagine it has something to do with geography and evolution over time. Perhaps Oladele can expand on my hypothesis when he returns back home?" Romulo said playfully, his eyes still on the young Nigerian. Oladele, too shy to respond, simply nodded.

"Perhaps. We should get going, there is much for us to discuss," Richard Wright cut in. "I have enjoyed speaking with you, Oladele. I hope I get to see you again before we all go our separate ways."

"Likewise, sir. It has been a pleasure."

Richard Wright winked at Oladele before disappearing into the crowd with Carlos Romulo and his procession. Oladele in turn walked back to the conference hall and took his seat. Rashid had returned, and he nodded when he saw Oladele.

"I was just about to go looking for you," Rashid said.

"I was about to do the same. Is everything okay?" Oladele asked. "You were gone for so long that I was starting to worry."

"Yes, I just had to take care of a little problem," Rashid replied. The conference resumed, and Oladele went back to taking his notes as Rashid looked on.

After two days of public addresses and four days of closed-door sessions, the conference finally came to an end. Summary statements were delivered by every committee, and speeches were given by the heads of the different delegations. The audience and press jubilated as the delegates shook hands with each other and spent the rest of the evening conversing before exiting the Gedung Mederka building.

Oladele almost lost himself a few times in the crowd, doing his best to stay right behind Rashid. After a long night of conversation, Oladele and Rashid finally returned to their hotel around midnight. Oladele walked into his room and plopped on his bed, smiling contentedly at the ceiling. He had learned more than he ever could have imagined! As he formed his thesis in his mind, the phone rang.

"Hello?"

"Are you tired yet?" Rashid's asked.

"Not at all," Oladele replied. "I am still trying to wrap my head around this whole experience."

"Well, why don't you meet me at the bar downstairs and we can wrap our heads around the experience together? I'm not tired either."

"Okay," Oladele replied.

Ten minutes later, Oladele met Rashid downstairs at the dimly lit bar. Soft blues played in the background, and a few guests conversed softly in the lounge. Rashid was sitting at the bar chatting with the bartender when Oladele arrived. It was obvious he had already had quite a bit to drink.

"There you are. What do you drink?" Rashid asked.

"Err, do they serve palm wine here?"

"Palm wine?" Rashid asked, raising his eyebrows. "No, not here. How about some bourbon? Or, if you don't want alcohol I know they make some good lemonade here."

"I'll try the bourbon."

The bartender poured Oladele a drink as he sat down. The whiskey was bitter, but felt hot and smooth down his throat. Rashid laughed as he watched Oladele's face pinch from the drink.

"You're not a drinker, I see."

"I like palm wine, it's not as aged," Oladele coughed.

"We all have our preferences," Rashid tipped his glass at Oladele. "So, you've accomplished your mission. Are you pleased?"

"Yes, I am," Oladele said with a smile. "I want to thank you again for all your kindness, Rashid."

"It was my pleasure. What did you think of the whole affair?"

"I thought it was very interesting, very colorful. I thought it was great. The real task now is to see what comes out of it all. A lot of the countries that were represented have very similar economies, so I'm not sure how they will benefit each other in the long run," Oladele replied.

"Interesting point. You should expand on that in your thesis."

"I intend on doing just that."

"Good. So overall, you feel your trip was worth it?"

"Oh, yes!" Oladele replied enthusiastically. "In the future I would like to teach children and young adults from experiences like this one, so yes, it was definitely worth it."

"Teach, huh?"

"Yes. Our people so desperately need this kind of information."

Rashid smiled and had the bartender pour him another round as he lit up a cigarette.

"I think I have a Nigerian nickname for you."

"Haha, what nickname?"

"It suits you perfectly—Oluko.[1] Your nickname shall be Oluko."

"Oluko? Haha, good one! So my new name is Oluko, eh? I like it."

"Thanks. When you become famous, don't forget to give me the credit for naming you."

"But of course," Oladele replied graciously.

A brief moment of silence passed between them. Rashid closed his eyes and made musical notes in the air with his finger as the jazz took him to another place. Oladele watched him quietly. He was intrigued.

"Mr. Rashid, what exactly is your job?" Oladele asked.

Rashid looked at Oladele, then turned his gaze toward two Indonesian women who had entered the bar. "I normally don't share

---

[1] "Oluko" means "Teacher" in Yoruba.

my personal business with people, but I guess you're pretty harmless," Rashid began. "I am a security contractor."

"Security contractor? What does that mean?"

"I get hired to protect people."

"Oh?" Oladele frowned. "Were you protecting someone at the conference?"

"Yes. Nehru is currently my client," Rashid answered.

"Nehru? The Prime Minister?"

"Yes."

"Wow! But how come you weren't next to him, then, if you're his bodyguard?" Oladele asked.

"I'm the kind of bodyguard you're not supposed to see," Rashid replied, wiggling his eyebrows mischievously, listing a little to the side as the scotch took effect.

"Wow, I'm blown away," Oladele shook his head. "Have you always been in that line of business? How did you become a bodyguard?"

Rashid grinned and gulped down his entire glass of scotch, lazily signaling the bartender for another round. "You're asking me to bring back some memories I'd prefer to forget."

"I'm sorry, Mr. Rashid. We don't have to talk about your past."

"It's okay, I like you," Rashid said slowly, eyes bleary. He raised his glass, eyeing Oladele over the rim, then took a sip. "When I was much younger, about your age, I belonged to a secret society

RASHID

"YOU'RE ASKING ME TO
BRING BACK SOME
MEMORIES I'D PREFER
TO FORGET."

ETEKA
RISE OF THE IMAMBA

called the Custodis. Our mission was simple: to protect the 'Chosen Ones' across the globe."

"The Chosen Ones?" Oladele asked, wide-eyed.

"Yes. Every region across the globe has Chosen Ones selected to perform one or a series of extraordinary, selfless tasks and to guide specific warriors selected by the 'Master.'"

"The Master? Who is the Master?" Oladele eagerly asked.

"I don't know. I never met him, or her, and I never questioned. I just did my job."

Oladele sat up in his chair and took a large sip of his bourbon. Maybe drinking would help him make sense of Rashid's story.

"So, you were a member of the Custodis?"

"Yes. We were also called guardians."

"And how did you come to join these people?" Oladele asked.

"I was born into it. My father was a Custodi, as was his father, and so on."

"You said you used to belong to them. What happened?" Oladele asked.

"I was in India, on assignment protecting one of the Chosen. We were in a crowd, and he was in front of me," Rashid shook his head. "Then it all happened so fast…" Rashid said as his voice trailed off and he stared into space. It took a full minute for him to come back to their conversation.

"It was a boy, a little boy. He couldn't have been more than six years old. He was running right at us as I escorted the Chosen to his temple. Those were dangerous times, not much different from today. I thought the boy was a suicide bomber, figured someone has strapped explosives to him, so I, I… I shot him."

Rashid gulped down his glass of liquor and signaled for another one. Shaking his head, he looked at Oladele. "The boy turned out to be running to his mother who was behind us, calling him. I can still remember his lifeless face looking up at the sky. The crowd almost lynched me—and sometimes I wish I'd let them."

"Is that why you are no longer with the Custodis?" Oladele asked.

"Yes. They banished me from the order, a small punishment compared to the nightmare of living with my mistake. For many years after that I became a useless drunk, wandering the globe, taking contract jobs here and there to get by. Then, I met the love of my life in Nigeria."

"So that's how you know so much about Nigeria!" Oladele remarked.

"Yes. She was beautiful," Rashid said dreamily. "Her name was Irati. We met in her village while I was taking care of a contract for the British in Nigeria. I had so much peace when I was with her. She was the first woman I had ever met who understood me, who understood my pain. We could talk for hours, from the sunset to the sunrise, about all sorts of things. She's one of the few good memories in my life," Rashid said with a slight smile.

"So, what happened?" Oladele asked.

"Well, I decided to stay on in Nigeria for about a year because I was in love. So, I stayed on in her village. We got married and eventually had two children, boys. They were beautiful," Rashid said as he rubbed his bloodshot eyes.

"So you had a family? Where are they now?"

Rashid shook his head while still smiling ruefully, and grabbed Oladele's shoulder. His grip was painfully strong.

"As you get older, 'Oluko,' you'll learn that life is a very complicated thing," Rashid said seriously. "Nothing is black and white. Things change, people change… I changed. I realized I was living a lie, thinking I had what it took to raise a family. Unfortunately, sometimes you don't realize you're on the wrong path until after you've started the journey. This is life," Rashid said, taking a long drag from his cigarette.

"Who knows?" Rashid sighed. "Perhaps staying married would have spared me the pathetic life I lead now, all alone. Who knows what I could have been had I chosen a different path?"

"What happened to your wife and your sons?" Oladele asked.

"I left them behind in Nigeria to fend for themselves. I ran away from being a man. I went back to Nigeria years later to try and find them. I learned that my wife had hanged herself because I left her. She was too heartbroken to go on. The boys were still in the village under the care of the elders, but by this time they were teenagers."

"What are their names?"

"The oldest is Amir, the younger we named Ade."

"Those are strong names," Oladele remarked. "What happened when you went back to see your sons?"

"I stayed on for about a year, teaching the boys the only skills I knew: weapons and killing. Amir was a bit more physical than his brother, he was always eager to try everything I taught him. But Ade, he was more of a thinker. More of a planner, a strategist. In the end I could not stay with them, so I left them there in the village."

"So, you're not in touch with them?"

"No," Rashid replied, standing up slowly, swaying as he found his balance. "It's late and I'm drunk. Thank you for listening to my sad stories. I never have anyone to share them with."

"Wait. You're trying to tell me that's all? You don't know where your sons are now?" Oladele asked.

"No, I don't, and I don't care to know. Besides, the oldest blames me for his mother's death. He hates that she married a foreigner—a foreigner who didn't even have the decency to stay. And the last time I tried to find them, I learned that they had both started moving with local gangs, and then just disappeared. Now they are untraceable and are nothing more than history to me," Rashid said bitterly. "I'm off to bed. You can stay down here if you want to drink some more. Do you want money for some hookers?"

"No," said Oladele, blushing. "I'll go to bed soon, Rashid, I should get some rest." Oladele stood up and walked with Rashid toward an elevator. After a short pause, Oladele asked, "Would you recognize your sons if you saw them today?"

"Maybe. The last time I tried to find them, I heard that they had new identities. No one I asked knew what had become of my oldest son, but they did tell me that Ade, my youngest, had changed his name."

"To what?" Oladele asked as they stepped into the elevator.

"Omega."

TRAINING DAY

Tambo International Airport. Johannesburg, South Africa. Africa.
1990.

Eteka and Cyrus, dressed in civilian clothes complete with
sunglasses, were asleep when their plane touched down in
Johannesburg, South Africa. Tucked deep in a briefcase on Eteka's
lap were the diamonds they had retrieved from Liberia. Resting on
the top of the briefcase was a newspaper, its front cover highlighting
the recent release of Nelson Mandela.

It was a hot, sunny afternoon and a special day for the
Imamba Brotherhood. At the beginning of every third week of each
quarter, the best new recruits in training were brought here, to South
Africa, for a final initiation. The ceremony itself was simple: each
new recruit would go one-on-one against a seasoned Imamba fighter.
The new recruits were required to stand their ground or overpower
their opponents by any means necessary. Eteka and Cyrus were now
seasoned fighters, and neither had ever lost. Only those Imamba
fighters fresh off a mission could choose not to fight in the initiation
process—ritual was important, but each fighter was an investment.

Forcing an exhausted or injured fighter into a sparring match was a poor return on that investment—anything could happen.

From the airport, Cyrus and Eteka were ushered into a waiting Land Cruiser with tinted windows and driven across the city of Johannesburg to the residential area of Soweto.[1] Outside, the view shifted from clean, orderly neighborhoods to crowded shanty shacks. The air was thick with exhaust fumes and the smell of fried yams, and the streets were full of people. Their car drove through a cluster of matchbox houses and hostels, and people standing on the side of the street pointed and stared at the expensive vehicle. After about an hour of driving, they turned down a quiet street and parked by a run-down house with boarded-up windows and graffitied walls. Eteka, Cyrus, and the driver stepped out of the car and walked up to the front door.

The driver knocked on the door four times.

"Name?" Oga's voice asked as someone inside cocked a gun.

"Bellum," the driver replied.

"Meaning?" Oga asked.

"War."

A heavy bolt lifted off the door and it opened laboriously. An Imamba in camouflage fatigues glanced outside and then ushered the mercenaries into the house. Inside they found Omega, Oga, and a newcomer sitting around a table. The unidentified man wore a bandana and had a wiry build—the kind of muscles that you get

---

[1] Soweto is an urban area in the city of Johannesburg. It is comprised of a mostly black population and was once home to Nelson Mandela and Desmond Tutu.

from hard work, not pumping iron at the gym. Eteka noticed that, just like Oga, the hair on the man's soul patch had a threading of grey. Handguns, assault rifles, and an RPG were stashed in one corner of the room. At the other end lumbered a scowling man so large his head nearly touched the ceiling. The room was hot and stuffy, and a small opening in the ceiling was the only source of ventilation. A small fan churned the thick air as Cyrus and Eteka walked over to the senior Imamba.

"Excuse our humble surroundings, gentlemen," Omega said in greeting. "I normally would have arranged for us to meet in one of the many well-appointed hotels in Johannesburg, but I wanted you to get acquainted with this safe house. We have just acquired it, and you will have access to it for any future missions you have in this area," Omega rasped as he puffed on a cigar.

"Do we have any other safe houses in South Africa?" Eteka asked.

"This is the first. I tried to secure one back in the '80s, but things worked differently around here back then, with all that apartheid nonsense. Thank God for Nelson Mandela," Omega replied with a grin.

"How was the mission?" Oga asked, his eyes on the briefcase in Eteka's hands.

"It went well. Here are the diamonds," Eteka replied as he placed the briefcase on the table.

Omega opened both cases and counted the diamonds with a big smile.

"Good, very good. I'm proud of you guys. Oh, where are my manners? This is Proditor," Omega said, gesturing toward the man sitting next to them. "He has been with us for a long time."

Eteka and Cyrus exchanged polite nods with Proditor while Eteka studied the man carefully. He was an older man, seemingly around Oga's age, with dark, creased skin and a nervous tic by his eye. Eteka found Proditor studying him intently and, with an effort, he turned his attention back to Omega.

"The rocks are all here. Good," Omega said, closing the briefcases. "Overdue payment for a job we did. This will help us with our expanding operations."

"What do you mean?" Cyrus asked.

"Don't worry about business for now, Cyrus. You are an assassin—a good one; leave the business side to me," Omega replied. "In two weeks, the two of you will be headed to Tanzania to deal with a resistance movement. Their leader is a woman known only as the White Witch, a name the locals in that area have given her. Our client has not been able to get any photos of her, so you must use whatever means necessary to find out who she is. When you find her, eliminate her and take a couple pictures of her dead body as proof. This is a cash job—$50,000 each. You'll be taking Mokin here with you," Omega gestured at the large man, who stepped up and nodded at both Eteka and Cyrus. Up close, they could see that Mokin was bald with tiny slanted eyes, jet-black skin, and heavy scarring on his face. Eteka was taken aback by Mokin's enormity up close, and Cyrus chuckled as he tilted his head back to try and look Mokin in the eye.

"You look like a bulldozer," Cyrus grinned as he looked at Mokin. "What country are you from?"

Mokin said nothing, fixing Cyrus with a deadly stare.

"He doesn't speak. He used to fight with ECOMOG,[1] but they let him go due to his extremely violent nature—he broke his captain's neck for no apparent reason," Omega said, puffing on his cigar. Cyrus and Eteka exchanged looks.

"Who is the client?" Eteka asked, keeping an eye on Mokin.

"As usual, you ask too many questions, Eteka," Oga answered as he stood up and handed folders to both Eteka and Cyrus.

"It will be a covert operation," Oga said as the mercenaries flipped through the contents. "Do not get trigger happy until you find the White Witch. Understood?"
Both mercenaries nodded their agreement.

"So, what's the next step?" Eteka asked.

"In two weeks, you'll both meet our contact in Tanzania," Oga replied. "Until then, I suggest you boys get some R&R. Two weeks is a short time, so use the time well."

"Sounds good," Cyrus replied, retrieving a rolled-up blunt from his pocket. "Will Pacman be coming with us?" he asked as he lit it with a match.

---

[1] The Economic Community of West African States Monitoring Group (ECOMOG) was an armed force created by the Economic Community of West African States (ECOWAS) and its soldiers were influential in many African civil wars.

OGA

"YOU ASK TOO MANY QUESTIONS."

ETEKA
RISE OF THE IMAMBA

"No. Pacman is taking care of a shipment for us in Jamaica. You two will be going alone. You will have some backup from local fighters once you get there. When you're done, you'll come back to South Africa and meet us in East London for your next assignments. The details for the hotel where we'll meet are also in your folders," Oga said.

Omega stood up and handed the briefcases containing the diamonds to a guard standing in the corner. The warped floor creaked as he walked up to the mercenaries.

"I can get you boys reservations at my hotel for the next two weeks. We have access to the best women in Johannesburg. In fact, I made arrangements for a few of them to stop by my suite tonight," Omega said with a grin as he led them outside.

"Just out of curiosity, where will you guys be while we're in Tanzania?" Cyrus asked.

"Well, I can't speak for Oga, but I will be heading to Ghana for a few days. I have some personal business to attend to," Omega answered.

"I'll be here in South Africa. I need to relax a bit. I like the beaches here," Oga added. They exited the house.

Eteka inhaled the fresh air, relieved to be out of the hot, congested room. As he wiped some sweat from his brow, his thoughts rested on Arewa. These next few weeks would be a good time to hang out with her. He pulled out her business card and began reviewing the details, although he had already committed them to memory.

"How many women?" Cyrus asked Omega as the men climbed into a black Mercedes with tinted windows outside the safe house. The car pulled out of the ghetto and onto the highway leading to Omega's hotel.

"More than you can handle, boy," taunted Omega. "You boys should swing by."

"I'm there," Cyrus said, taking a puff from his lit blunt, ignoring the older man's baiting. "Eteka, you'll be joining us, yes?"

"No, I'll be heading to Nigeria."

The other men looked at each other in surprise.

"Nigeria? What's in Nigeria, brother?" Cyrus asked. Omega and Oga exchanged glances.

"None of your business," snapped Eteka, jaw clenching.

At that, all the men laughed heartily. Cyrus was the loudest of all, and he began to make silly noises to taunt Eteka.

"Ooohhh! None of my business?" Cyrus snickered. "I thought we were brothers—don't brothers share?"

"I have something to take care of."

"Something? Or someone? A girl? Or are you being secretive because you're sleeping with men now?" Cyrus asked with a laugh, shoving Eteka.

"Leave him alone, Cyrus," Oga cut in, watching Eteka's fists clench. The last thing he needed was a fight.

Cyrus grinned, shaking his head and turning his attention to the blunt in his hand. Oga faced Eteka, rolling down a window to let out some of the pungent smoke.

"You can go anywhere you want to, Eteka. Just make sure you show up in Tanzania when it's time."

Eteka nodded agreement, grateful that the older man had silenced the teasing. He looked out the window at Johannesburg's urban landscape, his mind miles away.

"The initiations for our new recruits will be starting within the hour. I say we spend the rest of our afternoon supporting them. Perhaps you will entertain us with an exhibition," Omega said, his eyes resting on Eteka, who continued to gaze out the window, oblivious to the conversation around him. He didn't hear Oga sigh and exchange glances with Omega, who shook his head, chuckling silently.

After about 30 minutes, their car pulled up to a large factory, which had been gutted for warehouse use. It was located between two abandoned buildings in the northwestern suburb of Triomf.[1] Its large metal loading bay door was slightly ajar, leaving enough space for each of them to slip through, though Omega had to shove it open further to allow his bulk to enter. Inside was an empty space large enough to fit a midsize soccer field. Abandoned industrial machinery had been moved to the corners, leaving plenty of room in the middle for the Imamba initiation fights.

Nearly one hundred men formed a circle around the fighters, while a small contingent of new recruits stood to the side wearing only jeans. Two men fought in the center: the towering Maximus and his battered opponent, an athletic and ambitious recruit who'd seen in Maximus a chance to impress the other Imamba. Like most men, he'd presumed that Maximus's size meant that he would move slowly. Now, he was paying for his presumptions.

Maximus effortlessly grabbed his opponent by the neck with one hand and lifted him off the ground, to the cheers of the crowd around him. With a deep chuckle, he punched his opponent in the ribs, resulting in an audible crack.
The poor recruit yelled in pain, and Maximus threw him to the ground like a rag doll, laughing heartily, an ogre's amusement at catching a would-be Jack the Giant Killer. Omega's group moved to join the circle.

---

[1] Sophiatown was a key political and cultural center that was destroyed in 1954 by the apartheid regime through demolitions and forced removals. The apartheid regime renamed the suburb "Triomf" (Afrikaans for "triumph"). In 2006, the suburb's original name of Sophiatown was restored.

MAXIMUS

"THIS INSECT IS NO CHALLENGE FOR ME."

ETEKA
RISE OF THE IMAMBA

"Ah, Omega," Maximus said in a deep, booming voice that seemed to shake the very ground he stood on. "You should come and spar with me; you could stand to lose some weight."

"Maybe some other time, Maximus. Besides, you seem to have your hands full," Omega replied with a grin as he lit up a cigar.

"This insect is no challenge for me," Maximus replied as he effortlessly picked up the damaged recruit and lifted him above his head with both hands. "Shall I break him?"

"No," Omega replied. "The fact that he's been able to last with you for even a minute means he's good enough for our ranks— albeit a touch suicidal. Release him."

Maximus, smiling menacingly, threw the recruit to the ground and walked up to Omega. He wore a small ragged-looking cap on his head. Maximus's figure towered over everyone except for the equally imposing Mokin, who stood quietly behind the crowd, watching the scene with interest.

"I came here looking for a good fight and found none. How about you?" Maximus asked Mokin, receiving only a look of disdain in return.

"That would actually make for a good fight," Cyrus said.

"I agree," Omega cut in, "but not today. We are reviewing the recruits, and there is no time for gladiatorial games. Which recruits are next?"

Across the space stood two brothers in their early twenties. The older brother clutched his chest, in pain.

"You don't have to do this, Goncalo," the younger brother whispered in Portuguese. "We can walk away."

"No, we've come too far, Marcelino. We have only one chance, and this is it. I can do this," he reassured his brother, gritting his teeth with the effort of standing.

"But your heart—you haven't taken your medication in days! It's not fair!"

"We can't afford my medicine right now. I will finish off my opponent with my Taekwondo training. Remember, this is our destiny," Goncalo said.

"Who's next?" Omega called out impatiently.

"Let me go first, brother. You're not well. I'm sure they will understand if we explain your condition," Marcelino suggested. "It won't be a fair fight if you're sick like this!"

"Do you think they want to hear about fairness? No. My name is next on the list, and I must fulfill my duty. Don't worry, I'll be fine."

Marcelino shook his head mutely, worried. For Goncalo, it was a matter of honor, and stubborn as he was, nothing was going to move him.

"I will be with you in spirit," Marcelino said softly as his sibling straightened up and walked into the center of the circle.

✝

"Who is set to fight him?" Oga asked, watching Goncalo move to the middle of the circle. "He looks like he would make for good competition. Perhaps we should see how he goes against the mighty Maximus."

"No, Maximus would break him in half, and that would be messy. I want someone who is closer to his size. Deathstalker was originally supposed to test him, but I want to change the lineup a bit," Omega said. He turned toward Eteka. "Step in there and prove yourself."

Eteka looked from Omega to Goncalo. The man looked confident and had a good build. His fists were clenched and his breathing was hard. He was not relaxed. Fear? Stress? Eteka rolled up his sleeves, stepped into the center of the circle, and walked up to the recruit.

"What's your name?" Eteka asked.

"My name is Goncalo," the recruit replied with a strong Portuguese accent. "I am here with my brother, Marcelino." Goncalo inclined his head toward a dark-skinned young man with a clean-shaven face, pronounced cheekbones, and a shaved head.

"Where are you from, Goncalo? And why do you want to be an Imamba?" Eteka asked, unbuttoning the top button on his shirt and rolling his neck.

"We are from Guinea-Bissau,[1] and we were approached by your recruiters. We are smart and strong fighters, and will make the Imamba Brotherhood stronger than it already is. How long have you been with the Imamba?"

"I have been with the Imamba since I was a child," Eteka replied. "This is my life."

"Then it would be an honor to defeat you and earn my place within your brotherhood," Goncalo replied as he stepped back and assumed a signature Taekwondo fighting stance: feet shoulder width apart, bouncing on the balls of his feet with his heels slightly off the floor, elbows tucked in, and fists clenched and raised high. Eteka nodded in response and assumed a southpaw boxing stance, even though he was right-handed. Fighters were seldom prepared to face a left-handed opponent.

They circled, each man sizing the other up. Goncalo made the first move, feinting to his left and throwing a roundhouse kick at Eteka's head. Eteka blocked the kick easily, and Goncalo immediately followed with a low kick, driving his powerful foot deep into Eteka's thigh. The impact stung Eteka, sending him back a few paces. The crowd of men around them erupted with cheering.

---

[1] Previously known as Portuguese Guinea, this country underwent a recognized name change in 1974 to Guinea-Bissau.

"This should be a good fight. I would like to have a go with this recruit after Eteka is done losing to him," Cyrus heckled.

The two fighters continued to circle each other. Goncalo again initiated the attack, leading with a straight jab, then throwing his hips forward and planting a sharp front kick to Eteka's chest, sending him a few steps back. Regaining his footing, Eteka lunged forward with a straight right, blocked by Goncalo's left shoulder. Eteka followed closely with two left hooks that connected and then a right, but Goncalo parried the last punch, backing away, almost panting with the effort to catch his breath.

Eteka studied his opponent, scrutinizing Goncalo from head to toe. This man could use both his hands and legs. Plus, he was unpredictable. Goncalo threw another front kick followed by a crescent kick and a powerful back kick. Eteka sidestepped and blocked the first two kicks, but the third caught him in the stomach, sending him stumbling backward. Eteka dropped to one knee and looked up at Goncalo.

"Eteka may have met his match," Omega said under his breath to Oga. "Perhaps your protégé is not as great as you think he is."

Oga did not respond, but worry lines appeared on his forehead.

Eteka rose to his feet and resumed his stance. *Enough games*, he thought. Goncalo continued to bounce as they moved in a slow rhythm. Eteka closed the distance between them. After a flurry of punches and kicks by both men, Goncalo threw a side kick that

Eteka caught, countering with a powerful right hook that dropped the recruit. Goncalo quickly rolled off the ground and rose to his feet. The cheering around them hit a fever pitch. Goncalo threw quick kicks in succession at Eteka's legs, but Eteka blocked each one and countered with body shots. With time, the powerful body blows from Eteka slowed Goncalo down. With each successful punch, the crowd let out a loud cheer.

Goncalo began to hyperventilate as his vision blurred. His heartbeat was racing at a dangerous pace. He could not lose. He and his brother had been through so much to get here. This was their chance to start making some real money, to start living the dream they had both shared for so many years. No, he could not lose. He could not...

A powerful straight right from Eteka found its mark on Goncalo's chest. The powerful blow sent Goncalo flying backward. Goncalo landed hard and lay still on the floor.

"Goncalo!" Marcelino screamed as he rushed to his brother's side. "Somebody help! We need a doctor!" Marcelino screamed desperately.

Omega stepped forward and a medic, hired in case of emergency, began CPR. After several fraught minutes of compressions, the medic stood back.

"I'm sorry," the medic said, shaking his head. "There's no pulse—he's not breathing."

Marcelino lunged forward and grabbed the medic by the collar. "He can't be dead, he was sparring just a second ago! Help him!" He dropped to his knees by his brother, frantically trying to wake him.

"There is nothing more I or anyone else can do. It looks like his heart gave out," the medic replied.

Marcelino looked from his brother's body to Eteka. "You!" he said, lunging for Eteka's throat. Maximus collared Marcelino and hoisted him, flailing, into the air.

"You killed my brother!"

"That wasn't my intention," Eteka responded calmly, inwardly cursing his luck.

"Let me go!"

"Your brother did not look entirely well before he stepped in this arena," Omega interjected. "He was meant to die today, and you can be proud that he died as one of us. Perhaps you will complete his legacy."

Marcelino struggled against Maximus's grip, oblivious to Omega's words.

"Let me go!" he shouted.

"He is not stable now," Omega said to Maximus. "Get him out of here and don't let him back in until he calms down. And someone clean up this mess. We have to go on with our initiations."

The new recruits' eyes were wide as they watched two Imamba drag the body off to the side, out of the circle.

Maximus dragged Marcelino forcibly from the room, but not before Marcelino had locked eyes with Eteka—eyes full of vengeance.

"Looks like you've made a new enemy, Eteka," Omega said with a sneer.

Eteka said nothing, looking down at Goncalo's body. He had not asked for any of this.

c h o s e n

BASTARD

Mushin, Lagos. Africa. 1990.

Isatou sat across the room, curled up in a chair as she watched her latest client fast asleep. She lit a rolled-up blunt as she stared at the obese man snoring, his belly moving in all directions every time he breathed. Pig. The man was a prominent official in the Nigerian government, and he had traveled all the way from Abuja to here in Mushin, Lagos to fulfill sexual fantasies that his wife and multiple girlfriends could not provide. Isatou was a prostitute, part of an underground network that serviced the upper echelon of Nigerian society.

She stood up, her slender, naked body covered in sweat, and walked over to a mirror. She played with the short locks of her hair as she admired her body. She was a good-looking woman, with an air of confidence and a smile that promised to make men's dreams come true. She had even, dark skin and was tall at 5'9", with a strong, sensually curved frame and hands that were no strangers to hard work. Her eyes were deep-set and intense, even without the heavy eyeliner that she preferred. She cupped her full breasts in her hands and examined herself in the mirror, turning to look at the sleeping politician. If she weren't a prostitute, would a man like that have considered her for a wife?

Why did she even care?

She slipped into the bathroom, took a quick shower, and pulled on her working clothes. She grabbed her pocketknife from under the pillow without waking her client. She took his wallet out of his discarded pants, counting out the fee on which they'd agreed. After a beat, she tucked the wallet itself in her pocket. Without a backward glance, she slipped out of the rented apartment where she slept and entertained clients.

It was around 3 p.m., and the streets were alive with pedestrian activity. It had just rained, and the muddy ground made for a messy walk. She walked past all the familiar faces: Kinglsey, the unemployed young man who always catcalled whenever she walked by (he could never afford her); Yemi, the street hustler who constantly carried his pirated movies and fake watches around, trying to make a sale; Olabanji, the handsome gari seller on whom she had a secret crush (he could have it for free, as far as she was concerned); Gloria, the sweet old woman frying her yams and peppers; and Odebisi, more commonly known as Tribal, and his gang of armed robbers, who spent the whole day standing on corners or sitting in cars, scoping out people and houses to rob at night. Isatou's skin crawled whenever she got near them. She hated violence, even though in her world, violence was a fact of life. She spotted her pimp, PantiRaida, a few yards ahead. He was a tall, skinny man with wild twists and colorful beads in his hair, wearing a lime green sleeveless jacket that matched the beads. He was chewing on some boiled peanuts as she walked over.

"How far?[1]" PantiRaida greeted in pidgin.

"I dey, [2]" Isatou replied, handing him some naira bills.

"Na dis be all? The guy no give you interest?[3]"

"No. But here's his wallet," Isatou said as she handed PantiRaida the politician's wallet, shielding the action with her body.

"The guy een eye dey follow nyash. Now see how een money come dey ma pocket. Nyash na powerful oh, ha ha![4]"

"You sure say the guy no go give me wahala? Een see ma face as I chop am. I no wan trouble,[5]" Isatou said with concern. The last thing she wanted to do was to antagonize someone powerful.

"Make you no shake.[6] He can't touch you here."

At that moment, a police Jeep made a turn onto their street and pulled up across from them. Six policemen toting assault rifles climbed out, along with their commanding officer and another man. He was older, with balding grey hair, civilian clothes, and pronounced worry lines around his mouth.

"Your uncle dey come,[1]" PantiRaida said as the police party approached.

---

[1] "How are you?"
[2] "I'm fine."
[3] "Is this it? The guy didn't leave you a tip?"
[4] "The guy was mersmerized with your ass/booty. Now look how his money is in my hands. Your ass/booty (to Isatou, or women in general) is powerful!

[5] "You sure the guy won't give me trouble? He saw my face as we had sex. I don't want trouble."
[6] "Don't worry."

PANTI RAIDA

"THE GUY EEN EYE DEY
FOLLOW NYASH. NOW
SEE HOW EEN MONEY
COME DEY MA POCKET."

ETEKA
RISE OF THE IMAMBA

"Yeah, I see am,[2]" she replied as she hastily put out her blunt, grinding it into the mud under her sandal.

The commanding officer walked up to PantiRaida as his men stood on guard. The civilian man was not too far behind.

"Hello, Police Constable Isiaka. What are you doing here in Lagos? Isn't there crime to take care of in Ibadan?" PantiRaida asked in a painfully fake British accent.

"Watch your mouth," Isiaka replied as he glanced at Isatou. "Are your girls operating in this area today?"

"Oh, Chief, my girls have repented. I'm not in that business anymore," PantiRaida replied with a sardonic smile. "They hand out tracts for the churches—have you accepted Jesus as your Lord and Savior?"

---

[1] "Your uncle is coming."
[2] "Yeah, I see him (in this context)."

"I'm not in the mood for games. If we start raiding this place and we find your girls working, I will lock you up for a long, long time. So I'll ask again: Are your girls operating around here?" Isiaka asked again.

"How much you want?" PantiRaida sighed, pulling out a wad of naira bills from his pocket.

✝

As Isiaka and PantiRaida talked, the older man in civilian clothes walked up to Isatou. For a brief moment they looked at each other with no smiles. The old man shook his head, and was the first to speak.

"Hello, Isatou."

"Hello, Uncle Oladele."

"Why are you throwing your life away?" Oladele pleaded. "You're better than this."

"I'm not throwing my life away. I'm taking care of myself."

"You're not taking care of yourself. You're sleeping around, and living on the streets. It doesn't have to be this way."

"And what do you recommend I do? Huh?" Isatou asked.

"You can come back to Ibadan and work with me at my school. It's never too late, Isatou." His suggestion made her laugh.

"You're always asking me to come to your little school. And do what? Teach your students how to fuck? How to smoke cocaine, or use heroin? How to use a knife when a man tries to take advantage of you? That's all I'm good for—I got my mother's blood, my mother's looks, and she was an *ashawo*[1] like me."

"You also have your father's genes, and he did some school," Oladele countered. "You're not stupid."

She shook her head in disappointment.

"You know, I remember when I used to stand on the corner of his street every day, back in Ibadan. Watching his wife play with their son. Watching from a distance when he came home to his big fancy house, and watching you go there to sit and talk with him. And I remember feeling very left out, and wondering why this man got my mother pregnant and then just abandoned us. Clearly we weren't worth very much."

"Yisa didn't abandon you, you know that. You got money from your father through me."

"We got some money, whenever he felt like giving. But it doesn't matter now. My mother has lost her mind from doing drugs, and I have to fuck as many men as I can to have enough money to pay for her to stay in the psych ward where she won't get hurt or hurt anyone else."

---

[1] Common slang term in much of West Africa meaning "prostitute."

"God has a plan for us all. Hard experiences make us stronger," Oladele said, helplessly spreading his hands in placation.

"You still don't get it, do you?" Isatou demanded. "Look around. Do you see God? Why do we live like animals in these slums? Why aren't there any jobs available for us so we don't have to open our legs every time we want money to buy something to eat? You think being honorable and honest works around here? Look around, my dear uncle, and open your eyes. If God does exist, he forgot about us a long time ago. We have no money, and we have no jobs, so we do what we have to do."

Oladele took her recommendation and looked around. Mushin was a hard place to live in—a volatile, overcrowded, and underdeveloped part of Lagos that bred the worst that society could offer. He was no stranger to hard sights; living through the Biafran War had toughened his sensibilities, but seeing Isatou suffer like this was hard.

"You are allowing your environment to define you, Isatou," Oladele said. "You can become so much greater than all this. You don't have to live here, you have a home in Ibadan. Come back with me, please. I can't keep making all these long trips to look for you."

She shook her head.

"No. I'm not going back to Ibadan. I have big dreams, too. They may not be what you want for me, but they are my dreams. I belong here, in Lagos."

"All you're doing here is wasting your life away, hanging around these hoodlums," Oladele replied, nodding in PantiRaida's direction.

"This is coming from a man who was fucking his best friend's wife," she shot back, her sharp words causing Oladele to freeze for a moment.

"You're not any different from me, my Uncle 'Oluko.' You can write as many fancy books as you want, or preach your truth, but at the end of the day, you are just as fucked up as me and my hoodlum friends."

Oladele bowed his head in shame. Her words had hit home.

"There's nothing more to be said, then. My trip here, like all the others, has been a waste of time," Oladele said as he placed a hand on Isatou's shoulder. "I've always treated you as my daughter, and I'm sorry your life has been so hard. But you're still young, and there's so much more to experience. I hope you do not grow to regret some of the choices you will make, as I have."

Isatou felt her uncle pull her close, and she hugged him tightly.

"Be careful out here," Oladele said as they parted. "You always have a home in Ibadan."

ISATOU

"I HAVE BIG DREAMS TOO.
THEY MAY NOT BE WHAT
YOU WANT FOR ME, BUT
THEY ARE MY DREAMS."

E T E K A
RISE OF THE IMAMBA

She watched her uncle and the policemen walk away toward their vehicle. They exchanged waves as they pulled out, and then the closest thing she had to a father was gone.

PantiRaida walked over to her as she watched her uncle leave.

"You okay?"

"Yeah. Omo, give me a minute, I dey come,[1]" she replied.

She walked off, leaving PantiRaida behind as another prostitute walked up to check in. She walked past a few houses, crossed some gutters, and found a quiet corner behind an abandoned building, where she crouched down and wept.

---

[1] "Give me a minute, I'll be right back."

ASSASSINS

Tangier Boukhalef Airport.[1] Tangier, Morocco. Africa. 1967.

It was a bright, sunny Tuesday afternoon when Yisa arrived in a private jet at the airport in Tangier, Morocco. Oga was there to meet him in a limousine, and they were driven up the coast to a plush, five-star hotel on the beach in Oualidia. Palm trees and a beautiful coastline greeted them as they pulled up to the front of the hotel. Both Imamba sported shorts, linen shirts, aviator sunglasses, and sandals. A gentleman wearing a supercilious smile, a thinning mustache, and a hairpiece that danced in the cool breeze met them in the lobby.

"Hello, gentlemen. My name is Hassan. Mr. Omega is expecting you. Please, follow me."

Oga and Yisa followed Hassan across the lobby and into a beautiful garden overlooking a lagoon. The air was fresh and sweet, and a few of the hotel guests sat in cushioned wooden chairs, talking and enjoying the hotel's gourmet food and free-flowing alcohol.

---

[1] The Tangier Boukhalef Airport was renamed the Tangier Ibn Battouta Airport in 2003.

Omega sat at the far end of the garden, smoking a cigar. He had a gold Rolex watch on one arm and a thick gold ring on his pinky. Four men sat with Omega—experienced fighters with an impressive collection of knife and bullet scars. Three of them were white, while one looked more Latino. As Yisa and Oga approached, the four fighters stood up, shook hands politely with Omega, and walked off.

"Hello, boys. Welcome to paradise" Omega rasped.

"Hello, Omega. I trust you are well?" Yisa asked.

"I am. How was the flight?"

"Good," Yisa replied as they sat down. "Who were those men?"

"Mercs, like you. I helped them get a contract in Biafra.[1] They'll be working with you there."

"What kind of contract?" Yisa asked.

"We'll get to that in a bit. Cigar?" Omega asked, passing them a box of Cuban cigars.

Yisa declined as Oga eagerly reached for the box. Yisa waited patiently for Omega's explanation, enjoying the cool ocean breeze on his face and the scent of the tropical flowers surrounding the man-made lagoon.

"Good to see that you're enjoying life while we toil in barren deserts and steamy jungles," Oga teased, accepting a cigar cutter from Omega. He clipped the end of his cigar.

---

[1] Biafra was a secessionist state in southern Nigeria, the center of the Nigerian civil war from 1967–1970, and a hotbed for mercenaries from all over the world.

"Hey, everybody has their role. I take care of the clients and you get to take care of business. Speaking of business, how did it go in the desert with the Brits?" Omega asked.

"Good, until they flaked out on the second part of our deal. How's our money?" Oga replied.

"All's well. It's been deposited into your Swiss accounts. You can call the banks from the hotel to confirm when we're finished—I've set up a secure line for you inside."

"Good."

They paused as a beautiful Moroccan woman walked by in a sarong and bikini top on her way to the beach.

"So, what's all this about Biafra?" Yisa asked, breaking the silence.

Omega grinned and placed a folder on the glass-tiled table between them.

"Things in Nigeria have been a little chaotic with this whole Biafra business, and people have to die," he said, taking pictures out of the folder.

"Are we working with a particular side?"

"We work where the money is—we're not taking sides. We've received offers from both the Biafrans and the local government to eliminate some influential individuals, and that's what we'll do. We'll start with these two clowns," Omega answered, gesturing toward a picture of a Nigerian soldier and a photo of a priest in a clerical white collar.

"Who are they?" Yisa asked.

"The soldier is a Nigerian general, Mammadu Ibizna; the second is an Anglican priest that is very influential on the Biafran side, Reverend Nnewi. We've been watching them for some time now. Ibizna is currently in the city of Benin overseeing an offensive operation. You will go there and handle him first. Nothing messy."

"Are we taking any of our men?" Oga asked.

"Yes, but just one: Proditor. He will meet you at our safe house in Lagos."

"Ah, Proditor. I've worked with him before. I like him," Oga said, scrutinizing the picture of the soldier.

"Yes, he's one of our best. When you finish with Ibizna, you'll make your way to Warri in Biafra and deal with Nnewi. Fortunately, it looks like this war might go on for some time, so there will certainly be more contracts. You will leave for Nigeria in exactly one week," Omega said, collecting the photos and handing the folder to Oga.

"Sounds good. That'll give me some time to enjoy some of the women here," Oga replied as he licked his lips at two curvy women walking by.

"You can pick up your weapons at our safe house in Lagos. We got two silenced M16 rifles, an M40 sniper rifle, and two Beretta 25s with silencers, courtesy of our clients. The weapons are new, so don't worry about them jamming. When you're done, return the weapons to the safe house," Omega said.

Yisa looked from Omega to Oga, then back to the folder in Oga's hand. What was he doing here with these men when he could be home teaching his son how to play Ludo? Why was he planning to kill men he had never met when he could be home assisting Oladele with his writing and his work at the university? Why was he here at this exotic location, looking at half naked women when he could be home, making love to his wife?

"You seem deep in thought, Yisa. What's on your mind?" Omega asked.

"Nothing…"

"Yisa has been acting really strangely," Oga said snidely. "He does not believe we are doing what the Imamba Brotherhood was created for. He thinks we are killing innocent people and causing trouble."

Omega looked at Yisa with a placating smile.

"'Causing trouble'? Look around, Yisa; what trouble do you see?" Omega asked as he gestured around him at the beautiful sunset, the gorgeous women walking along the beach, the resort hotel, and the serene ocean.

Yisa had to admit, the view was nice. He never could have afforded this vacation—one of many—had he gone on to become a civilian in Nigeria. Yes, the scantily clad women were lovely—but they weren't Amina. The food here would only make him long for his wife's cooking. The wrongness of the situation pained him.

"Is this what it's come to? Do we get mixed up in the whole Biafra affair? We were supposed to fight for African unity, not kill our own people," Yisa said.

Omega grinned as he blew a practiced ring of smoke in the air.

"I think you're still living in the '50s, Yisa. Our activities have made you a very rich man, don't forget that," Omega replied.

Oga, in turn, patted Yisa on the back.

"You can't save the world, Yisa, so stop trying. Things will never change. We just have to play our part in this game, my brother," Oga said.

"Only lazy men talk like that. Things can change, and we can be a part of the solution. This is not what the Imamba was created for!" Yisa replied sternly.

"Say what you want, my brother, but your actions speak for themselves. And right now, you kill people for a living and are a part of the system, just like the rest of us. You are just one man, and you can't change anything. So relax and enjoy life, enjoy the fruits of your labor," Oga replied.

"If I really had brothers, they would not act the way you two do."

"It's a shame to hear you talk like that, Yisa," Oga replied in a paternal tone, "especially after all we have done together. You are one of us, whether you admit it or not. It's in your blood. You are an Imamba. Being anything else will get you killed."

Yisa shook his head again.

"I guess I know where you both stand."

Omega placed a heavy hand on Yisa's shoulder. Two French-speaking tourists walked by, hushing their voices as they walked past the Imamba.

"You've always known where we stand, Yisa," Omega said. "Enjoy this time off and relax. After the Biafra mission, go back home and spend some more time with your family. You will have another two weeks or so. Then we can all meet in London and discuss our next project. Deal?" Omega asked.

I told myself I would do just one more mission, yet now here I am accepting an invitation to review an additional one. I have to end this. I'm in too deep, Yisa thought to himself.

"This is not right, and was not part of our original agreement for the Imamba. But, I'll be a team player and tag along," Yisa responded, his expression clearly one of discomfort.

"Great! Good to see you're back in business. Now, let's go sample those women Omega was talking about," Oga said, heading back to the hotel.

The Imamba spent the rest of the evening drinking and seducing women, putting aside thoughts of the future. Yisa retired early for the night. Alone.

Two weeks later, Yisa and Oga arrived by bus in Victoria Island, Lagos[1] to begin their Biafran mission. On the way to the safe house, Yisa's mind once again wandered to his family. He recalled a

---

[1] Victoria Island is an "upscale" residential and business center in southern Nigeria. It is almost completely surrounded by water.

family trip they had once taken to the Matsirga Waterfalls in northern Nigeria. Tosin had been just a baby. It was a peaceful time; they'd had a picnic and enjoyed the scenic view of the falls. Just Yisa, his wife, and their baby boy. Amina's loving smile and Tosin's innocent eyes haunted him. What was he doing here?

Yisa and Oga walked past wave after wave of pedestrians on the overcrowded island. A young woman walked by, selling oranges and chin-chin[1] from a basket which she skillfully balanced on her head. Yisa stopped her and bought a few oranges, and the woman peeled them for him. The two men hailed a taxi and headed to an opulent high-rise apartment building situated next to a stretch of foreign embassies—in a pricey neighborhood. They took an elevator to the top floor and proceeded to a door at the end of a long hallway. Oga knocked on the door four times while Yisa finished his oranges.

"Name?" a voice asked from behind the door.

"Bellum," Oga replied.

"Meaning?" the voice asked.

"War."

A short, slim, muscular, dark man opened the door. He had deep-set, curious eyes that darted back and forth from Yisa to Oga. He wore a sweatband on his head, and many scars were visible on his chest through the gap of his unbuttoned shirt.

"Proditor! Been a long time," Oga said amicably.

"I know sha. How you guys dey?" Proditor asked in thick Nigerian pidgin as he shook hands with Oga and Yisa.

---

[1] Chin-chin is a popular Nigerian snack consisting of small pieces of fried dough.

"We dey, we dey, [1]" Yisa replied as they entered the room. Two other men were present, sitting on cushioned chairs. They sat up as the Imamba walked in.

"Who are they?" Yisa asked.

"Ma bredren. They'll be coming with us," Proditor replied with an anxious smile, revealing a gold tooth.

"No, they won't. This mission has strict guidelines. No outsiders," Yisa said.

"C'mon, bossman. They are not going to cause trouble, eh? Just assistance. And they don't want money, just rights to any goods we come across along the way," Proditor replied.

"Are your guys experienced?" Oga asked as he looked at the two thugs.

"Oh yeah, bossman, they fought with me in Liberia. They follow instructions well. You will see," Proditor said as the men nodded in agreement, striving to look useful.

Oga turned to Yisa. "We might need them."

"Oga, we're not following instructions. Omega said this mission should just be us."

"Stop being so uptight, Yisa. We're off to do a dirty job and we could use these guys to help clean up the mess. Calm down."

Yisa took a seat, frustrated at Oga's stubbornness. The old seat squeaked under his weight.

"Whatever you say, Oga. But if Omega is upset, I'm not taking the fall."

---

[1] "I know. How are you guys doing?" Reply (in this context) "We're cool, we're cool."

Oga faced Proditor. "Okay. Your friends can come along. Where are the weapons?"

Proditor got up and disappeared into one of the bedrooms in the apartment. He returned with a large instrument case, which he placed on the floor before them. Yisa opened it and found all their weapons, just as Omega had said.

"Excellent. We'll leave at first light tomorrow and head to Benin to deal with General Ibizna, and then we'll go to Warri and take care of Reverend Nnewi. We can get extra plane tickets for your friends, Proditor, that's not a problem," Oga said. "Proditor, you've made travel arrangements for us once we land in Benin, yes?"

"Of course, bossman. We paid a driver to take us to the army base. He'll be waiting for us when we land."

"Are you sure he is reliable?" Yisa asked.

"Oh yes, he is. He is my brother."

Yisa and Oga looked at each other.

"Seems you want all your people in on the fun," Oga laughed.

"Wherever there is money, we are there. Don't worry, bossman. Everything will be okay, you'll see," Proditor replied.

Oga stood up. "Good, then we are set. What are you boys up to tonight? Do you have any entertainment arranged for us?"

"Yes, some ashawos, dey come.[1] They'll be here in about two hours, so you just be ready," Proditor said while his friends chuckled.

---

[1] "Some prostitutes are coming."

PRODITOR

"WHEREVER THERE IS
MONEY, WE ARE THERE."

ETEKA
RISE OF THE IMAMBA

"That's my kind of man. Yisa, will you be joining us?" Oga asked with a grin as he turned to face Yisa.

Yisa stood up and grabbed his bag. He had been with prostitutes before, but tonight he wasn't in the mood.

"No, I'll be in my room. Just be ready tomorrow morning," Yisa replied as he walked into a vacant bedroom. "And don't make too much noise."

"I can't guarantee that, my brother, but we'll be ready tomorrow morning. Get some rest," Oga said.

Yisa nodded and walked into his room. He dropped his bag on the ground and threw himself on the bed.

Last mission, he thought to himself as he kicked off his shoes and retrieved a small photograph of Tosin from his back pocket. He smiled as he looked at his son. *Last mission and then I go home to stay.*

†

Around 6 a.m. the next day, Yisa, Oga, Proditor, and the two thugs hopped on the first flight from Lagos to Benin City. There, they met up with Proditor's brother, a sturdy man nicknamed Mango, and proceeded to make a 30-minute drive in a truck on deeply rutted dirt roads to the Ifon forest. They parked the truck about a mile from the army base and proceeded on foot, maintaining silence as they got closer to the base. By noon, they had set up a vantage point from which they could study the compound through binoculars. It didn't seem terribly busy at first sight: some trucks and a few soldiers peppered the dark green background.

"Okay, Proditor, wait here for us with your men and give us cover fire if we need it. We're going to get closer," Yisa said.

"Okay, bossman."

Yisa and Oga crept through the thick foliage to the top of a small hill overlooking the army base. They could clearly see several soldiers idling about, cleaning weapons, repairing their trucks, and cracking jokes. Yisa lay flat on the ground to put the sniper rifle together while Oga lay next to him, scanning the area below through his binoculars.

"Do you see him?" Yisa whispered. A small black snake moved past his leg and he flicked it away.

"Not yet," Oga hissed back as he scanned the area below. "The wind is bad. We should wait for it to die down—we'll get a better shot."

"Okay. How many soldiers are down there?" Yisa asked as he finished putting the sniper rifle together.

"Twenty, maybe 30. Is the silencer on the rifle?"

"Yes."

"Good."

"You want to take the shot?" Yisa asked.

Oga looked at him and shook his head.

"No, you take it. You have better aim."

Yisa took a deep breath and exhaled slowly, then got into position and adjusted his scope.

"How's the wind?"

"It's fine. The breeze stopped."

"I see our target," Oga replied after several long seconds.

"Where?" Yisa asked.

"By the large shed, north of the base. He's talking to two of his men."

Yisa moved his rifle and finally spotted General Ibizna through his scope.

"Got him."

"Wait for your shot. Let's get him when he's alone. We don't want to attract too much attention," Oga said.

"Okay."

It was ten long minutes before they got their chance. The commander had walked into a building and now sat alone in an office. Yisa had a tricky shot through an open window.

"I have a reading of one thousand and fifteen meters to the target. Head shot. Wind call?"

"Wind is good, 12 kilometers per hour right to left. Hold five meters right," Oga replied.

Yisa adjusted his scope, then slowed his breathing and tightened his grip around the rifle. The hot African sun left the dark skin on his hands moist with sweat. He zeroed in on his target, centering the crosshairs on Ibizna's head.

"Ready."

"Take the shot," Oga said.

Yisa looked at the General through his scope. He didn't know what the man had done, or why exactly he was about to end his life. He didn't know if the commander had a child, or a family. He didn't know if the commander was a good man.

He didn't know anything.

I'm sorry, Yisa thought.

Yisa closed his eyes and pulled the trigger. The silencer muffled the sound of the bullet's discharge to a soft "phut." When Yisa reopened his eyes, he saw Ibizna slumped in his chair, blood running down his shirt. It wasn't going to be long before his men discovered what had happened.

"Excellent shot. Let's move," Oga said as he crawled away.

Yisa took one last look at General Ibizna and asked God to forgive him before following Oga away from the base. A siren had begun to wail by the time they met up with Proditor, and in moments they were long gone.

Two days later, the Imamba found themselves driving through a thunderstorm, making their way through the city of Warri to complete the second half of their Biafran mission. The rusty old car made its way along the muddy road. Proditor and his brother Mango sat in front, while Oga, Yisa, and the two thugs were crammed into the back, all armed with machine guns: rusty AK-47s and M16s. Oga was whistling a tune and smoking a cigarette as the rest of them sat in silence. Even at this hour, evidence of the war could be seen. Taxis whizzed by them, the palm branches hanging out their windows signaling non-combatants. MFI-9B Minicons roared overhead: small civilian aircrafts that had been modified into fighter jets for the Biafrans.

"Okay, so I have a question for you guys," Oga said. "Why are you Nigerians always shouting? You guys even shout in regular conversation."

"What do you mean? We do not always shout," Yisa replied, ensuring that his tone was even.

"Yes, you do. Being in Lagos the other day almost drove me crazy. You people shout even when you're talking to the person next to you."

"There are loud people in every culture, Oga. I'm sure there are loud people where you're from," Yisa replied.

"Oga, we shout because that way the information enters your ears well!" Mango, the driver, said loudly. The other men stifled their laughter with limited success.

"Mango, what are you talking about?" Oga asked.

"Boss, make you no mind ma broda. Een jus' dey fool. And I beg, Naija people no always dey shout plenty, just dey depend for the person who you dey vibe with.[1]"

"Whatever, man. Hey Mango, how much longer?" Oga asked.

"About 15 minutes. Dis rain dey pour well well."

Oga took a drag from his cigarette and blew the smoke out of his open window. Rain or no rain, he was getting impatient with how slowly they were moving.

"If this damn road were paved we would get there sooner."

"You fit use some of that big money dem dey pay you to build the road, abi?[2]" Proditor suggested, eliciting laughter from the others.

"Funny guy. Or maybe I could kill you and use your money to build the road, what do you think of that idea?" Oga replied with an evil grin. The men went silent.

Proditor shook his head at Oga—he had to ruin the fun. Yisa watched them all in silence, focusing on the orange glow of Oga's cigarette in the dark. Suddenly, the car was rattled by a loud bang. He felt one side of their car give way as the vehicle skidded off the road. The men jumped out, guns ready.

"What the fuck was that?" Oga yelled.

---

[1] "Boss, don't mind my brother. He's just fooling around. And please, Nigerians are not always shouting. Just depends on who you're talking to."

[2] "You can use some of the big money they pay you to fix the road, right?"

Mango took the initiative and checked on the car tires, which were slashed with long, narrow cuts. He pointed to a row of spikes planted on the road.

"Armed robbers," Mango said.

"They picked the wrong guys. Where are they?" Oga asked angrily.

"Over there," Proditor replied, pointing at a van speeding in their direction, splashing water in every direction. It was full of young thugs carrying machetes and guns, and they screamed taunts as they approached the mercenaries. Oga grinned when he saw them coming, amused at these inexperienced thieves' attempt to rob them. He calmly reached into the car and pulled out the case with the sniper rifle.

"We don't have to kill them, Oga. They're just young, misguided kids," Yisa reasoned.

"Misguided, my ass," Oga replied, retrieving the sniper rifle from its case. "Proditor, when their van crashes, you guys go and finish them off. We'll use their van to get to the priest."

"I won't be a part of this," Yisa said.

"Don't be," Oga snapped as he balanced the sniper rifle in between his left arm and right knee. He waited for the van to come a little closer, and—

BANG!

Without the silencer, the rifle made a deafening noise. Oga had hit the driver right in the chest, and the van carrying the armed robbers veered sharply off the road and slammed into a tree. Oga stood up as Proditor and the thugs ran toward the van to finish the armed robbers off.

"My aim is not that bad. Maybe I should've killed that general in the forest when you offered," Oga grinned as he put the rifle back in its case. Several gunshots fired in rapid succession, and then there was silence save for the soft pelting of the rain.

"Morons," Oga said as he and Yisa started to walk toward their van. "They are a large part of the reason why so much violence happens here and people don't have peace."

We are a bigger reason, Yisa thought to himself.

Proditor and the thugs stripped the armed robbers of their belongings and left their bodies on the side of the road.

"The van is banged up from hitting the tree, but it'll get us to the priest. Let's go," Oga said.

They hopped in the van and continued up the muddy road until they arrived at a church at the end of a dark street. Loud singing was coming from within the building, and Yisa knew they would find more than Reverend Nnewi inside. The rain was still coming down hard, and thunder rumbled ominously.

"Before we go in, let's stick to a few rules," Yisa said. "We did not come here to hurt anyone unrelated to our mission. Understood?"

The thugs looked at each other, and Oga smiled.

"There's something wrong with you, Yisa. I don't know why you've suddenly become so soft."

"This has nothing to do with being soft, and everything to do with sticking to the plan. Stick to the mission," Yisa replied unflinchingly.

Oga calmly lit up another cigarette, grinning like a Cheshire cat.

"Okay, whatever you say. Let's move. Proditor, take your men and go through the back. We'll enter through the front," Oga said.

Proditor nodded and ran off with his men while Oga and Yisa walked up to the front door. The congregation was singing church hymns, and the sound made Yisa's stomach churn with anxiety. Oga kicked the door open, and the singing stopped. There were men and women in the room as well as several children. They all froze in fear when they saw Oga and Yisa standing menacingly in the doorway.

"Hello, ladies and gentlemen. We are looking for just one man: your priest," Oga said with a smile. Proditor and his accomplices emerged from the back of the church, swaggering down the central aisle.

A balding man with a calm demeanor and a warm smile on his face made his way through the group of people and stood before Oga. The man radiated peace.

"I am the priest here," the man said.

"Are you Reverend Nnewi?" Oga asked, blowing cigarette smoke in the man's face.

"Yes, I am."

"Good," Oga replied as he grabbed the man's arm and shoved him to the floor. A young man rushed to defend the priest, but Yisa pinned him to the ground.

"It'll be best for you to stay out of this," Yisa said quietly to the young man. The young man struggled for a moment, but could not free himself from Yisa's powerful grasp. He looked at the priest with a helpless expression, but Nnewi merely smiled and shook his head.

Oga, a taunting grin on his face, looked at the man. "It would be best for you to take his advice," Oga said with a chuckle, fixing his gaze on Nnewi. Yisa picked up the young man and shoved him in line with the other church members.

"Proditor, take these people outside and do what you want. Don't kill anyone, but you can take their things," Oga said.

"Okay, bossman. MOVE!" Proditor shouted as he and his thugs ushered the church members outside.

Yisa's stomach did another flip.

"There is only one reason why men with guns would show up here. I assume you're here to kill me," Reverend Nnewi said.

"You are absolutely right," Oga replied, shoving Nnewi onto a chair.

"Do you know why you've been sent to kill me?" Reverend Nnewi asked patiently.

"I don't need to know," Oga replied as he pulled rope from one of his side pockets and began to tie the priest's hands and feet.

"Of course you don't—you're puppets."

Oga ignored him. Nnewi looked at Yisa, a calm smile still on his face. Yisa became uncomfortable and looked away.

"Why don't you just shoot him, Oga? What's with the games?" Yisa asked.

"I want to have some fun," Oga replied, keeping his eyes on Reverend Nnewi. "Hmph. You religious people make me sick. You guys are a big reason why there is so much trouble in Africa," Oga said, facing the bound priest.

"I'm sorry you feel that way. It's my responsibility to care for and look after orphans of war and widows who have lost their husbands. I do my best to provide for others in need. So, I apologize if that causes trouble in Africa," Nnewi replied, a hint of irony in his rich, deep voice.

"Provide for others? You priests scam people out of money and sleep with women for so-called blessings, all in the name of the white man's religion. You're all liars and deserve to die," Oga said.

"You are right to some extent. There are many people who claim to work in God's name, yet abuse their responsibilities. But we are not all guilty and you cannot blame our faith. Men are the ones who commit evil deeds, who take good things and use them for evil purposes. And the Christian faith belongs to no one particular race, but to God."

"God? You're telling me about your God?" Oga laughed. "I do not believe in God. I am my own god."

"Your arrogance will do nothing but destroy you."

"The only one getting destroyed, my friend, is you," Oga replied as he drew his sidearm. "Your God does not exist. Where is He now, your imaginary friend?"

"He is with me wherever I go, even to the next life. This flesh is only temporary—the next journey is what matters," Nnewi replied calmly.

"Rubbish. You're delusional. I don't see your God. In fact, I've never seen Him and I'm alive and well," Oga said with a smirk. "Why hasn't your God revealed Himself to me?"

"Only you would know the true answer to that," Nnewi replied with a smile.

Oga became irate at his inability to intimidate or frighten the priest, slapping Nnewi across the face and sending saliva and a trickle of blood flying out of his mouth. Yisa flinched in empathy. It was as though the priest's pain were his own.

"You're beginning to piss me off. You religious people go around starting trouble and try to brainwash everyone to follow your rituals. You're all a bunch of hypocrites," Oga snarled.

"People follow of their own free will; that is the beauty of it. And as far as evil deeds go, as I said before, it is not the faith that is evil, but the inconsistency and the evil desires of men. If you saw things in the spirit, you would understand me," Nnewi replied.

Oga shook his head and stepped closer to the fearless priest.

"I am your god now, and it seems you are in a tight situation. When I pull the trigger, you will be a dead man, and none of this talk will matter."

The priest wore a bright smile on his face and looked upward.

"You are not my God; you are merely a young man lacking direction. All you can do is end this life. I fear the One God to whom I shall answer in the next."

Oga held his gun to the priest's head.

"When I pull this trigger, all you've been doing here will have been a waste of time. What if your imaginary friend doesn't exist?" Oga asked.

Nnewi shrugged. "Then nothing is lost. But I would never gamble with the outcome of my next life."

Oga's expression was pure evil as he stood with the gun to the priest's head.

Well, I gamble, and I never lose. Call me your god. Then beg for your life," Oga said, roughly shoving Nnewi, rocking the chair back.

"I cannot do that."

Oga struck Nnewi's head with the butt of his weapon with a thud which Yisa was sure they could hear outside. The priest collapsed against the chair, a big welt clearly already swelling on his head. The cut bled all down his face, leaving him a bloody mess.

"Beg for your life, or I will line this floor with your brains," Oga pronounced in a chilling tone as he held his weapon to the priest's head. Even in his pain, Nnewi managed a smile. His eyes rested on Yisa.

REVEREND
NNEWI

"ALL YOU CAN DO
IS END THIS LIFE.
I FEAR THE ONE GOD
WHOM I SHALL
ANSWER TO IN THE
NEXT."

ETEKA
RISE OF THE IMAMBA

"So be it. I'm ready," Reverend Nnewi replied, closing his eyes.

Yisa's heart raced. *We can't kill a priest—this is wrong,* he thought to himself.

Yisa wanted to tell Oga to stop, but as he raised his hand, the gun went off. Yisa felt like vomiting and tried desperately not to look at what was left of the priest.

"Gotta be careful around these religious types, they always try to convert you. If I were any weaker he would've got me," Oga boasted, putting his weapon away.

"I don't think you should have tortured him like that. You should have just shot him when we got here," Yisa replied.

"You could have shot him yourself, no one was stopping you," Oga replied as he walked to the main entrance. Yisa stayed behind, feeling a strange weight on his chest that he could not explain.

I'm sorry.

"Yisa, we should leave," Oga said from the doorway.

Yisa followed Oga out into the rain, knowing that the sight of Nnewi's crumpled body would haunt him for a long time.

FRIENDS WITH BENEFITS

Abuja, Nigeria. 1990.

Rain was mercilessly beating down when Eteka finally arrived in Abuja, a sprawling metropolis located in the heart of Nigeria. The muddy ground sucked at his shoes as he hailed a taxi from the airport. His luggage was light: a small suitcase containing clothes for the week, a map, and a revolver.

The taxi pulled up to Arewa's address in the early evening, and Eteka peered through the rain-spattered window at the two-story structure with a tall fence and a watchman at the gate. The watchman walked up to Eteka's window as he rolled it down.

"Yes, sah?"

"Is your madam there?" Eteka asked.

"Yes. Please tell me your name so I can tell her you're here."

"My name is Eteka."

"Oh, yes! Hello, sah! She told me that if you ever showed up, to let you inside. Please, come in."

"She told you that?" Eteka asked, surprised.

"Yes, sah," the guard responded as he opened the gate to let them through. Eteka stepped out of the taxi into the heavy rain. His heart raced with a strange mixture of anticipation and excitement as he paid the driver and was escorted by the watchman into Arewa's living room, wiping his shoes clean at the door.

"Please wait here, sah, so I call madam," the guard said as he headed to the back.

Eteka nodded, nervously dusting off his grey suit before looking around. She certainly had expensive taste: a large Persian rug covered most of the floor and a crystal chandelier hung from the ceiling. There were two large leather couches and a matching love seat in the room, as well as a glass curio cabinet containing expensive crystalware in a corner. A large-screen television and DVD player were at one end of the room, and pictures of Arewa with well-known Nigerian and British celebrities were all around. Eteka paused to look at a picture of her and her boss, Mr. Adeboyo. He had his arm around her, but she was not smiling.

"So, you came."

Arewa had entered the room and was studying him with her head tilted to the side. She was dressed in a loose-fitting dress made of kente[1] that accentuated her slender, curvy body. Her hair was plaited in neat rows, highlighting her beautiful face. Her smile took Eteka's breath away.

---

[1] Kente is a colorful fabric made from interwoven strips of cloth, in most cases silk. It's from Ghana, particularly the Akan people.

"I, uh, I apologize for not calling first," Eteka said, looking away shyly for a moment. Arewa smiled coyly as she made her way across the room, swaying her hips.

"That's quite all right. I was hoping you would stop by. How did you know I would be in Nigeria?"

"I took a chance."

"Well, it paid off. Have you eaten?" she asked.

"No, I came straight from the airport."

Arewa motioned for the security guard, who had been waiting for them near the door, to grab Eteka's bag.

"Your stuff will be safe here. Why don't we go out for dinner? I know a nice restaurant not too far away at the Sheraton. We can take my car," Arewa said as she linked her arm in his and led him outside.

She felt good on Eteka's arm, warm and soft, as she led him down a corridor and through a side door to her garage. They hopped in a silver '90 Audi Coupe Quattro, the latest model for that year, and Arewa started driving them to the Sheraton herself. The windows were rolled up, the air conditioner was on, and Sade's "Is it a Crime" was playing on the radio.

"So, how was your flight?" Arewa asked.

"Fine, thanks," replied Eteka, still a little stunned at how fast things were moving.

"Are you here for business?"

"No. I came to see you."

Arewa smiled as she bobbed her head to the smooth beat.

"I see. I like you. You're very direct with your answers, and honest. Most guys I've dated like to beat around the bush."

"Are we dating?" Eteka asked.

"We'll know by the end of the night," she replied mischievously.

Finally, they pulled up to the Sheraton Hotel. A valet took their car, and they were escorted into an elegant restaurant located on one of the top levels of the hotel. A hostess led them to a table by a balcony that offered a sweeping view of Abuja. The heavy rains had calmed down to a drizzle, and in the distance the city lights flickered, looking like little fireflies in a dark field. Light African jazz played in the background. Arewa leaned back in her chair and took out a Virginia Slims cigarette. She lit it up and blew a long line of smoke.

"You smoke?" Eteka asked, surprised.

"Yep. Been doing it for quite some time now. Do you?"

"No. That stuff can kill you."

"There are many things that can kill you, and I don't think I'm going to die from smoking anyway," she replied with a wink and a smile. Eteka enjoyed seeing her smile.

"So, here we are," she said.

"Here we are."

"I'm having dinner with a strange man I met in London who just randomly turned up at my place. Worse yet, his things are in my house. Most people would call me crazy," she giggled as she took another drag from her cigarette.

"Are you?"

"A little. You have to be when you work for a man like Mr. Adeboyo."

Their food arrived, and Arewa and Eteka smiled at each other as the waiter placed their dishes on the table. Underneath the table she brushed his leg with her foot, sending a nice tingle through his body.

"There was a man who wanted to kill your boss at the bank in London. Why would anyone want to kill him?" Eteka asked.

"No one is perfect. I'm sure he has his enemies."

"But not all enemies are out for blood."

Arewa paused as she put out her cigarette and took a bite of food.

"I don't get involved in Mr. Adeboyo's personal business. I just manage his money."

"How did you get the job?"

She gave him a lopsided smile as she chewed her food.

"Seems you've suddenly become talkative, eh, Eteka? You were not this talkative when we met in London. And why do you care how I got the job? What does it matter?"

"I'm just trying to get to know you."

There was a brief silence as she looked at him, her lips still curved in a smile. Eteka began to eat his food as well.

"My brother is an activist, and a popular singer in London."

"A singer?"

"Yep."

"What kind of music?"

"Jazz. Afrobeat. And some reggae."

"I see."

"Yeah. He sings a lot about injustices done all over Africa, and just became a UN spokesperson," Arewa explained, her voice rising in excitement. "But he wasn't always famous. Mr. Adeboyo discovered him here in Nigeria many years ago. In exchange for giving my brother exposure, I agreed to work for Mr. Adeboyo for free for a few years. The offer was appealing at the time because my parents had passed away a few years before and we were struggling to make ends meet.

"Mr. Adeboyo serves as my brother's manager," Arewa continued. "He takes a percentage of my brother's profits, and my brother can't sing or talk about certain issues. It's all at the discretion of Mr. Adeboyo and his associates."

"I see," Eteka replied thoughtfully. "So, if you aren't making any money with your boss, how can you afford the fancy house and all that?"

"He likes me. He's been trying to sleep with me for years, so I use my feminine charm to get him to give me nice things and a little pocket money. But, guess what?"

"What?"

"Our contract with him ends at the end of this year. And my brother found a new distributor and producer to handle his music, which means he'll be free to talk about whatever he wants and won't be on Mr. Adeboyo's leash. So, I won't have to work for him anymore!" Arewa said with a bright smile.

"You'll both be free?" Eteka asked, shaking his head in disbelief.

"Yes! Let's drink to that," she replied, raising her glass.

In the back of his mind, Eteka knew there was no way a man like Mr. Adeboyo would release Arewa and her brother that easily. He smiled at her, deciding to keep his thoughts to himself, because at that moment he could imagine nothing better than her happy optimism.

They watched each other eat for a minute, sharing bites from each other's plates.

"Enough about me, mystery man. Tell me about you."

"There is nothing interesting about me," Eteka replied, shifting his eyes away from her intense gaze.

"C'mon, it's not every day I get to have dinner with a handsome guy like you," she replied as she ran a finger across the backside of Eteka's palm. "You were protecting my boss when we met. Is that what you do all the time? Are you like a bodyguard for hire or something?"

"Something like that."

"See? That makes you interesting."

"There's really nothing interesting about me."

"Let me be the judge of that," Arewa teased. "If we're going to get along, you're going to have to open up some more and not be so secretive. Now, tell me what exactly it is that you do," she demanded, her slender finger still resting on the back of his hand.

Looking at her silhouetted against the window, the city lights reflecting on her skin, Eteka knew that this woman would eventually get the answer out of him. He just hoped she was ready for his revelation.

"I'm a mercenary for hire," he said, avoiding her eyes.

"What is a mercenary?"

"I get paid to solve problems."

"Does solving problems also entail getting rid of people?"

"Yes."

"Like the man back in London, at the bank?" Arewa asked, her eyebrows raised with apprehension.

"Yes."

"So, you're a contract killer?"

"That's one way of looking at it."

Arewa fell silent and fidgeted with her cutlery for a few seconds. She leaned back in her seat again and lit up another cigarette.

"Did my answer bother you?" Eteka asked. "If it did, I understand."

She gave an uneasy smile, blowing out two lines of smoke through her nostrils.

"No, not really. I don't judge people. Besides, I've always liked bad boys."

"I'm not a bad boy."

"If you say so. What made you get into that line of work, if you don't mind me asking?"

"I've been doing this since I was a child."

"Your parents were okay with you doing this as a child?"

"I have only vague memories of my parents. My uncle raised me."

Arewa nodded her head, taking another drag from her cigarette.

"Sounds like you've had to be strong from an early age. Not too many people can relate to that. Do you like what you do?"

Eteka thought hard on that one. In his mind, he saw images of the people he'd killed—the men, women, and children he'd seen murdered by one side or another. His mind finally rested on the blank stare on the face of the little girl in Detroit that had haunted him for months.

"No, I can't say that I enjoy it. And I can't say that I don't. I'm indifferent—it's all I've ever known."

"Well, someone once told me that it's wise to spend time doing the things you love."

"Are *you* spending time doing something you love?" Eteka asked, hoping to redirect the conversation.

"Well, I don't have a choice. Do you?" she coolly asked.

He didn't respond, and there was an awkward silence between them as Eteka looked out the window at the lights of Abuja. He liked the scent of the cigarettes she was smoking, as well as the perfume she had on. And he found something enticing about the way she fearlessly asked him all these questions.

"Where are you staying tonight?" she asked as she put out her second cigarette.

"My stuff is at your place."

"Yes, this is true. It's always good to be close to your things," she replied with a smile.

"Ready to go? Dinner's on me."

Arewa paid for their meal with fresh, crisp naira bills before they headed to her car and drove back to her place. The same security guard let them into her compound, and she parked her car.

"Care to come in?" she asked as she got out of the car and led Eteka back into her living room. Eteka leaned against a couch and watched her as she kicked off her high heels. She stepped into her kitchen, rummaged around, and returned with two glasses of wine.

"I like your lips," she said as she sat next to him and handed him his glass. He smiled, drawn to her lips, and then they kissed. It was a gentle kiss, and Arewa softly sighed with pleasure. Her lips felt perfect to Eteka, yielding and sweet, and as he kissed her he placed his hand on her inner thigh, slowly moving it up her leg under her skirt.

"Not so fast," she said, stopping his hand and standing up. She smiled at Eteka over her shoulder as she walked out of the living room, unzipping the back of her dress, and he followed her like a puppy. She led him to her bathroom, where she turned on the lights,

AREWA

"WHERE ARE YOU STAYING
TONIGHT?"

ETEKA

RISE OF THE IMAMBA

lit half a dozen scented candles, and began to fill a large bathtub with hot water, scented oil, and bubble bath.

Eteka eagerly watched her slender, naked body as she moved around her bathroom. He couldn't hide his arousal or his smile of delight at the proceedings. He'd hoped for dinner—he hadn't planned on dessert.

Arewa gracefully stepped into her bathtub and reclined. She turned her head and looked at Eteka, a sultry smile on her face.

"You coming?"

He grinned, taking off his shirt to reveal his chiseled chest. Arewa smiled as he stepped closer, eyeing him up and down appreciatively as he stepped into the tub. His body tightened with adrenaline as he felt her smooth, soft body next to his. They kissed again, his hands caressing her breasts while she ran her hands across his chest. Arewa kissed his neck as she artfully dug her nails into his strong back. His hands moved southward, and she purred as he began to tantalize her, carefully bringing her to the height of excitement.

Neither of them would do much sleeping this night.

Her head felt good on his chest. She was snoring lightly, and Eteka knew that she felt safe with him—trusted him. Why? Eteka was a man she had never known. Perhaps she had done this before, cuddled and fallen asleep with men she had never met. He could hardly judge her for it—heaven only knew how many hookers he'd been with over the years. This was something totally new. He lightly ran his fingers down her back. Her skin felt good. Her sheets felt good. Being here felt good.

He had to use the bathroom. He disentangled himself, slipping out of bed carefully, leaving Arewa fast asleep. The scent of potpourri greeted him as he entered her bathroom. Eteka looked at himself in the mirror. His reflection smiled back at him. He was happy that he'd made the trip to see Arewa.

By the time Eteka returned to the bedroom, Arewa was awake. She smiled when he climbed back into bed, scooping her into his arms.

"I'm sorry I woke you up."

"That's okay, I felt you leave. I was enjoying my cuddle time with you," she replied.

"Do you normally cuddle with men on the first date?"

"It depends. We both shared some personal stuff at dinner yesterday, so I'll assume we're at least friends. Friends with benefits."

"I see."

She ran her hands across his chest, gently kissing his shoulder.

"What does this tattoo mean?" she asked, scrutinizing the snake tattoo on his chest.

"It's nothing."

"C'mon, tell me!"

"You ask too many questions."

"And you don't give any answers," Arewa replied as she kissed his cheek. "Come on, Eteka, the world isn't going to stop if you tell me what it means. Please?"

"Now I see why they say women make men do bad things," he teased. "It's in your best interest not to know what my tattoo means."

"If you want to sleep with me again, you'd better tell me," Arewa said, this time kissing him on his lips. Her caress made him weak in his mind, made him forget promises and secrecy.

"I really shouldn't tell you," Eteka said, smiling as she placed her hand on his crotch.

"You sure?" she asked, fondling him. "C'mon, you know you want to. Is it the sign for your organization?"

He smiled and kissed her softly in relief.

"You're good. But you ask too many questions. Yes, it's the emblem for the brotherhood I belong to."

"Oh yes, I forgot about that. It was on your file. The Imamba, is it?"

"Yes."

Arewa sat up in bed and lit a cigarette, wearing a thoughtful look. Sunlight from the window brought her ebony skin to life, highlighting her polished beauty. She smiled at him, her full lips curving gently as she pondered her latest conquest.

"What made you join this brotherhood?" Arewa asked.

"My Uncle Oga raised me in it. He is one of the founders."

"Uncle Oga? Ha, that's a pretty cool name. So, they trained you how to fight? Is that how you got all these muscles?" Arewa continued, rubbing his thigh with her foot.

"Yes. I've trained here in Africa and abroad."
She flicked her ashes into a nearby cut-crystal ashtray. "Tell me about the first time you killed. What did it feel like?"

Eteka sat up to face her. It seemed like odd pillow talk, but she was hardly an ordinary girl.

"I'll never forget it," he said. "It was 1978, and I was a younger man, hanging out in Accra, Ghana. That day was to be my first hit, and I'd been training from childhood for it: learning how to shoot, wrestle, even how to box in Bukom, Ghana.

"The hit was on a foreign businessman. I wasn't told where exactly he was from. He was coming in to watch the African Cup of

Nations match between Ghana and Uganda. The stadium was packed, and everyone was excited about the game."

Eteka shook his head, feeling the memories surge. "I remember every detail. Young men painted in Ghana's colors ran through the streets, screaming cheers for the home team. It was a very hot day, and the parking lot was full of vendors selling frozen water in plastic bags. Young children ran through their parents' legs kicking soccer balls around, and pickpockets darted through the crowd, sticking their hands in whatever available pockets and open purses they could find.

"Oga, myself, and two other Imamba struggled through the sweaty crowd until we finally made it into the stands and found a pair of seats close to the VIP box. The businessman was in the box, standing with a few Ghanaian politicians. My heart was racing. I was sure everyone around me could hear it, even over the roar of the crowd. My left hand got sweaty from holding the gun in my pocket. I was quiet—it was probably suspicious how quiet I was—and kept my eyes on the VIP box the whole time, even when the other Imamba sang along with the crowd and cheered.

"Oga had hired a prostitute, and she made her way to the VIP box, right on cue. She fluttered around the businessman for a few minutes and then whispered something in his ear, and they left down some stairs away from the crowd, disappearing behind the stands. My job was to follow them, so I made my way through the crowd. I had to bribe the security guard at the exit to the VIP parking lot. The businessman was calling the prostitute a little black bitch as she gave him a blow job between two cars. He was so surprised when he saw me standing with my gun pointed at his head.

"My heart was pounding so hard," Eteka continued, "The prostitute ran away, and the man begged for his life. I had seen pictures of him, but it felt strange seeing him up close, in person. He had Caucasian features, a face that looked like it could use some sleep, and an accent that I found hard to place. He stopped begging for his life, and he looked so surprised and confused as he watched me watching him. Perhaps he thought I would reconsider what I'd set out to do. I closed my eyes and pulled the trigger. You couldn't even hear it over the crowd.

"I don't know why, but I thought I'd feel better once he was dead," Eteka said, shaking his head, his eyes distant. "I felt... sick, shaken. I felt like I'd committed the worst sin that a man could commit. I made my way back into the stadium to join Oga and the other Imamba. African drums and horns were playing, and the fans danced wildly in the stands—they had no idea what I had done. Then, Oga wrapped an arm around me, asking if the deed had been done. I said that it had, and he simply nodded. We watched the rest of the game as if nothing had happened."

Eteka had never spoken of these memories to anyone, yet with Arewa he could not stop talking. He had held so much inside, and it felt good to release it, to share himself with this woman he was beginning to care about. She sat there on the bed, captivated by her lover's tale.

"Wow. I'm stunned. I don't know if I find you sexier or scarier than I did before," Arewa said nervously, wondering if he'd ever killed a woman.

"You have nothing to fear from me," he replied, moving closer.

"Do you promise?" she asked as they kissed, reclining on the bed.

"I will never allow anything bad to happen to you."

Cuddled in his arms, Arewa fell fast asleep while Eteka remained awake, gazing blankly at the ceiling and anticipating his next mission—facing the mysterious White Witch.

SUPREME

On the road to Liati Wote. Volta Region. Ghana, Africa. 1990.

Omega sat quietly in the back seat of a Mercedes-Benz as he was driven toward the village of Liati Wote. Dense grasslands surrounded the car as it sped down a seemingly endless winding highway.

Omega toyed with one of the diamonds Eteka and Cyrus had brought to him from Liberia as he peered out the window at Mount Afadjato. Business with the Imamba was going well. He had left the Imamba brothers with directives on their next missions, and he was confident they would deliver as always. Now, it was time to revisit his past. He had been summoned by his older brother, Amir, now known as Supreme.

Around noon, Omega's car pulled into the village. It was a remote tourist destination, and prominent signs gave directions for tour sign-ups. Tour buses full of foreigners were pulling into the village, filled with wide-eyed travelers taking in all the scenery and snapping picture after picture. Omega's car stopped at the edge of the village. An old man Omega recognized as Kweku walked up to the car and smiled, revealing missing and rotten teeth. Omega wound his window down. The man reeked of alcohol.

"Hello, Master Omega. It's been a long time," Kweku said between coughs.

"I'm not sure what the Order of Zerachiel sees in you, Kweku. You're always drunk when I come here," Omega said.

"Looks can be deceiving, my Lord," Kweku said as he held out his hand.

Omega handed Kweku a little money and the old drunkard smiled and pointed toward a bushy area to his left. The Mercedes drove toward the bush, which parted (via hidden machinery) as the car approached to reveal a secret path going up the mountain. The path's composition soon changed from sand and grass to a smooth, paved road. Neatly trimmed shrubbery lined the road, backed by thick natural forest. After 30 minutes of driving, they pulled into a large paved clearing on a plateaued part of the mountain. Several cars were parked in the clearing, and stairs led to a large cave in the side of the mountain. Two men dressed in western clothes with Sterling submachine guns slung around their shoulders walked up to the car as it parked, and Omega stepped out.

"Hello, sir. Supreme is expecting you," one of the men said, politely gesturing toward the stairs.

Omega nodded, and they continued up the stairs and into the cave. Marble floors and glass panels greeted them as they took the walkway up to a large auditorium. Men similar to the two escorting Omega walked around, also toting submachine guns. Stalactite

formations hung from the ceiling, and four tall floodlights
illuminated the area.

In the center of the natural auditorium stood Supreme. He
was a man with a powerful build, standing well over six feet tall. He
was dressed in a long, flowing, sleeveless white tunic that reached
down to his ankles. He was bald save for a top knot and long pigtail.
Tribal scars resembled whitened cracks on his face, and an eye
deformity gave him eerily clear white pupils. Supreme wore
traditional Ghanaian sandals and held a long, black leather whip in
his right hand. In front of him stood a large, growling male lion,
baring its sharp teeth. The lion was partially restrained by a piece of
chain encircling its right hind leg. The chain was attached to an
immovable post, and in anger he swiped violently at Supreme, who
calmly watched the captive beast. Behind the defensive male lion
facing Supreme stood another, smaller male lion, two females, and
four cubs, all in chains.

Supreme observed the angry lion for a brief moment, and
then unleashed his whip. He raised the weapon, cracking it across
the lion's back. The lion grimaced in pain, and again lunged for
Supreme's face. But the metal chain tied around his leg pulled him
back into submission. Supreme slashed the animal again with the
whip, savoring his helpless rage. The other lions looked on,
expressing disapproval for their leader's treatment through low
pitched snarls.

This routine went on for about ten minutes before the
animal's movements slowed, his breathing heavy as he stared at

Supreme with wary eyes. Welts had formed on the lion's sides from Supreme's blows, and the other lions had become quiet. Supreme slowly approached the lion, and he cowered back in fear, crouching low. Supreme in turn placed a foot on his head and looked at the other lions, who all cringed away from him.

"If you ever want to conquer a people, take out the strongest man first and let his friends, wife, and children watch you do it," Supreme said to Omega, watching the other lions. His voice was deep and powerful. "The friends and wife will submit to you, and the children will grow up thinking being submissive is a way of life. Generations will serve you without question. Supreme has come to understand these things," Supreme finished, walking over to Omega as the lions were taken away by his men.

"Thanks for the lesson, Amir. What did you call me here for?" Omega asked, lighting up a cigar.

"My little brother. Always business as usual. Mother would have told you to relax and not be so tense, if she were alive."

"Well, she's not, and our father taught us differently."

"Yes… him. Let's take a walk, there is much to discuss," Supreme replied as he walked off. Omega shook his head, stood up, and followed.

They walked deeper into the large cave, passing beautiful rock formations and cave systems. Guards were everywhere, some sitting, some talking, most watching their leader walk with Omega.

"I've been hearing good things about the Imamba. I'm proud of what you have accomplished, although I wish you would have stayed with us," Supreme said. "We could have run the Order side by side."

"The Order of Zerachiel did nothing for me, Amir," Omega replied, "besides naming me Omega. We joined them when we were young because it made sense at the time. Times have changed."

"Indeed they have. You left us as soon as you learned about the arms trade, through a contact I introduced you to. I'm still a little bitter about that. But we are brothers, and I can forgive you," Supreme said.

"I'm all about making money, Amir," Omega said honestly. "The Order and I were not on the same page, so I left to do my own thing. You and your friends are a bit too radical for me."

"Focusing only on money makes a man one-dimensional," Supreme lectured. "I came to understand this when the Order found us all those years ago. We had been chasing money all along, but the Order made me see that having power is the cornerstone of judgment, the foundation for all things."

"Yeah? Well, money makes the world go round."

"And power determines when and in what direction the world should spin," Supreme countered.

They walked to an exit in the cave that offered a breathtaking view. The vast forest sat below them, sheltering the Tagbo waterfalls and Lake Volta.

"Why did you call me here, Amir?" Omega asked, puffing on his cigar.

SUPREME

"POWER DETERMINES
WHEN AND IN WHAT
DIRECTION THE WORLD
SHOULD SPIN."

E T E K A
RISE OF THE IMAMBA

"Times have changed, Ade, as you yourself said. It is time to make the world bow before us. This is what the Order requires."

"Get to the point," Omega demanded impatiently. "What do you need from me?"

Supreme smiled and nodded at a guard behind him, who handed Omega a folder containing a picture of a nervous-looking, greying man with Caucasian features, sporting a thick moustache and wearing large glasses.

"Who is this?"

"He is a Portuguese we've been studying for the past two years. His name is Professor Cayetano Ordóñez. He was one of three candidates sponsored by a missions program back in the '70s to study biology at Oxford. He went on to become one of the world's leading experts in the fields of biophysics, neurobiology, and virology. In 1983, a secret meeting was held at the NATO headquarters in Brussels among a few select generals in their defense sector. The purpose of this meeting was to set the strategy for the creation of a new weapon."

"I fail to see the connection," Omega cut in.

"The secret project was called OVERTHROW," Supreme continued, "and the weapon was meant to be a biological agent—a virus spread through mere touch that takes over the mind by cracking the brain's neural code and linking each infected subject to a master source for direction."

"Mind control…"

"Precisely. Top scientists from around the world were enlisted to work on the project, and Professor Ordóñez was brought on as the project lead. The project was tested and proved successful on lab rats and monkeys. Then the decision was made to test on live subjects at select locations here in Africa. This did not sit well with the professor, so he destroyed all the vials containing the virus, stole the log files and documentation of the project, and disappeared. But we found him."

"Where is he?"

"He's in Wales—Cardiff, to be precise—living under a new name," Supreme answered. "The folder in your hand has our observations to date and the profile we have built for him. Take that information and bring him to us."

Omega took another puff on his cigar, then closed the folder. "What made you approach me? You can get this done yourself."

"The Order of Zerachiel wants to maintain as much distance from this operation as possible. Besides, you and your Imamba friends could use the money. It is a win-win proposition."

"How much money is in this for me?" Omega asked.

"A lot," Supreme said as he nodded at another guard, who approached them with a large briefcase. The guard opened the case, revealing crisp stacked hundred-dollar bills.

"This is one million U.S. dollars. Think of it as a down payment, to get you started," Supreme said as the case was handed to Omega.

Omega, impressed by the gesture of good faith, nodded at his brother while puffing on his cigar. "An operation like this will take some time. We will have to plan to avoid any mistakes. When do you need this man brought to you?" Omega asked.

"There is no rush. For now, let's say no later than a year from now."

"That shouldn't be a problem. You have a deal. You'll hear from me with specifics regarding our strategy when we finish going through your folder and making our plans."

Omega nodded, turning without a goodbye and walking away accompanied by four armed guards. Supreme watched his younger brother leave, a sinister smirk on his face.

DETOUR

Ferry, en route to Zanzibar Island, Tanzania. Africa. 1990.

Eteka, Cyrus, and Mokin found themselves sitting on the back of a ferry headed toward Zanzibar Island. They had met earlier on the Tanzanian mainland in Dar es Salaam, en route to the White Witch, when Cyrus had requested that they make a quick detour to Zanzibar Island so he could take care of some personal business.

They sat on the ferry's deck, absentmindedly watching the assortment of locals and tourists on board. The sea breeze was strong, and waves tossed the vessel about as it made its way to Zanzibar. Cyrus had been a lot quieter than his usual self, wordlessly looking out to sea. Eteka daydreamed about the past few days with Arewa in Abuja. He missed the intense sensations he felt each time they made love. He missed holding her in his arms, and the soft texture of her skin. He missed the way she looked when she was sleeping. Most of all, he missed the way she expressed a genuine interest in who he was as a person. No one had ever treated him that way before. She exposed a sensitive side of him he'd never known existed.

They arrived at the Zanzibar harbor in Stone Town[1] and were greeted by Customs officials and large shipment containers. They walked through Stone Town's narrow streets as wave after wave of young street peddlers and hawkers ran up to them, trying to sell them their wares or convince them to sign up for a guided tour of the island. A unique blend of Indian, Middle Eastern, Moorish, British, and African architecture punctuated Stone Town, evidence of the different cultures that had once staked their claim over the land.

After an early lunch of Urojo soup, they hailed a taxi and set off toward the beach village of Matemwe, to the north of Zanzibar. It was a peaceful drive through Zanzibar's scenic countryside. They passed the Masingini forest, vast rows of palm trees, sparse housing, and roadside traders. The air was fresh and dry, a breeze blowing in off the ocean. Mokin sat in the front of the taxi due to his hulking size, and Cyrus and Eteka shared the back seat.

Eteka looked over at Cyrus. The latter hadn't said a word on the whole trip. "What's wrong with you?" Eteka asked.

"Huh?" Cyrus replied, snapping out of what seemed like an endless trance.

"You've been very quiet this whole time. What's wrong with you?" Eteka asked again.

"It's nothing, I'm fine."

"You're not fine, Cyrus. What's going on?"

---

[1] Stone Town was a focal point of both the Arab slave trade and spice trade in East Africa during the 19th century.

"It's nothing, Eteka. Let it go. I get like this whenever I come to these parts. It will pass," Cyrus replied. Eteka looked at Cyrus, now more curious than ever to know why he had been so quiet.

"So, how was Nigeria?" Cyrus asked, changing the subject.

"What do you mean?"

"Stop playing games, Eteka. I asked you how Nigeria was. Did you do whatever it is you went there to do?"

"I did."

"Was it a girl?" Cyrus asked as he retrieved a handgun from his side pocket and wiped it down with a rag.

"I already told you, it's none of your business."

Cyrus smiled at him as he put his gun away. "This is a beautiful island, this Zanzibar, although I would rather be back in Johannesburg at the hotel," Cyrus said. "You should have stayed with us, brother. Omega had a lot of women come by. I had a different woman every day for the two weeks I was there," Cyrus said with a yawn.

Eteka didn't respond as he fixed his gaze on the passing countryside. Indeed, it was beautiful. Endless rows of banana, plantain, and palm trees lined the highway, backed by lush vegetation.

"Why do you do this, Cyrus?" Eteka asked.

Cyrus shifted in his seat and turned toward Eteka. "Do what?"

"Why do you do this?" Eteka repeated. "Take these kinds of assignments? I've never known your reasons for being in the brotherhood."

Cyrus lit up a joint he pulled out of a side pocket. The smell of the burning weed quickly filled the car. He took a few drags, looking at Eteka seriously. Eteka had never asked him this question before.

"You certainly picked a nice day to get romantic with me," Cyrus said, offering his joint to Eteka. Eteka declined. "I do this because I love to kill, and I love power," Cyrus replied. "What else do you want to know? You want to hear how I came here, or what I've been through? You want to be my psychologist now?" Cyrus asked with a grin.

"No, but I'm interested in hearing what brought you here."

Cyrus blew smoke into the air, thinking. "I was about four years old when I came home one day from playing and found my mother and older sister dead," he began. "Their throats were slit from ear to ear and my mother had been stripped naked. We had just moved to Congo in 1962. There was a lot of fighting going on at that time."

"Did you ever find out who killed your family? Soldiers? Armed robbers?"

Cyrus hesitated as he smoked his blunt.

"Our neighbor saw everything. They were Belgian mercenaries. I don't know why they killed my family and left my mother like that, on the floor for me to see," Cyrus replied dully.

"I'm sorry to hear that, brother. What happened next?"

"Our neighbor took me in and raised me until she died just after I turned fourteen. I roamed the country for a while, learning how to fight. I fought with the Congolese army, and for some Ugandan rebel groups operating in the area. Then I went back to my mother's country, Liberia, where I was approached by Oga. I met you shortly afterward," Cyrus said.

"Yes, I remember that. Sounds like you've come a long way, brother."

Cyrus grinned as he took a long drag, the weed smoke somehow making the scar on his face stand out.

"How about you, Eteka? Why are you here?"

Eteka held up his necklace, the only physical link he had to parents he could barely remember. "I have a foggy memory of my parents. Like you, I was four years old when I last saw them. All I have to remember them by is this necklace, which I know my father gave to me. I remember a big fire, and that's it."

"A big fire? That's a shit story. You don't remember anything else?" Cyrus asked.

"I just remember fire, lots of fire, and that was it. I've been with Oga ever since."

"Did Oga tell you what happened to your parents?" Cyrus asked.

"He told me once that my real parents died in a car accident, and the people who adopted me could not afford to keep me. So they asked Oga to watch over me."

"And how did Oga know your foster parents?"

"I have no idea. They must have been friends."

Cyrus took another drag from his joint, regarding Eteka seriously. "That's an interesting story. I do remember you saying something about Oga finding you in Nigeria when we first met in the desert long ago. You are a man of mystery, Eteka. I wonder how we would have turned out if God hadn't put us on this path," Cyrus said as he put out the blunt.

"You think God put us on this path?"

"I have to blame someone."

"I thought you practiced your black magic stuff," Eteka teased. "You believe in God now, too?"

"I don't remember saying that I didn't. Let's not start a new discussion," Cyrus said dismissively. "I want to take a nap before we arrive."

"You've still not told me where we're going. What's this business you have to take care of in Matemwe?" Eteka asked.

Cyrus did not reply, and instead put on his sunglasses. Eteka watched him fall asleep, then resumed looking out at the beautiful Zanzibari countryside.

✝

After 45 minutes of driving, the taxi pulled into the village of Matemwe. Beautiful white sand beaches greeted the mercenaries as the taxi wove through the village's narrow streets. They drove past signs indicating a coral reef and a lagoon; lavish villas built to rent to tourists stood out like jewelry boxes next to the strictly functional houses of the locals. Children could be seen playing along the beach as fishermen pulled in canoes filled with fish. A few foreigners were walking along the beach, laughing and chatting as they searched for shells. The taxi drove up to a quaint little house, almost resembling a hut.

"Wait here," Cyrus said sternly, getting out of the car as Eteka and Mokin got out to stretch and stand by the taxi. Sighing, Cyrus walked up to the front door of the house and knocked. A pretty ebony-skinned woman opened the door. She was petite in frame, under five feet tall, with a certain air of gentleness about her. She did not seem particularly excited to see Cyrus, but hugged him nonetheless as a little boy walked out to stare at Cyrus.

Eteka watched Cyrus's face light up when he saw the child, and then Cyrus bent down, picked up the boy, and gave him a hug that lasted a few minutes. Eteka had never seen Cyrus show actual affection to anyone, and he leaned against the taxi as he watched Cyrus disappear into the house with the woman and the boy. After about an hour, Cyrus emerged from the house, the woman and boy not far behind. Cyrus and the woman spoke before Cyrus hugged the little boy again and walked back toward the taxi without looking back. As he got closer, Eteka saw that tears had filled Cyrus's eyes.

"Who are they?" Eteka asked as they got back into the taxi.

"That is my wife and my son," Cyrus softly replied.

c h o s e n

BAIT

Mushin. Lagos. Africa. 1990.

Isatou sat down on a bench in the main market in Mushin, playing with a lock in her hair. It was mid-afternoon, and the market was busy with all kinds of commercial activity. She smoked a cigarette as she watched two men argue over the price of sardines, both men exchanging insults in Yoruba. In another hour she had an appointment with another client, which meant she had some time to kill.

Gloria, the elderly woman who sold fried yams, sat in a stall next to Isatou. The old woman was having good business today: a steady stream of hungry customers had been buying her food all day, and now her yams were finished. She shut down a bit earlier than usual, and as she packed her cooking utensils, she looked up at Isatou.

"No business today?" Gloria asked.

"Later. I'm just relaxing for now."

"Why don't you relax at your place?"

"I use my place for work, not relaxing," Isatou replied. Gloria in turn gave her a motherly smile.

"You are a beautiful woman, Isatou. Why don't you find a good man and get married? You can't run around these streets forever."

"Get married?" Isatou asked with a raised eyebrow. "Madam, all men want to do with me is have sex."

"Not all men."

"No?"

"What about Olabanji?" Gloria asked as Olabanji passed by, pushing a cartload of fresh gari to his shop. He stood at 6'4", with broad shoulders, deep-set slanted eyes, and a smile that made Isatou's heart melt whenever she saw it. Olabanji smiled at both women as he passed, taking a little longer to smile at Isatou. Isatou blushed, smiling at her crush and taking some time to admire his derriere as he walked away.

"I've seen the way you and he smile at each other whenever he walks by," Gloria said. "He has his head on straight. I think he even teaches Sunday school at my church. He's a good man—a rare thing to come across these days," Gloria said.

"Yes, but he never talks to me, so I don't know if he likes me."

"You know how to get what you want from men. Maybe you should make the first move."

"Ah, Gloria. Okay, I'll work on it," Isatou said as she stood up. "Do you need help with your pots and pans?"

"No, I'll be fine."

"Okay. I have to get ready for my appointment."

Isatou waved goodbye and walked off through the sea of human traffic at the market. She bought herself a small bag of puff-puff[1] and munched on the tasty morsels as she made her way away from the market to a quieter part of the area. She walked down a street with apartment buildings on both sides and spotted PantiRaida reprimanding another prostitute named Lina.

"Weitin dey happen?[2]" Isatou asked in pidgin english as PantiRaida sent Lina away.

"It's okay, I no vex. Lina just dey find my trouble,[3]" PantiRaida replied, taking one of her puff-puffs. "She charged some guy the wrong price."

"Shit happens."

"Shit is not supposed to happen. You bitches are supposed to always have my money. Are you ready to service your guy?"

"I'll be ready, I just have to freshen up. That's what I came back here for."

"Good. Make sure your pussy is clean," PantiRaida said as another prostitute walked over and handed him some money. Isatou simply nodded in response, and they stood in silence for a few seconds, PantiRaida lighting up a blunt and Isatou absentmindedly staring at a stray mongrel across the street sniffing through some trash on the ground.

---

[1] Puff-puff is a very common Nigerian snack made from fried dough. In Nigeria, it is usually eaten with sugar. The Ghanaian variation of the same snack is called "bofrot."
[2] "What's going on?"
[3] "It's okay, I'm not angry. Lina is just getting on my nerves."

"Why you no dey your uncle een side?[1]" PantiRaida asked, handing the blunt to Isatou for a drag.

"Weitin I dey go do for my uncle een side?[2]"

"Oluko na efiko. The guy be jeje guy,[3] and he's always writing and talking about how Naija fit make better[4]. You don't have to live this life. You can learn a lot from him."

"What are you saying? You don't want me anymore?" Isatou asked with some concern.

"Stop asking stupid questions—you know you're the best girl I have. But you're wasting your time here. Oluko na sharp guy, and because he's done so much for the people, he has high street cred. If you decide to go and stay with him, people here on the street will still love you."

"I don't need to stay with my uncle. I can find my own way."

PantiRaida shook his head as he took the blunt back from Isatou and took a long drag.

"You are a foolish girl, but I'm sure you will learn that for yourself. Eventually. I have something else I want to discuss with you before you leave."

He paused to take another drag from the blunt before he spoke.

"Tribal and his boys have a little proposal for us. They want to use one of the girls for something, and specifically asked for you."

---

[1] "Why aren't you staying with your uncle?"
[2] "What am I going to do at my uncle's place?" (sarcastic tone)
[3] "Oluko is a smart man. The guy is gentle."
[4] "...always writing and talking about how Nigeria can be better."

"They asked for me?" Isatou asked in surprise. "I don't even talk to them."

"Well, somehow they know you, because they asked for you."

"You already know I don't want anything to do with them."

"Yeah, I know, but let's just hear them out. There's plenty of money involved."

"I don't care. They like shooting and killing too much. Can't you get another girl to use? What about Lina?" Isatou asked. Her suggestion made PantiRaida laugh.

"Lina na fugazi. Plus, she no dey hear word.[1] They asked me to bring you, so I need you to do this for me. When you finish servicing your next client, meet me behind the market at six o'clock. I'll be there with Tribal and his boys. Tribal said his boss is going to come and give the instructions himself, so make sure you're not late."

"Tribal has a boss?"

"Yes, I didn't know that either. Go get ready, and try to have a good time chopping[2] your client. We go yarn at six.[3]"

Isatou walked towards the rear of the market. Evening had arrived, and the sun had begun to set. The vendors could be seen packing and locking up their shops and stalls. She had finished business with her last client, listening to his moans as she thought

---

[1] "Lina is a wannabe/fake. Plus, she does not follow instructions."
[2] "...try to have fun having sex/sleeping with your client."
[3] "We will talk at six."

about the upcoming meeting with Tribal and his gang. Tribal, his nickname given to him due to the many tribal branding marks that covered the left side of his face, was a tough man and a notorious armed robber known for his violent streak. His gang had been responsible for many murders across Lagos, and were feared by even some segments of the police. She shuddered every time she walked past them, and never made eye contact.

She made it to the rear of the market, and found PantiRaida and the robbers sitting in a dark corner by some old cars. PantiRaida sat on the hood of one of the vehicles, deep in conversation with two other men. Next to them sat Tribal, eating pomo[1] and moi moi.[2]

"Thanks for coming," PantiRaida said to Isatou as she arrived.

"This be am?" Tribal asked. He was a short man with a stocky build and a round, mean-looking face. His facial scars stood out even in the dim lighting, and his eyes were bloodshot. He had a high tenor voice that belied his intimidating presence.

"Yeah, this be am," PantiRaida replied. Tribal walked up to Isatou.

"My boss dey come, na een wey ask of you,[3]" Tribal said.

They all waited for a few minutes in silence, and then in the distance a figure approached. As the figure got closer, Isatou opened her mouth in utter surprise. No, it couldn't be…

"Boss, how you dey?[4]" Tribal asked in greeting.

---

[1] Cooked cow skin.
[2] Nigerian bean cake.
[3] "My boss is coming. It was he who asked for you."
[4] "Boss, how are you?"

"I dey fine,[1]" Olabanji replied as he reached the group and rested his eyes on Isatou. The two locked eyes for a moment. What was he doing here? How did he know Tribal? Isatou remained puzzled as she stared at Olabanji.

"Hello, Isatou," Olabanji greeted.

"Uh, hello, Olabanji."

"Please. On the street I'm known as China."

"China? Umm, okay. I thought you sold gari?"

"I do sell gari."

"So what are you doing here?"

China looked over at Tribal and his men, and they all laughed. Isatou stared at China's tall frame and broad shoulders. Despite the strange turn in events, she still found him very attractive.

"I came here to meet you, and ask you to do something for us."

"Are you an armed robber?"

"What do you think?" China replied, stepping closer to Isatou as the other men looked on, stifling smiles.

"I don't know what to think. I also heard you go to church. You can't be an armed robber."

"The devil goes to church every Sunday, don't be surprised. There's a lot of money in this for you if you help us. And I would be personally grateful," China said, placing his hand on her arm.

"What do you want me to do?"

---

[1] "I'm okay."

China nodded at PantiRaida, and the pimp jumped into the conversation.

"Tomorrow, you are going to go to Ikoyi. Tribal and his boys will join you at the hotel the following day. This rich businessman called Yusuf Agbodzi who runs some of the bunkering operations in the Delta is going to be at the same hotel. He is supposed to be there for one week. You must watch this man. Make yourself look sexy, so he notices you. You are good at that. Get to know this man. Make sure you talk with adjebota English,[1] not pidgin. Make him want you. Then, bring him up to your room."

"And what do you want me to do with him in my room?" Isatou asked.

"Tribal and his boys will take it from there, you don't need to worry about that," China cut in.

Isatou knew what that meant. She had done many bad things in her life, but this... this was on a whole different level. If they got ahold of this businessman, she had an uneasy feeling that she knew what would happen to him.

"A beg, can't you get another girl to do this? I'm not comfortable with this."

"Weitin' be your problem? All you are doing is being bait. That's it. Just bring the guy to your room, and once we have him, you leave," Tribal said angrily.

---

[1] Proper English.

"Are you going to kill the man?" Isatou asked. At that, PaintiRaida slapped her hard, leaving her dizzily pressing her hand to her stinging cheek. He had never laid a hand on her before.

"Shut up! You will do as I told you, end of discussion! Go there, bait the guy, bring him to your room. That's it."

Her eyes welled with tears that she held back as she stared at all the men. China stood, a sardonic smile on his face. She suddenly didn't find him so attractive anymore.

"You leave tomorrow, so go back to your place and get some rest," China said.

✝

Three days later, she found herself in southern Lagos in the suburb of Ikoyi. She was in the hotel the men had spoken of, a five-star luxury venue that hosted a mix of wealthy Nigerians, expatriates, and foreign tourists. Tribal and his men had arrived the previous night, and had booked the room next to hers on the 10th floor. They, however, waited in her room whenever she went down to the lounge area to find Yusuf Ogbodzi. On this particular evening, she looked nothing like she did back on the streets of Mushin. PantiRaida had arranged for her to have a makeover: her hair had been relaxed and flat-ironed, she was wearing makeup suitable for a model, and her street clothes had been exchanged for an evening gown—a deviation from her normal tomboyish nature. Since arriving at the hotel, she had spent every evening in one of the hotel's bar lounges, looking out for Yusuf Agbodzi. Many men, both Nigerian and foreign, had tried to strike up a conversation with her, but to no avail. She was on the hunt for her prize, and she spotted the businessman this evening walking into the lounge area with two other men and his bodyguards. Yusuf was an average-sized man with big lips and narrow eyes, which he kept hidden behind a pair of designer glasses. He was dressed in an expensive agbada, complete with a matching cap. He had a loud, self-important voice, and waved his hands around as he talked. Two hulking bodyguards followed him around wherever he went. On this evening, he and his friends sat down at a table not too far from Isatou. She made sure she sat in his line of sight and elegantly sipped on a martini, occasionally reaching up to caress a loose strand of hair from her updo. Yusuf and his men laughed heartily, shouting at each other as if they wanted everyone in the lounge to hear their conversation. Isatou listened to them, tuning out once in a while to smoke a cigarette and to try and relax. She couldn't believe China was an armed robber. Even worse, he was Tribal's boss. How could this be? She'd seen him every day at the market—selling gari, smiling at people, and, best of all, smiling at her. Had he been leading her on all this time? The main reason she had found him attractive was because he didn't carry himself like most of the men she knew back in Mushin—he hadn't seemed like a thug or a fool. But now that China had revealed this darker side of himself, she saw him in a completely different light, and saw the disguise for what it was.

"Well, well. Hello, sweetie."

Isatou was shaken out of her thoughts. Standing in front of her stood Yusuf, smiling from ear to ear. She found him quite ugly up close—not that it had ever mattered.

"Hello," she purred throatily.

"I hope you know CPR, cuz you take my breath away!" Yusuf said, followed by a loud burst of laughter, a drop of his saliva hitting Isatou in the face. He sat himself down next to her without her permission. He reeked of cologne—it smelled like he'd poured the whole bottle over himself.

"So, how are you doing?" Yusuf asked.

"I'm fine, how are you?"

"Oh, I'm fine, just in town making some big deals worth millions of American dollars. Can I buy you a drink, or do you just want the money?"

"I'm still drinking this one, but maybe when I finish you can buy me another," Isatou replied. "Your agbada looks very nice on you."

"Thank you, sweetie. My personal tailor made it for me. I also bought this Rolex in Dubai," Yusuf said, flashing a fancy gold watch in front of her. "If you want, I could take you shopping in Dubai and New York sometime."

Oh, Lord, Isatou thought to herself while keeping up a fake smile. "What girl doesn't love shopping? I would love that."

"Are you married? Is that why you're here sitting by yourself? If you are married, then we have to be very careful."

"I'm not married."

"That's good, that's good… you know, it seems like I have seen you somewhere before," he said, pausing theatrically, waiting for her to ask the question.

"Where have you seen me?" Isatou supplied.

"In my dreams," he delivered the punchline. "My pastor said I would meet the woman of my dreams today. Praise the Lord, he is correct. I think you and I are very compatible. What do you think?" he asked, peering at her through his prescription glasses.

Isatou giggled to herself. Clearly, Yusuf had been drinking before he'd even arrived at the bar.

"Yes, I think we are compatible. But you've not even told me your name," Isatou said.

"I am so sorry. My name is Yusuf Agbodzi. What is your name?"

"Fatima," she answered. "What are you doing now?"

"Just having some drinks with friends of mine. You can come and join us. I would like to show them my new babe," Yusuf said with a smile, revealing a gap between his front teeth.

"I have a better idea. Why don't you give your friends five more minutes of your time, then follow me up to my room? I would like to see exactly how 'compatible' we are," she replied, stroking his leg under the table with her foot.

Yusuf beamed from ear to ear, his large teeth standing out in all their glory. He stood up and quickly walked over to his friends while Isatou finished her drink. As Yusuf filled his friends in on his latest feat, Isatou walked over to the bar and placed a call to her room. Tribal answered.

"I dey bring am come,[1]" Isatou said in pidgin.

"Good. We dey wedge you.[2]"

She hung up and walked back to her seat. Internally, she was distraught. Yusuf had no idea what was waiting for him upstairs. He was a fool, but a harmless fool. The businessman strutted back, a look of accomplishment on his face. As Isatou and Yusuf walked out of the lounge area and toward the elevators, Yusuf's colleagues watched them leave. No doubt Yusuf felt like a winner, having impressed his friends by picking up a beautiful woman.

As they climbed floors in the elevator, Yusuf leaned in to kiss her. Reluctantly, she allowed him to, for the sake of the mission. He had bad breath—a combination of halitosis and garlic—and his tongue felt like sandpaper. Soon, their elevator arrived on the 10th floor, and they exited.

As they walked toward Isatou's room, a range of thoughts flooded her mind, mostly revolving around what Tribal and his boys planned on doing with Yusuf. From her limited experience, she knew that it was likely they would kidnap him, and if their demands were not met, they would torture and then kill him. And here she was, helping them. This went against everything she had been taught by Oluko growing up. It went against every moral fiber in her body. Everything in her told her this wasn't right, yet she knew that if she backed out now, China, Tribal, and their gang would come looking

---

[1] "I'm bringing him."
[2] "Good. We are waiting for you."

for her. The money in it for her would be good if she did as they asked—better than anything she had made before. But was it worth a human life? She had to make a decision quickly; her room was only a few doors away.

She stopped Yusuf in his tracks.

"I changed my mind. This is not a good idea. You should go back to your friends," Isatou said in a hushed tone. Her suggestion made Yusuf laugh loudly.

"Why are you whispering?"

"Please, just go back downstairs."

"I knew it. You are married. I can smell a married woman a mile away. It's okay—we are already here, and your husband will never know. Just lead the way to your room."

"Shut up and listen. In my room are five men waiting to kidnap you. You must go—now!"

Her last statement made Yusuf's smile turn into a frown. Fear suddenly distorted his facial expression, and he froze in his tracks.

"Fatima, is this a joke?" Yusuf asked apprehensively.

"My name is not Fatima. Now please, just go before they hear us."

No more words needed to be said. Yusuf, trembling in fear, quickly turned around and walked back to the elevator. Isatou nervously watched him leave, glancing frequently between him and her room door. Had any of the armed robbers overheard their brief hallway chat? What if one of them walked out now? She watched as

315

Yusuf disappeared into the elevator. Then she was alone, standing in her fancy dress in the hallway. Should she go in and confess to Tribal that she had let Yusuf go? Should she make up a lie about what had happened between her and Yusuf after she hung up with Tribal? Either way, trouble lay ahead. She couldn't go back to her room. And she couldn't go back to Mushin. Word of what she had done would get back to China. No, she had to go far away.

She heard some movement coming from her room. Time to go. She ran to the elevator, pressing the summons button nervously as she kept looking back to see if anyone would emerge from her room. After what seemed like the longest minute in history, the elevator doors opened and she dashed in, sighing with relief. On the first floor she walked through the lobby, nervously looking around. She spotted a frightened-looking Yusuf surrounded by what appeared to be the hotel manager, his colleagues, and two policemen. No doubt he was recounting his recent experience on the elevator with them, evidenced by the way he flailed his hands around and pointed repeatedly at the lounge area. To avoid being seen, Isatou stepped back into the elevator and took it down another level to the swimming pool, spa, and gym area. She walked past a few hotel patrons, through an exit, and up some stairs that led to the rear of the hotel. It had just rained, and the weather was overcast, the ground wet. As she walked toward the main road, two police Jeeps pulled into the hotel parking lot, and seven policemen toting machine guns filed into the hotel.

She walked to the main road and flagged down a taxi. The driver was an old Hausa man, whose smile revealed some crooked teeth. She sat down in the taxi. She had to get away from here. As far away as possible.

"Madam, where are you going?" the taxi driver asked.

"Ojuelegba."

GOOD COMPANY

Ibadan, Nigeria. Africa. 1967.

Yisa walked up to his front door on a quiet Sunday afternoon, exhausted both mentally and physically. His family had had no word of his coming—he wanted to surprise them. After greeting the house help, he stumbled inside and crashed on a couch in the living room. No one was home—it was Sunday, and going to church was part of the culture in this region.

Their last assignment in the Biafra region really troubled him. That priest had done nothing wrong. Storming into that church, accosting all those helpless, innocent people, and allowing Oga to beat that priest was just not right. Not right at all. This guilty feeling had haunted him ever since they'd left Biafra, and Yisa felt like less than a man. The Imamba had returned to their safe house in Lagos, dropped off their weapons, and gone their separate ways: Oga further inland to Benin City, and Yisa back home to Ibadan.

Yisa shifted on the couch, still wearing his traveling clothes and boots. He had a nice home. The latest sports cars lined his driveway. His family was well taken care of. He had an enormous amount of money in two Swiss bank accounts that Omega managed. He had all these things, yet he had a tortured soul. At his core, he was a good man. He had a moral center. He wasn't like Oga, who could kill without remorse. And he wasn't like Omega, who was only focused on getting money by any means necessary. Yisa was getting tired of being an actor—the man in the mirror always appearing to be a different version of himself.

Fatigue caught up with him, and he fell asleep.

Yisa was awoken by the sound of the main door opening, and little feet quickly scurrying his way.

"Daddy!" little Tosin screamed as he ran into the living room and jumped on his father. Amina and Oladele were not far behind, followed by a woman Yisa had never seen before.

"Ah, my boy, you feel heavier each time I see you," Yisa said, hugging his son close. Amina joined them on the couch as Oladele and the lady sat in adjacent chairs.

"What are you doing here?" Amina asked as she kissed her husband.

"My last assignment was over early, so I wanted to surprise you all," Yisa replied, glancing over at Oladele. "Hello, Oladele."

"Good to see you, Yisa. This is Bayinna Kikwete—she's visiting from Tanzania and is a good friend of mine. She gave a wonderful talk at the university today," Oladele said with a smile as Yisa and Bayinna locked eyes.

"It's so nice to meet you, Yisa. I've heard so many good things about you," Bayinna said in a very soothing, low-pitched voice. She was an albino woman, short in stature and slightly overweight. A warm smile lit up her face, and she had a certain presence about her. Yisa felt at peace as he spoke with the woman. She had a good spirit.

"The pleasure is all mine, and you are most welcome in our home," Yisa responded. "Amina, why don't you have some lunch made for us all, so we can eat?"

"Look, he's been home only a few minutes and he's already bossing me around," Amina teased as she headed for the kitchen. Everyone laughed, and a servant appeared from the kitchen with drinks and refreshments for all.

✝

Later that evening, Yisa sat alone in his bedroom. The restlessness and anxiety had left him, and he felt at peace. Oladele and Bayinna were downstairs. Yisa could hear their laughter as little Tosin entertained them. It felt so good to be around good company. Yisa smiled to himself as he put a robe on. Amina walked into the room with a small box in her hands.

"Hello, my love," Amina said as she sat down behind Yisa and wrapped her arms around him.

"Hello, my queen."

"I have something for you, to keep us on your mind when you go on your travels," she said as she opened the box. In it were three pieces of string braided into a cord and a few polished beads.

"What's this?"

"We have to start getting your mind off violent things as you prepare to come home for good," she answered.

"Who said I'm coming home for good?"

"I'm saying it. You can't do anything if you don't start acting on it," Amina said wisely.

Yisa smiled. Amina was right. She truly was his better half. "So, what am I supposed to do with these beads?"

"This, my dear, is your next project," Amina said gently. "You're going to make a beaded necklace for your son. If you finish it before you leave, I'll get you more so you can make another necklace for me."

"Ah, I see. That sounds doable," Yisa said, taking the box from her. "I love you, Amina."

"Awww," Amina said, her eyes welling up with tears, despite the levity of her tone.

"I know that me leaving has not been easy on you and Tosin. I will stop my travels and come home soon, I promise."

"Really?" Amina asked.

"Yes."

Tears rolled down Amina's face, and she hugged her husband tightly. She felt good in his arms.

"I'm so happy," Amina said.

"Me too," Yisa replied. "Let's go downstairs, musn't keep our guests waiting." They kissed one more time and walked downstairs, hand in hand. In the living room, Tosin stood between

Bayinna and Oladele, making them laugh as he tried to lecture them on why cars could only drive on four wheels.

"Okay, that's enough of that. Time for bed," Amina said as she scooped up little Tosin.

"But Mama, I have to hug Auntie Bayinna! And Uncle Oladele!" Tosin cried out.

Amina smiled and released her boy. He ran up to Oladele first and gave him a hug, and then turned to Bayinna.

"You are such a sweet young boy," Bayinna said, "and I will miss you."

"Can't you stay longer? You can play that mind game you showed me before!" Tosin said, tugging on her blouse.

"No, I have to go back home," Bayinna replied with a smile. "But we will meet again," she said as she gave Tosin one last hug and stood up. She paused as she smiled at the three adults, and then her eyes settled on Yisa. She looked at Yisa for what seemed a long time before Yisa exchanged confused glances with his wife and Oladele. It was then that Bayinna spoke:

"You have a good heart," Bayinna said, still staring at him, "but you've committed grave sins. Events are about to transpire in your life that will change everything, all for the greater good."

TOSIN

"CAN'T YOU STAY LONGER?
YOU CAN PLAY THAT MIND GAME
YOU SHOWED ME BEFORE!"

ETEKA
RISE OF THE IMAMBA

Her words left Yisa stunned. It was as if she could see right through him. What did she mean? How did she know about anything he had done? No one, not even his wife or Oladele, knew the details of his missions. Despite his confusion, Yisa quietly accepted her words, nodding. Bayinna smiled, hugged Yisa, and then hugged Amina.

"Why don't we all get a picture together, eh? Hold on, let me run upstairs and get my camera," Yisa said as he ran up to his bedroom, grabbed his camera, and returned. Amina summoned a servant to take the photo as they all grouped together, and after three takes to ensure that they got at least one good shot, they were done.

"I have to drop Bayinna off," Oladele said. "Let's meet tomorrow or the day after, Yisa. I want to show you around the school so you see the things we've been doing," Oladele winked as he walked Bayinna out of Yisa's home.

That night, after Tosin had been put to bed and after Yisa had made love to his darling wife, he stayed up, unable to sleep as he wondered about Bayinna's words.

Two days later, Oladele pulled into Yisa's driveway in his old car and blew his horn twice. Tosin was in school and Amina was inside taking a nap. It was the perfect time for the two old friends to take a ride together and connect. Yisa, dressed in a short-sleeved white shirt, khaki shorts, and sandals, walked out to the car and got comfortable in the passenger seat.

"What's that in your hand?" Oladele asked as they pulled out of Yisa's driveway and headed toward Ibadan University.

"I'm making a bead necklace."

"Things are not that bad, Yisa, you don't have to start making trinkets to sell. I'm sure I can get you a job at my school or the gas station."

"Funny guy. I'm making a necklace for Tosin."

Oladele looked at him with a raised eyebrow. "You? Making a necklace? I must be dreaming."

"You're not dreaming," Yisa assured him. "What you are is jealous because you've never made one yourself."

"Jealous? Ha! If those are the only life skills you have to offer, then perhaps I should rethink the idea of you coming back home for good."

The two friends laughed as they made their way through Ibadan. They drove past primary schools with children walking to and from classes and construction sites with laborers, their bare muscles glistening in the sunlight, wielding heavy pickaxes and hacking at the ground like human jackhammers. The streets were overly crowded, filled with pedestrians, traders, and exhaust fumes—which made for a very unpleasant and congested commuting experience. Military personnel were all over the city, either in army Jeeps or in small groups on various street corners. News posters and signs were everywhere, highlighting the Biafran War currently in progress. Oladele shifted his car into third gear as he cruised down a wide road.

"There is so much happening here in Nigeria, and in Africa, my brother," Oladele said, a serious look on his face.

"I know."

"I know you are aware, but I'm not sure you understand the big picture."

"What do you mean?"

They made a right turn onto an empty street in which some children, mostly barefoot, were playing mock football with a torn, beat-up soccer ball. Oladele blew his horn and the children scuttled out of the way.

"Like our friends all over Africa, the colonists invaded us from all sides. In addition, especially here in Nigeria, we were already a divided people. And conflicts like this Biafran War only increase the divide."

"What's your point? That it's the colonists' fault we are so broken?" Yisa asked. "I've heard that before."

"No. I do not make excuses, my brother, you should know that. Our problems all come down to the allocation of resources, forced borders, failed leadership, and the decay of our unified identity. Everything else—the corruption, ethnic and religious tensions, underdevelopment, foreign and local parties taking our resources, and so forth—are by-products of those realities."

They drove for 20 more minutes, then pulled up to the front gate of Ibadan University. A security guard let them in and they pulled into a large parking lot lined with lush greenery. A single-story structure stood behind the parking area, which hid the many buildings behind it that made up the university campus. Students walked to and fro, carrying books. A few older people, likely professors and faculty members, walked in and out of the buildings. They made quite a picture as they walked toward the buildings: Yisa with his tall, commanding posture and the shorter Oladele with his head bent and his hands behind his back. Different people greeted Oladele and called him by his well-known nickname, Oluko.

"It seems you're a celebrity around here," Yisa said.

"My nickname, Oluko, represents my body of work, not me as an individual," Oladele replied. "That is what the people here acknowledge and respect."

They walked down a long corridor, past a few administrative offices, and into a two-story building. The first floor housed two rooms: a classroom and a lab of some sort. In the classroom, three students surrounded by a group of onlookers were engaged in a heated discussion. Yisa spotted an interesting-looking man standing behind the body of students. He wore long robes and a round Fulani hat, and had white pupils that resembled cataracts. He held some beads, which he flicked between his fingers. The man watched Oladele tap Yisa's shoulder to draw his attention to the debate between the students as they stepped into the classroom.

"I'm telling you, the most important thing we need is education and money. In fact, these are the most needed things in most of Sub-Saharan Africa. We need governments to put more money toward formal education so our people can have employable skill sets," the first student said.

"No. We are where we are because of the injuries we've had to endure from colonial oppression. Our lands and people have been plundered to build the infrastructure of Europe and America. We need to come to terms with this fact and focus on our past. This is the only way we can move forward," the second student said.

"You are both wrong. We need good leadership across the board. Once there is good leadership at the top, everything else will fall into place," the third student said.

The students turned to Oladele. The second student spoke first, "Oluko, sir. What do you think?"

Oladele smiled and approached the students. He looked at each debater, as if to add extra effect. "I commend you all for having such a discussion amongst yourselves. These sorts of debates build critical thinking skill sets. Now," Oladele continued as he faced the second student, "I applaud your Afrocentric view. Our people have had to face some harsh realities that should never be forgotten.

However, continuously latching onto our past sufferings will have no significant impact on our current and future economic and political standings, and that's a reality with which we all must come to terms. We have to think *proactively*, not retroactively. We should never forget the past, but our focus should always be on making progress. And making progress means we have to be open to good ideas from any source, even from those who once oppressed us."

He turned to the first student.

"You are right when you say education should be a priority in every African nation, and the world, for that matter. However, be careful when you speak of education. We must not aim to create a system that trains future leaders not to think outside the box. And we must also make sure the educational system we employ drives value for our culture and society. And with your point on money, I'll advise you not to look at money as the solution to our problems. Having more money only makes a man more of what he already is. The heart of a man must change in order for any meaningful progress to happen," Oladele said before facing the third student.

"Your suggestion encompasses everything your friends have said, to a small degree. Yes, good leadership from the top can influence positive change on a macro level, but for policies to be truly effective, we also need effective leadership at all levels of society. We need personal accountability. A leader, no matter how good he or she is, can only do so much from the top. All the pieces need to be aligned if a unified vision is to follow."

Oladele smiled and faced the rest of the students in the room as Yisa looked on.

"Africa has many things to be proud of, but it also has many problems—too many to be covered by these three themes alone. However, I applaud you all for having this discussion. It is through the exchange of ideas that solutions are born."

The students nodded at his every word, and watched open-mouthed as both men left the room.

"I'm impressed. You spoke well," Yisa said as they walked away.

"Thank you," Oladele said. "However, you should be complimenting the students, not me. These are the young minds we need to nurture. These are the minds that will hopefully drive our political agendas, industries, and technology, which will give us a competitive advantage in the future."

As they walked, Yisa noticed the man in the long robes following them. Sensing danger, Yisa clenched his fists. Oladele noted Yisa's anxiety and placed a hand on his shoulder.

"There is no need for alarm. He is our friend."

"Who is he?" Yisa asked, keeping his eye on the mysterious man behind them.

"I do not know his name. I met him through Bayinna. He just showed up at my house one day and has been following me ever since. He helps me around my house and has gotten me out of trouble with some violent people on a few occasions."

"Is he looking for money?" Yisa asked.

"No. I've offered him some on a few occasions. He takes nothing, not even food."

They walked into the adjoining lab. One student stood by a large table, a screwdriver in his hand as he worked on various electronic parts around him. A second student sat across the room. On a table in front of him were two large glass panels wired to four colored cells.

"What are they doing?" Yisa asked.

"These are the university's brightest physics and engineering students," Oladele said proudly. "I tasked them with making solar panels and converters for household use. We've been blessed with all this sunlight—might as well use it."

"I don't understand."

"They are attempting to make solar panels that we can fit onto the roofs of houses here, and converters that can transform the harnessed energy for household use.[1] The next phase, if they are successful, would be to somehow sync each converter with our national power grid. This could save a lot of money and also give our people a steady source of power for their homes. I plan on presenting their creations to the government. Hopefully, we'll be able to get a grant that would allow us to produce them on a larger scale. Imagine if we could build manufacturing plants for our finished product? Imagine if we could have research labs manned by our own people to continuously enhance our inventions? It would

---

[1] Solar power inverters are part of solar electrical systems that help convert the sun's energy into usable power. In its raw form, solar energy is harnessed as DC (direct current) electricity. An inverter converts that DC voltage to the AC (alternating current) format that most people use in their homes.

create jobs for a lot of people and stimulate our economy. Innovation is the key to our economic development, Yisa."

They moved on, going up some stairs and into Oladele's small office, the mysterious man sitting outside the door on the ground.

"You have quite an interesting setup here at this school," Yisa said as they sat on hard mahogany chairs.

"Yes," Oladele said proudly. "I am trying to create good leaders for tomorrow. Our students come from all over, so I'm blessed with the opportunity."

"You seem very driven."

"Weren't you at one point?" Oladele asked.

"Yes, but things have changed."

"The only thing that's changed from the '50s to now is the stage of the war, not the war itself."

"What do you mean?" Yisa asked.

"It is now a war of ideas, not guns, my brother."

Yisa stood up and walked over to a window that overlooked the lab. He could see both students working hard on their innovations. Yisa wanted his son to do the same when he grew to be their age.

"I created the Imamba with my partners for what I thought were noble reasons," Yisa said. "I'm the one who actually came up with the idea for the brotherhood. I just wanted to make a difference."

"Your intentions were noble, I'm sure, but you didn't think it through. You chose to go with the way of the gun, and now you have created a monster that you cannot control."

Yisa digested Oladele's words, playing them over and over again in his mind. His friend was right. Nothing good had come from the Imamba, and he was a part of the mess.

"It seems that I've become a victim of my own design," Yisa said bleakly.

"We all have the freedom of choice, Yisa. You can always walk away from that dirty business," Oladele replied.

"It's not that simple, my brother. It's not something you just walk away from."

Oladele leaned back in his chair and sighed deeply. Then he stood up and joined his friend by the window. "Look at those two boys out there," Oladele said. "I know you had to have imagined Tosin as a young man in their shoes."

"I did."

"Imagine if Tosin could be responsible for creating some groundbreaking invention, or coming up with a unique theory or something that changes the world as we know it, and be celebrated and endorsed here at home for it. Wouldn't that make you proud?" Oladele asked with a smile.

"That would be nice, and I would be proud."

"That's what this is all about, Yisa," Oladele said. "A good idea is more important than money or anything money can buy. I have dedicated my life to creating an environment here in Nigeria in which good ideas can flourish."

He moved closer to Yisa and placed a hand on the mercenary's shoulder. "Come home, my brother. Your wife needs her husband, your son needs his father, and I need my friend," Oladele said as a tear rolled down Yisa's cheek. "We could do so many great things here! Your expertise as a fighter would be so valuable!"

"How so?" Yisa asked. "I am skilled at destroying lives, nothing more."

"Not true. You have knowledge of weapons, guns, that sort of thing. We could take that knowledge and use it to improve some of the weapons for our military. There are also a lot of young men who would benefit from hearing your stories."

Yisa nodded and turned back to the window. Then he shook his head. "You have always been a good dreamer, Oladele, but we have to also consider reality. There are a lot of powerful people who benefit from original ideas being suppressed. There are a lot of people who like the system as it is, and would pay good money to have anyone who upsets the balance killed. Men with good ideas are sometimes considered dangerous. I have killed a few such good men myself. Why would I want such a fate for my son?"

Oladele smiled at the question. "When Tosin grows up, he will choose his destiny. That is out of your hands. Until then, you must show him how to be a man. My program," Oladele said, pointing to the lab, "is in the business of making men."

Yisa looked at Oladele intently. His words sounded good. Motivational, in fact. But there would be so many hurdles to cross. Cultural barriers, government support, ostracism, death threats. This would take some serious consideration.

"You should be careful. Men who follow the path you're on are sometimes marked for death," Yisa said.

"When and how I die is not that important. What matters is how I live."

Yisa nodded and resumed observing through the window. The student working on the battery cells stopped his work and walked out of the room. The other student called after him in Igbo and asked him to pick up a snack from wherever he was headed.

"I will give your proposal some serious thought," Yisa said. "I have to go to London in a few days; from there we shall see."

"Don't think too long," Oladele replied as he walked over to his desk and retrieved two glasses and a green bottle from a drawer. "Come, let's take our minds off of serious affairs and have some palm wine."

Both men spent the rest of their time getting tipsy over palm wine in Oladele's little office, putting aside the reality of what was to come.

c h o s e n

THE WHITE WITCH

Northwestern Tanzania. Africa. 1990.

The sun was scorching hot, leaving the land parched and begging for moisture. Four men made their way toward a village in Northwestern Tanzania: Eteka, Cyrus, the hulking Mokin, and a man called Ibrahim. All four dripped sweat as they made their way up a steep hill, cutting through some grassland with grass up to their shoulders. They were making their way to a small village on top of the hill, where the White Witch supposedly resided. The mercenaries were posing as tourists, wearing Hawaiian shirts and carrying backpacks concealing AK-47s, some rope, semi-automatic handguns, and knives.

As they trekked in the intense heat, Eteka looked over at Cyrus. He had been the closest thing to a friend Eteka had ever had, but Cyrus had never spoken about his wife and child. When they'd left the beach village in Zanzibar, Cyrus had acted like nothing had ever happened, remaining silent for the rest of the journey. Eteka was never one to force a conversation. Perhaps there were some aspects of his life that Cyrus wanted to keep to himself, and Eteka could respect that.

Cyrus wiped down a handgun as they walked along, mumbling something indecipherable under his breath. This was not the first time they had made such an arduous trek.

It was a hot day in June, 1982. Eteka and a group of young men on a training mission walked across the sands in the Nubian Desert. They had been walking for the past six hours without stopping, with large sacks of sand on their backs under the merciless sun. Fatigue crept into their muscles and their throats were parched. The men were chained together at the waist in pairs of two and wore black trousers with no shirts or shoes. A man's voice came through large speakers mounted on a truck that followed them, yelling instructions and taunts at the group of men in Arabic. Eteka's shoulders ached from the heavy sack of sand on them, a feeling made worse by the scorching sand against his tired feet. Four Bedouin[1] men on horseback came up behind the group and lashed at them with long whips. The whip sent a searing-hot streak of pain through Eteka's side as he struggled to hold up the sack of sand. Another hour passed before Eteka noticed a Jeep approaching. As it got closer, he could see Oga, Omega, and a driver sitting in the car. The Jeep pulled up next to their procession, and its occupants got out.

---

[1] "Bedouin" is Arabic for desert dweller.

"These are a nice bunch," Omega said to Oga as the Bedouin's whip continued to punish the young men.

"They are the toughest ones I could find. They will make fine additions to our brotherhood," Oga replied as he took off his sunglasses to examine the young men.

"Good. We will have to test them mentally as well."

"They have been through many mental trials already," Oga replied as they walked to keep up with the group. The sand crunched under their feet, their footprints washed away by small wind gusts that churned the dunes.

"Don't worry, I have my own special tests for each one them."

Oga signaled at the Bedouin on the horse, who blew into a horn, a signal for the men to stop. The young fighters dropped their sacks and fell to the ground. Young boys jumped out of the truck and brought the men lambskins of water, bread, and habuck herbs. The exhausted men ate heartily as Omega and Oga stood before them.

"Each one of you has made a unique journey to come here," Oga said. They stopped eating and focused their attention on Oga. "Some of you have come from the eastern regions, like Uganda and Somalia, while others I found in places like Liberia and Congo. Even places like Mali and Tunisia have representatives in your ranks. Some of you may even have fought on opposing sides and are now here chained together." The men looked at each other, curious to learn where the others were from.

"It matters not where you came from or who you were," Oga continued. "You left all that behind when you joined us. Each of you has specific skill sets and a certain level of character, which is why you were selected to join the brotherhood. You are Imamba now, and you must forget your past." Oga's eyes rested on Eteka for a moment.

"What does Imamba stand for?" one of the young men asked.

"The Imamba is a Zulu word for a very dangerous snake. In English it's called the black mamba. The black mamba is widely considered one of the most deadly and venomous snakes in the world," Oga replied as he lit up a cigarette.

"To be one of us, you must think like the black mamba," Oga explained. "It is secretive, cunning, fast, and accurate. You must make no compromises and be prepared to shed your old skin. It is self-sufficient and does not provoke confrontation, but it will strike if it is provoked—and when it strikes, it always kills. Today, we, the Imamba, are the most powerful organization in all of Africa, yet few people know of our existence, and that is the way we want it. Our reach is growing, and we're getting clients from all over the world. You will soon see that working with us far outweighs the life you knew before."

Oga walked closer to the men as the skies darkened. Evening was coming, and the Bedouins began to erect their tents for the night.

"You are all chained together in pairs. Get to know the man you're chained to, as he is your brother. The next time you train here in the desert, you will be chained to someone else. He will be your brother as well. You will have a unique experience with each brother. We will camp here for the night and resume our trek tomorrow," Oga finished, heading back to the Jeep.

Eteka looked at the man he was chained to. He seemed to be the same age, a slim dark man in good shape. A scar ran across his right eye and his dark skin was drenched with sweat. On his right pinkie finger was an unpolished gold ring. He looked at Eteka without saying a word as the men around them talked, finding common dialects.

"I am Eteka."

"I am Cyrus," the man replied with a distinct Liberian accent.

There was another brief silence while they finished their meal. The sky was dark now, and their escorts had lit little fires around their tents on the desert sands.

"Where did you come from?" Eteka asked.

"Oga found me in Liberia. You?"

"Nigeria."

"Nigerians…" Cyrus replied with a chuckle.

"What's so funny?"

"Nothing. I used to have a Nigerian friend. He always addressed me as 'my friend.' I found it very funny whenever he said it with his accent."

"I see."

"I've always liked the way Nigerians think," Cyrus said, grinning. "You guys are very determined, no matter what it is you're doing."

"You think so?"

"I do. I'm sure we will get along just fine."

"Time will tell."

The sunset brought with it cooler temperatures. A scorpion ran by Cyrus's feet and he picked it up by its tail, holding it up to his face as it thrashed back and forth.

"You know what that thing can do to you if it stings you?" Eteka asked, watching Cyrus study the arachnid.

The scorpion swiped at his finger and drew a little blood with its pincers. Cyrus chuckled. "What's life without a little risk, eh?" he asked, and with that he put the scorpion in his mouth and crushed it between his teeth. Cyrus ate the scorpion with no hesitation, then threw the tail into the sand. "Now, I have conquered the scorpion and have his power," Cyrus said, wiping his mouth.

"I guess you have," replied Eteka, rolling his eyes at the display.

They watched the other Imamba talk and rest on the desert sands. The sky was clear and beautiful, and a shooting star streaked across the horizon. The scent of roasted meat and baked bread wafted from the nearby campfires.

"What I would give for some real food," Cyrus said, licking his lips.

"We can't, we are training. Our minds must be sharp."

"You're right."

Cyrus rubbed the chain linking their waists and looked at Eteka.

"So, we are brothers now it seems," Cyrus said to Eteka as he held up the chain.

"It would seem that way," replied Eteka, noncommittal.

"Then let us make a pact as brothers," Cyrus continued, extending his hand. "Next to our Imamba Brotherhood, nothing will be as important as our bond. Agreed?"

"Yes, why not," Eteka replied, and they both shook hands.

They spent the rest of the evening cracking jokes and laughing with the other young men. It was a good night, as neither of them had ever had a brother before.

Eteka focused on the present as they reached the top of the hill. The village shimmered in the heat from this distance.

"It's about time," Cyrus said. His body was drenched with sweat. "You said you have a contact in the village, right? Your contact knows how to get to this White Witch?" he asked Ibrahim.

"Yes. We have to move carefully. I hear that she has plenty of guards," Ibrahim replied in a thick Arabic accent.

Cyrus put his backpack down for a second, withdrawing a pistol from the back of his shorts, cocking it, and replacing it underneath his clothes.

"Brother, I suggest we lay low until we find out exactly who she is. What d'you think?" Cyrus asked Eteka.

"I agree. Let's hang around the village until the time is right."

They resumed their trek and arrived at the village 15 minutes later. The village was set up in a communal style, with the huts arranged in a circle around a large open space. There was hardly any grass on the ground, just sand and dust. The village had a well and a wooden structure that appeared to be a makeshift telephone and telegram center. Women walked around with small children tied to their backs in makeshift slings, and a few mysterious men wore long robes and Fulani hats, holding long, polished sticks and sitting by a grey hut.

The townspeople stared as the Imamba approached and a few children gathered around them, tugging at their unfamiliar clothes. Eteka studied each smiling face, looking for anyone that bore any resemblance to a witch or a white woman. As they stood in the center of the growing crowd, a short man with a mischievous grin walked over to them. He was dressed in a long-sleeved shirt and wool trousers that were hiked up all the way to his chest; Eteka wondered how comfortable the man could be in the heat. The man walked over to Ibrahim and both men exchanged a few words in

Bemba.[1] After a few laughs, Ibrahim introduced the man to the two mercenaries.

"This is Chimba. He will be taking us to the White Witch," Ibrahim said, patting the man on the back.

"Does he speak English?" Cyrus asked.

"No. He tells me that your people are paying some locals to help you in case a lot of fighting starts. They are nearby, ready to move when it's time to strike," Ibrahim replied.

"We don't need help, we just need to know where this White Witch is so we can finish this mission," Cyrus replied tersely.

"Okay," Ibrahim said. "Chimba told the villagers that you are visiting here from England, so they prepared a place for all of you to sleep when night falls. Early tomorrow before anybody wakes up is the best time to attack the White Witch—her guards will be sleeping."

Cyrus faced Eteka, who was scrutinizing the mysterious men with the Fulani hats.

"Are those the guards?" Eteka asked.

"Yes."

"And I assume the White Witch is in there?" Eteka asked, nodding at the grey hut that stood out a ways from the others. Ibrahim asked Chimba and the latter nodded repeatedly.

"Well, then, I guess we wait. Do they have any food prepared for us? I'm hungry," Eteka said.

---

[1] Bemba is spoken by the Bemba people in Zambia. It is also widely used throughout Tanzania.

Ibrahim exchanged a few more words with Chimba and turned back to Eteka. "They have made some ugali[1] for you to eat. Chimba will take you to your beds where you will sleep. He will also bring you the food," Ibrahim said as he walked away.

"And where are you going?" Eteka asked with a raised eyebrow.

"To get the local boys ready for our move tomorrow morning," Ibrahim replied. "Don't worry, Chimba will take care of you. We will meet up tomorrow morning at 5 a.m. on the dot, by that tree," Ibrahim continued as he pointed to a large mahogany tree in the compound. "Just be ready."

The mercenaries watched Ibrahim disappear into the distance, dust licking at his heels, before Chimba ushered them into a brown hut not too far away. As they walked along, Eteka felt the White Witch's guards staring at him. There was a menacing presence about them, and Eteka felt a twinge of unease—something was wrong.

When night fell, the village was very dark save for the few small fires burning around the village. Faint conversations between people in their huts and the few people sitting outside could be heard, along with crickets singing their love songs. Eteka rested by the entrance to the hut, looking at the moon in the clear night sky. Everything seemed peaceful. Eteka sighed as he stretched his back and yawned. He would have given anything to have had Arewa there

---

[1] Ugali is a dish that is native to East Africa. It is made from ground-up maize that is cooked and usually shaped into a ball. It is normally eaten by hand and served with an assortment of stews and sauces.

with him. She would have been a welcome addition to the peaceful night he was enjoying. With that thought, he fell asleep.

It was just before 5 a.m. when Eteka received a rough shove on the shoulder from Cyrus. He quickly retrieved his AK-47, handgun, and knife. The mercenaries slipped wordlessly from their hut, clad in camouflage fatigues, and made their way to the mahogany tree that Ibrahim had pointed out. The White Witch's guards were absent from the front of her hut, and Ibrahim and his men were nowhere to be found.

"He's supposed to be here," Cyrus whispered to Eteka.

"Perhaps we should wait," Eteka replied.

"Light will be here soon. We do not have much time."

"Let's give them another ten minutes."

They crouched behind the tree and waited, keeping their eyes on the grey hut. Eventually, even the crickets stopped chirping.

"Something doesn't feel right," Eteka whispered.

"I agree. It's been about ten minutes, I say we make a move. We don't need Ibrahim and his goons to handle our business," Cyrus replied.

"Okay. I'll go in through the main entrance of the hut, you two flank me on both sides. Make sure the guards aren't hiding around in the brush," Eteka said.

The men nodded and moved to their positions. Eteka's adrenaline spiked as he cautiously approached the entrance to the grey hut. He tightened his grip on the assault rifle as he stopped a few paces from the entrance. Mokin and Cyrus circled around the hut, weapons drawn, and quietly disappeared into the darkness. Eteka took a deep breath, stepping into the grey hut. There was no light inside—the hut was empty.

Something isn't right, he thought to himself.

Suddenly, two gunshots went off outside, followed by three more.

Eteka spun around and headed for the door, but he didn't get far. A figure appeared out of the darkness and hit him with so much force that he flew headfirst into a wall. He picked himself up off the floor, slightly dazed, and swung his weapon in the direction of his assailant, firing indiscriminately. The bullets poured from the muzzle in rapid succession, lighting up the room like ignited fireworks and leaving a trail of holes through the ceiling and walls.

Eteka, his heart beating fast, reloaded his gun and readjusted his eyes to the dark room, but his attacker had disappeared. Outside, he could hear a few gunshots and a struggle, and he began to back out of the room. Something moved on his right, and Eteka spun to defend himself just as another hidden attacker came at him from the left. He felt a sharp pain in his head as it met with a hard object, dropping him to the ground. Then, two dark figures loomed over him, and he made out the outline of two men wearing robes and large hats.

It was the men in the Fulani hats.

His eyes still blurry, Eteka could see the hand of one of the men reaching for his collar while the other kicked his gun out of reach. He rolled away from both men and stumbled to his feet. The guards circled around him, confusing his vision in the dark room. Eteka pulled out his dagger, but it was knocked out of his hand. A guard lunged at Eteka with a clenched fist, which Eteka dodged and countered with a sharp elbow to the man's face. Eteka would bet that he'd broken the man's jaw as his attacker let out a howl and crumbled to the ground. The second guard slammed his stick down on Eteka's shin, causing him to stagger. The guard tried to tackle the Imamba, but as he grabbed Eteka, the mercenary reversed his hold, picked him up off his feet, and slammed him headfirst into the clay wall to the side, sending both men through it.

Pain coursed through Eteka's body, especially his injured leg, but at least the guard had been knocked out. He got to his feet, dust and clay in his eyes. Eteka knew he needed a weapon in his hand, and fast. Before going back through the large hole in the side of the hut, he spotted Mokin carrying a wounded Cyrus, moving through a field and firing rounds at a large mob of men in hot pursuit led by Chimba, their one-time guide.

What's going on? Eteka thought as he stepped back into the bullet-riddled hut and frantically looked around for his gun. The first guard was still holding his mouth and moaning in pain, lying on top of Eteka's AK. Eteka shoved him off his weapon, cocked it, and limped back outside, searching for the other Imamba.

The mob had disappeared, along with Cyrus and Mokin. The early morning was once again quiet, with only the occasional sound of gunshots in the distance. Eteka tried to follow the mob, but his leg hurt too much. He leaned on one knee in the center of the open compound, using his assault rifle for support.

This can't be happening... we've been set up, he thought to himself as he looked up at the full moon disappearing toward the horizon.

Eteka spotted another of the White Witch's guards emerging from the brush. The guard came up to Eteka, silhouetted in the moonlight like a glowing ghost. This particular man was different from the others. He had beads tied to the side of his robe, and his Fulani hat seemed to be taller than the others. His long robe blew softly in the cool breeze, and as he stood he reached into his garments and pulled out two long sticks.

Not another one, Eteka thought to himself, rising to his feet. The villagers were watching from the windows of the huts surrounding him, and it was obvious that they had been given some warning of the ambush. Eteka kept his eyes on the man, his fingers tightening around the trigger of his gun. As Eteka whipped up his assault rifle, the guard quickly moved within striking distance of Eteka, using one of the sticks in his hand to knock the assault rifle out of the way and striking Eteka's injured leg with the other.

Eteka grunted in pain as he was forced to one knee. The guard spun and kicked Eteka squarely in his chest, knocking him to the ground and taking all the wind out of him. Pain throbbed through him as he lay faceup on the ground, looking at the stars in the clear night sky. He panted for a few seconds as the guard circled around him, sticks drawn. Eteka slowly got to his feet. The guard allowed him to stand as he continued to circle. Eteka tried to see his face, but his wide-brimmed Fulani hat was tilted downward and covered everything but his lips. The mercenary crouched and clenched his fists, hoping to shrug off the pain. The villagers watching grew in number, some even coming out of their huts to watch the fight. The guard circled Eteka one last time, then stopped in front of him.

"Let's finish this," Eteka said, limping toward the man.

The guard said nothing, standing still as Eteka approached. Eteka stayed alert, watching for any sudden movements. His eyes darted from the man's head to his arms, but the man remained eerily still. Eteka hesitated for a moment, feinted to his left, led with a right jab, and threw a ferocious left hook at the man's face. The guard fell for the feint, and Eteka's jab caught his jaw, rocking his head backward. As the follow-up left hook reached the guard's face, he blocked it with the stick in his right hand and took two steps back. Eteka got back in a guarded position and waited. Eteka wished he could use his legs to fight as well, but he could hardly stand. He took a painful step toward the man, feinted to his right, and threw another left hook at the man's face, but this time the guard was ready. He blocked the left hook and delivered a sharp kick to Eteka's already damaged shin, which dropped the mercenary to his knees. As Eteka grabbed his right shin in excruciating pain, he looked up to see the side of the man's stick approaching his head with alarming speed. He briefly wondered whether Cyrus and Mokin had escaped.

†

He was back in Detroit. The little girl with whom he had exchanged glances held the body of the man he'd helped kill in her frail arms. She looked up at him, tears of blood streaming down her face. She was wearing Eteka's necklace.

Eteka shouted as he woke with a start. He was lying in a bed with a bandage wrapped around his head and a second one encircling his shin. He tried to make sense of his surroundings while his mind did its best to suppress the aches and pains he felt throughout his body.

He was in a hut. Bright sunlight poured into the room from one of the windows and he could hear children playing outside. There were two chairs by the hut's entrance, one of which was occupied by the guard that had incapacitated him. The guard was looking out of the hut's entrance, and the beads that were on his side earlier were now in his hand. The man was smiling beneath the large hat he wore as he watched the children playing outside.

I have to get out of here.

Opposite his bed, his AK-47 was propped up against the wall. Eteka tried to sit up, but he couldn't move.

"Stop trying to move, you can't," an elderly, soft female voice said from behind him in a thick East African accent. He tried to turn his head in her direction, but he couldn't seem to do that either.

"My herbs have temporarily paralyzed your limbs, but they will speed the healing process," the woman said.

He heard footsteps, and a little woman with a large, fluffy white afro was suddenly sitting next to the guard near the entrance. She was dressed in a simple gathered skirt and faded blouse, and her hair was tied back in a colorful hair band. Her back was to Eteka and he couldn't see her face. The skin on her hands was as white as the hair on her head. She watched the children playing outside and chuckled every so often.

"Children are so peaceful and innocent. They do not worry or fight over the petty things we do. They are pure and truly beautiful, wouldn't you say?" she said as she turned around and smiled at Eteka, her teeth as perfect as those of a much younger woman. Her small eyes were mischievous, hooded by folds of aging skin. Eteka was taken aback by her classically African features, which which were framed in pale, unpigmented skin. She appeared to be an albino—at first he wondered if he'd stumbled across a Caucasian woman living with the villagers.

"Unfortunately, for many reasons, some of which are still mysteries to us, these children will grow up and, in some way or another, evil will become a part of them. You were like these children at one point in your life, young man. Do you know that?" she asked, her eyes resting on Eteka's necklace.

Eteka kept his eyes on her but said nothing. He wasn't sure if she was playing mind games with him.

"Don't worry, I'm not playing mind games with you," she said with a grin as she turned her attention back to the children playing in the courtyard. Eteka's eyes grew huge.

How did she know what I was thinking?

"All your questions will be answered in time, whether here or on your journey to come," she said without looking at him. "For now, you need to rest."

Strangely, Eteka did not feel threatened in any way. As he watched the woman and her guard, his eyelids began to flutter and he soon fell asleep.

When Eteka awoke, he was alone in the hut. Night had fallen, and it was dark all around. He could hear voices outside talking in Bemba and Swahili. He could also see flickering light from fires through the windows in the hut. He wiggled his toes and, realizing he could move, slowly sat up. The bandages were still on his head and shin. Most of the pain was gone, but the healing herbs had left Eteka feeling groggy and weak, so he sat up slowly and looked around. His camouflage fatigues had been replaced with a loose-fitting white kanzu[1] and his head had been shaved smooth. Eteka looked around the hut for his weapon, but that was gone as well. Realizing there was nothing left for him to do in the hut, he cautiously stepped outside into the compound.

It was a cool night, with a soft breeze blowing. There was no trace of the fierce battle from the night before. The village was immaculate; they had even repaired the wall of the grey hut that Eteka and the guard had crashed through. A few fires with men

---

[1] A kanzu is a robe/tunic worn by men in East Africa.

sitting around them lay scattered across the village. He had to find that old woman who had spoken to him earlier.

Eteka spotted the mysterious man with the beads sitting with some of his friends by a tree a few yards away. Sensing he was the leader of their group, Eteka made his way across the compound in the guard's direction. A few men looked at him as he passed, but no one got up or seemed threatened by his emergence from the hut.

As Eteka approached the guard, he passed the man whose jaw he had broken. A bandage had been wrapped around his head to support the broken bones in his face. The head guard lifted his hand and pointed at a small hut as Eteka approached. A soft light flickered from within, possibly from an oil lamp or candle. Eteka nodded at the man and walked toward the hut, the stones and pebbles on the ground pinching his bare feet. Unlike the other huts in the village, this one had a door that was shut. Eteka stepped up to the entrance and knocked lightly on the door.

"Yes?" asked the familiar voice of the old woman.

"Hello, uh, this is the man you treated earlier."

Footsteps sounded and the door was opened by yet another guard. It was the first time Eteka had seen any of them up close, and he noticed that this one had tribal marks on his face and white pupils. The guard ushered Eteka into the room and stepped outside without saying a word.

The albino woman sat smiling in a chair while a young woman washed her white hair. On the ground close by sat a little girl reading a storybook. There was an empty chair next to the old woman and a table with a lit kerosene lamp. In another corner of the room, a mosquito coil had been lit, the scented smoke making abstract symbols in the dimly lit room.

"Sit down."

Eteka took a seat in the empty chair. He still felt a bit groggy, and the whole experience up until this point had seemed somewhat surreal.

"My, my, my, look how big you've grown."

"Excuse me?"

"You've turned out to be a fine young man," she replied, the big smile still on her face.

"What do you mean? We've never met before."

"You were very young the last time we spoke, so I do not expect you to remember. Nonetheless, I am not supposed to explain your past to you, so forget about that. How do you feel?" she asked.

"Fine," Eteka responded, still confused.

"Good."

"Why can't you explain my past to me? Who, then, will explain it?" Eteka asked.

"I am one of a few Chosen Ones on your path. The next of the Chosen you meet will fill you in on the missing chapters of your life."

Eteka leaned back, thinking, but nothing she said made sense to him. Movement from the guard outside caught Eteka's attention.

"What's with the men in the hats?" he asked.

"What about them?" she asked with a girlish giggle.

"Who are they? I have never seen their kind before."

"They are called Custodis. They are an ancient line of warriors, also called Guardians. They protect us, the Chosen, wherever we may be. I don't know much else about them, they just show up and follow me around," she replied as she swatted a fly away from her face.

"It is because you have a good spirit, Auntie. The Master sent them to take care of you," the woman washing the old woman's hair said with a laugh.

"Yes, the Master did send them, although I don't know if it's because I am a good person. There are some things I am meant to do, and the Custodis protect me while I do them. When it's my time to go, I will go," the White Witch replied.

Eteka was still trying to piece together what was going on. "Who are you?" he asked.

"I am the woman you came here to kill," the old woman replied with a smile.

The White Witch.

"I prefer Auntie Bayinna. That's what my people call me," she replied in her uncanny way that answered his unspoken questions. Eteka looked at her curiously. She continued to smile at him without saying a word, her head tilted back to enjoy the young woman's ministrations. Her eyes rested on Eteka's necklace.

"Did you think about what I said to you earlier?"

"What did you say to me?"

THE WHITE WITCH

"I AM THE WOMAN YOU CAME HERE TO KILL."

ETEKA
RISE OF THE IMAMBA

"That you were once an innocent child," she replied. "A good boy with a future."

"No, no, I didn't."

"That is what your parents wished for you, back in Nigeria." Eteka sat up, his heart racing. How did this woman know about his parents? Was this a trick?

"What do you know about my parents?" Eteka asked defensively. The guard posted outside sprang into the hut at Eteka's tense tone, but Bayinna shook her head and waved for the guard to leave. The young woman shook out a worn towel and began drying Bayinna's hair.

"The details of your past will be answered in good time. And, with my gifts, I knew you and your friends would be sent to kill me long before you did, Eteka."

"So, you really are a witch," stated Eteka, palms sweating.

Bayinna laughed. "No, I'm not a witch and I do not practice black magic, or any other kind of magic, for that matter. People call me a witch because they have no explanation for my gifts. But, neither the Master nor spirits operate within the boundaries of logic."

Eteka's head felt light from the effects of the herbs in his system. The dim light in the room combined with the smell from the burning mosquito coil and Bayinna's abstract words only added to his delirium.

"What do you want with me?" Eteka asked.

"We will get into that tomorrow. For now, you should get some rest—you must be very weak. Tomorrow, when you have recovered, we will talk and then you may leave. My men will take you to Dodoma.[1] From there, you'll have to find your own way."

Eteka stood up and made his way to the door, each step bringing sharp pains and a heavy feeling to his head. He needed to lie down and get his thoughts together.

"Thank you," he said, stepping outside. Eteka slowly limped back to his hut. Chimba and Ibrahim were sitting together around one of the fires, and they nodded at Eteka as he passed. Even though Bayinna had been hospitable, Chimba and Ibrahim had misled the Imamba and almost gotten Eteka killed. Reaching the hut, Eteka reclined on the bed and let out a long sigh, enjoying the feeling of the light sheets and wool-stuffed mattress. He turned his head to the

---

[1] Dodoma is the capital of Tanzania.

left and looked out one of the hut's windows before he fell into a deep sleep.

Eteka woke up to bright sunlight hitting him in the face. He sat up in bed, stretched, yawned, and rubbed his eyes. The bandages on his head and shin had been removed. The swelling on his head had vanished, and his shin felt as good as new. His camouflage fatigues had been cleaned and folded on a chair near his bed. As he picked up his clothes, a little girl with big, beautiful brown eyes and a bright smile entered the hut. She waved at Eteka and motioned for him to follow.

The girl held Eteka's callused hand and led him out to the village, which was filled with children playing, racing around the compound after each other. They made their way down a path that led around the village, through some vegetation, and up to a beautiful river. Some women washing their clothes in the water exchanged waves with the little girl. The girl led Eteka by the hand along the river to a secluded pond surrounded by a few low-hanging acacia trees. A towel, a bar of soap, two chewing sticks,[1] lime to serve as deodorant, and some sandals were laid out on a large stone near the water.

"Baf," the little girl said proudly as she gestured grandly at the pond.

"Baf? Oh, bath!" Eteka replied with a smile. "Thank you."

---

[1] Chewing sticks have been an important part of oral healthcare for thousands of years by people in Africa, the Middle East, and Asia. The sticks are taken from the barks of specific trees and cut into small strips. These are then chewed on the end until they become frayed, and the frayed ends are then used to "scrub" the teeth.

The girl giggled and then turned and ran, leaving Eteka alone. He looked around and took a deep breath, enjoying the scenery around him as he stripped off his clothes and got into the water. The pond was clear and cool, and the sunlight provided him with a natural mirror on the water. He felt peaceful and refreshed for the first time since leaving Arewa in Nigeria. A toddler sat by the edge of the pond, having wandered away from his hardworking mother, and was sticking grass in his mouth as he curiously watched the scarred fighter wash. Eteka enjoyed the child's company and found himself smiling by the time the child's mother came and dragged him away, scolding.

Eteka cleaned himself thoroughly, donned his freshly washed clothes, and began the trek back to his hut. Halfway there, he noticed a lagoon off another path where some fishermen stood in the water with open nets. He could see what looked like dolphins gliding in and out of the water as they drove in schools of fish, which the fishermen trapped in their nets. Eteka had never seen humans interact in such a way with animals before, and he sat on the grass for some time, keenly watching the fishermen laugh amongst themselves as they worked with their maritime friends to bring in nets full of fish.

Finally, Eteka made his way back to his hut, where a young boy brought him a bowl of porridge, fresh baked bread, and a cup of herbal tea, which Eteka heartily enjoyed. When he was done eating, Eteka stepped out into the village. Some older children had set up a makeshift soccer pitch and were in the middle of a game, playing in the sand with their thickly callused bare feet. He walked past some women cooking and laughing, who giggled when he walked by as he looked for Bayinna or her guards.

Quickly, he came to the edge of the village. Men herding cattle on a hillside waved at him as he walked by. The little girl that had served as his guide earlier walked with one of the herdsmen, who appeared to be her father. She waved at Eteka and pointed to a house in the distance surrounded by the men with Fulani hats.

As he approached the house, the guards made a path for him. Eteka walked between the men, who stood with their heads bowed so he could not see their faces. Their leader, the guard with the beads, stood closest to the entrance. With his head still bowed, the guard opened the door of the house and ushered Eteka inside. Eteka stepped in to find Auntie Bayinna hugging another albino woman who was crying hysterically, screaming words in a dialect Eteka didn't recognize. Auntie Bayinna looked up and nodded at Eteka while she rocked the woman back and forth in her arms, making gentle, soothing sounds to the distraught woman. Two young girls stepped into the room and helped the crying woman away. Auntie Bayinna shook her head sadly and stood up, grief etched on her face.

"Let's take a walk, there is something I want to show you," Auntie Bayinna said.

They left the house and walked through a maize field to a cluster of houses, escorted by Bayinna's guards. Bizarrely, everyone in this area seemed to be an albino—men, women, children, babies—and many of them were missing limbs, and had bruises or cuts and scrapes on their skin. Others cowered in fear or rocked back and forth, obvious victims of psychological trauma. Ibrahim and Chimba were amongst the villagers, attending to some of the people.

"Do you know why you were sent here, Eteka?" Auntie Bayinna asked.

Eteka took a moment to think, glancing at a little boy with a blank expression on his face. He was missing the lower half of one of his thin arms—a crude amputation that looked as though it had been performed by a heavy machete or meat cleaver.

"There are evil people in this region who buy and sell body parts for black magic and the dark arts," Bayinna began. "Albinos especially are in high demand. These evil men harm and often kill people like those you see in front of you for their wicked schemes. They deal with other evil men—not just here, but also abroad. Around here, my men and I are the only things that stand between those killers and these innocent souls," Auntie Bayinna said as she cupped the little boy's face in her hands.

"Do you have a heart, Eteka? Do you have feelings?" Bayinna asked.

"I... I do what I'm told."

"That is your training, but you are meant to be a leader. To lead, you must first learn to serve, and you have been doing that. Now, it is time to move to the next stage of who you really are."

"I don't understand."

"The men you work for and the men who commit these atrocities do not understand what love is. But you do—you know love. You know it very well," Bayinna said, fixing him with her intense gaze.

Arewa.

"Yes, her. The Master purposefully put her on your path. She has shown you how much more you can be, that you have feelings. You are capable of caring for others."

Eteka looked from Bayinna to the little boy. Somehow, he knew she was right. Arewa had awoken a part of his heart that he had thought to be long dead.

"Who is this Master you keep referring to?"

"You're not ready to know about the Master, as there is still much you have to overcome within yourself," she answered as she kissed the boy on his forehead.

"They sent you to kill me because I protect these people, not because I'm evil," Auntie Bayinna continued. "You should assess the motives of the people you work for."

Eteka tried to digest what she was saying. Was she trying to trick him? Was she trying to get him not to trust Omega and his fellow Imamba? And Oga, the man who had raised him from childhood? What if this was a mind game she was playing with him? His emotions, long stifled, were overwhelming.

"Why should I believe these things you say? Why should I trust you?" Eteka asked.

"After everything you have heard and seen here, I think the better question to ask is why shouldn't you believe me? I gain nothing from deceiving you, my child."

I have to leave, he thought to himself.

"I can understand your confusion," Bayinna said sympathetically. "This is a lot for one day. My job is to plant the seed; the next Chosen One you meet will water the plant. As promised, one of my men will drop you off at Dodoma, and from there you will be able to find transportation to your people in Johannesburg," she said, laying a comforting hand on his arm.

"Thank you."

"You're welcome. It's been such a joy seeing you again," she said with a smile as she opened her arms for a hug.

Eteka looked at her, hesitated, and then carefully held her small, frail frame in his arms. As much as he felt strange around her, he also felt a connection that he had never felt before. It was as if they had indeed met before. The Custodis led Eteka out to a barren road and into the cab of an old pickup truck, while Auntie Bayinna and a few children stood by the roadside to say their goodbyes.

"You are a good boy, Eteka—you just don't know it. The events that have transpired in your life, the pain you have suffered, have happened for a much bigger purpose. You are not who you think you are, remember that. There is a lot of good you can do in this world; your perspective just needs to be enlightened."

Bayinna waved as the leader of Custodis started the truck, and Eteka watched them shrink into the distance as the truck set off for Dodoma.

☨

They arrived in Dodoma a few hours later. For the whole ride, a range of emotions had run through Eteka. What had Auntie Bayinna meant by her last words? What did she mean, he was not who he thought he was? How did she know what he had been through? Her words, as confusing as they were, felt good to him. In fact, in his whole life, no one had ever said anything that had felt so good, so full of hope. It was a strange feeling.

Dodoma was very different from the rural area they had just left. The streets were filled with sweaty pedestrians and car smoke. Although nowhere near as populated as Lagos or Abuja, the city was busy nonetheless. The two men drove through Dodoma's dusty streets to a bus terminal. Taxi drivers stood by the entrance of the bus stop and yelled at incoming visitors to hop in their cars, while a few women sat by the roadside selling fried fish and other snacks to the hungry travelers. As the pickup truck pulled to a stop, Eteka looked over at the Custodis warrior. The man reached into his robe and handed Eteka a package wrapped in a brown cloth containing money and one of Eteka's many fake passports.

"The money should be enough to pay for your trip to Johannesburg," the Custodi warrior said in Yoruba—Eteka's childhood language. He had a flat, smoky voice, and he smiled at the look of shock on Eteka's face at hearing the familiar language. "You will have to catch a bus from here to Dar es Salaam. The trip will take about four hours. Then, from Dar es Salaam, you can catch a plane to Johannesburg," the man finished with a nod.

The man did not turn toward Eteka as he spoke, and it became evident that the conversation was over. The Imamba opened the door and stepped out.

"Thanks for the ride," Eteka said through the dusty truck window. In return, the Custodi warrior gave a slight smile, put the truck in gear, and sped off, leaving behind a trail of dust. Eteka watched him leave, then turned and made his way into the bus terminal.

EVERYTHING HAS A PRICE

Brixton, London. England. 1990.

It was a cool Monday afternoon. Arewa had just left a lunch date she had set up with three of her girlfriends at a trendy Ethiopian restaurant in Brixton, London. It was a typical meetup among girlfriends, with the usual talk of work, clothes, and men over a tasty meal of Awaze Tibs.[1] One of her friends had entertained them with stories of how she'd reported a married man to the human resources department at her job for sexual harassment. Her story made the other girls at the table exchange covert looks, as only a few weeks earlier this same girl had not been able to stop talking about the same married man, and how she had the biggest crush on him but felt he never reciprocated her flirtatious advances or gave her the attention she desired. They ignored the discrepancy.

Hearing her friend talk made Arewa appreciate the fact that she did not have to deal with much drama at work.

---

[1] Awaze Tibs is a tasty Ethiopian stew typically made with spiced lamb.

She walked by the Brixton Academy, where long lines had gathered to watch the set being built for a music video shoot later that day. It was a grey, misty afternoon, the sun hidden behind clouds. She entered the Brixton subway station and followed an Indian couple onto her train.

The couple reminded Arewa of Eteka. She missed his strong arms, laying her head down on his chest, holding his broad shoulders, and enjoying his calmness. She missed the way they talked when he stayed with her. She missed the sense of security she felt around him, and the time they spent making love was unforgettable. Was he thinking about her as she was about him? Did he have other women he was seeing on his travels? Sure, they hadn't established anything official between them, but she had to admit, in a strange way she felt they were together. As she got off the train, she realized she couldn't wait to see Eteka again. She missed him.

Arewa hailed a cab to take her to Mr. Adeboyo's mansion. The mood had definitely changed since her brother, Fallal, had made his grand announcement about leaving Mr. Adeboyo. Her boss had not engaged in much casual conversation with her since that day. She felt she was walking on eggshells and worried that Mr. Adeboyo would fire her unexpectedly. After finishing her cigarette, she walked into the mansion, said hello to Mr. Adeboyo's butler, and headed to her office. As she sat in front of her Mac, she looked at the picture of her and Fallal with a heartfelt sigh, then set to work on her large stack of folders. Almost immediately, her phone rang. It was Mr. Adeboyo.

"Hello, sir?"

"Stop by my office when you have a moment," Mr. Adeboyo said.

"Sure. Is everything okay?"

"Yes. Just stop by." And with that, he hung up.

Arewa looked at the phone. His answers had been short, very unlike his usual gregarious self. Was he calling her to fire her? Steeling herself for the worst, she left the files and walked down the long hallway toward Mr. Adeboyo's office. A bodyguard stood by the door and let Arewa into the room. Inside, Mr. Adeboyo stood looking out the window, holding a piece of paper in one hand and absentmindedly tugging on his suspenders with the other.

"Hello, sir. You wanted to see me?"

"Please, sit down."

Arewa took a seat by Mr. Adeboyo's large oak desk. He walked over and stood beside her, placing the piece of paper on the desk so she could see it. She could smell his expensive cologne and what had to be whiskey on his breath.

"That's your brother's freedom, right there," Mr. Adeboyo said, softly knocking on the desk as he said so. "If your brother wants to leave, that's fine, but he will have to sign this document."

"Oh, what is it?" Arewa asked.

"It's an opt-out contract," Mr. Adeboyo replied. "I managed and am responsible for a lot of the work your brother has done to date, so I'm entitled to my share of his royalties. This document just protects us both."

"I see," Arewa said as she picked up the paper and glanced over it. "Have you shown this to Fallal yet?"

"No. I thought you should see it first."

"I think it best if Fallal and a lawyer look over it before he signs anything, don't you?" Arewa asked, trying to remain deferential. Mr. Adeboyo grinned and walked to his seat.

"Do whatever you think is best, but I need that signed by next week," he replied as he sat down and pulled a bottle of whiskey and two shot glasses from a drawer. "Drink?"

"No, thank you, sir."

Mr. Adeboyo nodded and poured himself a glass.

"Lawyers," Mr. Adeboyo said resignedly. "After all I've done for you and your brother, you still cannot trust me. You two would be living in some fucked-up, two-cow village somewhere in

Nigeria if not for me. I brought you both out of the slums and gave you lives many people can only dream of," he said as he gulped down the first shot of whiskey and poured another glass.

"Your little brother is making a big mistake," Mr. Adeboyo continued. "He doesn't have the business acumen that I have. These new friends of his will bleed him dry, believe me. The world out there is not as nice as you may think."

"Fallal is his own man," Arewa said nervously, "and I have to let him make his own decisions, sir. We are very grateful for everything you've done for us."

Mr. Adeboyo gulped down his second glass and poured himself another. He looked straight into Arewa's eyes and she looked away.

"And how about me and you, eh, Arewa? You've always given me a tough time, even after all we've been through."

"What do you mean, sir?" she hesitantly asked.

He stood up and walked over to her side of the table, leaving his glass of whiskey. "You know I've had my eye on you all these years, yet you always play hard to get. Even with your brother leaving I've still kept you on board," he said as he placed his hand on her shoulder. His hand felt heavy and she cringed at his touch.

"I don't understand. I do good work for you, don't I? What do you mean I play hard to get?"

"You think I give you things because I just like you?" Adeboyo chuckled. "Tell me how many accountants out there have their bosses pay them good money, give them good housing, and take care of their family? Huh?"

Arewa shrugged his hand off and stood up, backing away. "I'm not sleeping with you, sir."

"I know about all your little boyfriends," Mr. Adeboyo continued, taking a step toward her. "None of them have given you what I have, yet you sleep with them. Why?"

"What I do in my personal time is none of your business!"

"It is my business," Mr. Adeboyo said as he grabbed her arm. "You live on my property, and anything that happens on my property is my business."

"Please, get your hand off me!" Arewa said, attempting to remove his grip from around her arm, but he was too strong.

"You people take and take, but never think of giving back," Adeboyo said, his voice raising. "You and your brother think you can use me 'til the time is right and then leave? You're fucking crazy if you think you can. Everything has a price, and it's time I got paid."

He threw her against the oak table, lifting her legs as she did her best to push him away.

371

"Please, sir, you're drunk. It doesn't have to be like this," she pleaded, but he ignored her as he shoved her legs apart and began to lick her neck.

"Just relax, you'll like this."

He continued to lick her neck, the alcohol on his breath making her stomach churn. This couldn't be happening. She never thought she would be the victim of rape, but now here she was, with a man almost twice her size on top of her, licking her neck. She felt his hands squeezing her breasts, then he began to fumble toward her waistline. She frantically grabbed his hand.

"Please, sir. Don't do this. Please."

"I said just relax. I'm good in bed, you'll see," he replied. He continued to lick her neck as he unbuttoned her pants.

Arewa knew she had to act now. She awkwardly kneed him in his groin, causing him to roll off her. She immediately made for the door, but Adeboyo held onto her arm again. He pulled her back and slapped her violently, knocking her down. A trickle of blood began to flow from her nose.

"Why the fuck did you do that?" Mr. Adeboyo asked in an angry tone as he regained himself and stood over her. He knelt down on top of her and slapped her again and again until his face was replaced by white flashes and her ears began to ring, blurring out sound.

MR. ADEBOYO

"EVERYTHING HAS A PRICE,
AND IT'S TIME I GOT PAID."

E T E K A
RISE OF THE IMAMBA

"I was trying to make this a nice experience for you, but now you've pissed me off," Mr. Adeboyo said as he began to take off her pants again. She tried to stop him, twisting and struggling, but he held her down by her throat. His now-blurry face began to fade around the edges as she gasped for breath.

"I told you everything has a price. You don't fuck with me and think you can get away with it," he said as he yanked down her pants, revealing her bare skin. She watched in horror as he began to unzip his trousers. This could not happen.

With all her strength, Arewa reached up and dug her nails as deep as she could into his face. She clawed at him with all her might, her nails sinking into his skin. He howled in pain, tightening his grip on her neck and shaking her. The bodyguard barged into the room upon hearing the commotion and stopped in shock at what he saw.

Seizing her moment, Arewa shoved Mr. Adeboyo off and crawled desperately toward the door, her clothes half off and missing a shoe.

Adrenaline pumping, Arewa pushed the stunned bodyguard at Mr. Adeboyo as she got to her feet, kicking off her remaining shoe. She ran down the hallway to her office as she pulled up her pants and quickly buttoned her shirt, shaking violently with her sobs. She stopped only long enough to grab her purse before darting outside, running past the surprised butler. Running past the gate, as fast and as far away from Mr. Adeboyo's mansion as possible, Arewa replayed the assault over and over in her mind. She hailed a cab when she felt she was a safe distance away from the mansion to take her back to her apartment. In the back seat, she wept like she had never wept before.

MOB ACTION

Ojuelegba, Surulere. Lagos. Africa. 1990.

The taxi pulled into Ojuelegba on the Lagos mainland after about an hour due to heavy traffic. It was a little past 10 p.m. when Isatou was dropped off in a busy commercial area filled with people, cars, and noise. Tired, Isatou got out of the taxi and looked around. Ojuelegba was not far from Mushin, and she knew China and his gang could have spies in this area on the lookout for her. She had to get out of town, but she had no money. Thankfully, she had a friend who lived in this area, a former prostitute called Nneka who now made her living assisting a car parts trader. Nneka had always been like a sister to Isatou: the two girls had started working for PantiRaida around the same time, and they both came from educated backgrounds. Isatou's plan was to lay low at Nneka's place for the night and then get out of town the next day. She made her way through the crowded transit section, receiving curious stares due to her formal appearance, toward a residential part of the area. After 15 minutes of walking, Isatou walked up to an old shanty building.

Some women were sitting on some benches by the front door, and they eyed Isatou up and down as she knocked. It was Nneka who answered.

"Isatou? What are you doing here at this time? And where did you get that dress?" Nneka asked as they hugged.

"A beg, make we talk inside,[1]" Isatou replied in pidgin, hurriedly moving past Nneka and stepping into the house. Nneka, confused, closed the door and followed.

"Weitin dey do you?[2]"

"My sister, some wahala come catch me.[3]"

"Weitin happen?[4]"

Isatou sat down on a couch in Nneka's living room.

"I don't even know where to start… some days ago, PantiRaida asked me to do some work for Tribal and his boys."

"Tribal? The armed robber?" Nneka asked.

"Yes. And by the way, Tribal is not even the boss of that gang. Do you remember Olabanji, the gari seller?"

"The fine guy? Yeah, I remember him."

---

[1] "Please, let's talk inside."
[2] "What's wrong with you?"
[3] "My sister, I'm in big trouble."
[4] "What happened?"

"He's the boss of that gang. And his criminal name is China."

"Whaaaatttt?" Nneka exclaimed in disbelief. "Are you sure?"

"My sister, I no dey lie you. Masef I shock.[1] They asked me to go to Ikoyi and seduce some rich guy. They put me in some hotel and wanted me to bring the guy up to my room, where Tribal and his boys were waiting."

Nneka sat down next to Isatou. This was the last thing she'd expected to hear tonight.

"Did you do it?"

"No, that's why I'm here."

"You should have asked them to use another girl."

"I did," Isatou said, "but they didn't listen."

Nneka stood up and paced about the room, shaking her head.

"Isatou, trouble dey call you, oh! Wey kind wahala be dis?[2]"

"I had nowhere else to go, that's why I came here. Please, all my money and things are at my place in Mushin. If you can lend me some small money, just so I can travel to Ibadan tomorrow, it will help. Please, Nneka," Isatou pleaded.

---

[1] "My sister, I'm not lying to you. I was also shocked."
[2] "Isatou, you are looking for trouble! What kind of trouble/madness is this?"

Nneka stopped pacing and faced her friend.

"You want to go to Ibadan and see Oluko? Oluko is a good man, don't bring this trouble to him," Nneka said. "Go somewhere far, like Onitsha or even up north, and just lay low for some time."

"But I don't know anybody in Onitsha, or in the north."

"Then try another country. The point is, you have to get out of this area, because Tribal and his gang are going to come looking for you. You can stay here tonight, but tomorrow early in the morning you'll have to leave. This is all I have," Nneka said, reaching for her purse and handing Isatou a few naira. "It should be enough to get you out of Lagos, but after that you're on your own."

"Thanks," Isatou said, taking the money. She then began to cry, and Nneka sat back down to comfort her.

"What did I do? Why does God like punishing me? I didn't ask for any of this," Isatou said between sobs.

"Shhh, everything will be fine," Nneka said, hugging her friend. "Sometimes, trouble comes when it's time to start something new."

$$\dagger$$

The next day, Isatou left Nneka's house at 8 a.m. and headed back to the Ojuelegba station. She wore a scarf to hide her hair, an old dress of Nneka's, and face-concealing sunglasses. She decided to heed Nneka's advice and catch a bus headed to Onitsha. Isatou nervously looked around as she walked along the streets. The area was already crowded and bustling with commercial activity. She walked over to a ticket booth and bought a ticket for the next bus to Onitsha, leaving in two hours. Two hours was a long time. China's gang members could be anywhere, and she was a sitting target out in the open. She had to lay low. She nervously picked a seat next to some mechanics fixing a broken-down danfo as she waited for her bus to arrive.

An hour passed. Then suddenly, through all the daily commotion, an unmistakable scream could be heard. It was a call that any true Nigerian from the streets would recognize—the sound of someone who had just been robbed.

"OLE! OLE! THIS BOY STOLE MY MONEY!" a middle-aged woman screamed as she pointed at a startled young boy, who looked no older than 12. Almost instantaneously, an angry mob formed and surrounded the poor boy. Most of the crowd was made up of young, hardened men, bored and looking for an excuse for violence. Armed with clenched fists, some carried wooden clubs and others glass bottles, and a few even displayed knives as the crowd closed in on the hapless boy. Isatou had seen this form of justice before, a long time ago when she was a little girl being driven around town by Oladele in Ibadan. Back then, an angry mob had lynched an alleged thief. Oladele had tried to stop it, but the mob had not listened to him, and they killed the suspect. The scene back then had made her sick to her stomach, especially when Oladele had explained the senselessness of it all. Her uncle had told her that community justice in the form of lynchings had been a part of life within cultures the world over, including places like America and England. In fact, her uncle had told her that there was a time when simply being black could get you lynched by whites in America. The cultures in these places had morally evolved from ignorance to a better appreciation of human life in recent years. But it seemed that here in Ojuelegba's streets, this evolution had not taken place.

Isatou watched as the young boy received slaps and punches to his face and stomach from these grown men. The boy pleaded his innocence, with blood dripping from his busted lip.

"A beg, I didn't steal anything. This is my own money that my mama gave me to buy some eggs. Please, I didn't steal anything," the boy cried as he was yanked by his collar. He was given a few hard slaps for his words.

"He is lying. It is my money he stole," the woman claimed, malice in her eyes.

"LET US ROAST HIM!" yelled a large bald man holding a club. He seemed to be one of the leaders of the mob.

"YES!" the rest of the crowd shouted ecstatically.

Isatou spotted two men carrying tire irons approaching the crowd. If no one did anything, the poor boy would be cooked alive.

This was street justice in its truest form unfolding before her, and it made her stomach turn. Something in her urged her to get up, to save the little boy. But her fear also whispered in her ear. It was a big crowd, made up of mostly rowdy men looking for blood. If she stood up for the boy, they could hurt her as well—women were easy targets. They could even kill her if she annoyed them enough. But she could feel Oladele staring at her. He would have jumped in and defended the boy. That is what he did, her Uncle Oladele, always standing up for the less fortunate with no regard for his own safety. Was she of the same mold?

The same large man leading the mob raised his club to smash the little boy's face in. But before he could do so, the club was knocked out of his hand from behind. He turned around to face Isatou, who had moved between him and the young boy.

"You craze?[1]" the man growled at Isatou. His look frightened her, but she kept her poise.

"Weitin dis boy do you?[2] He said he did not steal anything."

The crowd gathered around the large man and the smaller Isatou. Many of the men had raised their weapons, and were ready to kill.

"They said he stole that woman's money, so he must die."

"Who is 'they'?" Isatou asked.

---

[1] "You crazy?"
[2] "What has this boy done to you?"

"That woman said he is a thief, that he stole money. So we will roast him," the large man said, pointing to the woman who'd started the commotion.

"And how do you know she herself is not lying?" Isatou asked, looking at the woman.

"Look, move, or we will roast you, too," the large man replied gruffly as he bent down to grab his club. But Isatou kicked it away.

"This boy is not even half your size, yet you've come with all your friends, grown men like you, to kill this small boy. As a man, don't you respect yourself? Of all the enemies we have to fight, why do you want to kill this small boy? Don't you know children like him are Nigeria's future? Nigeria has enough problems—we don't need you adding to them. Let the police come and handle this boy," Isatou said, maintaining her stance. She smiled to herself. She'd never imagined in her wildest dreams that she would ever sound so much like her uncle.

The mob had suddenly grown quiet, as its leader had become deflated by Isatou's words. The little boy, trembling in fear, latched onto Isatou like white on rice. The large man gave Isatou a bloodcurdling glare, and for a moment Isatou thought she would be killed along with the boy. But then a squad car full of policemen pulled up, and the angry mob began to disperse. Last of all was the large angry man, who looked at Isatou meaningfully before picking up his club and walking off.

Isatou watched the mob scatter, and then turned around to face the young boy.

"Thank you, madam," the battered young boy said.

"Are you okay?" she asked, cupping the boy's face in her hands as two policemen walked up.

"I'm fine, madam. Thank you," the boy said again as he was escorted away by the police officers. She stood in place, right were the big mob had been. She had single-handedly diffused what could have been a lynching, and saved the young boy's life. She felt lighthearted, and a good feeling that she could not explain filled her with joy. If only her uncle could have been here to see this; he would have been proud.

"You did well," an old, raspy voice said from behind her. She turned around to find a short, elderly man smiling at her. He looked well past 70 years of age, or maybe even past 80, which was ancient around here. He was dressed in rags, and his smile revealed a few missing and rotten teeth. An unkempt afro topped his head, and a messy grey beard covered much of his face. The old man held himself upright with a short wooden stick, and he reeked of alcohol. At first glance, Isatou took him for a beggar.

"Thank you. But I don't have any money for you."

"That's okay, I don't want your money," the old man replied, stepping up to Isatou. "You did very well today."

"Thanks," Isatou said again. For a beggar, he spoke surprisingly good English.

"You took a risk stepping up to the mob like that. Most would have just watched from the sidelines. It shows there is a leader in you," the old man continued.

"Thanks," Isatou said, as she turned to walk away.

"What I find even more interesting is that you knew exactly who to confront in order to control the mob," the old man said. Isatou stopped in her tracks and turned around.

"You went straight to the source of the problem, instinctively," the old man said, pointing his wooden stick at the large man who led the mob, who was now laughing with some of his friends by a pair of vehicles in the distance.

"Thanks," Isatou said, keeping her eyes on the large man. "I was just trying to do the right thing. I don't know why some people don't value human life."

"People hear what they want to hear, and see what they want to see," the old man replied. "Most of these people are not going anywhere, and have nothing meaningful to do. They are zombies seeking purpose in an environment that cannot provide it. This is why, at the slightest public commotion, they quickly form their mobs, like a swarm of flies seeking shit on which to settle. But I did not come here to give a lecture. I came here to look for you."

His last words made Isatou turn and face him with a raised eyebrow.

"What do you mean, you came here to look for me?"

The old man grinned and took a step closer.

"You do not have to go to Onitsha. I can take you to a far better place."

Isatou took a step back, her heart racing. Who was this strange old man? How did he know about her plans to go to Onitsha? Had Nneka gone and told people about her predicament? Was China watching her, and did he send the old man to taunt her?

"How did you know I was going to Onitsha?" Isatou asked, looking around frantically. "Did China send you here?" The old man laughed at her questions.

"I'm tempted to feel insulted that you associate me with petty criminals," the old man answered.

"They are not petty. Everyone here knows China's gang."

"My dear, the man has his house, the ringleader his posse, the king his kingdom, and the emperor his empire. Not everyone can be a leader, and we must all decide on which level we shall function. Your armed robber friends are nothing but breadcrumbs to us. Your mind is what we are most concerned with."

"Who are you?" Isatou asked.

The old man coughed a few times before responding.

"I go by many names. Some call me Kweku, others call me Anansi, yet still others call me Spider. It all depends on to whom I am speaking and in what form I choose to reveal myself," the old man answered.

"And what shall I call you?"

"You can call me Spider," he replied. "It's a pleasure to finally meet you, Isatou. I've been watching you for a long time."

"How do you know my name?"

"If you come with me, I shall show you many mysteries, and unlock a power you never knew existed within you. You won't have to worry about your little armed robber friends anymore."

At that moment, the call for Isatou's bus to Onitsha came in, and the bus began to load. She looked at the bus, then back at the old man.

"You're not trying to trick me, are you? Are you a member of some cult or something? Because I'm not interested in that nonsense."

"Come with me, and you will see for yourself who we are."

"And who are you, exactly? You keep on saying 'we.'"

"You may call us the Order of Zerachiel."

NOBLE DECISIONS

Knightsbridge, London. England. 1967.

Oga and Yisa were sitting in a dimly lit restaurant at a plush hotel in Knightsbridge, London. Yisa was dressed in an all-white suit, drumming his fingers on a table; Oga was dressed in black, smoking a cigarette. A bottle of white wine sat between them, along with a pack of Newports.

"Ah, they just took Muhammad Ali's title from him… shame," Oga said, reading out loud from his newspaper.

"What? Really? Why?" asked Yisa absently.

"Are you serious?" Oga asked. "My brother, where have you been? Anyway, what time did Omega say he would meet us?"

"Right about now. There he is, right on time." Yisa replied, looking down the hallway. Omega casually approached, laughing heartily with a white man.

"Hello, boys," Omega greeted when he reached them. "This is Mr. Grange, an American businessman."

"Nice to meet you, Mr. Grange," Oga said, shaking his hand.

"Nice to meet you as well," Mr. Grange replied. He was handsome and tall, possibly in his late twenties or early thirties, with jet-black hair and a striking, white-toothed smile. Yisa nodded in greeting.

"I was just discussing Ghana with Mr. Grange," Omega said. "He may have some more projects for you in that region in the future."

"Yes, we have heard nothing but good things about the way you boys handle business, so we have you in mind," Mr. Grange added.

"Great, we look forward to it," Oga replied.

"Well, I have to dash off, but it was nice meeting you both," Mr. Grange said. "I'm sure we'll meet again soon."

"Okay. We'll speak soon," Omega said.

Mr. Grange walked off and Omega joined the Imamba at their table. "So, how was the trip?" Omega asked, pouring himself a glass of white wine.

"Successful. We had no problems," Oga answered.

"Good. As usual, your money has been deposited in your accounts. How is your son, Yisa?" Omega asked.

"He is well, thank you."

"Excellent. He must have been thrilled to see you."

"He was."

Omega smiled and looked back at Oga. "And Proditor, he turned out to be reliable?"

"Yes," Oga replied.

"Great. Well, while you guys were having fun in Nigeria, I was making some moves here with our oyimbo[1] friends," Omega said. "There's a big, fat contract on a hit in South Africa. That leader they imprisoned has some connections here in London who are very influential. Many people with large pockets want them taken out," Omega said as he looked at the menu.

"Go on," Oga said, as Yisa looked on.

Omega smiled privately as they received strange, annoyed looks from passing hotel guests. Just then, the hotel manager walked over to the three men with a large, placating smile on his face.

"Hello, gentlemen. Would you mind moving to the rear of the restaurant? Some of our prominent guests are complaining of a disturbance," the manager said. He was white, in his mid to late forties, and overweight, with a squint in his left eye and a pompous handlebar moustache. All three men looked at each other in surprise.

"A disturbance? We are not disturbing anybody, just discussing business," Omega said with a cordial smile.

"Our patrons are a bit disturbed by your, er, kind, sitting here. These are prime seats."

"Our 'kind?'" Oga jumped in, bristling.

"Yes, sir. If you could kindly move to the rear of the restaurant, we will settle this whole issue. I'll take ten percent off of your final bill to make up for the inconvenience of having to move to a new table."

---

[1] Nigerian vernacular: word commonly used to refer to Europeans, but also applicable to anyone not in tune with Nigerian/African culture.

Omega retrieved a cigar from his shirt pocket, clipped it, and lit it up. He blew a line of smoke at the manager, who was still standing with a rictus of a smile on his face.

"You go back and tell your patrons to enjoy the view. We are not going anywhere."

"Sir, please do not cause trouble. We need you and your friends to move to the rear of the restaurant," the manager repeated, this time with a frown on his face. "You're disturbing our other patrons."

"You should walk away, my friend," Omega warned. "Perhaps you think I do not know of the Race Relations Act.[1] We are allowed to sit where we choose, free of harassment. Now, I suggest you leave," Omega said calmly as he blew cigar smoke into the manager's face. The manager grimaced, looked at all three men, and then walked away to explain matters to his other guests.

"I should kill him," Oga said. "Make the world a better place."

"No," Omega said brusquely. "He came here to taunt us, to try and get a reaction out of us. Don't fall for his bait; it's not worth our time. Let's get back to business. As you both probably know, Willem Botha is getting sworn in next month as South Africa's new president, and some of his apartheid friends want this man, Abel Tony, dead," Omega said, holding up a picture of the proposed kill. He was a middle-aged black man with a medium build, rough-looking hands, and a small, styled afro.

---

[1] The Race Relations Act of 1965 was the first act/legislation in England to outlaw racial discrimination.

"Who is this Abel Tony, and why is he significant?" Oga asked.

"He's one of the many sponsors of the black guerrilla groups in South Africa. He's been supplying weapons and supplies to the ANC.[1] And he lives here, in London," Omega replied. "You guys will head over to his apartment in Brixton and sort him out. Make a statement when you do; our clients want this to be messy, to send a message to anyone else who might consider this man's path."

"That can be arranged," Oga said, smiling cruelly as he lit up another cigarette.

Yisa shifted in his chair uncomfortably. "The ANC cause in South Africa is a just one. Why are we siding with the enemy and bidding to kill our own people?" Yisa asked. This type of mission only served to confirm his decision to leave the Imamba. Omega and Oga exchanged annoyed looks.

"Here we go with Yisa and his noble talk again. What makes you think the ANC's cause is just? They are killers, just like us," Oga said.

"They are freedom fighters, fighting for a just cause," Yisa said. "What we're planning to do is not right."

Omega sat up in his chair, the smoke from his cigar casting a haze over the Imamba.

"We keep on going back to this," Omega said. "We are where the money is, Yisa. We are not taking sides. Stop being so

---

[1] The African National Congress (ANC) is the ruling political party in South Africa today, and played a key role in South Africa's fight for independence.

emotional and start thinking like a businessman—not a Sunday school teacher!"

"I can be a businessman and still have ethics, still have morals," Yisa said vehemently. "I don't have to kill my own people."

"You are Nigerian, Yisa. These are South Africans," Omega shot back.

"And we are all African. This is not what I envisioned the brotherhood becoming. We've become a cancer to our own kind."

Omega fixed Yisa with an impatient stare while a grinning Oga looked between them. They were calling attention to themselves with their tense conversation and thick smoke. Passing guests looked at the Imamba nervously as they went about their business.

"I see that being with your son did nothing to clear your head, eh?" Omega said as he sat up.

"Leave my son out of this. I just don't like the direction this organization is taking," Yisa replied.

"What are you really saying?" Oga asked.

"I think I've said what I'm really saying."

"Enough!" Omega growled, slamming a heavy hand on the table. "There's no time for these games—we have clients waiting. Tomorrow, you two will head to Brixton and sort out this Abel Tony. We'll meet the next day at 2 p.m. to discuss the hit and our next move. We can sort you out then, Yisa. Here is the folder with the guy's address and the location of our safe house in Brixton. Your weapons are already there," Omega said, tossing an orange folder onto the table.

Oga took another drag from his cigarette and picked up the folder.

"We'll take him out. See you soon," Oga said. He stood and walked out of the restaurant. Yisa sat for a moment longer, his eyes locked on Omega, and then he too abruptly stood up and followed.

✝

Yisa drove a blue Fiat 125 through driving, pelleted rain toward a flat in the Loughborough Estates in Brixton, Southwest London. Oga cocked his weapon, a Colt Python revolver made with blackened steel, from the passenger seat as they listened to a football match on the radio. They pulled up a block away from their destination and then proceeded to walk toward the 16-story housing complex. Outside the entrance, the pleasant aroma of fried plantains and Jamaican ox tails wafted from a takeout restaurant on the ground floor.

"Wait here a minute, I want to place an order. You want anything?" Oga asked.

"No, thanks," Yisa responded, shaking his head. He couldn't believe that Oga had an appetite when they were here to torture and kill a man. His own stomach was clenched like a fist at the thought of what was to come.

Yisa looked around warily while Oga placed his order. This was a perfectly average neighborhood. A few boys played a game of football in the rain between some cars, and a barbershop across the street was full of Brits chatting while their barbers lathered them up with foam. After a few minutes, Oga returned.

"Okay, let's go."

Their target lived in an apartment on the sixth floor. Oga took the lead, his weapon in his hands as he listened through the apartment door. The muffled sounds of a conversation in Swahili between two men could be heard from beyond the door.

"They're inside," Oga whispered. "Get ready."

Yisa nodded, reaching for his silencer. Oga shook his head.

"We're here to make a statement; no silencers. Loud and messy."

Oga leaned back and violently kicked the door open. Two men were sitting at a table eating lunch as the Imamba swarmed into the apartment. The men sat in shock as both Imamba stood before them with weapons drawn. One of the men reached for a pistol hiding under a newspaper, and Oga shot him dead.

The shot reverberated through the apartment building, and all murmurs of life from outside stopped. The man slumped over in his chair, a bullet hole in his chest. His friend shouted something in Swahili and wrapped his arms around his dead friend as Oga and Yisa towered over him. The remaining man was their target, Abel Tony. The man turned toward the mercenaries, tears in his eyes.

"What do you want? If it is money you want, you could have just asked. There was no need to shoot him," Abel Tony said.

"We don't want your money... we're here for you," Oga replied with a smirk.

"Daddy? Please come, I'm scared. There's big sounds," cried a little girl, no older than four, as she walked into the room. She froze when she saw both mercenaries standing in front of her father, guns drawn.

"Bonnie, no! Go back to your room!" Abel Tony screamed as Oga walked up to the little girl. Oga stood in front of her and smiled as her eyes widened fearfully.

"Things just got interesting," Oga said as he grabbed the little girl's arm and dragged her over to her father. She began to cry from the rough treatment, and Abel Tony clutched her close, shielding her with his own body.

"Why are you doing this?" Abel Tony asked, his voice strained.

"Seems like you've pissed off the wrong people back in your home country, Abel," Oga replied, waving his gun in their faces. Yisa was uneasy at the whole situation. Tosin was not much older than Bonnie, yet here he was, letting Oga terrorize both her and her father. It did not feel right.

"I don't understand. You work for the government in South Africa?" Abel Tony asked.

"Shut up. Yisa, care to do the honors?" Oga asked, signaling for Yisa to shoot both father and daughter. Yisa looked at Abel Tony as he clung to his little girl, and then at Bonnie, her eyes wide with uncomprehending fear. She was a pretty little girl with even chocolate skin, large brown eyes, and curly hair in little pigtails, complete with yellow and pink ribbons. He could imagine Bonnie playing with Tosin, walking with him to school. There was enough innocent blood on his hands. No. He wouldn't do it. He couldn't do it…

"No."

"What's that?" Oga asked, looking at Yisa.

"No. I won't do it this time."

Time seemed to stop as Oga lowered his weapon and looked at Yisa with a raised eyebrow.

"Yisa, kill these people so we can torch the place and be on our way. The police will be here soon."

"No, I won't do it."

Oga looked at Yisa with a half-confused, half-angry look. "What's gotten into you, Yisa? We can talk about your concerns once we've finished the job, but for now, let's be professionals."

"No," Yisa replied, relieved to have finally taken the plunge. "I'm not killing anyone anymore. Particularly not a child."

Oga studied Yisa angrily. Police sirens were approaching and they were running out of time.

"You're a fool, Yisa," Oga hissed. "Fine, I'll shoot them myself."

"No, you won't," Yisa replied, stepping in front of Oga's weapon.

"Get out of the way!"

"You'll have to shoot me first."

"Yisa, I said get out of the way!"

"We're not killing these people, Oga. For once, we'll do the right thing."

"You can do whatever you want—I wash my hands of you and your problems—but I have a job to do. Now, get out of the way!" Oga said again, cocking his weapon.

"No."

As the two mercenaries argued, Abel Tony stealthily reached under the table, retrieving a sawed-off shotgun. He carefully brought it to his front, pointing it at Yisa's back.

"MOVE!" Oga yelled, shoving Yisa to the side and firing with precision. He shot four times, catching Abel Tony squarely in the chest.

Tony slumped to the floor as his little girl let out a loud, bloodcurdling scream. Anyone with a soul would know there had been trouble.

"We have to kill the girl," Oga said. "She knows our faces."

"Leave the girl alone. She has nothing to do with the hit. The police will be here any minute. We have to go."

"No," Oga replied, his eyes on the little girl. "Our orders were to leave a message. She must die," Oga said as he pointed his weapon at Bonnie's face. Yisa swiped the gun away.

"Not today, brother. We must go, the police are here."

Sure enough, four MPS[1] squad cars had pulled into the parking lot, and seven officers scrambled out and rushed into the

---

[1] MPS: Metropolitan Police Service (commonly known as MET Police). The MPS is one of the two branches of the London police force; the other is the City of London Police.

building with weapons drawn. Oga gave Yisa a disgusted look and regarded Bonnie. She had avoided the bullets that had killed her father, but not the spray of blood. Her yellow dress was spattered up and down with blood, and her eyes stared at the two men, almost catatonic with fear.

"You've gone mad, Yisa. Fine, the child will live for now."

"Good," Yisa snapped. "We have no time. Let's use the window and scale to an apartment on a lower floor. We can leave through the back entrance."

After locking the front door, both Imamba moved past the little girl, who was cradling her father's head in her lap, and climbed out of the window in the apartment's kitchen. They effortlessly climbed down three floors. As they reached the third floor, they could hear the police banging on Abel Tony's main entrance. Oga and Yisa climbed through an open window into a startled elderly woman's apartment. The woman almost had a heart attack as both mercenaries walked by her and out into the interior hallway, Oga winking at her as she clutched her chest. A minute later they were outside, calmly strolling past police squad cars and a small crowd that had gathered at the scene. They walked around the crowd and Oga picked up his takeout from the Jamaican restaurant. Back in their car, they sped off, heading toward their safe house.

"You crossed the line, Yisa," Oga said, placing his gun in his lap and putting a piece of ox tail in his mouth.

"The line was crossed a long time ago," Yisa replied, shifting the car into a higher gear and turning onto a road leading to Central London. Oga shook his head as he continued to eat.

EXPENDABLE

East London, South Africa. Africa. 1990.

Oga and Omega sat alone in a large conference room on the top floor of a five-star hotel in East London, South Africa on a cool Thursday evening. Glass windows offered a breathtaking view of Gonubie Beach. They were playing a game of oware[1] at a polished oak table. Omega grinned as his thick fingers moved the beads on his turn, trying to outsmart Oga. It had been a few weeks since they'd sent Cyrus, Mokin, and Eteka to Tanzania to kill the White Witch. The first two had returned a few days ago, but they had received no word from Eteka.

"How are Cyrus and Mokin doing?" Omega asked.

"They are fine. Cyrus took a bullet in his side. He's healing quickly and should be up and about in no time," Oga replied as he counted the beads left on the oware board.

"And Mokin?"

"Nothing can stop Mokin," Oga chuckled. "He's fine."

---

[1] Oware, a game similar to mancala, is commonly played in Ghana, throughout West Africa, and in the Caribbean.

"Good. Still no word from Eteka, eh?"

Oga sighed and looked up. "No, no word."

"Do you think he's dead?"

"Eteka is a skilled fighter and a survivor. I'm sure he's fine and on his way here."

"Shame about Tanzania. Somehow, our intelligence was intercepted. The White Witch knew we were coming. Do you think we have a rat?" Omega asked.

"No, our brotherhood is secure, and the Tanzanian contacts only knew of the mission when our boys arrived there, not before. Something else interfered."

"Something else?" Omega frowned at the board. "Like what?"

"I have no idea, but I will find out."

Omega played his turn and took a big puff from his cigar. An evil grin materialized on his chubby face. "Let's move on. Three new assignments have come up, one long-term while the other two need to be taken care of on short notice. They are all very lucrative."

"Start with the long-term one," Oga said. "What's that about?"

"Some friends of mine want us to help them pick up a package for them from Wales."

"Pick up a package? That's it? Why can't they pick it up themselves?" Oga asked.

"They don't want to get too close to the mission, and the job will require professionals."

"I see. Must be a special package," Oga said as he moved his beads.

"It is."

"Do you have a plan?"

"Not yet," Omega replied as he slid the folder from Supreme across the table to Oga.

"Who is this?" Oga asked, looking the picture of the man inside the folder.

"He's the package."

Oga looked through the folder while Omega played his turn. "Who are your friends that want this man?" Oga asked.

"I can't tell you that," Omega said shortly. "All you have to worry about is the cash coming in, and they've already given us one million American dollars as advance money."

Oga lit up a cigarette and studied Omega, who had his eyes on the oware board. Omega had always shared who their clients were before.

"Who did you have in mind to send up to Wales for this assignment?" Oga asked.

"I want Dark Moon to take care of this for us. This needs a woman's touch."

"Dark Moon... yes, she's a good choice," Oga replied. "What were the other two assignments?"

"There's one in New York and another in Nigeria, both of them very worthwhile."

"Go on," Oga said.

"Our old friend, Mr. Adeboyo, is offering good money for us to take care of an activist singer," Omega said. "Something about an unpaid debt the guy owes him. The singer's supposed to be performing in New York in a few weeks."

"If this singer has a high profile, he could attract unwanted attention to our group."

"Not if the job is done properly, which is why the right people have to take care of this."

"The right people," Oga said, playing his round, "would be Cyrus and Eteka. Or Deathstalker and Eteka. Stealth would be paramount."

"No, we'll have Cyrus and Mokin take care of him. Deathstalker is taking care of a contract in America, and when he's done I want him to stay there for some time, in case we get more business in that region. Besides, I thought Eteka would be a perfect fit for the last contract."

"What's the last contract?" Oga asked.

"Money has been put on the table to take out another activist in Nigeria," Omega said with a ghoulish smile. "It was an open bid that I worked hard to get. He's been leading a few peaceful protests against some oil companies there. Some pretty influential people want him taken out, and want it done quietly. This is where we come in. I want Eteka to handle this one."

Omega placed a folder on the table. He opened it and shoved a picture toward Oga.

Oga studied the photo. It was a man about his age standing with some children. His clothes were old and worn, and he had grey hair in his thinning beard.

"This man looks familiar, although I cannot place where I know him from."

"He's a pretty popular activist in Nigeria. You may have seen his face in a newspaper or on television."

"Perhaps. Let me find someone else to handle this contract. We don't know when Eteka shall return, and when he makes it back, he will need some rest, and possibly treatment."

"Very well. But if Eteka is still alive like you believe, I would like him to carry out the hit. It would be a good test of his mental stamina."

"You already know Eteka is one of our best. His stamina should not be questioned."

"Yes, but Eteka is also your little pet, and he cannot receive special treatment. We don't want to give the wrong impression to the other Imamba. I told you many years ago that I would give each Imamba a final test to prove their worthiness to us. This will be Eteka's."

"Eteka's already one of us. He's done more for the Imamba Brotherhood than most of the others. I don't think it's a good idea. You should think of some other way to test him. When he returns, he should rest."

Omega regarded Oga seriously. His reasoning was irritating. "I've made my decision, Oga. End of discussion." Omega stormed toward the exit, his big belly jiggling. As he opened the door to leave, he turned around and looked at Oga.

"And one more thing," Omega said harshly. "Just remember that I am the sole reason that we, the Imamba, are in business. I put together the deals and find us clients. In other words, the money comes through me. Skillful and trained as you are, you are just a brute with a gun, and expendable. There are many experienced fighters who would love to be in your shoes, just remember that."

Omega walked out, slamming the door behind him. Oga turned to look out the windows at the beach below. His temper boiled just beneath the surface. If any other man had spoken to him in that manner, it surely would have resulted in a bloodbath.

But Omega was right. He was expendable.

A tired Eteka caught a flight from Johannesburg to East London, South Africa. His mind was racing, and he slept very little on his flight despite his exhaustion. So many unanswered questions. How did Bayinna know so much about him? How did she know of their mission? Why had she shown him all those maimed people? Why was he so instantly comfortable around her, and what did she mean when she said everything in his life had happened for a bigger purpose? Why should he question the motives of Oga and Omega? What was the point of these missions he went on? Who were his parents? Oga would have the answers he needed, and he was going to get them, but these questions (and others) tormented him throughout the entire flight.

Eteka arrived at the hotel in East London late that night. The cool beach air was soothing to his ragged senses as he exited the taxi and walked up to the main entrance. The front lawn was lit up with lights and a majestic water fountain greeted him on his way in, a stark contrast to the wilderness he had experienced in the Tanzanian village. He hadn't had a chance to shower in two days, and he looked filthy in comparison to the guests milling about the lobby.

He made his way into a waiting elevator and up to the 10th floor, where his fellow Imamba were supposed to be waiting for him. Maximus's hulking figure greeted him when the elevator doors opened. The giant Imamba, dressed in jeans and a short-sleeved shirt that exposed his enormous arms, wore his signature joker's smile as he patted Eteka on the back. With Maximus was a familiar, disgruntled-looking Imamba dressed in a sharp black suit. He was a tough-looking young man with chiseled features and a low-cut mohawk.

"Good to see you, Eteka," Maximus said in greeting. "Omega and Oga were not sure you would be back. They're hanging out at a lounge on the beach."

"Thanks, Maximus," Eteka said, slapping Maximus familiarly on the shoulder. "I'll get cleaned up first. Do you guys have a change of clothes for me?"

"Yes. Omega reserved room 10G for you, just in case you made it back. There are some clean clothes for you in there. Here is the key," Maximus said, handing Eteka a key card. "I'll wait for you by the elevator."

Eteka nodded at Maximus and made his way down the hall to his room. Sure enough, a clean denim shirt, slacks, and sandals were on the bed, and in the closet was a dark grey suit, all to his exact measurements. They had even left him a gun, which lay next to his clothes. Eteka stripped naked and took a long hot shower. The water and scented soap felt good against his tired, dirty body, and as he cleaned himself he noticed a scar on his shin from his fight with the Custodis. Memories from Tanzania came swarming back to him. He had to stay focused and get his answers from Oga.

He finished his shower, put on some fresh clothes, and made sure to conceal the loaded gun. Feeling fresh, he met Maximus and the other, irritable Imamba at the elevator.

"Hello, gentlemen," Eteka said. "Have we met?" Eteka asked the Imamba with the mohawk, who he couldn't place.

The man shook his head angrily and stalked away.

"Who's that guy and what's his problem?" Eteka asked as he and Maximus got in the elevator.

"His name is Marcelino. You killed his brother," reminded Maximus.

"I killed his brother?" marveled Eteka, trying to remember.

"Yes," Maximus nodded, "when we were at the new recruit initiations. I don't think he's particularly fond of you. I wouldn't be if I were in his shoes," Maximus replied in his booming voice, a smirk on his face. It took a minute, but Eteka remembered the training exercise he had been involved in when the recruit he had been fighting had collapsed and died. Yes, he remembered the recruit having a brother.

It was a breezy night as both men trudged through the sand toward a lively venue on the beach. Smooth kwaito beats met them at the door as they entered. The club was full of young people, mostly white, dancing to the music as a black DJ with short dreadlocks worked the turntable. Maximus led Eteka to a VIP room in the back, where they walked in on Omega with two women on each arm, doing his best to grind on them with his huge belly. Oga, on the other hand, was sitting on a couch with two Imamba brothers, smoking a cigarette. Both men looked up as Eteka walked into the room.

"Ah, Eteka! You're alive!" Omega yelled over the music, cheerfully doing his best to monopolize four women at once.

Eteka nodded at Omega as he made his way over to Oga.

"How are you?" Oga asked, concern deepening his wrinkles.

"I'm well," Eteka replied as he stood over Oga and the other Imamba.

"Want a drink?"

"Not in here," Eteka replied, impatiently nodding toward the door.

Oga regarded Eteka carefully as he finished his cigarette and stood up, leading Eteka to the exit. After picking up two bottles of Guinness at the bar, they exchanged the loud music and cigarette smoke for the fresh night air on the beach. Oga studied Eteka as he sipped his beer.

"We heard about what happened," Oga began.

"Did Cyrus and Mokin make it back?" Eteka asked.

"Yes. Cyrus took a bullet to his side, and he's getting some treatment in Johannesburg. Mokin is fine. What about you? What happened out there?"

"Things got complicated," Eteka said, running a hand through his hair.

"Did you encounter the White Witch?"

"I did, actually."

"And? What happened?"

"She healed me, then she asked me to reflect on why I do what I do," Eteka replied, taking a sip of his own beer. Oga stared at him, nonplussed.

"You know why you do what you do, right?"

"No," Eteka said honestly. "I've never given it much thought before."

"You are an Imamba. This is what we do."

"The White Witch seemed pretty harmless to me. In fact, she's protecting people out there," Eteka said as Omega emerged from the club and scanned the beach, looking for them.

"Your job is not to question the morality of your targets," Oga said. "Your job is to simply execute."

"But the White Witch said she knew my parents! She also said that I'm not who I think I am, and that I should question the motives of the people I work for. What did she mean?"

"Could be sorcery, or mind tricks—they call her the White Witch for a reason. The bitch really got into your head," Oga said. "Let's pick this up later," he advised, spotting Omega.

"Eteka!" Omega shouted, approaching them faster than it seemed his girth would allow. "We didn't know if you'd made it out. How are you?" the large man asked as he patted Eteka on the shoulder. Eteka managed not to roll his eyes—Omega hadn't thought to ask after his health when he'd been busy with those girls at the club.

"I'm fine."

"Great! Cyrus and Mokin are fine, too," Omega said.

"When will they join us?"

"You will see them when the time is right. For now, I have a new project for you, my young friend."

"I'm ready to serve," Eteka said without hesitation.

"Good!" said Omega, smirking at Oga's annoyance. "You'll be heading back to Nigeria to sort out a radical activist that's pissed off a few of our friends there," Omega said. "He is a notorious troublemaker that masquerades as a teacher. You are to go there and kill him. I have a folder with all the details back at the hotel. Lots of money in it for you, my young friend."

The thought of going to Nigeria for a new assignment made him think of Arewa. Handling a mission there meant he would have the chance to see her again. He missed her already.

"What's the target's name?" Eteka asked.

"They call him Oluko. He lives in Ibadan. Like I said, the folder at the hotel has the details," Omega said.

"Consider it done," Eteka nodded.

"Great! Let's use our time here to party and enjoy the women, eh? Let's go back to the club and dance!" Omega said as he started back up toward the club.

"Wait," Eteka said as the White Witch's words came back to him—what were Omega and Oga's real motives? "The White Witch could have killed me, but she let me live. And she was kind to me. She told me many things that made sense," Eteka said.

"And you believed her? She tricked you into believing her nonsense so that you wouldn't kill her," Omega said.

"That's exactly what I told him," Oga cut in.

"Like I said, if she wanted me dead, she could have easily killed me."

"Look," Omega said impatiently, "I don't know what that bitch's intentions were or why she let you live, but it's clear that she tricked you. Don't worry; we'll sort her out in good time."

Eteka looked between Oga and Omega, then out at the ocean. The moon shimmered over the water's surface and he could smell the salt in the air. This was becoming an overwhelming internal struggle for Eteka. The White Witch sounded convincing, but so did Omega and Oga. No matter—he would get his answers as soon as he took care of this Oluko in Nigeria.

"Will any Imamba be joining me?" Eteka asked. "Or will I be going alone to Nigeria?"

"You'll be going alone," Omega replied. "I have Cyrus and Mokin signed up for an assignment in the States a little more than a week after your assignment. They're going to take out a singer called Fallal at his concert in New York. The other brothers are busy with important assignments."

"When will I have the green light?"

"In a week. Your flight details should arrive in the next few days," Omega replied with a smile.

"I'll leave earlier," Eteka replied, his mind drifting to Arewa. If the hit was in a week, perhaps he could go see her first. He wanted to hold her again and listen to her voice.

"You'll leave ahead of time? Like the last time we were in Johannesburg and you left us for Nigeria without an explanation?" Omega asked with a laugh.

"I want to try some of the hookers in Abuja and relax a little before I head out," Eteka replied defensively, keeping Arewa a secret. "I'll make sure I'm there to finish the job when it's time."

"Whatever works for you, my young friend," Omega said with a shrug. "Now that we've settled business, why don't we head back to the nightclub? There were some nice ladies in there."

"You guys go ahead. I'll be in my room," Eteka replied, turning to walk up the beach toward the hotel.

Oga and Omega watched Eteka walk back to the hotel in silence. When Eteka was out of hearing distance, Oga threw his empty Guinness bottle in the sand and lit up a fresh cigarette.

"He's not ready to go out on a fresh mission. He needs to rest his body and his mind," Oga said.

"Eteka is strong, and he will pass this test. He will kill this Oluko man and get us our money, and then he can rest all he wants," Omega replied, puffing out large smoke circles as he looked out at the ocean. "Besides, I've arranged for Proditor, Pacman, and a few local boys to follow Eteka just in case."

A wave of worry swept over Oga, startling him; he hadn't realized just how fond he was of Eteka. The young man was like a son—and now he was deeply concerned for his son's safety. Omega smiled and patted Oga on the back.

"Relax, old friend," Omega said. "My plans are always well thought out, leaving no room for error. That's why I am the only irreplaceable element within the Imamba. And if, by some mysterious chance, Eteka is affected by this unsuccessful mission in Tanzania, he is expendable," he said as he leaned in to whisper to Oga, "just like you."

The large man grinned maliciously as he patted Oga's back again and headed up the beach toward the nightclub. Oga watched Omega leave, then turned his gaze back toward the ocean as he smoked his cigarette.

DEAD MAN WALKING

Leicester Square, London. England. 1967.

It was a rainy day as Yisa walked into a gleaming hotel in Leicester Square, London. He was dressed in his usual white suit and felt light in spirit. Smiling broadly, he cradled the beaded necklace that he had made for Tosin in his right trouser pocket. After all the teasing from his friend and wife, he had finally completed the project. He strode into the hotel, past the people milling about in the lobby, and straight into the hotel bar. Omega was already seated and waiting for him in a dark corner. Oga sat next to him, sipping on a glass of bourbon with a single large chunk of ice wandering around in it like an iceberg. It had been two days since they had killed Abel Tony, and the story had been all over the news. Yisa took a seat next to them, and there was a moment of tense silence before anyone spoke.

"Oga tells me things became a little dicey on this last mission. Is this true?" Omega asked in a low voice, keeping an eye on the bar's other patrons.

"You'll have to be more specific," Yisa replied calmly, with the arrogance of the righteous.

"You could have gotten us both killed," Oga cut in sharply. "If you were not prepared for the job, you should have stayed in the car. I could have handled him myself."

"I'm sorry," said Yisa unconvincingly.

"Being sorry is not enough!" Oga shot back. "This is business, Yisa. You need to wake up and stop playing games—you are going to fuck things up for the rest of us."

"I said I'm sorry," he repeated, a muscle twitching in his jaw. He sounded even less sorry than he had the first time he'd said it.

Two white men sat just a few tables away from the Imamba. The first was young, early twenties, unshaven, and wearing a worn-out grey overcoat. The second man was so thin he looked like he could do with a good meal. He sported a Charlie Chaplin moustache and slicked-back hair, and he was wearing a suit that was too small for his lanky frame—his ankles and wrists escaping from his jacket cuffs and pant legs. They hunched over the table and talked quickly to each other, as if their conversation were of the utmost importance.

"What exactly went wrong, Yisa? Was it the target?" Omega asked.

Yisa sighed. "This Imamba Brotherhood, this thing we created—it's become something else. It's not what I expected."

Omega and Oga looked at each other with an air of almost parental disgust.

"Here we go again. Please, explain," Omega requested as Oga lit up a cigarette.

"We've had this conversation many times before. I'm not happy with anything that we do. Our activities are not helping me or my family or Africa," Yisa replied, standing up.

"Where are you going?" Oga asked.

"Home, to my wife and son. It seems we no longer share the same interests, gentlemen—if we ever did. So, I leave the Imamba to you and wish you luck."

Omega and Oga stood up with surprised looks on their faces.

"Wait," Omega said. "Yisa, don't you think you're overreacting? We have big money on the table for this next job."

"That's the way it was last time. There was big money then and there will be big money the time after that and the time after that. It never ends," Yisa replied as he started to walk away.

"You'll lose every cent of the money in your Swiss accounts if you leave us, and there's a lot of money there waiting for you. Don't be foolish," Omega threatened.

"Keep it. I have enough."

Oga reached out and grabbed Yisa by his shirt. In a sense, Yisa had been the only friend he'd ever had.

"You're just going to walk away, after all we've been through together?" Oga asked.

Yisa smiled and nodded in response. "Omega can never understand what we go through—his hands stay so clean. You've been a brother to me, Oga, but this life is killing me and tearing my family apart. They come first, or life is not worth living."

For the first time in his life, Oga felt genuine betrayal. His eyes welled up with tears and his hands trembled ever so slightly as he looked at Yisa, who was smiling calmly. Family? What did Yisa mean that his family was being torn apart? With whom did he spend the majority of his time? With whom did he have the most intense of experiences: shootouts and quiet conversations about life and purpose in the most obscure of places?

"So, what are you going to do now? You're just going to be a normal civilian? You can never change, Yisa. I know you, better than most. You're a born killer," Oga said.

"I can try, Oga."

Oga put out his cigarette in an ashtray and stood toe to toe with Yisa as Omega placed an order with a passing waiter.

"So, this is it, then? You're just going to walk away?" Oga asked.

"Yes."

"And throw away everything we've built? Can't you see how powerful we are becoming? Even the oyimbos are beginning to fear us."

"I do not care who the oyimbos fear. I have bigger things to think about."

"You're making a mistake, Yisa. You know the rules of our brotherhood," Oga said.

"Yes, I know. It's a chance I'm willing to take. I hope you understand, brother," Yisa replied, extending his hand for a peaceful handshake.

Oga looked at Yisa's hand for a moment, and then grinned. The two men shook hands as Omega continued to watch them from behind.

"You sure you don't want to rethink your decision?"

"No. I've made up my mind."

"So, civilian life it will be, eh?" Oga asked.

"Yes."

"Well, I wonder how an Imamba will survive without its fangs."

Yisa smiled. "It will have to adapt, as all creatures do."

"I guess it will."

There was a brief silence as both men locked eyes with each other, one last time.

"So long, my brother. It's been an interesting journey, working with you," Yisa said as he turned around and walked out of the hotel into the rain. He smiled to himself as he left his colleagues behind, happy that he had accomplished what he'd come there to do.

As Oga watched Yisa leave, part of him was angry, leaving a heavy feeling in his heart as his former partner walked away. He and Yisa had developed a unique relationship from all the time they had spent together. This was not the way he had imagined things would play out. With a sigh, Oga rejoined Omega at their table.

"You know what this means, right?" Omega asked as his food arrived.

"Yes."

"Good. He knows too much and could be a problem in the future."

Oga frowned and ran his fingers through his beard. For the first time in his life, he had doubts about what he had to do. But, business always came first. At least with Omega it did.

"Not in London."

"No, too risky," Omega replied as he took a bite of his Beef Wellington. "Besides, I don't want to give our oyimbo friends here any reason to think that we're having internal trouble. Follow him to Nigeria, and do it there."

"I might need backup. Yisa is not a typical target. He's dangerous, even for us."

"Then take Proditor with you," Omega replied, "and his thugs. Oh yes, and Maximus. We don't want to risk any more of our Brothers."

"And his wife and child?"

Omega looked at Oga, his mouth full of food. He shook his head and downed the mouthful with a sip of red wine. "Were you planning on adopting his family, Oga?"

"Of course not."

"So why are you asking me about his family? Take care of them as well. We need to send a message to the other Imamba about the cost of deserting us."

"Done. Shame we lost him," Oga replied, taking a sip of his bourbon.

"Yes, he's worth a lot," Omega agreed. "It'll be a real shame if another outfit picks him up, which is why you have to take care of business quickly."

Oga looked at a pretty waitress attending another table, her curvy figure commanding his eyes, but not his mind. "Yisa is a good fighter and he has experience. I've fought with him for many years. Don't you think we should try to convince him again? Maybe he needs some more time to think about it."

"No. Kill him."

"As you wish. What will happen to his accounts?" Oga asked.

"We can split his money," Omega replied with a smile.

"Good. I'll find someone to replace him, don't worry," Oga said as he stood up and put out his cigarette.

Omega smiled. "I think you and I will do well together. We think alike."

"I'll contact you when the deed is done," Oga replied without emotion, turning to walk out of the restaurant.

Omega smiled as he watched Oga leave. Losing Yisa meant one less person to challenge his authority within the Imamba. It would only be a matter of time before he had complete control over the brotherhood. He gulped down his drink and finished his meal, alone.

BETRAYAL

Ibadan, Nigeria. Africa. 1967.

It had been two days since Yisa had left London, and much of his time since then had been spent contemplating his decision to leave the Imamba Brotherhood. He knew that he was now a threat to the brotherhood—after all, he knew the locations of all their safe houses, he knew the logistics of their operations, and, most importantly, he knew how to reach the elusive Omega. And Omega was a strategist who did not like leaving loose ends. Yisa knew he would have to be careful and watch his back, for his own sake as well as that of his family. Plans were in motion to relocate his entire family to the Cayman Islands. They needed to start a new life with new identities as soon as possible. He had already purchased land and a new house, but he still needed to tell Amina, and very soon.

His decision to leave was bittersweet. Contracts with the brotherhood had afforded his family a very comfortable lifestyle, and his life, while dangerous, had been very exciting. How would he adjust to a civilian life, to being a family man? Would it even be possible? For so many years he had been able to come and go as he pleased. Now, he had made the tough choice to subdue his alter ego and live a peaceful life of routine and responsibility. The thought of the mental transition scared him, but a part of him felt good and argued that it was the right thing to do. Perhaps the Caribbean would be a good place to start from scratch.

He sat alone in his bedroom on a Friday evening after spending the afternoon cleaning his cars. The Biafra conflict was still in full swing, and the sounds of bomber jets flying overhead was commonplace. Downstairs, he could hear Amina chatting with her friends on the front porch in Yoruba. The friends genuinely laughed with each other as they talked, probably gossiping about news around town.

Women...

Yisa took the thought back as he looked at himself in a mirror. There were also men who gossiped as women did, sometimes even worse. What Amina and her friends had were genuine connections with each other, and he rarely experienced that. A familiar little face peeked at him from the bedroom's doorway.

"What are you doing, Daddy?" little Tosin asked.

Yisa smiled at his boy's innocent little face.

"I am..." Yisa said as he shifted toward Tosin, "... COMING FOR YOU!" he finished in a roar as he snatched up a wide-eyed Tosin and threw him on the bed. Yisa proceeded to tickle his son, who laughed hysterically as they played together. Eventually, Yisa stood up.

"I have a surprise for you, Tosin."

"A surprise? What is the surprise, Daddy?" asked Tosin.

Yisa walked over to a drawer with a mischievous smile and pulled out the beaded necklace he had made for Tosin, then removed his wedding ring and looped it onto the necklace. Engraved on the wedding band were the initials "Y.M." He walked back to Tosin and placed the necklace around his neck.

"I made this for you myself," Yisa said proudly, admiring the necklace. "Do you like it?"

"Yes, Daddy!" Tosin replied, running to the mirror to examine it. Yisa followed him, and they both admired the gift in the mirror. "I will always wear it, Daddy. Can I go and show Mummy?"

"Wait, I want to talk to you," Yisa said, picking up his boy and returning to the bed, where he placed him on his lap. It was time for a man-to-man chat.

"Tosin…"

"Yes, Daddy?"

"I want you to know that I am very sorry that I have not been in your life all this time," Yisa began. Tosin looked at his father with a curious grin, his eyes blank, his young mind not knowing what to do with Yisa's words. Was there another way of life in which daddies were around all the time—like Mummy? Yisa saw his confusion, but continued anyway.

"I won't be traveling again. I will be in your life from now on. I will be a good father, and I will teach you how to be a man—a *real* man," Yisa said as he placed a hand on Tosin's shoulder. "I want you to know that I love you. I love you very, very much. Understand?"

"Yes, Daddy. Can I go and show Mummy my new necklace now?" Tosin asked, itching to jump off his father's lap.

"Yes, you can," Yisa replied softly as he watched Tosin climb down and dart out of the room. Yisa shed a tear as he watched his son disappear. A deep sadness enveloped him, a sadness he could not explain. He looked at his reflection in the mirror and he tried to smile, but the Yisa in the mirror didn't smile back.

The next morning, Yisa woke up to the sight of his lovely wife placing breakfast by their bed: scrambled eggs, porridge, bread fresh from the oven, some yogurt, and tea. She wore a sexy lace outfit and sat on the bed, leaning over to kiss Yisa's forehead.

"Hello, my king."

"Hello, my queen," Yisa replied as he bit a piece of the buttered bread she'd fed him.

"I'm so happy you've decided to stay home for good."

"So am I," he replied after a moment's hesitation.

"And I saw that necklace you made for Tosin last night," she continued.

"Did you like it?"

"I love it, and so does he. Why did you put your wedding ring on it?" she asked with a raised eyebrow.

"I thought it would be a nice touch."

"Okay, it can stay on for today, but it will have to come off tomorrow. Tosin might lose it, and more importantly it has to stay on your finger. Now that you're home, there will be a lot of women making advances at you, and we can't have them getting any funny ideas," Amina said as she rolled her eyes. Yisa smiled as he ate, and kissed her on her cheek.

"The only woman I'm here for is you."

She looked lovingly at her husband, slight worry creases forming at the corners of her eyes. "He's really excited that you're home."

"Who? Tosin?"

"I wish you would call your son by his proper name once in a while. He needs to hear it more often, especially from you," she replied.

"I've never called him Eteka before. I like Tosin[1]; it's my pet name for him."

"Well, it's about time you started calling him by his proper name," Amina said, shaking her head. "Eteka is not a baby anymore, and he needs to identify with his proper name."

"Okay, my love. Your wish is my command," Yisa said, giving her another kiss on her cheek. "There's something serious I want to talk to you about…" Yisa put the food away and stood up. After staring out of their bedroom window for a brief moment, he faced his wife.

"It's time we left Nigeria."

---

[1] Tosin is a Yoruba name (short version of Oluwatosin) which means "God is worthy to be praised."

"Huh?"

"We have to leave Nigeria. Tomorrow. I got us some property in the Caribbean. I want us to start our lives afresh, over there."

Amina stood up, confused and angry.

"Is this a joke? If it is, it's not funny."

"It's not a joke. I decided to leave my organization, as I said I would. But I don't think the men I work with will let me go just like that. I know too much."

"I don't understand. What do you mean by they won't let you go?" Amina asked.

"I work with dangerous men, Amina, in a dangerous business. My decision to leave puts us all at risk. So we have to go. Besides, the Caribbean will offer us a better lifestyle than what we have here in Nigeria with all this Biafra fighting going on. I don't want my son growing up in the middle of a war."

"I'm with you, but Eteka is just a child. This is so sudden, to just strip him from everything he knows. You gave us no advance notice."

"I know, and I'm sorry—it was a spur-of-the-moment decision. That's why we're leaving tomorrow, not today. It gives us some time to pack, and have a sit-down with Eteka this evening to explain things."

"What about me?" Amina asked. "What will I do in the Caribbean? My friends and my life are here, in Ibadan. I know this

Biafra thing is going on, but it hasn't affected us, not yet. Can't we just move to another state?"

"It's too dangerous to stay here in Nigeria, Amina. I need you to start packing our things to leave tomorrow. End of discussion."

"And what about our cars, and the house? What about our maids and gardeners?"

"We were doing just fine by ourselves before they all came to us. We will be fine," Yisa said, holding his wife's hands and putting his forehead to hers. "This will be our chance to start life over, the right way."

She held his head and kissed him firmly. She could see the tension in his posture, the underlying message that if they didn't leave quickly, they might not ever leave at all.

"You're my husband, and I love you. You lead our family, so if you think it's time to go, it's time to go. When will you tell Oladele?"

"He said he wanted to pick me up later this afternoon and show me some stuff at the university. That'll be a good time to break the news to him."

"You'll break his heart. He really wanted you to get involved with his students," Amina said.

"I was looking forward to that, but those plans will have to wait."

"Eteka was supposed to have some classes today."

"On a Saturday?" Yisa asked.

"Yes. I enrolled him in some extra classes for elementary English because he needs more work in that area."

"Why didn't you just get Oladele to teach him?"

"Because Oladele already does more than enough for us, and he has a life of his own. I want Eteka to ride with you on your way to the market."

"The market?"

"Yes. We need packing boxes for some of our things, and we don't have any here at home. You can drop Eteka off at his classes while you and Oladele go pick up some boxes for packing, that'll give you some one-on-one time to tell Oladele what's going on. You can pick Eteka up on your way back, and we can all pack together. While you're gone I'll start organizing things and cook us some lunch," Amina said.

"I don't want to leave you guys alone. We have to stay together."

"And we also have to make the best use of time, which we can't do if we are all together," Amina replied. "If we are leaving tomorrow first thing then there are a lot of things that have to be done. We need those packing boxes from the market, and I have to organize things here and make us food to eat."

Yisa nodded and walked over to a closet drawer set. He opened the bottom drawer, which squeaked as it came loose. In the drawer was a revolver and a case of bullets.

"I want you to hold onto this. Just in case." He showed her how to load it, taking her through the steps several times until she was proficient.

"You know I don't like guns. Is it necessary?" Amina asked.

"Yes, it is."

"Okay," Amina said as she took the weapon and placed it on top of a dresser. "But I don't think I'll have to use it."

"Let's hope you're right."

That afternoon, Yisa, Amina and little Eteka stepped outside as Oladele pulled up to their gate, blowing his horn. It was unbearably hot, the Nigerian sun casting its blinding rays over the parched land. Oladele stepped out of his car as Yisa and his family walked up.

"Hello. Are you ready?" Oladele asked, looking at Yisa.

"Yes. Eteka is coming with us. Let's drop him off at his school, then head to the market. I have to buy some stuff for the house," Yisa said.

"The market? I thought the plan was for me to show you around the university today." Oladele's smile wavered.

"We can do that some other time. I'll explain in the car," Yisa replied.

"That's fine," Oladele said, looking down and smiling at little Eteka. He noticed the elaborate necklace around his neck. "What's that around your neck, Eteka? Is that one of Yisa's contraptions?" he asked with a laugh. Amina chuckled while Yisa shook his head.

"Eteka, tell Uncle Oladele how much you like the necklace I made for you, so he can be jealous," Yisa retorted with a grin as he nudged his son.

"I like my Daddy's necklace," young Eteka said with a giggle as he held it up to Oladele for inspection.

"Added your wedding ring, I see," Oladele said, examining Yisa's handiwork. "Nice touch. Let's hope Eteka doesn't lose it when he plays with his friends at school."

"He won't. Let's get going. We'll see you later," Yisa said as held his wife close and gave her a kiss. "I love you," he said softly as they parted lips.

"I love you, too."

As Yisa and Eteka climbed into Oladele's car, Oladele exchanged a smile with Amina that Yisa couldn't see. She smiled back, then looked away.

They left Amina waving at the gate as they drove off toward Eteka's school. The regular activities of any Saturday morning in Ibadan were in full swing: roadside vendors shouted at passersby as they promoted their products, and young girls walked the streets balancing large boxes and basins on their heads as they carried babies on their backs, wrapped in cloth. Buses were so packed with passengers that a few were even hanging out the doors.

They wove through the busy streets with little Eteka babbling away, excited that his father was in the car with them. They finally arrived at Eteka's school and pulled into the main compound. Little children scurried around, closely supervised by the teachers, most of whom were women. Many of the children waved at Oladele as they pulled up. Yisa stepped out of the car with Eteka and knelt down in front of him as one of the teachers came to take his boy away.

"You be a good boy, okay?"

"Okay, Daddy. Will you come and pick me from school?" little Eteka asked.

"Yes, I'll be here, my son. And you'll be leaving early today so we can spend time together."

"YAAAAAYYYY!" little Eteka squealed as he gave his father a tight hug. Yisa held his son close and kissed him on the forehead. He stood up, ushering Eteka toward the teacher.

"Please keep an eye on him. We'll be right back," Yisa said to the teacher, who nodded in response.

Yisa pulled Eteka close for one last hug, then stepped back into the car with Oladele. The duo pulled out of the school compound and began the drive toward the market.

"It made me happy to see you hug Eteka like that," Oladele said as they drove along.

"Why is that?" Yisa asked.

"Because Eteka thinks the world of you. It will be interesting to see how your presence impacts his development."

"I have something to tell you."

"What?"

Yisa took a deep breath as he looked at his friend. "I won't be staying in Nigeria."

"Huh?"

"I made plans to relocate Amina and Eteka to the Caribbean," Eteka said. "It's too dangerous here."

"What?"

"I said I made plans to move my family to the Caribbean. It's for their safety."

"I, I don't understand," Oladele said in disbelief. "I thought you planned on staying here for good."

"I want to," Yisa said sincerely, "but I walked away from my Imamba brothers and they know where I live, and if we stay here it puts Amina and Eteka at risk. I already bought a house on the Cayman Islands right before I came back home."

"I don't believe what I'm hearing," Oladele said as he made a turn. "What about coming back to work with me?"

"I thought about that," Yisa replied. "You'll always have my support, and we'll still work together. I just won't be around as much."

"So, just like that I won't see Amina or Eteka again?" Oladele said in a strained voice. "You know they've been like family to me while you've been gone."

"You'll still see them. You can come visit us," Yisa replied. "I'll need your support on this, Oladele. You're the only link I'll have back to Nigeria when I leave. I'll need you on my side."

"Yes, of course," Oladele said absently, frowning at the road before them. "Can't you just go to another state in Nigeria? Or a neighboring country? Why do you have to move so far away?"

"It's for my family's safety, Oladele. Don't worry, you'll know how to find us."

"Does Amina know of your plan?" Oladele asked.

"Yes. We'll have to move fast, so we can help Amina with packing."

"We?"

"Yes, you're going to help us. Use those muscles instead of your brain for a change."

They arrived at the market and within 30 minutes had purchased the packing boxes needed. They began the drive back toward Eteka's school and Yisa's residence, but the traffic in town had built up, and they found themselves moving at a snail's pace. Yisa impatiently tapped his fingers on the car's dashboard as they slowly moved along. He really did not like being away from his family, a feeling which was amplified by the sea of vehicles in front of them. Yisa pulled out another set of beads and string from his pocket and started putting them together, to take his mind off the traffic. Oladele laughed when he saw Yisa with his handiwork.

"You seem really bent on making cheap trinkets, Yisa. What's with you and all these beads?"

Yisa smiled as he looked up at his friend. "I'm making a bracelet for Eteka. There was some leftover string from the necklace I made for him."

"I see. Are you going to say goodbye to your daughter?" Oladele asked.

"Not now, Oladele," Yisa responded angrily. "This is not the time to bring her up."

"Her name is Isatou," Oladele continued, looking at his friend. "I thought you might want to know her name, in case you never see her again." Yisa remained silent, briefly looking out the window before resuming his work on his son's bracelet.

They purchased the packing boxes from a market vendor and continued along. Finally, after being stuck in traffic for an hour under intense heat, they came to a crossroad with extensive traffic on both sides. Making a left would take them to Eteka's school. Making a right led to Yisa's residence. Yisa had to make a decision for the sake of time.

"You go ahead and get Eteka," Yisa said, grabbing the bundle of packing boxes and stepping out of the car.

"Where are you going?"

"Making good use of time. I'll catch a local bus back home. I have to help Amina pack. I'll meet you back at the house."

Before Oladele could respond, Yisa had already taken off, running after a local bus heading in his home's direction.

Sitting on the empty passenger seat next to Oladele was the incomplete bracelet. Yisa had absentmindedly dropped it.

Amina stood by the gate in an outfit that tightly hugged her curvy body as she watched the car carrying the three favorite men in her life drive off. She scratched a row of plaited hair under her headscarf. Yisa's last words had left her perplexed. Moving across the world, on such short notice? The plan sounded crazy, yet exciting at the same time. Was her husband's job really that dangerous? What would this mean? Giving up the luxuries that came with her husband's money, including the servants, cars, and nice house? Saying goodbye to friends she had made in the neighborhood over the years? Her son saying goodbye to all his classmates? No more satisfying her sexual urges with Oladele? This unexpected change would affect so much of her life. But she had been praying for her husband to settle down and spend time with the family, and if it took traveling across the world to make that happen, then perhaps that was God's way of answering her prayers—and of removing the temptation of Oladele from her reach.

She headed back into her home, an agama lizard perched on a rock nearby nodding as if in approval of her appearance. Two of her house servants, both girls, washed clothes by hand behind her home while a male house servant reverently cleaned their cars outside with a bucket and sponge, the radiant sun exposing large sweat stains on his dirty short-sleeved shirt. Another servant, an elderly woman with a motherly demeanor, smiled at Amina from the doorway, the sweet aroma of well-seasoned pepper soup emanating from within. She was the best cook they'd ever had. It seemed like a perfect day, and Amina was happy. Change was good. She summoned two housemaids and gave them the task of folding some clothes for their trip while she went around the house removing paintings, pictures, and anything of value. When Yisa returned with the packing boxes, they would begin packing.

An hour passed. Her husband, her son, and Oladele hadn't yet returned. She knew they would be hungry when they got back, so she decided to take a break from packing to do some cooking and headed to her kitchen. Pepper soup was brewing on the stove, but she opted to make some egusi soup with pounded yam for her husband and Oladele. Yes, she would season it well—add in some goat meat with smoked shrimp and perhaps some fish. The thought of the dish alone made her lick her lips, wash her hands, and get started. Then she would fry some seasoned, diced plantains and save them for later in case little Eteka wanted something to snack on. He was often hungry after class.

Another half hour passed and her egusi combination was brewing on the stove. Amina had already chopped up the plantains and had some olive oil simmering on the stove. Just when she was about to start throwing the plantains into the hot oil, a vehicle pulled up in front of the house. She heard some male voices outside and decided to investigate, walking into her living room to look through a window.

Three men were walking toward the house. Following the first three men were three more men dressed in worn street clothes, and another three sat comfortably in a truck parked by the front gate. The men in street clothes looked rough, and could very well have passed for street thugs or armed robbers. The first three men were clearly the leaders of the group, and looked even more menacing than the others. The first was a shorter man with a hard face and a grey and red bandana on his head. He had unsettled eyes that darted to and fro as he observed his surroundings. The second man was a hulking giant, with wide eyes and a strange smile on his face. The third man walked in the lead. It was clear that he was the leader from the way the others looked to him, and he sported dark aviator glasses and a full beard. A cigarette dangled loosely from his mouth as he walked up to the outside veranda and knocked on the front door. Amina became alarmed. Who were these men? They did not look like good people. Were they her husband's associates? Why did they have to show up now, when Yisa was not around? She gathered her courage and stepped out to meet them.

"Hello. Can I help you?" Amina asked, stepping onto the porch to meet the men. The one with the beard smiled when he saw her and took his time before responding, eyeing her up and down.

"Good afternoon, madam. We are looking for Yisa." He did not sound Nigerian.

"Yisa is not here right now. Who are you and what is your relationship to Yisa?"

The man smiled as he ogled Amina's body. She stepped backward, appalled by his open lechery.

"You must be his wife. Nice, very nice. Yisa always did have good taste."

"Sir, I said Yisa is not here. If you give me your name, I can tell him you stopped by."

"That's okay, we can wait for him." Before Amina could even blink, the man had opened the door and stepped into the house. The shorter man followed suit, while the other thugs stayed outside. The giant stayed outside as well, a strange, sadistic smile on his face.

"You can't just barge into my home!"

"Don't worry, Yisa and I are like brothers," the man replied. "My name is Oga, by the way. Did Yisa ever tell you about me?"

"No," Amina answered, now worried.

"Of course he didn't," Oga said, blowing out some smoke. Outside, the thugs brandished very visible weapons, causing the servants to cower in fear.

"What do you want?" Amina asked, hoping she sounded braver than she felt.

"I told you, we want Yisa."

"But he's not here. Why don't you come later, when he is around? He may not be home for a while."

"That's okay. Come, sit next to me," Oga said with a grin as he patted the cushion next to him.

"No. You and your friends will have to leave, now," Amina said firmly, doing her best to hide her fear.

"I told you we will wait for Yisa. If you won't come and sit by me, at least bring us some of that lovely food you're cooking, eh?"

Seeing no alternative, Amina walked into her kitchen and stood by the stove, the oil she'd put on earlier for the plantains now bubbling energetically in the pan. What was she going to do about these men? What was taking Yisa so long? Nothing about them felt good. How could she reach her husband? Her mind went to the gun Yisa had left her. She had set it on her dresser in their bedroom upstairs. To get to it, she would have to go past the men.

"So, are you going to serve me food, or what?" Oga had followed her into the kitchen, startling her by grabbing her ass. She reflexively swiped his hand away and faced him. Her heart was beating fast now.

"Don't touch me," she said, trembling in fear despite her best efforts.

"Yisa and I have shared many women on our travels," Oga said in return. "I'm sure he would be fine if I tasted you."

"I don't know who you are or what you want, but my husband will be home soon. Now please, leave me alone," Amina replied as Oga moved closer. There was little space for her to move.

"I want to taste the woman that took Yisa away from us. Only something that tastes really good could make him want to stop being with the brotherhood," Oga said, grabbing her ass again. She pushed his hand off, but he grabbed more forcefully and pulled her to him. He was strong, just like Yisa, only he did not use his strength with her lovingly. He yanked her close and began to feel her breasts.

This isn't happening, Amina thought. She pushed as hard as she could, but Oga wouldn't budge. He began to lift her dress and unzip his trousers. No, this couldn't happen.

Amina grabbed the handle of the frying pan with the sizzling oil and, in a flash, covered half of Oga's face with the burning-hot liquid. The Imamba screamed in pain, letting her go and clutching his face as he dropped to one knee. He continued to scream and she darted out of the room, right into Proditor's arms. She kicked, flailed, and screamed as loud as she could, but all to no avail. The second Imamba held her fast as he watched his injured comrade.

Oga stood up and doused his face with cold water from the faucet, trying to stop the burning. The oil had seared through his skin and burned off half his beard, his raw flesh partially exposed in some areas, flaring up into tiny bubbles in others. Oga clutched his face, moaning in pain as another thug walked into the house.

"I hear somebody dey shout. How the bossman dey?" the thug asked in pidgin as he caught a glimpse of Oga kneeling on the kitchen door.

"He dey. Just some small wahala.[1] Go back outside," Proditor replied as he held onto a panicked Amina.

The thug left the room, and Oga suddenly became quiet. He stood up, a deathly glare on his face, and after wrapping a random kitchen towel around his burn, he approached Amina.

"You should not have done that, you bitch," he said as he retrieved a large knife from a utility belt and placed it on a table. Amina nervously glanced at the knife, then back at Oga.

"Turn her around and hold her down," Oga said, unzipping his trousers again. "We will all have our chance at her." Proditor bared his teeth in a grin and signaled for the thugs outside to join them in the house.

---

[1] "He's cool. Just a little problem."

✝

The bus Yisa had caught was moving too slowly, so he had hopped out and caught a taxi instead and now sat in the back of an old blue and yellow taxi as he made his way home. The streets were alive, teeming with life. It was almost impossible to navigate through the heavy traffic, and he wished the way would clear so he would have enough time to make it home and get some packing done with his wife while it was just the two of them. He hummed along to a song by Ebenezer Obey[1] blaring on the car's radio. As expected, signs and random newspapers depicting the Biafra conflict lined the streets—violence of which he no longer had to be a part. It was good that he'd left the Imamba—now he could enjoy his wife and son. He looked forward to leaving Nigeria and leaving his past behind to start a new life. They would leave first thing tomorrow morning. He had already paid for the tickets in advance.

The taxi dropped Yisa off right in front of his home. An old, rusty, banged-up Toyota Stout truck was parked a few yards away from the front gate. Suspicious, he walked over to investigate. It was empty. *Visitors for the neighbors, perhaps. Or maybe workers,* Yisa reasoned as he stepped onto his compound. It was eerily silent. He'd expected to at least see the house help walking around, conducting their daily chores.

Where is everyone? Yisa wondered as he walked up to his front door. Did they all go out? Were they all in a room somewhere else in the house? He could not recall any time he had come home to

---

[1] Ebenezer Obey was instrumental in popularizing the juju musical genre in Nigeria.

complete silence. Usually, at least one person could be seen walking or sitting outside. He stepped inside his home—not a sound. Something delicious was cooking on the fire—overcooking, in fact, as smoke had begun to fill the living room. He put down the packing boxes and dashed into the kitchen, turned off the gas, and discovered a huge mess. A frying pan was on the floor, and a combination of oil and plantains was splattered all over the kitchen. This was bizarre. Amina would never stand for a mess like this, especially in her own home. What was going on? He picked up the pan and placed it in the sink. Something didn't feel right.

Yisa felt tempted to shout his wife's name, but decided to investigate first. Pulling out and cocking a pistol he had on him, he walked cautiously into the living room. The furniture had been shifted around, and near a broken flower vase he found a spatter of blood.

Amina! Yisa began to panic. What was happening? Were the Imamba here? Was this some other criminal act? Had there been an accident?

Please, God, don't let her be hurt, Yisa prayed as he scoured the living room. Behind a couch, he noticed a foot sticking out. The foot had painted nails. He rushed to it and uncovered his wife lying underneath some couch cushions. She was naked from the waist down and lay with her limbs akimbo, as if she had been tossed like a hastily discarded rag doll. Her face was blank and her eyes stared lifelessly at the ceiling. He had seen that expression before in many eyes, eyes belonging to people whose lives he himself had taken. His heart missed a beat as his throat swelled and the world around him suddenly became fuzzy. Yisa reached out to his wife with trembling hands. This couldn't be happening. This just could not be happening. Not now, not when he had given up the brotherhood. Not Amina.

No, no, no, no, no. Yisa held her lifeless body in his arms. Blood had pooled around her body.

"Please don't leave me, please, my queen. I'm here. I came back, I'm here," he said softly in her ear, tears streaming down his face. This was his wife, the love of his life. Her skin had gone cold. He had just kissed her smiling face and told her he loved her only a short while ago. Why was this happening? He had decided to choose the right path, to be a good man, to do the right thing. Was this the reward good men had to look forward to?

Why did I leave her? How do I fix this? Oh God, this is not happening, he thought to himself.

Movement behind him caught Yisa's attention. He spun around in time to see an athletic man with skin as dark as midnight barreling toward him at full speed. Yisa lowered Amina's body and quickly spun around, firing off two shots from his pistol into the man's chest. His assailant fell without a fight.

Yisa knew he needed to get to his bedroom upstairs—he had stashed an assault rifle there and he needed that level of firepower if the Imamba were here. The chances were high that he was being watched, so he quickly ducked behind another sofa just as he heard a loud bang. A bullet ricocheted off the wall right above his head, followed by two more gunshots that ripped through the sofa, narrowly missing his chest. He could tell that there were two shooters, one right here in the living room and the other somewhere outside.

A few more shots ripped through the sofa, and Yisa knew he could not rely on it for cover much longer. He visualized the room and did his best to guess where the interior shooter was. As soon as the next shot went off, Yisa spun around the sofa and fired a shot toward the gunshot's origin. A man standing by the living room's entrance fell dead.

Another gunshot went off and narrowly missed Yisa as he took cover to reload his pistol. Maximus emerged from behind another sofa and rammed Yisa with his shoulder, knocking him through a door and into an adjacent room. Splinters of wood cut through Yisa's skin, and he felt a sharp pain go through his chest as they hit the floor. Maximus pinned Yisa down by his throat and slapped his pistol away. The man was built like a rock, and his eyes were bloodshot.

"Good to see you again, Yisa," Maximus said with his cruel joker's smile.

Yisa tried to shove him off, but he couldn't – it was like trying to shove a brick wall. Maximus punched Yisa in the head, smiling broadly. His fist felt like a slab of concrete against his skull, and Yisa almost blacked out from the impact. His vision got blurry, and blood began to leak from his nose. He knew his head could not take another hit like that. Maximus picked Yisa up easily off the ground and shoved his head into a wall. He slammed it two more times, each time generating a large crack in the wall. Yisa began to black out. Maximus was too strong, and he could not take much more of this punishment. Feeling around with his hands, Yisa grabbed as much dust and insulation from the broken wall as he could. As Maximus cocked his hand back for one final blow, Yisa threw the dirt into the giant's eyes. As Maximus reached for his eyes, Yisa punched his throat and the large man released his grip around Yisa's neck. Yisa fell to the floor as Maximus gasped for air. Yisa stood up groggily, his nose bleeding from Maximus's punch, and picked up a large wooden plank. With as much strength as he could muster, he struck Maximus on his head. The giant reeled back, and after another hit, Maximus fell to the ground with a loud thud.

Eteka! He couldn't let these people get to his son. Eteka would soon be home with Oladele.

Another gunshot went off and hit Yisa in the leg, going right through his shin.

He screamed as he fell, clutching his leg. He saw two men running in his direction, both holding M1 Carbines. A third was right behind them with a machete.

He frantically looked around and spotted his pistol a few feet away. It was his only chance. He rolled on the ground and grabbed the gun as the first thug pointed his weapon at him. The other two were still running and were now only a few feet away. It was all a question of aim and how many bullets were in the pistol.

Two shots went off at the same time as Yisa and the first thug exchanged gunfire. A bullet hit the ground only inches away from Yisa's head. The first thug slumped to the ground, a bullet in his head. Yisa quickly turned and, as the other two thugs loomed over him, closed his eyes and let off another two shots.

Both thugs slumped to the floor, and Yisa rolled away to avoid the falling machete. He lay on the ground for a few seconds and checked the pistol to see how many bullets he had left—none. Numbness spread through Yisa's leg, and he knew he'd lost a lot of blood. He grabbed a Carbine off the body of one of the thugs and then walked over to his wife's body, painfully picking it up and beginning to walk toward the stairs. He had to get to higher ground and into a defensive position. As he began to climb the steps, he felt a sharp pain in his stomach—a bullet. He'd been shot again.

He let out a cry of pain as the impact from the bullet thrust him against the side railing. He hadn't heard that shot go off, and he didn't see the shooter. Sniper with silencer. Yisa only knew of one other Imamba that was proficient with a sniper rifle: Oga.

Staggering numbly up the stairs and into his bedroom, Yisa set Amina's body down on the bed. There was blood all over his clothes, and his vision was very blurry. His knees had stopped working by the time he'd cocked the AK-47 and he had to crawl to get to the doorway. Footsteps came from downstairs.

"Yisa, we can do this the hard way or the easy way," Oga said from down the stairs.

"I figured you were the one who shot me," Yisa replied in pain. "You coward, sending amateurs to do your job."

"These guys were expendable, local boys not worth anything to us. And with Maximus, well, you got lucky. I was actually looking forward to watching him kill you with his bare hands."

"Why did you come to my home to do this? Did you have to kill my wife? She knew nothing about the Imamba!"

"I'm sorry about your pretty wife, but it was necessary," Oga replied. "If you must know, I gave her a good time before I killed her. We all did, actually."

Oga's cruel words cut through Yisa. His adrenaline spiked and his heart grew heavy at the thought of Oga and his thugs raping the most sacred woman in his life. He wanted, with all his might, to go downstairs, gun blazing, and kill Oga, but his training kicked in. Eteka and Oladele were still out there. Going downstairs now would be suicide and it would get the last two important people in his life killed.

"You should come up here and say that to my face," Yisa spat.

"Don't be angry with me, Yisa. You're the one who decided to leave the brotherhood. You knew there would be consequences," Oga replied.

"Is this how brothers treat each other?"

"You stopped being my brother the moment you quit on us. Now, you're the enemy."

"My wife had nothing to do with my decision. You could have left her alone."

"Well, I did not want to leave her alone. None of us did," Oga replied. "You know, I could have killed you as you climbed the stairs, yet I let you live."

"No, you're just a horrible shot."

Both men laughed, even though the situation was anything but funny. Tears streamed down Yisa's face as he laughed. Yisa couldn't remember the room being so cold.

"I'm happy you can laugh at your own funeral," Oga said.

"I'm happy you can laugh at yours," Yisa replied.

"I already spared your life once, back when we met in Algeria."

Yisa could hear movement in his living room, like furniture being moved around.

"What are you doing?" Yisa asked as his body got weaker.

"Well, my brother, the best way to catch game when it won't come to you is to smoke it out," Oga replied from the bottom of the stairs.

Yisa tried to stand, but his leg was completely numb now—he had lost too much blood—and the rest of his body was getting numb as well. He could smell the kerosene and knew they were going to burn the house down. If the flames reached the propane on which the appliances ran, the entire house would explode. After tearfully kissing his dead wife goodbye, Yisa started to drag himself toward an open window in his bedroom. He had to live, for his son.

"You should not have left us, Yisa," Oga called from down below. "You made a foolish mistake. You knew we could not let you live."

"On the contrary, I have done nothing but live in the short time I've been home," Yisa replied, still crawling toward the window.

"Well, it has been an honor working with you, my friend. I'll see you in Hell, I'm sure."

Footsteps made their way toward the front door, and as the front door slammed a sense of urgency ran down Yisa's spine. He frantically dragged his body along the floor, desperately doing his best to reach the open window. His heart raced, and he fought with all his strength to make it, his bloody hand finally making it to the window ledge.

But he ran out of time.

Oladele pulled up to Eteka's school and ran inside to grab the little boy. Soon they were on their way to Yisa's home, little Eteka seated on the passenger side as Oladele did his best to weave through traffic.

"Where is Daddy? I thought he said he would come to pick me up," said Eteka.

"Your Daddy had to rush home to help your mother. Don't worry, they are both waiting for us," Oladele replied.

They drove over the busy dirt roads, and Oladele sang along to a gospel track on the radio as little Eteka tried to mimic him.

"Heh, what are you doing, Eteka?" Oladele laughed as Eteka bounced around the front seat.

"We are going to eat with Daddy!"

"You are just excited that your father is home, that's why you are jumping around like a little rabbit, isn't it?" Oladele teased, rubbing Eteka's head.

As Eteka wiggled, the necklace Yisa had made for him bounced around on his neck, reminding Oladele of the unfinished bracelet Yisa had left in the car. He'd placed it in his pocket, with the intention of handing it to Yisa when they got to his place.

"Do you like the necklace your Daddy made for you?"

"Yes! I will never take it off!" Eteka replied, holding the necklace up to his uncle.

"That's good, I'm sure your father would be happy to hear that."

They continued to drive through the urban sprawl that was Ibadan. A bomber jet flew overhead, its engines roaring. As it passed, everyone on the ground looked up at its menacing figure, a painful reminder of the turbulent times in which they lived. Oladele kept his eyes on the road but glanced at the plane, watching it as it disappeared beyond the horizon. Conflict. War. All the violence did was cripple innocent people and the nation's progress.

They made the turn onto Yisa's street, the house visible just down the road.

"Okay, home sweet ho—"

A loud explosion rocked the neighborhood, making Oladele and Eteka's ears ring. Windows shattered and smoke filled the air. The eruption knocked Oladele's car off the road and into a neighboring gate, destroying both the gate and the front end of the vehicle. Oladele and Eteka coughed as they sat in a daze, choking on the thick smoke.

"ETEKA! Are you okay?" Oladele asked.

A stunned Eteka simply nodded his head.

"Okay. Stay here, okay? Don't move."

Oladele stepped out of his car and followed a trail of debris that led to the heart of the wreckage: Yisa's home. Oladele's heart grew heavy with fear.

No, no, no. Please God, no. Oladele approached what was left of Yisa's home. He coughed and waded through fires and rubble, spotting charred human remains.

"YISA! YISA! AMINA!" he screamed as he walked through the compound. His heart was pounding and he feared the worst for his best friend and his wife, the woman with whom Oladele had fallen in love. Was this all a dream? Where was Yisa? Where was Amina?

Oladele walked into the house, or what was left of it, and searched for the remains of the master bedroom. When he got to what was left of the bedroom, a raging fire forced him backward. He wanted to jump through the flames, but the heat was too intense and scorched his skin. He desperately looked through the flames for any sign of life, calling their names, but he got no response.

Oladele frantically rushed down the stairs, and as he got down to the first floor he was struck in the head by a metal pipe, knocking him to the floor. A thug wearing a bandana yanked Oladele by the collar and picked him up, slapping him awake with a heavy hand. Oga stood behind the thug, flanked by two more men. Oga had wrapped a bandage around his damaged face, and he glared at Oladele through his one good eye.

"Who are you, and how do you know Yisa?" he growled. He towered over Oladele, looking menacing.

"My name is Oladele. Yisa is, is my friend," Oladele replied, still in a daze. "Who are you?"

"I am the mighty Oga," Oga replied as the men around him grinned. "Do you live around here?" Oga asked. The fire intensified as the building continued to fall apart.

"No, I am a teacher. I picked his son up from school, and we were on our way back to have lunch together," Oladele replied in between coughs.

"Ah yes, Yisa did tell me he had a son. Where is the boy now?"

Oladele realized his error in involving Eteka with this conversation, and thought up a lie.

"I left him at the school."

"I don't believe you. Don't try to lie to me. One way or another, I will get an answer from you."

"Bossman, abeg make we jus' finish am den lef,[1]" the man in the bandana said in pidgin, adjusting his grip on Oladele's collar.

"No, Proditor. I want him to tell us where exactly the boy is."

"Uncle Oladele?"

All the men turned to find a frightened Eteka standing by the front door. Oladele's heart sank.

"Ah, and this must be Yisa's lovely boy," Oga said with a smile. He turned and shook his head at Oladele. "I usually skin men alive for lying to me when I want information, but in honor of Yisa, I'll let you live, for now," he whispered in Oladele's ear. He turned around and faced Eteka.

"Why are you grabbing my Uncle Oladele? And where is my Daddy? Where is my Mummy?" Eteka asked in a frightened tone.

"Your uncle is not feeling well, so we are going to take him to the hospital," Oga replied as he signaled his men to take Oladele to the back of the house for a sound beating.

"Where is my Daddy? Where is my Mummy?" Eteka asked again between sobs as Oladele was dragged helplessly away.

Oga walked up to Eteka and bent down.

"Listen. How do I say this? Your Daddy and Mummy had to go somewhere far away, so they asked me to look after you."

"Mummy and Daddy would not leave me. My Daddy said he will be home from now on."

---

[1] "Boss, please let's just kill him and leave."

"Yes, but things change. Grown-ups never mean what they say."

"MUMMY! DADDY!" Eteka screamed in a panic, looking helplessly at his burning home. His sense of security and his source of love were suddenly nowhere to be found. Eteka's young eyes frantically scanned the chaos around him.

"They are not here, my boy," Oga said, placing an arm around Yisa's son.

"Can we go to where they are? I want to see my Daddy and Mummy," little Eteka managed.

"We'll go to them soon. My name is Uncle Oga, and I am your Daddy's good friend."

"My Daddy never told me about you," replied Eteka uncertainly.

"Yes, your Daddy had a lot of friends he never told you about. Your Mummy and Daddy told me to take care of you. Don't worry, they will join us soon."

Eteka peered at Oga, tears pouring down his chubby cheeks as the fire continued to rage behind them.

"What about Uncle Oladele? I want him to come."

"Your Uncle Oladele is not feeling well. When he gets better, he will join us, I promise," Oga replied as he took hold of Eteka's hand and led him to a waiting car outside. Proditor and another thug emerged from the back of the house, panting and with bloodstained shirts.

"Bossman, I no fit say this be good move, movin' the guy een pikin," Proditor said. "We for jus' finish am', leave no trails. [1]"

"No," Oga replied, closing the car door behind Eteka. "Yisa was my brother, even though it came to this. I can train his son to be a better version of his father. What did you do with the uncle?" Oga asked.

"Oh, we maja am. Een try rack plas we, but we mess am up well well.[2]"

"Good job, Proditor. Let's get out of here, then," Oga replied.

The men hurriedly jumped into their vehicle and drove off as bystanders gathered around the destroyed residence. Eteka clutched the necklace his father had made for him as he watched his burning home disappear through the rear window.

---

[1] "Bossman, I don't think it's a good idea, taking the guy's child. We should just finish him and leave no trails."
2 "Oh, we put fear in him. He tried to fight with us, but we beat him up very well."

REVELATION

Nnamdi Azikiwe International Airport. Abuja, Nigeria. Africa. 1990.

Eteka touched down at the Abuja airport on a very hot Friday afternoon. He had left Oga and Omega behind in South Africa the day after their meeting. His first stop was at the Imamba safe house in Lagos, where he picked up some ammunition, a bulletproof vest, and his favorite handgun: a Taurus PT 92. A bribed customs official at the Lagos airport allowed him to smuggle his weapons onboard, and a few hours later he found himself in Abuja, sitting in a taxi on his way to Arewa's house. He had called her earlier, and she had confirmed that she was in Nigeria and eager to see him.

Eteka arrived at around 3 p.m. The same security guard who had met him before walked up to the taxi.

"Good afternoon, sah."

"Good afternoon. Is your madam there?"

"No. Madam said she will be back around five."

"Good," Eteka replied as he paid the cab driver and got out of the car. He immediately started to sweat in the hot sun. "I will wait for her inside," he said as he handed the watchman some money. The security guard smiled when he saw the crisp naira bills and let him in. Once inside, Eteka dropped his bags in her bedroom and took a long, cool bath. Wearing just a towel, he plopped onto her bed to watch some television, and before long he was asleep.

✝

He woke with a start to find Arewa smiling at him from the doorway. She looked beautiful in the suit she was wearing, and Eteka rubbed his eyes as he smiled back. The sun had begun to set, evidence that he had been asleep for well over an hour.

"Hi," he said as he sat up. "What time is it?"

"Six o'clock."

"And how long have you been standing there?"

"About ten minutes. You looked so peaceful as you slept and I was enjoying watching you, especially since you're only wearing a towel."

"Come here," he said softly with a devilish smile. She dropped her handbag on the floor, walked over, and sat on his lap. She moaned as they began to kiss, breathing deeply as she ran her fingers across the stubble on his chin before pushing him back on the bed.

"I've missed you," she said in between breaths.

"I've missed you, too," Eteka said, nibbling on her ear as he took off her clothes, layer by layer. He ran his hands across her back as she straddled him on the bed, their lips locked in a passionate kiss. She kissed his neck, then the corners of his lips as she held onto his powerful shoulders. Gently, Eteka drew her to him and took her nipple to his mouth. Arewa writhed with excitement, roughly tearing the towel from his waist and tossing it on the floor. She eased herself onto him, and they both sighed as she moved in ecstasy.

Eteka woke up late the next morning. It was drizzling outside, and the rain-cooled air wafted through the open window. Arewa slept on Eteka's chest—her smooth skin felt good against his. He lightly kissed her forehead and then looked through the open blinds. In a few hours, he would be on his way to kill another man. He had done this so many times before, and this would be no different. He began to go over his attack plan in his mind, imagining how he would find his target and assessing different scenarios...

"What are you thinking about?"

His eyes were still on the window, and he hadn't noticed her wake. Arewa stretched on top of him and nibbled on his earlobe. Eteka looked down into Arewa's brown eyes and snuggled her closer.

"Huh?"

"What are you thinking about?" she asked again, running a finger across his chest.

"You."

"Is lying one of your job requirements, Mr. Mystery Man?" Arewa giggled as she tugged on his beaded necklace with one hand, gently drawing circles with her index finger on his arm with her other hand. "Eteka?"

"Yes?"

"Why did you come back here? Simply to have sex with me again?"

"No."

She raised her head and looked at him. "Then why? I'm sure a guy like you has women in many places."

"I missed you."

Arewa smiled shyly. "Really?"

"Yes."

She kissed him passionately before getting out of bed. He watched her bare, light-coffee body stride across the bedroom before she put on a robe.

"Geez, it's twelve-thirty already. Are you hungry?"

"I am," Eteka replied as he sat up.

"Why don't you go freshen up and I'll fix us some lunch, okay?"

"Okay," Eteka sighed as Arewa left the room. Leaving would be difficult—he felt calm and peaceful here with her.

Fifteen minutes later, Eteka made his way to the dining room. Arewa was still in the kitchen, and he could smell a savory egusi stew. After a few minutes, she emerged from the kitchen dressed in a bathrobe and carrying two pots holding pounded yam and the egusi stew. They sat down together to lunch with a bottle of wine.

"So, how long are you here for? I have to leave for London in a few days," said Arewa.

"Don't worry, I have some business to take care of in Ibadan. I won't be in your way."

"Oh, hush, I never said you'd be in my way. Why Ibadan? Protecting another client?"

"No," he replied.

"Then what? Can I ask?"

"Business."

Arewa narrowed her eyes at him over her spoon. "Are you keeping secrets from me now, Eteka? That's no way to treat someone you're sleeping with."

"You don't want to know what I'm going to do."

"Try me," she replied, smiling.

"Okay. I'm going to kill a man."

Arewa gaped at him as he calmly finished the meal, cleaned his hands in a bowl of water, and poured himself a glass of wine.

"So you're heading to Ibadan to go, um, kill this person?"

"Yes."

"Do you have to kill him?"

"Yes."

She lit up a cigarette, shaking her head. "Will killing him solve anything?" Arewa asked.

"It's my job."

"Can't you, like, warn the guy and then let him go? Do you have to kill him?"

"Yes. He must die."

"Jesus, I can't believe I'm having this conversation," she said between drags. "It was one thing to hear you talking about being violent for work, but it's another to actually hear you talk about planning to kill somebody."

"I'm sorry if I upset you."

"You don't have to be a killer, Eteka. Can't you do something else?"

"I live by the code of the gun, Arewa. You would not understand. You have a simple, spoiled life," he replied heartlessly.

Arewa bristled at his words, leaning back in her chair as she took another drag of her cigarette. "Stop judging me," she shot back. "Just because I'm a woman and I make good money doesn't mean I don't know anything about right and wrong. It's wrong to kill people, period."

"If it's so wrong, how come you work for a man who is involved in that business?"

"Mr. Adeboyo?"

"Yes."

She shook her head as she flicked some ashes into an ashtray. "I won't be working for Mr. Adeboyo anymore, so let's just get that out of the way. Besides, criticizing me because I worked for him is not fair. I did simple accounting, I wasn't going around shooting people," she retorted.

"You don't work for Mr. Adeboyo anymore?"

"No."

"What happened?"

"I'm not ready to talk about it," she replied as she stood up and walked over to a window.   Eteka stood up and joined her, hugging her from behind. "I'm sorry if talking about my job upsets you," he said as he kissed her cheek. She turned around and wrapped her hands around his neck.

"Please don't kill this person in Ibadan," Arewa begged. "It's just not right. Promise me you won't do it."

"But it's my job."

"I can't see you again if you keep on killing people. Promise me."

Eteka smiled as he looked into her big brown eyes. "Okay, I promise."

"You mean it?"

"Yes."

She drew him close as they kissed again, and he picked her up in his arms and headed to her bedroom. They spent the rest of the afternoon making love and watching Nollywood[1] movies.

Three days later, Eteka found himself sitting in the back of a danfo in Ibadan. It was late in the evening, and the van was packed with people—men, women, and even a large woman selling cured fish. As the van made its way through the city's busy streets toward his destination, he played his conversations with Arewa over in his mind. She had asked him what killing this man would achieve, and

---

[1] Nollywood is the nickname given to Nigeria's film industry.

honestly, outside of doing his job, he could not think of anything. But business was business, and he had a job to do.

His adrenaline spiked as his stop approached and the outside world seemed to fade away. Even the big woman—her fish bumping into his side and crowding into his seat—the many potholes in the street, and other distractions did not catch his attention. The bus driver made one more sharp turn before he finally pulled up to Eteka's stop.

Eteka climbed out of the bus and looked around as it drove off. It was dark now, and one lonely flickering streetlight gave a little brightness to the dusty street lined with large fenced houses. It was quiet, which was much different from the commercial area through which he'd come, and the street was deserted other than a stray mongrel looking for food and some watchmen chatting.

After cocking his sidearm, Eteka walked up to a two-story house with a large concrete fence around it. This was it. Eteka scaled the fence without much difficulty, making sure to stay out of sight of the watchmen. Inside the compound, an elderly watchman was fast asleep on a bench next to a small radio softly playing some music. Eteka quietly moved past him and onto the front porch.

Eteka peeked through a window into what appeared to be the living room. All the lights were off except one in the hallway, and he found that the front door was open. For a rebel leader, Eteka found Oluko's house very easy to break into. As he carefully made his way inside, Eteka noticed that the living room was filled with books. Their subjects ranged from leadership to economics, government, and politics, and included authors such as Dostoevsky, Shakespeare, Ken Saro-Wiwa, and C.S. Lewis.

There was a light on in a room down the hallway, and someone was moving inside that room. Eteka made his way down the hall and stood behind the door. The door was slightly ajar, and Eteka peeked through the small opening. A television was on in the room, and it seemed its occupant was watching the news. Eteka pushed the door open and stepped inside.

It was a large room, stifling hot and poorly ventilated, and the only window in it failed to catch even the slightest draft. Oluko had been reading the newspaper, but now it lay discarded as he ate his pepper soup and watched the news, clad in a light pair of sleeping shorts. The glow of the television reflected off his bare chest as he listened intently to the newscaster. Without hesitation, Eteka crept into the room and aimed his weapon at Oluko's head. He planned on making this job a quick one.

Suddenly, his gun was knocked out of his hand by a long staff. The sound of the impact made Oluko jump and turn to face Eteka, who turned to see who had hit him. Standing in the doorway was the same Custodi warrior that had knocked him out in Tanzania. The warrior stood silently, his Fulani hat masking most of his face as he flicked some prayer beads between his fingers.

"You!" Eteka said in disbelief. "What are you doing here?"

ORION

"YOU WILL NOT BE KILLING
ANYONE TODAY."

ETEKA
RISE OF THE IMAMBA

"You will not be killing anyone today," the Custodi warrior said in Swahili as he moved between Eteka and Oluko. Oluko, still in shock, took a few steps back.

"Did the White Witch send you? How did you know I would be here?" Eteka asked. The Custodi warrior did not respond.

"I'm not sure what's going on, but you need to get out of my way," Eteka said as he attempted to shove the Custodi warrior to the side, only to be pushed back.

"You were kind to me in Tanzania, so I don't want to hurt you," Eteka said as he got into a fighting stance. "But I have a job to do, and I will move you if I have to."

The Custodi remained silent as Oluko dashed out of the room. The Custodi maintained his stance as Eteka slowly moved closer. After feinting a few times and getting no response, Eteka threw a ferocious right hook at the Custodi's face, which the Custodi parried with his staff. Eteka followed it again with a jab and a straight punch, both of which were also parried. The Imamba then spun and threw a roundhouse kick, under which the Custodi warrior ducked.

The two fighters circled each other, Eteka breathing heavily. Eteka pulled out a large knife and reversed his grip on the blade's hilt. The Custodi warrior changed his stance and began spinning his staff in large circular motions. Eteka lunged forward with his blade, but the Custodi defended himself, knocking Eteka to the side and hitting him with the other end of his staff. The Custodi warrior pointed his staff at Eteka as the Imamba inched forward. Again, Eteka attacked with his blade with a forward thrust. The Custodi warrior blocked the attack, but caught a follow-up haymaker to the face, sending his Fulani hat flying off his head.

Gathering himself, Eteka took the opportunity to study his opponent. The Custodi's white hair had been wrapped in long dreadlocks under his hat, and it now flowed freely down past his shoulders. He had a long, chiseled face, and his eyes had white pupils. His skin was weathered, and Eteka sensed that he was much older than his looks and movements would suggest.

The Custodi stood still and placed one hand inside his robe as Eteka approached with his blade. Eteka struck again, but the Custodi warrior blocked the strike with his staff, and suddenly threw a white powder directly into Eteka's face. The move caught Eteka off guard, and he stumbled backward as the sedative began to take effect. He became dizzy and fell to the ground.

Not again… Eteka thought to himself as the darkness enveloped him.

The room was bright, the sunlight like needles behind Eteka's eyes. Slowly, he recalled that he was in Oluko's house, and he had been fighting the Custodi leader, and then… nothing. His wrists and ankles had been tied to the bedposts. A headache worse than any he had ever had before left his head ringing, and his body felt immensely weak. What was the Custodi leader doing here? Had Oluko escaped? Why was it so quiet? He tried to sit up but couldn't even move his arms.

This is the second time I've been knocked out in a strange place.

Conversation and laughter drifted in from another room. On a table next to him was a bottle of Coke and some chloroquin tablets,[1] and next to the table was a bucket containing a little vomit. He shifted in the bed as he tried to loosen the ropes around his wrists and ankles, and accidentally knocked the tablets onto the floor. The conversation outside stopped and footsteps came toward the room.

Oluko walked in. He wore a big smile as he greeted Eteka. "My, my, my… I can't believe it's you. After all these years…"

"Huh?"

"When I was told you were still alive, I could not believe it. Now here you are. It's a miracle."

"What the fuck are you talking about?"

---

[1] Chloroquin is commonly used to treat and prevent malaria.

"They told me you would come to see me. I didn't know you were going to come here to try and kill me," Oladele said with a laugh. "Do you remember when we used to have English lessons together? Or how about when I used to drop you off at school?"

"Old man, are you crazy?"

Oluko, still smiling, picked up the tablets. "You've been out for the past day and a half."

Eteka could not understand what was happening, and his eyes darted around the room, frantically looking for a weapon. Was this man going to hurt him? Was that why he was tied up? Why was his body so weak?

"What have you done to me?" Eteka asked as he continued to struggle with his ropes. Oluko took a seat and faced Eteka. He seemed really happy to see him.

"I've done nothing to you, Eteka. Seems you picked up malaria. You probably were bitten by a mosquito sometime before you got here, and the illness is now in full swing. Don't worry; we'll take care of you."

Eteka felt extremely weak, and his spinning head made it hard to make sense of all that was happening. The heat in the room didn't help; neither did Oluko's smile. He decided to relax and kept his eyes on Oluko. He did not trust this man and he wished he had his weapon by his side.

"Today is one of the happiest days of my life. I cannot believe it's really you," Oluko said with a smile as he wiped a tear from his eye.

"You're crazy, Oluko," Eteka said warily. "When I'm free, I'll finish what I came here to do."

Oluko let out a loud belly laugh, much to Eteka's chagrin. "Oh, boy," he said, wiping a tear from his eyes. "That was a good one. You know, if you were someone else I would take you seriously, but you're little Eteka, so I find that amusing."

"How do you know my name?"

Oluko laughed again.

"What's so funny?"

"My little Eteka who I used to take to school is now a grown man, unbelievable," Oluko replied with another laugh. "My real name is not Oluko."

"What's your name?"

"I am your Uncle Oladele," he replied with a smile.

Eteka blinked at him. For a good five minutes he studied the man in front of him in silence. The skin around the old man's eyes had creases, and he had a full beard with patches of grey hair. He wore a very warm smile on his face, and had a calm demeanor. His hands, even though they were rough, had no scars or any of the usual marks that experienced fighters carried. He looked more like a professor than a rebel leader, and most importantly his name rang a bell. Eteka vaguely remembered having an uncle, and the familiarity he began to sense with Oladele created a certain peace inside of him. But another part of him told him that the man was lying.

"Your name... I've heard it before," Eteka said with a cough.

"Of course you have. You used to say it all the time," Oladele replied as tears streamed down his face.

"Enough with your lies! Stop trying to confuse me!"

"I am not trying to confuse you, Eteka," Oladele said gently. "What would I gain from confusing you? If I wanted you dead, don't you think I could have killed you already as you slept? I was your father's good friend."

Both sides of Eteka's inner character waged war with each other. Oladele, sensing Eteka's confusion, dashed out of the room. He returned with an old photo album and took a seat next to Eteka.

"Here, look," Oladele said as he excitedly opened the album. "That's you when you were a baby," he said, pointing to an infant in a photo. "And that's me, your father, and…" Oladele paused and sighed before he continued. "That's us and your mother when we were in university, before you were born," he said, pointing at a worn photo of a beautiful woman with long braided hair and a handsome, athletic man with a moustache. Oladele stood between them. Eteka looked on, transfixed by the images. These people did seem familiar.

As Oladele flipped through the album, a particular picture caught Eteka's attention. It was a picture of Oladele, the man and woman he claimed were Eteka's parents, and a short albino woman.

"Her," Eteka said, pointing at the picture. "She looks familiar, too—I've met her before. How do you know her?"

"You met her recently? Where?"

"In Tanzania. She's the White Witch."

At that, Oladele let out a loud laugh that both amused and annoyed Eteka. "White Witch? She's no witch. That is your Auntie Bayinna, and she's the most peaceful woman I know. I brought her to visit you and your parents when you were just a little boy. And yes, she is from Tanzania. It's quite remarkable that you met her as an adult, how did that happen?" Oladele asked.

"I was sent to kill her."

"Oh. You did not harm her, did you?" Oladele asked, looking concerned.

"No, I did not."

"Good!" Oladele exclaimed with a sigh. "Here, I have something else to show you."

A very excited Oladele walked out of the room again and almost stumbled over himself on his way back. He carried an old shoebox, and he placed it on his knees as he began to forage through it. It seemed to contain a lot of old jewelry. Eteka looked on, curious to see what he was looking for.

"It has to be here, it has to be… GOT IT!" Oladele shouted with excitement as he pulled out a small bracelet made up of beads and string. The bracelet looked as if it could use some work.

"Your father and I were in my car as he made this bracelet for you. He left it accidentally the day he was murdered," Oladele said, offering a sad smile as he held up the unfinished bracelet. "I've kept it all these years, praying that one day I would see you again and you could finish what he started," Oladele said, tears gathering in his eyes.

"Wait, wait, wait… you said my father was murdered?"

"Yes, Eteka—your mother, too."

"That can't be possible. My father died in a car accident, with my mother."

"Not true, my boy. Your parents were murdered, and you were taken."

It couldn't be. That wasn't what Oga had told him. "My Uncle Oga told me that my parents were killed in a car accident."

"Your Uncle Oga? No, my son, you've been lied to. Your parents were murdered in cold blood," Oladele said sadly. "I'll take you to their grave when you've had a chance to rest."

"Why should I believe you?"

"Because I was there when it happened," Oladele answered.

"It's true," a flat smoky voice said from behind them. They turned to see the Custodi walk into the room and take a seat on the floor. "You must believe this man," the Custodi said in English.

"What is your name?" Eteka asked the Custodi warrior after a brief moment of silence.

"Orion."

Eteka frowned. His parents were murdered? It couldn't be. Oga said they'd died in a car accident, somewhere here in Nigeria. But Oladele had pictures of him and his family, physical evidence that Oga had never shown him before. What was happening? Who was telling the truth? Eteka bowed his head in confusion. Oladele held the unfinished bracelet in his hand next to Eteka's necklace.

"Look, they are made of the same materials," Oladele said gently.

Eteka's heart skipped a beat as he noticed the resemblance. Oladele was right, they were made out of the exact same materials: the same color string and the same combination of beads. A perfect match. A wave of happiness swept through Eteka's body, and he found himself believing in and enjoying everything Oladele was showing him. He looked at the photo of his parents for close to 30 minutes without saying a word. His eyes scanned every little detail, from the texture of his mother's hair to her slanted eyes, her beautiful ebony skin, her smile, her slender figure, and the tie-dyed outfit she had on. Then, he studied his father's image, from his haircut and strong hands to his intense eyes, his broad shoulders, and his perfectly pressed clothes.

"Sorry I tied you up," Oladele said as he untied Eteka. "We just didn't know what to expect when you came to."

Eteka sat up in bed, ignoring the dizziness from the malaria as he held onto the photo album. Overwhelmed with emotion, a few tears rolled down his cheeks.

"These are my parents?"

"Yes. We were in school back then, and when that picture was taken your parents were dating. You weren't even an idea then," Oladele replied, and they both laughed. Eteka began to enjoy Oladele's company.

"And you, you're my uncle?"

"Yes, I am your uncle, my boy. You and I used to be the best of friends. I took you to school every day, and the last time I saw you you were only four," Oladele replied, patting Eteka's shoulder. "Here," he said, handing Eteka another album.

Eteka flipped through the photos, stopping at another photo of his mother.

"This was my mother?"

"Yes."

"She was very beautiful."

"Yes, she was," Oladele replied, a sad smile on his face. "Her name was Amina."

"Amina," Eteka said softly as he ran his finger across the picture. "What was my father's name?"

"Yisa."

"I want to know exactly how my parents were killed."

"Let's not get into heavy talk just now."

"No, I want to know."

Oladele let out a deep sigh and stood up. "You should rest. When you're stronger, we will try to fill in all the gaps."

"I am fine. I want to keep talking," Eteka shot back, his eyes glued to the album.

"Get some rest, Eteka," Oladele said as he walked out of the room. "It's good to have you back."

Eteka nodded at Oladele and resumed perusing the photo albums as Orion sat in silence on the ground by the room's entrance, flipping his beads through his fingers.

†

The next day turned out to be a cool, misty Tuesday. Eteka stayed in bed until late in the morning and felt a little stronger. Oladele brought him some porridge with bread, and Eteka did his best to eat it all. After his meal, he summoned the strength to take a bath. His uncle had prepared a bucket of hot water and a sponge for him, and after cleansing himself he wrapped a towel around his waist and decided to look for Oladele.

Moving slowly, his search led him outside into the bright sunlight. Oladele was standing by the main gate, laughing with two watchmen and a short man wearing a police uniform. Across the street, a few more policemen stood next to a parked police car. They all turned and watched Eteka as he gingerly walked toward them.

"Ah, Eteka! How do you feel?" Oladele asked with a wide smile.

"A little better, still feverish."

"Good. The illness should clear in a few days. Allow me to introduce my friend, Isiaka," Oladele said as he gestured toward the man in the police uniform. "He is the police chief for this region."

"It's nice to finally meet you," Isiaka said warmly as he shook hands with Eteka.

"Likewise," a groggy Eteka replied.

"You don't look too good," Oladele said. "You should rest while you recover. Let's go back inside so you can lie down. We can catch up later."

"Okay."

"I will take my leave, then," Isiaka announced. "I have to attend to some matters at the station. Call my office phone if you need me to escort you anywhere," he said to Oladele. Isiaka smiled at Eteka. "It's good to see you. We've all been looking forward to this day. I'm sure you have many questions for your uncle."

"Thank you," Eteka replied.

Isiaka waved goodbye and walked off toward the police car. Oladele said something in Hausa to the watchmen, and they smiled as they walked away. He then turned to Eteka and the two of them walked back into the house. Still feeling weak, Eteka took a seat on a chair in the living room while Oladele went into his kitchen and fetched bottles of Coke for them. After pouring them both glasses, Oladele took a seat facing Eteka.

"Orion left early this morning, by the way."

"Why did he leave?"

"I don't know," Oladele shrugged. "He doesn't explain himself to me. He serves a higher power." Oladele paused to run a hand through his hair. "My, look how big you've grown. Your father would be impressed if he could see you now—he was tall, too."

Every word from Oladele sounded good to him. It was almost as if his own father were talking. Oladele, still smiling, noticed the scars on Eteka's body. "I see the apple doesn't fall too far from the tree," Oladele said.

"What do you mean?"

"You're covered with scars. Your father put his body through similar abuse."

"Tell me about him," Eteka requested as he took a sip of his drink.

"What do you want to know?"

"Everything."

Oladele smiled, savoring the cold Coke. "What can I tell you about Yisa? He was a quiet man, very much like you. He had a strong, firm handshake and an intense stare. He was very ambitious and had good manners. He was a good man," Oladele said.

"All I remember about him is that he traveled a lot."

"Yes, he did travel a lot. Your father was part of your Imamba Brotherhood," Oladele said as he glanced at Eteka's Imamba tattoo. "He was one of the founders."

"The Imamba? You're saying my father started the Imamba?"

"Yes."

"That can't be possible. Oga and Omega started the brotherhood."

"I remember the man called Oga, but I am not familiar with Omega. Regardless, it was your father who came up with the original idea for the brotherhood."

"How do you know this?"

"He told me himself."

There was a brief silence as Eteka digested Oladele's words.

"Your father wanted to do good for us all," Oladele continued, "especially for you, Eteka. Those were different times back then, and he thought the Imamba would fight against the oppression we all faced. But there was never any chance of the Imamba doing any good for Africa, or for Yisa. Your father's partners twisted his good intentions, took his noble ideals and turned it into a money-making scheme. Yisa chose to do business with people he did not really know."

Eteka took a sip of his Coke. All his life, he had worked with these people. What was Oladele talking about?

"You know that I am an Imamba myself?"

"I know. The man who took you was one of them."

"The man who took me?"

"Yes. The man with the beard who took you from your parent's house while it was burning. The one you call Oga. He had a nasty burn mark on his face when I saw him. I'll never forget it."

"All I've known my whole life is the Imamba. Why should I believe you?" Eteka asked, angered at Oladele's revelation about Oga.

"After all I've shown you, you still don't believe me?" Oladele asked. "Ask yourself, how do I even know about the secretive Imamba in the first place? Ask yourself how I knew about your necklace, or your mother. Have I not proven my credibility? Yisa tried to get out of his corrupt organization, and they killed him for that—killed your mother, too."

Eteka seethed with rage. How could Oga, the man who had served as his mentor and taught him so much, lie to him? He could see Omega lying, but Oga? As a child, he had called him Uncle Oga and Oga had taken care of him.

"You said you were there when they took me. Why didn't you help me?"

"I tried to help, but they beat me and left me for dead behind your father's burning house. If it wasn't for some kind neighbors, I would have died," Oladele answered as he shook his head.

"And you're certain that my parents were killed that day?"

"Yes. I can take you to their grave if you want—they were buried together."

Eteka fixated on the Coke in his hand, his entire world turned upside down. He clenched his fist as he remembered Omega's smiling face and Oga's convincing words. Looking up, Eteka said, "I would like to visit my parents' grave, and my old home."

Oladele smiled wistfully and stood up. "You should get some rest. I'll take you to both places later this evening. I'm going to prepare some eba and okro soup for us to eat. I hope you have an appetite," Oladele said with a slight laugh, walking toward the kitchen. The older man stopped in his tracks and turned around.

"It's really good to see you, Eteka. Your father was like a brother to me, and the closest thing to family that I ever had."

Eteka watched him leave as his uncle's words took the heaviness in his heart away.

The evening was much cooler as Eteka, his Uncle Oladele, Isiaka, and two policemen drove through the streets in a police car. Oladele knew he was being watched and didn't want to drive alone. Most of the streetlights were out, and little lamps illuminated the roadside vendors selling their fried yams, roasted groundnuts, roasted corn, and chin-chin.

Finally, they pulled into a graveyard on the outskirts of the city. The graveyard had not been maintained well, and weeds had grown over many of the tombstones. Oladele and Eteka got out of the car to walk down a trail through the cemetery, while Isiaka and his men stayed behind to keep watch. Eteka still felt weak, and Oladele had given him a staff to help him walk. They walked along for a few minutes until they came to a large concrete tombstone at the center of the graveyard. The names on it were still visible through the weeds:

R.I.P. Yisa and Amina Rasaki
1932–1967 | 1937–1967

Eteka studied the tombstone in silence as mixed feelings of sadness and relief ran through him.

"We buried them together on a Tuesday evening. It was very quiet, just me and a few of the neighbors," Oladele said as they looked at the tombstone. "I remember Isiaka had to bring me in a wheelchair. It took most of my savings to raise enough money for their burial. I invited many people that I thought were your parents' friends, but none of them showed. It's funny how fickle people are—and I suppose they were afraid."

"Thank you. Thank you for everything you've done."

"You're welcome. I'll leave you alone. We will be by the car."

Eteka nodded as his uncle walked away. His parents were here, right here in front of him. After so many years of them being a mystery, he had found them. So many memories came flooding back as he knelt by their grave on that cool evening. He suddenly remembered how nice it had felt whenever his father came into town from his travels, how much he had enjoyed his father's company the last time he'd seen him, and how much he had looked forward to having his father home for good. He remembered what it had felt like to receive loving hugs from his mother, and to be with her every day as a child. All that had changed on that fateful day. On this evening, he felt the most peaceful he had felt in years. He could finally close a painful chapter of his life. He knelt by the tombstone for about half an hour, tears streaming down his face as he said his goodbyes, then walked solemnly back to the car.

Two days had passed, and Eteka had begun to feel stronger. The chloroquin had done a good job of fighting off the malaria in his system. It was a sunny afternoon when Eteka got out of bed, feeling well for the first time in many days. After taking a bath he walked out to the living room, drying his hair with a towel. Oladele was nowhere to be seen. The watchman and another man were standing by the main gate, and Eteka decided to ask them where his uncle was.

"Hello," Eteka said, as he approached the men. They both turned around and smiled.

"Hello, sah. My name is Faruk, and I am one of Mr. Oluko's assistants," the newcomer said. He was a tough-looking guy with a tribal scar etched onto his face. "He told me to drive you to his office when you got up."

"Oh. Let me put on some clothes and we can go, okay?"

Eteka went back inside, got dressed in some of Oladele's clothes (he had to leave the shirt open and let out the drawstring of the shorts to make them fit), and joined Faruk in his car. The weather was bright and sunny as they drove through the city's streets, through a busy outdoor market, and into a compound with a single-story building, a mango tree, and a couple of bicycles leaning against a wall. The grounds themselves were very sandy, and dust flew in the air as the car pulled to a stop. Oladele stepped out of the building as Eteka approached. They smiled broadly as they greeted each other.

"Ah, you finally decided to wake up," Oladele greeted as they shook hands. The old man had excited eyes, and his beard had been shaved off. "Thank you, Faruk."

"You're welcome. I'll be in the lecture hall," Faruk replied as he walked off and left the two men outside. The building seemed in dire need of repairs: it was weathered, and the paint on its concrete walls had corroded, leaving large patches of raw concrete exposed. It was covered by a battered aluminum roof, and weaver birds had made a nest in the mango tree next to it.

"What is this place?"

"My office," Oladele replied. "I used to have a space at the university, but I got this building a few years ago. It's not exactly what it used to be, but I make do. Come, let's head inside."

They entered the structure, walked down a corridor, and passed a few rooms in which men worked at an offset printing press, cutting, sorting, and packing books and journals. In another room, what appeared to be students sat in a class led by an elderly woman with kind eyes. They finally made a right turn and stepped into Oladele's office. It was a small, messy space, with papers and books all over the place. Pictures of Oladele with various people were on the walls, and Eteka noticed many literary awards on his desk. A small fan was doing its best to cool the room, but to little avail.

"Please, have a seat," Oladele offered, clearing some papers off a chair for Eteka. Both men sat down. "Look at you. The more I look at you, the more I see so much of your father."

"Really?" Eteka asked, happy to hear of the association.

"Yes," Oladele nodded happily. "You know, he and I used to sit just as we're doing now and talk for hours. I still can't believe I'm talking to you."

"What did you two talk about?"

"I'll tell you everything, with time. How do you feel?" Oladele asked.

"Better, much better."

"Good. Banana and groundnuts?" Oladele offered as he pointed at some snacks on his desk. Eteka peeled a banana and began to eat it along with some of the groundnuts, which he picked from a small plastic bag. Oladele helped himself to some as well, and the two men sat in silence as they enjoyed their snacks.

"Is this a school?" Eteka asked.

"Yes. My school. I used to run a department at the university, but we lost our funding, so I came here and set up my own special school for young men and women," Oladele replied.

"Are you a teacher?"

"Among other things, yes."

"What do you teach?"

Oladele grinned at the question. Outside, students walked the hallways, and a young woman in her twenties began to sweep the floor directly outside Oladele's office.

"Leadership, philosophy, business, innovation, those sorts of things. I try to get the young people from an early age. They are our future leaders. And young men like Faruk, whom you met, assist me."

Eteka nodded as he scanned some books and journals on Oladele's desk. They all had Oladele's nickname "Oluko" on them.

"And what of these?" Eteka asked as he flipped through one of the books. Oladele grinned, his mouth still filled with food.

"Those, my boy, are books and journals I try to distribute to the masses. Not just here, but all over Africa and some parts of Asia. Just a few studies I have done. They are also the reason I believe your superiors sent you to kill me."

"You think there's money on your head because you write articles?" Eteka asked skeptically.

OLUKO

"IDEAS, MY BOY, ARE THE MOST
DANGEROUS WEAPONS A MAN
CAN HAVE."

ETEKA
RISE OF THE IMAMBA

"There's money on my head because I pass out so-called propaganda—positive propaganda. Ideas, my boy, are the most dangerous weapons a man can have. Here, let me show you something I've been working on," Oladele said excitedly as he opened a drawer and pulled out a large folder containing hundreds of papers.

"Do you know what this is?"

"Looks like paper and scribbled notes to me."

"It's a lot more than that," Oladele replied, running his finger across one of the papers. "I've been working on a research project for many years, a study that I started right around the time you were born. I've been trying to understand the broad pattern of human history."

"I don't understand."

"Why did human history unfold the way it did? How is it that we were the conquered and not the conquerors?" Oladele asked with a smile as he placed the big stack of papers back in the drawer.

"I never gave it much thought. Why?"

"Human beings developed at different rates around the world. The differences in development rates among various races and cultures can be attributed to unique differences in each environment. These differences would shape historical patterns and determine the outcomes when disparate cultures and people would eventually collide.[1]"

"Collide?" Eteka asked, enjoying the wisdom in his uncle's words.

"Yes. Exploration, colonization, disease, genocide... the ripple effects from these events can still be felt today, all over the world."

"If you say human beings developed at different rates, then history was supposed to happen the way it did, right? What use is all this research you've done?"

"Be careful with your words, Eteka. The whole point of my life's work is to teach our people how to think critically and outside the box, beyond the norms of our culture. And the only way to develop critical thinking skillsets is to study processes, ideas, and systems. Understanding why and how things happen will empower us to see the big picture and be all we can be. Of course, our moral

---

[1] The answer to why Western civilizations became hegemonic and why history followed different courses for different peoples has been tackled by many scholars. The most notable attempt to date was by Pulitzer Prize winner Jared Diamond in his celebrated thesis, "Guns, Germs, and Steel: The Fates of Human Societies."

compasses have to be in order, so our solutions exist for the greater good."

"This all sounds very interesting, uncle. What made you want to do so much research on this subject?"

"It was asked of me many years ago by a very important man I met in a land far away," Oladele replied as his mind drifted back in time for a brief moment and recounted his chance meeting with Carlos Romulo and Richard Wright in Indonesia many years ago.

Eteka nodded as he glanced through another book full of essays and reports, with topics ranging from leadership, urban conflict, and human evolution to mercantile exchange.

These were all subjects with which Eteka was unfamiliar, and they caught his attention. Oladele smiled as he watched as his nephew sift through the publication. It was just like the old days, when Yisa would come into his office and do the same.

"Is this dangerous writing?" Eteka asked, pointing to the header that read "Mercantile Exchange.[1]"

Oladele laughed. "Anything can be perceived as dangerous. It depends on who's doing the perceiving."

Eteka thought for a moment. Being with Oladele made him feel happy and peaceful in a way he couldn't ever remember feeling. He could picture his uncle and his father having these sorts of conversations many years ago. "Was my father in agreement with your ideas?"

---

[1] Mercantile/commodities exchanges are central marketplaces where businesses which buy and sell major commodities can meet to set quality and quantity standards and establish rules of business. For an exchange to be successful, conditions such as having a strong financial sector, transparency and large trading volumes have to be present.

"Yes, yes he was," Oladele said excitedly. "We spent much time sitting together, discussing Africa's future. He was a fighter in his mind, and a peaceful man at heart."

"And that's why they killed him? Because he wanted to do the right thing?" Eteka asked.

"Possibly. I honestly don't know why he was killed, but I do know he made the decision to leave your Imamba Brotherhood so he could spend more time with you and your mother."

Eteka shook his head. "There is no way to leave the Imamba. Once you're a member, you're a member for life." Glancing out the window, Eteka clenched his fists. Outside, on the dusty school grounds, two young men walked by Oladele's office, talking in Igbo.

"I'm going to kill the men who have lied to me all these years."

"Kill them?" Oladele asked with a surprised expression. "And tell me, Eteka, what will killing them achieve?"

"It will avenge my parents, and make me feel better," Eteka replied, seething with anger.

"You don't need revenge," Oladele said gently. "You know, your father did not want to kill anymore. He realized that killing his own people wasn't helping anyone, and he decided that he would use his anger in a positive way—as an impetus to help others," Oladele said as he got up and walked over to the window. After looking out of it for a moment, he turned and faced Eteka.

"You must forgive, Eteka. Forgive, forget, and move on," Oladele said, walking back over to Eteka and placing a hand on his shoulder. "Anything else makes you a slave to emotions, and not to reason. Your enemies will get what they deserve. The equation of life will balance them out."

"I don't know if I can forgive these men, Uncle."

"You must try."

Tears stung Eteka's eyes. How could he simply forgive people who had betrayed him to this extent? How could he forgive people who were involved in the murder of his father and mother? What his uncle was asking of him was surely impossible. What he wanted to do was grab a gun, shove it against Oga's head, and ask him why before blowing his brains out. But something good in him reckoned with his uncle's words. Oladele, sensing Eteka's inner turmoil, patted his shoulder and sat back down.

"Let's do something fun today to lighten the mood," Oladele said brightly. "I got us tickets to a fuji music concert happening in town. Your father and I used to go to a lot of concerts, and we could do the same. It'll be fun. And until then, you can follow me around here as I do my work and learn a thing or two. Sound good?"

Eteka agreed reluctantly, and spent the rest of the day learning about Oladele's enterprises and his aspirations for Africa.

†

It was around midnight when Oladele and Eteka returned from the fuji concert. The performance had been at a local football stadium packed with hundreds of spectators. The band played good music and the crowd loved every bit of it. It was one of the best experiences Eteka had ever had in his life—being able to shout and cheer as loudly as he wanted with a man he considered family. Both men had the time of their lives, and returned to Oladele's home in high spirits.

"Ah, that was good. Did you enjoy yourself?" Oladele asked.

"I did," Eteka replied, sitting down on the couch in his uncle's living room. And he meant it—he was having the best time of his life.

"Good. Care for some palm wine?"

"No, thanks."

"Your father and I used to drink palm wine from these very calabashes," Oladele said, placing two small calabashes on the living room table. "Somehow they were not destroyed in the fire at your home. I saved them as a memory of a favorite pastime with your dad. Sure you don't want a drink?" Oladele asked again with a wink.

"Sure, why not?"

Oladele left for the kitchen and returned with a large gourd of palm wine. He filled both of their calabashes with the chilled white liquid, and they both raised their drinks for a toast.

"To new beginnings."

"To new beginnings," Eteka replied. The palm wine felt good as it massaged its way down Eteka's throat, leaving a cool feeling in his neck and chest.

"Ahhh, that was nice," Oladele said.

"This is probably the best time I've ever had in my life."

"Well, I'm honored to be a part of it. What now?" Oladele asked.

"By tomorrow I should be fully recovered. I can leave then."

"Leaving so soon? Why don't you stay a little longer? We still have a lot of catching up to do."

"No, I must go," Eteka said, shaking his head.

"Okay. So you'll leave, and do what?"

"I, uh, I really don't know."

"Why don't you stay here and work with me?" Oladele offered. "There is a lot you can do around here."

Eteka shook his head. He hadn't considered staying in Ibadan as a civilian and honestly did not know what he would do with himself in this strange, academic environment.

"I'm not a teacher, Uncle Oladele. I'm a fighter."

"That was the same thing your father said. You don't have to go back out there," Oladele replied.

The thought was certainly appealing. It seemed peaceful here in Ibadan, and he liked the idea of being around his uncle. But, he needed to face the men who had betrayed his trust—he knew it would haunt him until he did.

"You and I both know that I have unfinished business to take care of."

"Don't fall for the devil's bait, young man," Oladele replied. "You have the chance to walk away. Do it and don't look back."

"You do not just walk away from the Imamba. I must face them, or what happened to my father will also happen to me," Eteka said.

Oladele sighed in frustration. "Very well. Every man must find his own way. Doing what I suggest may not be God's plan for you. Just remember that I'll always be here for you if you need me."

"Thank you."

They sipped on their palm wine in silence for a moment, both men thinking of the future. The one light provided only dim lighting, and in a corner of the room the smoke from a lit mosquito coil danced in the air. Eteka looked at his uncle, smiling peacefully at him from across the room.

"You think people want you dead because of your writings?" Eteka asked.

"And the school, yes."

"Yet you still do it. Why?"

"Ha, your father asked me the exact same question, many years ago," Oladele replied as he took another sip of his drink and tapped his chin. "That's a good question. I certainly don't get paid much, and I get death threats from time to time. There are a lot of foreign and domestic parties that would prefer that I keep my big mouth shut."

"So, why do you do it? Doesn't sound like there are many benefits for you," Eteka said.

Oladele paused in thought as he continued to tap his chin. It was the sort of question that would make any man on this journey stop and ask himself whether character, selflessness, sacrifice, and nobility were really worth the heavy—and sometimes mortal—price tags they usually came with.

"I must confess: I lost the passion to continue my work many years ago. I doubted myself after seeing so little progress in society, and really lost hope after your parents were killed. I began to question myself… all these dreams I have… my desire to create a society driven by innovation and morals… am I fighting a losing war? Is it even a war worth fighting? Is there a place for idealists in the complex world in which we now live? And am I even qualified to be the authority on morals to begin with?" Oladele said, his mind briefly drifting to Amina.

"I lost my desire to continue, and even considered shutting down the school. But seeing you after all these years has put a fire in me that I have not felt in a long time."

After a long pause, Oladele continued.

"I do what I do because it's not about me. I am dedicated to my people. If we all had a spirit of selflessness and responsibility, the world would be a much better place, and you would not have lost your parents the way that you did. There is a lot of work to be done, and I refuse to believe that our people are condemned to feed at the bottom of the barrel."

"You sound like a man on a mission. Now I see why you're a dangerous man," Eteka said teasingly.

"I'll take that as a compliment."

"You know, your enemies will eventually get to you. After I leave, someone else will come in my place to finish the job," Eteka replied with a look of concern.

Oladele smiled complacently as he took another sip of his palm wine. "So, let them come. Maybe, like you, I'll be able to charm them into a moral life," he replied. They both laughed at that, but the laughter was bittersweet for Eteka.

"Don't you fear for your life? Are you sure this is what you want to do?"

"Fear?" Oladele asked with a laugh. "Young man, fear is one of the main reasons many people do not do what they were born to do. Death comes to us all, we cannot change that. I'm more worried about how I live."

"But surely there must be some other, safer way to do what you do. Isn't there another way to get your message across without being so visible?" Eteka asked.

Oladele smiled peacefully, setting down his drink.

"You sound so much like your father. My boy, no strong man chooses the direction in which the winds of life will blow. He simply plays his part and makes the best of it, no matter how painful the direction may be."

"Pain... why would you want to expose yourself to feeling pain, Uncle? You can choose to lead a peaceful life. It's not as if you're a fighter," he protested, looking at the smaller man.

"Eteka, pain is the one human predicament from which no man escapes. No one goes through life without experiencing it in one form or another. True power comes when you beat the odds and keep your character rather than succumbing to your environment and becoming what it dictates. You should learn that."

Oladele stood up and yawned as he stretched.

"Let's get some rest. You'll need it for your journey tomorrow," he said, helping Eteka to his feet.

The following morning was sunny and beautiful with clear blue skies. Eteka, dressed in his camouflage Imamba fatigues (the only clothes in this house that fit him), made his way to the front of Oladele's house carrying a duffel bag containing his weapons. He felt as good as new, with no traces of malaria in his system. He stepped outside and was greeted by two policemen, police chief Isiaka, and Oladele.

"Good morning, Eteka," Isiaka greeted. "Your uncle told me you will be leaving us today. I have arranged for one of my men to take you to the airport."

"Thanks, I appreciate it."

A policeman led Eteka toward a car, and as Eteka loaded his things into it, his uncle walked up to him, tiny wrinkles creasing his eyes as he beamed up at his nephew.

"This is for you," he said, handing Eteka a plastic bag filled with meat pies, mangoes, and oranges. He also handed Eteka some naira bills. "Where will you go from here?" Oladele asked, standing in his signature pose with his hands behind his back.

"I know someone in Abuja. I'll be with her until I figure something out."

"Her? Little Eteka has a girlfriend now?" Oladele asked with a laugh.

"She's just someone I'm seeing."

"I see. These are dangerous times for you and I, so be careful. These people are very dangerous."

"I know. I'm one of them."

"Not for long, hopefully."

Oladele gave Eteka a warm hug. Tears streamed down both men's faces as they embraced each other. This was the only man Eteka knew who had ties to his family, and a part of him didn't want to leave. He had found an essential part of himself that had long been missing, and he wanted to get to know this side a lot better. But first he had to confront Oga. He would go to Arewa's place to clear his head and think up a strategy for confronting the Imamba. More importantly, Eteka wanted to ensure Oladele's safety. He knew that once the Imamba found out that he hadn't killed his uncle, they would send someone else to finish the job.

"I'm really happy that I met you, Uncle Oladele."

"The feeling is mutual," Oladele replied. "You have family here, Eteka. Those men you are with do not have good intentions for you. Come back here and learn who you really are."

"I intend to. We have a lot to discuss."

"You know how to find me," Oladele said, "so don't be a stranger. And consider what I said about coming here to work with me. I won't be around forever, and I could use a strong young man like you to help run things."

"I will. I'm concerned about your safety. The Imamba are no joke—don't underestimate them."

"Don't worry about me," Oladele said. "Isiaka and his men will be here keeping watch over me."

"Your uncle will be fine," Isiaka chimed in. "Like he said, my men and I will be here to make sure he's protected. You don't have to worry about him."

"See? You go take care of what you have to do, and when you're done, come back so we can pick up where we left off. Deal?" Oladele asked hopefully, his eyes still glinting with tears behind his glasses.

"Okay," Eteka replied, getting into the car. "I'll come back as soon as I can." He and his uncle exchanged one last hug.

"So long. I'll see you soon." Eteka waved and the car sped off, leaving a trail of dust in its wake.

"So long, my boy," Oladele replied, watching his nephew leave, the car fading into the distance.

"There he goes, your long-lost nephew," Isiaka said as they watched the car disappear.

"Yes, there he goes."

"Did you tell him about Isatou?" Isiaka asked.

"No. Too soon. He already had a lot to take in with the revelations he received. When he returns, I'll tell him about his sister."

"You think he'll return?"

"Yes. His soul and heart are here. He still has some unanswered questions, and he's yearning for guidance. Let's just pray that God protects him."

"And us. Come on, let me sample whatever palm wine you have left," the police chief said with a grin. "If you haven't drunk it all already."

"Yes, of course," Oladele replied absently, closing the front gate and heading back into his house, Isiaka and the two policemen following closely behind. He had some more writing to do, and meeting Eteka had inspired him with all sorts of new ideas.

Pacman, Proditor, and two other Imamba waited in a car across the street from Oladele's house as Eteka's car drove away. They watched Oladele and Isiaka walk into the house, followed by two armed policemen. After a few minutes, the mercenaries got out of their car, readied their weapons and headed for Oladele's residence.

No Way Out

Abuja, Nigeria. Africa. 1990.

Eteka arrived back in Abuja. So many emotions and thoughts had run through him during his trip—even his dreams were disturbed by vivid images of the life he had almost forgotten. Sometimes he was tempted to doubt his uncle's words, but they had to be true. How could Oladele have known so much about him—and the Imamba? And what of the pictures? Everything made sense, and the truth felt good. He had never been this emotionally distraught in his entire life, and he needed to be around a neutral person—Arewa. He called to inform her of his arrival ahead of time.

His taxi pulled up to her front gate in the early evening. Her watchman, recognizing Eteka, saluted and let him in with a knowing smile. She was away at a meeting in the city, so Eteka took a short nap and got dressed in a sharp charcoal-grey suit with an ivory shirt and jet cufflinks. He skipped the tie. He had never heard of any Imamba fighter going against orders, and it was widely understood within the brotherhood that the punishment for betrayal was death. He would have to move quickly, especially because his presence put

Arewa at risk. Eteka planned on having a chat with her, then vanishing for a while as he figured out the best way to handle Oga and his other Imamba brothers. He would go somewhere quiet, maybe Canada or somewhere remote in Asia. Hopefully, Arewa would come with him, and it would be more of an extended vacation and less of an exile.

After grabbing a chilled bottle of Gulder from her fridge and checking the windows, Eteka sat on a couch in Arewa's living room and watched a bit of television while flipping through a Nigerian lifestyle magazine. An article in the magazine caught his attention. The headline read "Oladele Akinjide, a.k.a. Oluko, is at it Again." It described a recent journal publication by Oladele discussing the role of foreign aid in Africa, and included a picture of his uncle giving a lecture in a university classroom. Eteka smiled when he saw the photo and reclined in his seat. He looked forward to spending more time with his uncle back in Ibadan, after he dealt with the Imamba.

After 20 minutes, Arewa's car pulled into the garage. Arewa came through the front door and smiled when she saw Eteka sitting in her living room, throwing her handbag on the couch.

"Hey, mister," she said as she walked over to Eteka and sat on his lap. She was dressed in a sleeveless tie-dyed shirt and dark-wash jeans, her long earrings dangling.

"Hey."

"Miss me?"

"Of course," he replied, kissing her.

She got off his lap, kicked off her shoes, and sat next to him. "You look nice. Going somewhere?" she asked, admiring his outfit.

"I am," Eteka said, holding her at arm's length, "but first we need to talk."

"Um, okay. What do you want to talk about?" she asked as she helped herself to a sip of his beer.

"My trip."

"Yes! How did it go?"

"It went well. I had a good time—the best time of my life, in fact. I was at peace," Eteka replied with a smile.

"I take it you did what I asked you not to."

"No, I did not kill anyone."

"I'm confused. What made the trip so good, then?"

"I found out the truth."

Arewa raised an eyebrow and lit up a cigarette as she looked at him. "Okay, I'm not psychic, Eteka. What happened out there?"

"The man I was sent to kill is actually my uncle."

"Your uncle?"

"Yes, and he proved it."

"Okay, you sound really crazy right now. How did this person prove that he's your uncle?" Arewa asked.

"It's a long story, but I believe him, and that's what matters."

"Okay, so good for you, you found your uncle." Arewa smiled at him. "We should celebrate."

"Not so fast. I didn't kill him, and the punishment for not carrying out an assignment for the Imamba is death."

Arewa nervously tapped her foot on the ground as she took a few more drags from her cigarette. "What are you saying, Eteka?"

"I plan on disappearing for a while, going somewhere quiet. I want you to come with me."

"Come with you?" she asked, overwhelmed as she stood up and began to pace the room. "Eteka, I barely know you! We just started seeing each other! I mean, I do like you, and you're cute and all, but I can't just get up and go with you wherever you're going. I have my own life, you know."

"What life? You don't work for Mr. Adeboyo anymore. There's nothing holding you back."

"True. And he'll want this house back soon, I'm sure. But still, I have plans with my brother. I can't just run off with you."

"It's not safe for you here or in London, Arewa. You don't know the Imamba. They'll hurt anyone to get to me once they find out what I've done."

"Why do I always pick the weird guys?" Arewa grumbled to herself. Rounding on Eteka, she demanded, "Who is this uncle of yours anyway, and why were you sent to kill him?"

Eteka picked up the magazine from the table and showed her the article about Oladele. Arewa's mouth fell open in shock.

"Wait a sec, your uncle is Oluko?"

"Yes, why? You've heard of him?"

"Heard of him? Everyone around here knows Oluko! I love his writing," she replied as she ran off to her bedroom and returned with a handful of journals and books by Oluko, favorite passages highlighted carefully. "He's a very smart man, and he has a lot of fresh ideas for Africa. He used to give lectures in Lagos, and I would go listen to him before I started working in London. I can't believe he's your uncle!"

"Well, believe it."

"If your friends want him dead, then there must be a price on his head. Will he be okay out there on his own?" Arewa asked anxiously.

"He should be fine," Eteka assured her. "His friend is a police chief, and he has a few policemen watching over him until I get back out there and figure out what to do. But for now, I have to disappear, and the only reason I'm here is because of you. Please, come with me. It's not safe for you here."

Arewa put out her cigarette and sat down. "I can't go with you, honey," she said, placing a hand on his face. "I have too much going on here."

"Like what? The stuff with your brother?"

"Yes. He signed with a different label and needs me. I'm the only person he can trust. Plus, I don't work for Mr. Adeboyo anymore, so I need to find a job to support myself. I'm not even supposed to be in this house anymore, I just came here to get away from London for some time. There's too much happening, so I can't go with you."

"You're making a mistake. Please, come with me. We can leave tonight."

"Let's just drop this subject, okay? I'm sure you can talk to your Imamba friends and get them to give you a break. You're probably making this a bigger deal than it really is."

"Arewa, I'm not maki—"

"Shhh! It's my brother, Fallal. There, look!" Arewa said excitedly as she pointed at the television. She stood up and began to clap her hands happily as she watched the news report about her brother.

Eteka, taken aback, looked at the television. Fallal was a tall, young black man with a large afro and an eclectic fashion sense. He was familiar for some reason—Eteka knew he'd heard his name before. As the story came to an end, it hit him: this was the man Omega had sent Cyrus and Mokin to kill. Eteka looked at Arewa. She was still smiling, excited that her brother was on the television.

"When is his concert?" Eteka asked.

"This coming Saturday in New York. I'm going! You should come if you can—he's amazing."

"Is there any reason why anyone would want to hurt your brother?" Eteka asked. Arewa frowned at his words as she sat back down.

"What kind of question is that?"

"Just answer it, please."

Arewa fidgeted, tapping her foot on the floor again. "Well, Mr. Adeboyo obviously wasn't happy that my brother ended their relationship."

"I was thinking the same thing."

"Is there something you want to tell me?" she asked seriously, her brow furrowed in concern.

"Yes. I think two of my associates are in New York right now, making preparations to murder your brother on the day of the concert."

"What! Why would anyone want to hurt Fallal?"

"They are trying to make a statement on behalf of your old boss, I think."

"How would you know that? That can't be true!" Arewa yelled, launching to her feet. "We have to do something. I have to call the police in New York."

"I doubt they'll be able to do much, but call anyway," Eteka said. "Also, call your brother, warn him and tell him to cancel his concert. And then we have to get out of here."

"Okay, okay," she replied nervously as she rushed to her room to find a phone card to call her brother.

Eteka pulled a gun from his bag, cocked it, and placed it in the back of his trousers, tucking the suit over it. Arewa came running out of her room and darted toward the landline in her living room, but the phone rang before she could get to it. She stopped in her tracks and gave Eteka a surprised look.

"You going to get that?" he asked as it continued ringing.

"I'm not expecting any phone calls," she said nervously.

"Well, answer it."

She stared at the phone for a few more rings, and then answered it. "Uh, hello?" The blood drained from Arewa's face as she listened to the receiver; then she handed the phone to Eteka. Eteka had never seen her look so scared before—she was ashen and shaking. "It's for you."

Eteka, puzzled by her response, took the phone from her and held it to his ear. "Yes?"

"Hello, Eteka," Omega's husky voice said on the other end. Eteka bristled. If Omega was calling him here, then they were being watched. "How did you find me?" Eteka asked as he looked out of a nearby window and drew the curtains.

"The Imamba have eyes everywhere, you know that," Omega replied. "I see you did not finish your assignment as we agreed."

"We need to talk."

"We're talking now. I want to know why you didn't complete your mission. Your weakness disappoints me, Eteka."

"Where's Oga? Put him on the phone," Eteka demanded.

"Oga will talk to you when I want him to. You need to answer my questions, for the sake of yourself and that pretty little bitch you're staying with."

Eteka glanced at Arewa, who was standing behind him clutching his sleeve.

"Oh, yes," Omega continued, "we know all about her and her foolish brother with the big mouth. We've been watching them for quite some time, at our client's request. I advise you to answer my questions if you don't want anything bad to happen to her in the immediate future."

"If you try anything, I'll kill you myself," Eteka growled into the phone.

"There, now, that's the Eteka I know," Omega chuckled. "Now tell me, why didn't you complete the hit in Ibadan? He was worth quite a bit of money, you know. Your actions will cost us."

Eteka clenched his jaw. Leave it to Omega to always worry about the money. "Where's Oga? I need to talk to him. Now."

"Oga can't talk to you now. In fact, no Imamba can. You broke the rules, and you must pay."

"You sent me to kill my own uncle, and you knew it all along. Now you're threatening me and my private life? Why don't you come here and threaten me to my face?" Eteka said, gripping the phone as if it were Omega's throat.

There was a brief pause over the phone before Omega spoke.

"Your uncle? What are you talking about?"

"The man you sent me to kill was my own uncle! You tricked me, and now you question why I didn't kill him?"

OMEGA

ETEKA
RISE OF THE IMAMBA

"I don't know what you're talking about, but I can see you're no longer of any use to us," Omega mused. "You certainly had a lot of potential, I must say. Oga I'm sure will miss you."

"I WILL KILL YOU!!!" Eteka screamed into the phone.

"Correction," Omega replied calmly, "we will kill you. You're a dead man walking—you just haven't been buried yet."

"Omega!" Eteka said. The phone replied with a dial tone— Omega had hung up on him. Eteka put down the phone and looked at Arewa. She was jittery, and had gone through at least six cigarettes since coming home.

"Wh-what happened? Who was that? How did they know where you were?"

"Grab your car keys and all the money you can get quickly. We should leave, now," Eteka said firmly. She nodded and grabbed her purse and shoes, and they made for the Audi parked in her garage.

"Give me your keys," Eteka said sternly. She handed him her keys with trembling hands, and after the garage doors opened, they hopped into the car and sped off. It was around eight-thirty and darkness had fallen. The roadside vendors were up to their usual business, selling their wares to pedestrians walking by. The speeding Audi roared past them, and everyone on the road jumped out of the way and looked on in amazement at the reckless driving.

"Where are we going?" Arewa asked.

"To the airport. I'll get us on a flight to Canada, you'll be safer there. We can try calling your brother once we get to the airport."

"I'm scared," she whispered. Arewa did look frightened—her face was drawn and pale, and her hands shook slightly.

"Don't be scared. I won't let anything happen to you."

Eteka shifted the car into fifth gear as they merged onto a highway. He worked the clutch as he wound his way through traffic effortlessly, but noticed a traffic jam up ahead. Spotting a side street, he made a quick detour.

"We can cut through some side streets and get to the airport faster. That traffic jam will hold us up."

They drove down a bumpy dirt road and made a left onto a street in a residential neighborhood. Large fenced mansions lined the street and huge palm trees sat on perfectly mowed lawns. They continued to speed along when they heard machine gun fire.

"Put your head down!" Eteka shouted as the bullets tore up the rear of the car. In the rearview mirror, he could see two pairs of men on okadas—Nigerian-style motorcycles—followed by a black BMW. The men on the Okadas appeared to be street thugs, which he could tell from their clothing. The men in the rear seats of the Okadas were firing the assault rifles, the outbursts sounding like firecrackers going off. Arewa was screaming and crying hysterically, unaccustomed to being under fire and totally unnerved by the night's events.

Another string of bullets hit their car, punching a few holes in the back window. Seeing a right turn ahead, Eteka pulled up the handbrake and dropped to first gear to make the sudden sharp right turn. The car spun violently, and as soon as it was aligned with the street, he released the handbrake and pumped the gas, boosting the car down the street and throwing the okadas off. The BMW driver had no trouble following and sped down the street in pursuit. Someone leaned out of the passenger side window and started shooting at them with a shotgun.

The blasts shattered all the car windows, and little shards of glass cut their arms. Eteka's heart raced as he spotted another left turn ahead that would lead him into an area with some unfinished buildings. He made the left turn, whipped out his gun, and fired off a few rounds at the pursuing BMW. The BMW was momentarily thrown off their trail, and Eteka sped down the dark street.

"Are you okay?" he asked as he glanced at Arewa's hunched figure. She had a few cuts on her face and arms from the shards of glass flying about, but she managed a smile as she looked at him. They came up to a T-intersection and made a right turn onto a dirt road that had no streetlights. The two motorcycles suddenly cut onto the road from between some houses and approached them from behind, guns blazing. The bullets tore through the battered car, ripping holes in the back seats.

Eteka slammed on the brakes, bringing their car to a screeching halt. One of the okadas slammed into their car, throwing one man into a wall and the other onto the street. The second okada barely missed the rear end of the Audi as it skidded, slamming into the front gate of a residence. Not wanting to waste any time, Eteka revved up what was left of the car and drove off, leaving the thugs behind. He came up to another T-intersection and made a right onto a tarred road. Their engine was smoking and one of the tires was punctured.

"We need to switch cars," Eteka said to Arewa, who was coughing from the engine smoke. The car rocked suddenly as they were hit violently from behind by the BMW. The impact knocked Arewa's head against the glove compartment, and she winced in pain as Eteka swerved left and right, desperately trying to shake off their pursuers. An Imamba leaned out of the passenger side of the BMW and fired more shots at their car.

The blasts tore through what was left of the car, leaving large holes on the sides, roof, and rear of the vehicle and ripping across Eteka's face and arms. Grimacing, he noticed an abandoned warehouse ahead to his left. He dropped the car from fifth to third gear, pumped the gas, and made the sharp left turn with the help of his handbrake. The unexpected turn sent the BMW sailing down the street, and gave Eteka enough time to park the car at a quiet spot by the warehouse and turn off the headlights.

"We have no time, let's go inside," Eteka said, opening his door. But there was no response. He looked over and saw Arewa writhing in pain as blood oozed from shrapnel in her sides and a gunshot wound in her neck.

No, not her, this can't be.

Arewa looked helpless and terrified as blood began to leak from her mouth. He got out of the car, pulled open the passenger door, and crouched by her side, unfastening the seat belt. He picked her up in his arms, knowing that their time was very short.

"You'll be fine, I promise. I love you, just hold on," he said reassuringly, looking around as he made his way into the dark warehouse. His suit was dirty and stained with her blood as he hurried through the ground floor of the building. It was empty except for a few heavy generators humming in the background, and the squeak of distant rats.

As Eteka's eyes adjusted to the darkness, he spotted a stairway leading to the second floor of the structure. He ran up the stairs with Arewa in his arms, even as he heard the BMW pull up to the warehouse. The second floor was another large, empty space accented by structural pillars. Eteka carried Arewa to one of the corner pillars and set her down. Fear was in her eyes, and her mouth was filled with blood as she tried to speak, choking in her desperation for air. Blood also pumped out of the hole in her neck, and she shook violently as she clutched the sleeve of Eteka's suit jacket tightly. She was trying to talk, but all she could do was gurgle on her own blood. Eteka panicked, all he knew of first aid blurring at the sight of her injuries. Here lay the only woman he had ever had any feelings for and she was losing her life, right next to him. He tore off a piece of his sleeve and wrapped it around her neck. Her heartbeat was getting slower, and blood continued to leak out of her slack mouth. Downstairs, he could hear a noisy okada pull up and some faint male chatter.

"I'm so sorry," Eteka said softly to her as he stroked her hair. Arewa kept her eyes on him as she tightly clutched his sleeve. "This is all my fault," he continued, shedding tears of fear and anger. She was still shaking, but she shook her head in disagreement.

"Please don't leave me," he said softly to her as he rocked Arewa back and forth in his arms. She tried to respond but could only give a faint smile as she held onto him.

Eteka heard voices and footsteps coming in their direction, shouting taunts and curses in Yoruba, Igbo, and pidgin English. He could also hear some scraping, like a machete being dragged noisily along the concrete floor. He checked the clip in his handgun—only two bullets left. There were no other exits on this floor and he would have to face them. He looked back at Arewa. She had stopped shaking and was looking at him. She was unable to lift her head, but with her finger she wrote in the dust on the concrete floor: SAVE

MY BROTHER. Eteka wiped tears from his eyes as she continued: I LOVE YOU.

The Imamba had climbed the stairs and were in the room. It would be a matter of seconds before they spotted them in the corner. Both lovers locked eyes for a moment, a moment that seemed like an eternity. All of their experiences—seeing each other in London, her crush on him and his infatuation with her, meeting in Abuja, the timeless hours they'd spent making love, their plans for the future—all that had come to this. Life had dealt its hand, and there was nothing Eteka could do. He gave her one last smile, caressed her cheek, and stood up to face his pursuers.

The first figure Eteka spotted was a lean man carrying a machete. The blade gleamed in the dark from moonlight streaming in from a torn opening in the wall. Eteka aimed his gun carefully and fired off one shot that caught the man squarely in the eye. The figure slumped to the ground as the other three turned their heads in Eteka's direction. Eteka moved as quickly as he could around the room as two of the figures opened fire. The flashes from the gunfire lit up the dark room as the gunshots left trails along the walls. Eteka aimed his gun at one of the shooters and shot him right in the chest, knocking the man into a pillar. Dropping his now-useless gun, he ran along the wall straight toward the shooters.

As he got closer, Eteka could make them out: two young thugs, one of them with a piece of cloth around his head, a see-through undershirt, and an automatic weapon, the other with short dreads and a machete. Both men were having a hard time tracking

Eteka, and obviously weren't professionals. The man with the AK shot at Eteka as he approached them, each shot lighting up the room. Eteka jumped out of the way of the gunfire, but a bullet caught him in his side a moment before he reached cover. He winced as he propped himself up behind a large pillar, silently praying that the men would not stumble across Arewa. His discarded gun lay next to him and he picked it up.

"Omo, where he dey?[1]" the thug with the AK asked his partner in pidgin.

"I no sabi sef, but ebe like e go dat side. Move slow sha,[2]" the second thug said.

Footsteps moved in Eteka's direction. He picked up a nearby piece of wood with his left hand, holding his empty gun by its muzzle in his right. When the footsteps were close enough, he threw the piece of wood across the room. It clanked against a wall, and the thug with the AK opened fire in its direction, spraying the walls indiscriminately with bullets. Eteka spun around the pillar and threw the pistol as hard as he could at the gun-toting thug's head. The weapon hit the man in his temple with so much force that it knocked him off his feet, sending him sprawling, unconscious, to the floor.

The second thug watched his friend fall to the ground with disbelief, then charged at Eteka with his machete. The blade flashed as the man took a swipe at Eteka's head. Eteka ducked and kicked him in the knee, dropping the man to his knees with a crunch of breaking bone, then grabbed his head and gave him a jumping knee

---

[1] "Yo, where is he?"

[2] "I don't know, but I think he went that way. Move slow."

to his temple, slamming his head into the pillar with a cloud of dust and concrete particles. As he tried to stand up, Eteka kicked him as hard as he could on his chin, shattering the man's jawbone.

Eteka caught his breath and grimaced from the pain from the gunshot wound to his side, then began to limp toward Arewa when he heard a soft sound behind him—the scuff of a shoe crossing the floor. He grabbed an AK from one of the thug's bodies and slowly turned around. Without warning, Eteka took a powerful blow to his side that knocked the gun out of his hand and threw him to the ground. Eteka quickly scrambled to his feet as Pacman emerged from the darkness and kicked the AK away. Pacman was dressed in a short-sleeved shirt, buttons open, and black trousers, with his long dreads tied into a ponytail. Each man sized up the other.

"Hello, Pacman."

"Whaapm,[1] bredren," Pacman replied cordially in his Jamaican patois as he took off his shirt and exposed his ripped upper body and his voodoo charm, the gold chain with animal hair.

"This is what it's come to, eh?" Eteka asked as he took off his suit coat and rolled up his shirt sleeves.

"Sorry about your woman," Pacman said as he whipped out a large knife from his side sheath. "But we gotta do what we gotta do."

"No weapons. We can settle this like men."

Pacman thought about it, eyed the spreading red wound on Eteka's side, nodded, and threw the knife to the ground as they

---

[1] Jamaican Patois greeting: "What's up?"

began to circle each other. Pacman started to perform the ginga, a traditional fighting stance, rocking back and forth as he circled Eteka. Following Pacman's snakelike movements, Eteka got into a southpaw stance. Pacman rolled and threw a sweeping kick, which Eteka dodged. The Jamaican threw another sweeping kick and followed it with a straight kick which caught Eteka in his chest, sending him a few steps backwards. Eteka stepped back and kept his eyes on his opponent as he dusted Pacman's footprint off his shirt. Pacman continued to rock back and forth in the ginga, then performed an inverted Aú sem Mão[1] at Eteka. Eteka dodged the attack while Pacman landed on his feet and kept his back to his opponent. Eteka fell for the bait and charged at the Jamaican. Pacman threw out a reverse kick that caught Eteka square in the chest, and followed the kick with an S-Dobrado[2] that swept Eteka off his feet and sent him flying to the ground.

Pacman spun to his feet and resumed his ginga. Eteka stood up and clenched his fists. He had so much adrenaline pumping through his system that he felt nothing from the scrapes and grazes of previous injuries—even the bullet wound on his side had faded to so much background noise.

---

[1] The Aú sem Mão is an advanced Capoeira move which is essentially a cartwheel with no hands.
[2] The S-Dobrado is another advanced Capoeira move which is a ground sweep that rolls into a spring backflip.

PACMAN

"WE GOTTA DO WHAT
WE GOTTA DO"

ETEKA
RISE OF THE IMAMBA

He had to finish his opponent off fast, before blood loss claimed him. Every second wasted was a death sentence to Arewa. He got into his southpaw stance again and threw a jab at Pacman, but Pacman was so low that the punch was ineffective. Eteka threw a powerful right hook, but Pacman rolled away from it and countered with a powerful roundhouse kick that sent Eteka reeling headfirst into a wall.

Eteka felt pain surge through his head and neck as he dropped to one knee. A trickle of blood oozed from his forehead as his vision got blurry. Pacman approached, and Eteka stood up with clenched fists. He timed Pacman's movements, watching him sway left and right—a cobra waiting to strike. Eteka threw a lead left jab followed by a powerful right hook and a right knee. Pacman successfully spun away from the jab and leaned back to evade the right hook, but he did not see the right knee coming. Eteka felt some ribs break as his knee dug deep into Pacman's side. The Jamaican let out a howl of pain as Eteka kneed him again, trying to drive the broken ribs into the man's lungs.

Eteka summoned all his remaining strength and picked Pacman up. Carrying Pacman on his shoulders, he let out a loud shout and ran toward a nearby pillar, slamming into it and knocking the wind out of Pacman, who slumped to the ground. Eteka threw a series of punches at Pacman's face, enraged by Arewa's injury and how Oga had lied to him. After a few minutes he stood up, out of breath, as Pacman's body slumped in front of him, his face a bloody mess. Eteka's fists were swollen from hitting Pacman, and blood covered his hands and shirt. He walked groggily toward his discarded AK-47, but before he could pick it up, he heard a gun cock.

Eteka looked up, right into the muzzle of a shotgun held by Proditor. Proditor looked at Eteka with menace, his finger on the trigger. Then he grinned and shook his head.

"Too many Imamba don die today," Proditor said, lowering his weapon and looking at Pacman's inert body. "Today I go lef you make you commot. But ma guy, if I see you again, you go die. [1]"

He turned and walked away, leaving Eteka panting and sweating, trying to fight off the dizziness of blood loss and the adrenaline leaving his system. Eteka walked over to an open window overlooking the front of the building and watched Proditor. Proditor opened the car door, and after pausing to look up at Eteka one last

---

[1] "Too many Imamba have died today. Today I'll let you go, but if I see you again, you'll die."

time, he got in, revved up the car, and reversed out of the warehouse parking lot. Then it was quiet.

Eteka turned around and made his way to where he had left Arewa, hoping against hope, but she was lifeless. Her skin had gone cool and stiff, and the blood had clotted around her neck and mouth. Her eyes stared into space blankly, filmed over. Eteka shook her, checking for her pulse over and over again, hoping it would somehow come back, now that they were safe.

"Arewa! Arewa! Arewa! Please," he whispered hoarsely as tears fell from his eyes, but she was gone, far away and never to return. He held her in his arms and wept for hours, her once warm, pliant body now cooling and stiffening. He buried her that same night outside the warehouse, digging a makeshift grave with a discarded scrap of metal that cut his hands until the blood ran down into the ground around her, mingling with hers.

Eteka arrived in Ibadan a day and a half later. The little money he'd had on him had barely managed to get him across Nigeria, but in the end, it was enough. He was a tired mess, emotionally, physically, and mentally. Arewa's death had taken its toll, and he wept in anger for much of the trip to his uncle's place. It seemed that any good thing or person around him was doomed.

It was around 9 p.m. when Eteka's danfo dropped him off on the corner of Oladele's street. Normally around this time the street would be filled with the usual street vendors selling their wares, but tonight police officers patrolled the street in pairs, talking in low voices and keeping a sharp lookout for trouble. Eteka, tired, dirty, and in pain, limped toward the house. The gunshot wound in his side was still fresh and needed medical attention. He had managed to patch it up with a roll of duct tape that he'd found in Arewa's abandoned car, but the combination of sweat and unavoidable dirt had begun to infect the wound. The edges of the wound were red and puffy, and the wound itself had started to leak a clear fluid and smell. He was a real mess, with visible bruises and cuts, bloodstains all over the tattered remains of his suit. Two policemen, dressed in the traditional black and green Nigerian police uniforms, noticed the limping, exhausted mercenary approaching the house. They drew their weapons and walked up to Eteka.

"What's your business here?" one of the policemen asked in a thick Yoruba accent. The other cocked his weapon. "You are not allowed in this area."

"I am here to see my uncle. This is his house."

"My friend, you don't sabi English? I SAID COMMOT![1]" the same officer yelled in pidgin.

"I said I'm here to see my uncle. Please," an exhausted Eteka replied, swaying on his feet.

"Wait!"

Eteka looked up. Standing by the gate was Faruk, one of Oladele's students. His eyes were swollen from crying, and his face was drawn. Something was wrong.

"Please, officer, he was a friend of Oluko's. He is fine."

---

[1] "I said get lost!"

"Give me sumtin' small and he'll be fine, abi?" the policeman replied as he opened his hand and smiled. Faruk exchanged looks with both policemen, and then reluctantly shoved twenty nairas into the policeman's hand. The policeman smiled again, gave Eteka one last look, and left.

"Sorry about that," Faruk said as he walked up to Eteka. "You look really bad."

"I'll be fine. What are all these police doing here? And where is my uncle?"

Faruk, unable to control himself, sat down on a nearby stoop and began to weep.

"Faruk, what's going on?"

"I'm very sorry. But Oluko, he was…"

"Spit it out!"

"He's dead. Some guys came here the day you left and killed him."

Faruk's words felt like a dagger through his heart. Eteka suddenly felt sick to his stomach, and slumped to the ground. Why was this happening to him? In the span of only a few days, he had lost the two most important people in his life. He tried to say something, but he couldn't—the words were just not there. This was worse than any physical beating he had ever taken. Everything he had hoped to do with his Uncle Oladele—rekindle their relationship, learn about his father, work with him on his writing projects, and find peace in this life—had been taken from him. After so many years, he had come so close to finding peace and it was as if he had been cheated, robbed of the experience. Eteka cried as he knelt on the road, broken.

"I am sorry. I am so sorry. He was a father to us all," Faruk said, wiping tears from his own eyes. "No one knows why they attacked Oluko, he was such a good man. They attacked Isiaka and two other policemen as well. Isiaka was the only survivor."

"Where is Isiaka now?"

"At the hospital. I went to see him yesterday. He took a gunshot wound to the head and a few to his body. He is in critical condition."

After the tears stopped, Eteka simply knelt there on the ground. There was nothing left. He had been robbed of his dreams, robbed by the same people responsible for his father and mother's murders and all the lies he had been fed.

"I looked through his study yesterday after the police finished ransacking it and I found his will," Faruk said. "You were listed as the sole benefactor of all his estates, including the school."

"Thank you."

"You're welcome. I will be organizing a funeral for him as well—I hope that's okay. There should be a lot of people attending. It'll probably be in about two weeks. And I'll be saving most of his journals, including his unreleased works. Since you are the boss now, you will have to guide our decision making with the publisher, and the leadership meetings he had with us."

"Me? I don't know anything about publishing or leadership. I am a fighter—I kill people."

"I can teach you."

Oladele's endeavors were not on Eteka's mind at the moment. Arewa's final request to him was to save her brother in New York. He would have to worry about his uncle's business later—this was a matter of life and death.

"I need some money. What do you have?"

"Er, here, take this," Faruk replied, handing Eteka some naira bills with a surprised expression. "May I ask what the money is for?"

"I have to leave for Lagos as soon as possible. I leave my uncle's business to you for now."

"Wait, you can't be serious. Your uncle just died, and you're leaving?"

"Yes," Eteka said. "There are some things I have to take care of. I'll see you when I get back."

"And when will that be?"

"Soon."

Faruk grabbed Eteka's arm. "Listen, I know I do not know you that well, but I feel you should at least stay behind for a day or two. Please, there are some matters here that require your attention. Like organizing his funeral and some paperwork. You can't just leave."

"You handle everything. I have to go, time is not on my side," Eteka replied, shrugging Faruk's hand off.

Faruk watched as the mercenary limped away.

REDEMPTION

John F. Kennedy International Airport. Jamaica, New York, NY.
United States. 1990.

  Eteka's flight touched down at JFK at 2:30 p.m. sharp. He had slept for most of the flight, and he felt slightly rejuvenated as he made his way through customs and baggage claim. His fake passport had gotten him through with no delays, but unlike back home, he couldn't bring any weapons with him. He proceeded slowly in the line for foreign nationals to get his fingerprint scanned. The last time he'd been in New York he hadn't had to worry about being picked up by security, as Omega had had all the appropriate arrangements in place. But now he was certain that he wouldn't be afforded that luxury anymore. There were even armed guards patrolling the airport. Perhaps it was a good thing he hadn't tried to sneak any weapons through customs.

  The Imamba had a safe house in Manhattan in an upscale apartment overlooking Central Park, and he was certain there would be a good supply of weapons and cash there. But there was no telling if Mokin, Cyrus, or any other Imamba would be there as well. Once he was armed, Eteka had to stop them from hurting Arewa's brother. He knew the concert was scheduled to take place on this day, but he had no idea where.

After leaving the airport, Eteka took the E train to the Port Authority in Manhattan. Anger consumed him as he thought about the Imamba. He would have to stop them, every single one. As Eteka walked through the subway terminals, he spotted many of New York's unknown musicians playing instruments or singing for money from passersby. He passed by a pretty African-American girl singing Sade's "I Never Thought I'd See the Day," and a lump formed in his throat. Her song reminded him of that night in Abuja when he and Arewa had gone on their first date. The singer had a captivating voice and had drawn a small crowd. Her eyes made contact with his, and she smiled at him. Eteka watched her and, for a brief moment, he could see Arewa's face in place of hers. The lump in his throat got heavier. There was no time to get emotional. After tossing a few dollars in the girl's guitar case, he turned and walked out of the Port Authority onto 42nd Street.

The crisp autumn air felt good against his face as he looked down at his watch. It was almost four o'clock, and he was running out of time—he still didn't know when the concert would start, and he was unarmed and nearly out of money. Eteka hailed a cab and made his way from the heart of Manhattan to the Upper West Side. The cab dropped him off in front of an elegant apartment building with stylized art deco glass and metal doors. Eteka walked in past the doorman, but the front desk clerk stopped him on his way to the elevator.

"Hello, sir. Is someone expecting you?" she asked with a smile, revealing a full set of braces. They matched her outfit, alternating pink and purple elastics to go with her pink and purple sweater.

"Just here to see an old friend," Eteka replied pleasantly. He did not want the girl to call upstairs and alert anyone to his presence.

"Which apartment, sir?"

"12F."

"Okay, sir. Please take a seat in the waiting area, I'll have to call upstairs to verify. Your name, please?" she asked with a hint of steel in her voice.

"It's a surprise, I'm an old friend. Is there any way you could just let me up?"

"No, sir, that's against the building's security policy. If you have a telephone number for your friend, perhaps you could call them and tell them you're here?"

"No, it's okay. Thank you," Eteka replied, walking out of the building. Restaurants and shops up and down the street were bustling with activity, and Hispanic nannies watched a group of children racing around on a nearby playground. Eteka walked around the building, each step aggravating the slow-healing gunshot wound in his side. He spotted a door leading to the rear entrance of the building, which was locked.

Damn. Eteka sat down on some stairs near the rear entrance just as the door opened and an elderly white woman stepped outside with some bags of trash. She smiled at Eteka as she threw the trash into a nearby dumpster.

"Trying to get in?" she asked as she held the door open for him.

"Yes, ma'am. Thank you."

Eteka stepped into the building and walked past a laundry room to the elevator. His heart began to race as he stepped into the elevator with the old woman and pressed the button for the 12th floor. Eteka leaned against the rear wall as the elevator climbed, clenching his jaw in preparation for battle. The elevator stopped on the 11th floor, and the old woman stepped out. She turned around and smiled at Eteka, her pale blue eyes fixing on his face.

"You be careful now, young man."

"Thanks. You, too."

"I mean what I said," she replied as the elevator doors closed. He frowned at her oddly appropriate admonition. The elevator continued up and finally stopped on the 12th floor. The doors opened and he walked down a long hallway toward apartment 12F. Faint chatter and television commentary came from the apartments as he passed. The gunshot wound in his side still hurt, but he ignored the pain as he arrived at door 12F in the middle of the hall.

Eteka put his ear against the door to listen for any sound. Nothing. He quietly turned the doorknob, but the door was locked.

Holding the doorknob, he leaned back and slammed his shoulder into the door twice, breaking it open. The apartment appeared to be empty, the only movement coming from silk curtains dancing in front of the open windows. A kitchen with a stocked mini bar was just inside the door. Past that was the living room, filled with a large-screen television, a sound system, and a Sega Genesis. Elaborate, hand-carved African tribal masks hung on the walls, and a large glass table filled the center of the living room. The remains of a hand-rolled blunt sat in an ashtray on the glass table, next to a fine dusting of white powder.

After scanning the living room, Eteka checked out the two bedrooms. The first was empty, and the bed had not been made. By the bed was a case containing a shotgun, two machine guns, a revolver, duct tape, and bullets. Eteka slipped the pistol into his pocket and moved into the second room. There was a figure lying under the covers, and he drew out the pistol as he moved slowly toward the bed. The person rolled over, unaware of Eteka's presence. Eteka grabbed the edge of the sheets and threw them off the figure, ready to blast whoever was underneath, but to his surprise he found the naked body of a richly curved Hispanic woman with long black hair. She woke up with a start and froze when she saw Eteka with his gun pointed at her. Her pupils were dilated and her skin sweaty—sleeping off the effects of too many party drugs, Eteka imagined.

"Who are you?" Eteka demanded.

She continued to stare at him in shock and her mouth began to tremble, her full lips quivering with fear. He stepped closer and slapped her lightly across the face.

"Who are you?" Eteka repeated.

"Uh…"

"Answer the question."

"My, my name is Mariella," she replied with a thick Spanish accent.

"What are you doing here, Mariella?"

"I was called by the guys who stay here."

"You're a prostitute?" Eteka asked.

"An escort, yes."

Eteka lowered his weapon and looked around the room. It was a mess, and a few used condoms lay on the floor. Next to the condoms lay a crumpled gold sequined dress, a push-up bra, and a pair of thong panties.

"Where are the guys now?"

"I don't know. One of them said somethin' about going to a show."

"Did they tell you where the show is happening?"

"No. But I think there's a flyer for it in the bathroom. One of the guys took me in there last night. Oh, my head hurts," she said, wincing.

Eteka walked into the bathroom, and just as she'd said, a flyer for the concert was on the floor. The concert was scheduled to start at 6 p.m. and was being held at Pier 26 by the Hudson River. As

Eteka studied the flyer, the naked woman walked up to the bathroom door. She leaned against the doorframe and pulled her shoulders back to show her heavy breasts to their best advantage.

"Are you their friend, papi? If you wanna have some fun with me I can get cleaned up and hook you up at a discount," she said, licking her lips.

"Put your clothes on and get out," Eteka said without looking at her.

The girl rolled her eyes at Eteka. She quickly put on her clothes, muttering under her breath in Spanish, and left the apartment, slamming the broken door behind her, though it wouldn't latch. Eteka put the flyer in his pocket and stepped out of the bathroom. It was almost five, and he knew he was running out of time. Since Arewa's brother was the main act, he would probably start his show around six-thirty after someone else opened, but with the Imamba after him, anything was possible.

A red stain colored Eteka's shirt, and he realized he had to change the dressing around the wound on his side—it had been too long. He stepped back into the bathroom and found a full medical kit in a drawer. After applying fresh gauze and antibiotic ointment and taping it in place, he cocked his gun. As he opened the door to head out, he was met by Mokin. Eteka took a step back as Mokin glared down at him. Mokin's powerful frame towered over Eteka, and the son of Yisa had to look up to see into the giant's eyes.

Damn. Mokin grabbed Eteka's gun-bearing hand with his left hand and his throat with his right. The vice grip around Eteka's throat tightened as he lifted Eteka off the ground effortlessly and stepped back into the apartment, carrying his opponent. Eteka choked, his legs flailing around like a helpless child's. Mokin studied Eteka expressionlessly as he squeezed Eteka's gun-holding hand so hard that Eteka dropped the weapon, his bones crunching under the strain. With a little grunt, the large man threw Eteka across the kitchen, slamming him headfirst into the stainless-steel refrigerator. Eteka winced as he felt a welt swell on his forehead.

For the next few minutes, Mokin threw Eteka around like a rag doll, slamming him into the apartment's walls and onto furniture. Shards of glass and wood splinters cut through Eteka's clothes and into his already battered skin. He was bloodied from the hits, and his attempts to shake off Mokin had no effect. Sporadically, Mokin would hold Eteka's head up to a wall's surface, then slam his fist into the side of Eteka's face, driving the smaller man's face through the wall. His knuckles felt like the cold, hard surface of a hammer— utterly impervious to injury.

The room swam in front of Eteka. His left eye was nearly swollen shut, and he tasted blood. Mokin took a break from pulverizing Eteka and threw him effortlessly across the room. Eteka coughed blood onto the ground and twitched in pain as Mokin calmly stood still and looked at him. The silent killer had a look on his face that reminded Eteka of a cat's playful sadism with a small mouse. Eteka watched his opponent with his one good eye. What could he possibly do to stop this monster? Eteka could barely move, and his head began to feel numb. Sharp pains ran through his whole

MOKIN

"..."

ETEKA
RISE OF THE IMAMBA

body, and the broken glass on the floor cut his fingers as he tried to prop himself up. He watched helplessly as Mokin calmly walked into the kitchen, stalking his prey.

Eteka had to think fast. With his good eye, he frantically scanned the area around him. The gun he'd been carrying earlier was on the ground a few feet away, but there was no way he could reach it before Mokin got to him.

Eteka noticed a thin, pointed piece of glass by his feet, part of the broken coffee table. He picked it up and concealed it in his sleeve as Mokin reappeared from the kitchen. In the giant's hand was a large cleaving knife, its sharp edge gleaming. Eteka did not want to imagine what he planned on using it for, and knew he had to act fast.

Mokin stepped up to him, picked him up with one hand, and propped him up against a wall. His small, bloodshot eyes studied Eteka's weakened state. Satisfied that Eteka was too weak to resist, he raised the cleaving knife as he prepared to split Eteka's head open. With his useful eye, Eteka watched the blade rise until it reached its apex, and then he swung the concealed glass in his sleeve with all his strength at Mokin's head. The pointed shard went directly into Mokin's ear, penetrating deep into his eardrum. The giant reeled back in pain and let out a strangled squeal, similar to that of a pig being slaughtered. He clutched his ear and howled in pain, releasing Eteka from his powerful grip.

Eteka fell to the ground, and with his remaining strength he scuttled toward the gun lying a few feet away. Mokin held the side of his head as blood spurted out of the wound in his ear. When he saw Eteka reaching for the gun, he grabbed the cleaving knife off the floor and charged toward Eteka.

Eteka grabbed the revolver and turned to face Mokin. His back was against a wall in the kitchen as Mokin's menacing figure approached. Eteka pointed the gun at his enemy and began to fire off rounds. Each shot slowed down Mokin's advance, but he kept on coming, the cleaving knife in his hand stained with the blood from his ear.

The bullets tore away at Mokin's clothes, drenching his body in blood and open wounds, but he kept on coming, and was only a few feet away from Eteka now. Mokin shook as the bullet wounds took their toll on his body, but he managed to stand over Eteka. He raised the cleaving knife in his hand to strike. Eteka knew he'd be dead if he didn't make this last shot count. He pointed the gun at Mokin's head and squeezed the trigger.

The bullet hit Mokin in the center of his forehead. The shot knocked his head backward, and pieces of his brain matter spattered the room. He took a step backward, the hand with the cleaving knife still in the air, wobbled for a moment, and then came crashing down on top of Eteka. Eteka rolled out of the way, just narrowly missing the knife in Mokin's hand. The giant fell facedown with a loud thud, twitched a few times, and then remained still.

Eteka groaned as he shoved Mokin's huge body off of him. His head felt light and in intense pain at the same time. He could still taste Mokin's knuckles mixed with the blood from his busted lip. His left eye had swollen completely shut, he had cuts all over his face and body, and the gunshot wound from before had reopened. He stood up gingerly and made his way across the apartment toward the bathroom. The apartment was a mess: destroyed windows, broken tables, glass, and pieces of wall littered the floor.

Eteka had to move fast. The concert would have started by now, and the cops would surely arrive at any moment. After quickly cleaning the blood off his face in the bathroom sink, he applied some rubbing alcohol to his cuts and bruises. He picked up a new shirt from the other room's closet, wrapped some ice in a paper towel, grabbed the concert flyer, and stepped out of the apartment. The neighbors peeked through their chained doorways and peepholes at Eteka as he limped down the hallway, closing their doors as he passed. He staggered into the elevator and went down to the first floor.

In the lobby, two policemen were questioning some residents, one of whom was the elderly woman who had let him into the building. She was describing the gunshots and fighting she had heard. Eteka stepped back into the elevator and pressed the button for the basement. The elevator opened in the basement, and he limped down the narrow hallway past the laundry room to the exit. It was now around six-fifteen, and darkness was falling.

Eteka limped to the street and hailed a cab. As he got in, he could see more police cars pulling up to the apartment building and policemen sealing off the area. He ducked down in the car as the cab driver, a young Indian man, looked at him in the rearview mirror.

"Where are you headed, sir?"

"Pier 26. The faster the better."

The cab driver studied Eteka's battered face and then looked back at the cops. Obviously making a connection between the two, he paused for a second and kept his eyes on Eteka, who met his gaze.

"Please go," Eteka requested desperately.

The cab driver took one last look at the cops behind him and drove off, mumbling under his breath at his peculiar passenger. The car sped through Manhattan before finally arriving at the pier ten minutes later. Eteka paid the cab driver, tipping him as much as he dared, and stepped out of the car. The venue was packed with tourists and fans of the various bands that were set to perform. Throngs of people lined the large boardwalk, and in the distance stood a large stage. Behind the stage flowed the Hudson River, beautifully illuminated by the boardwalk lights and boats. A band was already performing, and the lively crowd erupted in deafening cheers every few seconds.

As Eteka looked around, he spotted a few people walking around with T-shirts bearing Fallal's name. Huge posters of Fallal also decorated the space. Eteka shoved his way through the people toward the entrance, trying to imagine where Cyrus would be. If it was going to be a hit, then it wouldn't be out in the open. Cyrus was too smart for that. Eteka looked around and spotted a large building overlooking the stage.

There, Eteka thought to himself, and he pushed his way toward the building. A female security guard stood at the entrance of the building, and he knew there was no way he would get past her looking the way he did. Then, a van from a catering company called E-Vance Catering pulled up. Two young men in catering uniforms stepped out and wheeled a cart stocked with snacks and drinks from the van. They headed toward the door with the security guard and were let in.

Eteka watched them disappear into the building, then turned his attention to the parked van. He walked up to the van and peeked in through a window. There were extra catering uniforms and some food in the back seat. He tried the back door, and surprisingly it was open. He quickly grabbed a catering jacket and some food on a tray and approached the same security guard.

"Yes?"

"Hi, I'm with E-Vance Catering," Eteka replied politely.

The security guard studied him, taking an extra moment to look at Eteka's battered face. "They already brought the food for the performers."

"Yes, I have to help them set up the food stand for the concert. I was just fixing a few things in the van."

"What happened to your face?"

"I got in a fight before I came to work," Eteka replied, smiling as disarmingly as possible.

The security guard studied Eteka for another brief moment. "Hold on, I'll have to check with my manager," she said as she picked up a walkie-talkie on her waist. She called for her manager, but got no response.

"Dammit. Okay, go ahead," the guard said. "Down the hall, first door on the left—that's where they're setting up," she said as she stepped aside and let Eteka into the building.

Thanking the guard, Eteka walked down the hall. When he was out of sight, he walked past the catering room. He felt a lot of pain from the beating he'd taken from Mokin, but he couldn't be weak now—he had to find Cyrus. Somewhere in this building, he was certain that Cyrus was getting ready to murder Arewa's brother, if he hadn't done so already. He knew that Arewa's brother would be set to perform at any moment.

I have to think like him. What would I do if I came here for the same mission?

"Ladies and gentlemen!" Eteka heard the concert's MC shout through the wall. "The moment you've been waiting for is finally here! Please welcome to the stage your favorite, Africa's native son, FALLAL!"

Outside, the crowd erupted as Fallal came onto the stage. Fallal being out in the open on stage meant Cyrus could pick him off very easily. Eteka knew he had to find Cyrus quickly. He looked around as caterers and a few production engineers scuttled around him. Then he noticed some movement through a window on the floor above him. Someone was fidgeting in a back office that overlooked the stage outside. Could it be? Eteka walked up to a door below the office. On the other side, he found himself looking up a long flight of stairs. He ran up them as fast as he could, fighting the pain in his side. At the top of the stairs was a door labeled SECURITY. It was slightly ajar, and Eteka silently stepped up to it. He took deep breath and slowly pushed it open.

Sprawled on the floor was the unlucky security guard. Blood trickled from a slash around his throat, and his eyes stared fearfully into space. The room was filled with television monitors and switches. Cyrus was kneeling at the opposite end of the room loading a sniper rifle in front of a large glass window that overlooked the concert happening down below. He was dressed in a black suit with no tie and had cut a hole in the window for his rifle. A lit blunt sat on a desk next to Cyrus, and its smell filled the room. He looked up as Eteka entered.

"Good to see you, brother," Cyrus said as he returned to loading the rifle. Eteka took a step closer.

"You don't have to do this, Cyrus."

Cyrus glanced at Eteka. He took a drag from the blunt and replaced it on the desk next to him.

"You look like shit," Cyrus said with a grin. "I'll assume that you had a nice meeting with Mokin. And I'll also assume that Mokin is dead, since you managed to make it this far. Impressive. I didn't think anyone could defeat Mokin. Or maybe you didn't run into him—maybe you got hit by a truck instead."

"I did run into Mokin, and he's dead."

"Shame," Cyrus sighed. "I liked Mokin, he did not complicate things. He was obedient, did not talk, and followed orders—the ideal soldier. You could have learned a lot from him, Eteka," Cyrus said as he scratched the menacing scar that ran across his eye.

"Brother, we've been tricked."

"We? Or you?" Cyrus replied as he finished loading the rifle and set it against a wall. He picked up the lit blunt and took another drag from it. "I heard about you and how you've turned your back on us."

"I had to, brother."

"A foolish decision. Why? Because of some slut you met in Nigeria?" Cyrus asked, crossing his arms. "Omega told me over the phone. I was disappointed. Are you so weak that you let a bitch control you? No pussy is that good!"

"She had nothing to do with my decision. Omega and Oga are responsible for killing my parents."

"Bullshit. Those men took us in when we had nowhere to go."

"It's true."

"It's true? What is truth, Eteka? Stories you've heard from witches and old men? Anyone can make up stories. Your reality is what you had, with us. I thought you were smarter than that," Cyrus replied with a laugh as he glanced out the window at Fallal down below. Fallal seemed happy as he danced around the stage, oblivious to the fact that his sister was dead in Nigeria and his own fate was being decided upstairs.

"You've always been a bit soft, Eteka," Cyrus said. "Always been the one to stick to the plan and not take any risks. Yet you chose not to stick to the plan when it counted. D'you know how much I'm getting for this hit? Seventy thousand dollars, cash. One more payday and I can move up in the brotherhood. I won't have to go on these hits anymore. I will be able to make decisions, like Oga and Omega. You think I'll let you get in the way of that?"

"Don't do this, Cyrus. That guy is young enough to be your brother. He may even have a son, like you."

Cyrus flinched. He bowed his head briefly, then, as if shrugging off his conscience, he shook his head and reached for his rifle. "And who is this singer to you? He's insignificant, just another of the many that we kill. He means nothing to you."

"Let me be the judge of that."

"I don't know what happened to you since we last saw each other, but you need to wake up and get back to business. You've caused enough trouble as it is."

"I'm serious, brother, I can't let you kill him," Eteka replied as he took a step closer. His body ached. Cyrus clenched his jaw and cocked the sniper rifle.

"I don't want to hurt you, brother. Don't think you can get in my way. You're no match for me, especially in your current condition. I'll do you a favor and let you live. If you want us to stop being brothers, so be it. Just walk out that door, and never let me see you again," Cyrus said as he got down on one knee and aimed the rifle.

Eteka lunged at Cyrus and knocked him off his feet. Both men fell to the ground, the impact sending a sharp pain through Eteka's side.

"You fool!" Cyrus shouted as he shoved the weakened Eteka off of him.

Eteka grabbed Cyrus's leg as he tried to stand, and both men wrestled around the security booth, knocking over tables, chairs, and folders filled with loose paper. Then, Cyrus shoved Eteka against a wall and put a knife to his throat. The sharp edge of the cold blade nicked at Eteka's skin, releasing a small trickle of blood.

"Don't make me kill you, brother," he said as he stared Eteka directly in the eyes. "We have fought many battles together. I would hate to take your life. Please leave, now."

CYRUS

"JUST WALK OUT THAT DOOR.
AND NEVER LET ME
SEE YOU AGAIN."

ETEKA
RISE OF THE IMAMBA

He released Eteka, threw him to the ground and got back into his sniper position. Eteka watched him walk off. He wanted to get up, but his weakened body told him to stay put—he had nothing left. Then he thought of Arewa. Her last wish was for him to save her brother. He had to stop Cyrus, at any cost.

Eteka summoned his entire will and stood up. As Cyrus fixed his aim on Fallal, Eteka lunged at him again and tackled him to the ground. Cyrus lost his temper and threw Eteka off him. He picked Eteka up, punched him in the face, violently shoved his head into a wall, and threw him over a table into some computers nearby. Eteka fell to the ground with a loud crash as monitors, desktop units, and printers came crashing down on him. The bandage over his head was knocked askew and the gunshot wound in his side throbbed with pain.

Cyrus climbed over the desk and effortlessly picked Eteka up by his collar. The look of rage on Cyrus's face was only enhanced by the scar that ran across his eye.

"I warned you," he said in a cold tone as he threw an elbow into Eteka's face, knocking out a few of his teeth. The impact had Eteka seeing stars. Cyrus kneed him in the groin, doubling Eteka over in pain while Cyrus held him up.

"I gave you a chance to leave. I'm not as stupid as Mokin, brother. I do not know why he couldn't finish you off, but I will rectify his mistake," he said, throwing Eteka to the ground. The crowd was cheering for Fallal as Cyrus drew his gun and pointed it at the fallen warrior. Eteka, bloodied and beaten, could barely lift his head.

"I gave you a chance," Cyrus repeated, shaking his head as he stood by the window overlooking the concert.

"You don't h-have t-to d-do this, brother," Eteka said softly as he slowly raised a hand at his former comrade.

"You've left me no choice. You turned your back on me and our Imamba brothers, and you must pay," Cyrus replied, cocking the gun.

Eteka's whole life flashed before his eyes. He looked one last time at Cyrus and closed his eyes. He had failed Arewa, and it was all over. He hoped that she forgave him, wherever her spirit had gone.

At that moment, the door of the security booth crashed open and three NYPD officers filed into the room, guns drawn. Noting the dead body of the security guard, they turned their attention to the two Imamba at the other end of the room. What they saw was a man dressed in black pointing a loaded weapon at a wounded man on the ground. Cyrus did not flinch, keeping his gun on Eteka.

"POLICE! DROP THE GUN! DROP THE GUN!" the officers screamed as they trained their weapons on Cyrus. Cyrus grinned and winked at Eteka.

"It seems I'm in a tight situation… brother."

"It-it-it d-doesn't have to end here, brother," Eteka replied in pain. "Drop your weapon, we can fix this."

Cyrus didn't respond, and the officers continued to scream at him to lower his weapon, inching forward. Cyrus slowly lowered his weapon and turned his head toward the concert downstairs. The band was still playing, and the crowd was as loud as ever, oblivious to the drama playing out in the security booth above.

"DROP THE GUN, NOW!" the NYPD officers continued to scream as they got closer.

"I came here on a mission and I will carry it out. That is what we Imamba do," Cyrus said calmly, looking back at the police officers.

"Don't be foolish, brother. Your juju charm won't help you here," Eteka replied, knowing that Cyrus would attempt to take out the officers and then complete his mission. Cyrus smiled again and leaned over to kiss the gold ring on his finger. His grip tightened around the gun in his hand as he gave Eteka one last look.

"What's life without a little risk, eh?" He grinned as he winked at Eteka. "I'll see you in Hell." He spun around and opened fire at the officers. Two rounds caught one policeman in the chest, throwing him to the ground. The other officers opened fire, and their shots tore through Cyrus's body.

Cyrus fell back against the large window overlooking the concert. A shot from the police pierced the glass and his body crashed through it, falling 40 feet to the stage below. As Cyrus fell through the window, the battered Eteka reached for his legs, but he was too weak, and he could only watch helplessly as his Imamba brother sailed through the air toward the crowd below. Cyrus slammed onto the stage, right next to Fallal. Blood splattered the singer, who froze in horror.

The crowd fell into a shocked silence as Cyrus's bloody body twitched for a moment, then remained still. More NYPD officers filed onto the stage and surrounded the body as the crowd grew frantic. People screamed, panic erupted, and the police began to file people out of the building. Eteka looked down at Cyrus's body. He hadn't wanted him to die, at least not this way.

Two police officers sat Eteka down as more officers charged into the security booth, and a police photographer began to take pictures of the crime scene. A tall man in a suit walked into the room, and after having a word with a few NYPD officers, he walked over to Eteka.

"Hello. My name is Agent Grange. I'm with the CIA," the man said, studying Eteka. He was a white man, clean-shaven, with greying hair and wrinkles around his eyes. Eteka looked at him without responding. Grange smiled. "I know all about you, Eteka."

He had Eteka's attention. "How do you know my name?"

"I've been waiting a long time to meet you," Grange said. "Let's just say I have unfinished business with Omega. I also knew your father, albeit very briefly."

"How do you know my father?"

"We can get into all that later. You are a very important piece in a big puzzle, and we need your help."

"What are you talking about?"

"We can talk later, after you've had your wounds looked at," Agent Grange said as he waved a paramedic and two policemen over. They picked Eteka up off the ground and escorted him downstairs. Camera flashes blinded him as they made their way through the large crowd on the boardwalk on the pier. Eteka caught a glimpse of Cyrus's body being zipped into a body bag. The gold ring that Cyrus wore as a juju charm was stripped from his hand and placed in a plastic bag by a police officer. So much for magical invincibility.

Eteka watched with a heavy heart as they put his brother's body in the back of a waiting police van. In the distance, he saw Fallal being escorted into a limousine by a bodyguard. Fallal paused as he entered the limo and exchanged looks with Eteka. There was no way to tell if he knew about his sister's fate, but as both men locked eyes, the rest of the world seemed to freeze around them. Then, the singer nodded at the fighter and disappeared into the limo.

Eteka was led past a swarm of reporters to a waiting ambulance. He was ushered into the vehicle, followed by three police officers and the medic. He was made to lie down on a stretcher as the medic began her work, cleaning his wounds and patching Eteka up. Outside, police sirens blared amidst all the commotion.

Finally, Eteka was escorted to a waiting police car. The future was uncertain, and he had no idea what intentions the Americans had for him. But that was the least of his concerns. He had lost so much, in such a short time. Most of the light in his life had been extinguished, and the men responsible for blowing out the candle were still at large. There was definitely unfinished business on the table.

DISCUSSION QUESTIONS

1. Who was your favorite character, and why?

2. Refer to the Peer Pressure chapter. What real life personality from African history does Judas bring to mind?

3. In your mind, what ideology/concept does Supreme represent?

4. In your mind, what ideology/concept does Omega represent?

5. In your mind, what ideology/concept does Oluko represent?

6. What do you think was the significance/symbolism between Oladele and Richard Wright's chance meeting in Bandung?

7. Discuss Yisa's internal battle. What was his dilemma?

8. The Cold War era was a unique period in history. Discuss your knowledge of proxy wars fought in the Americas, Asia and on the African continent.

9. Discuss the Bandung Conference of 1955. In retrospect, was it a success?

10. How many times does Anansi reveal himself in the story?

11. At the end of the Father Figure chapter, Anansi expressed interest in Eteka's kinsman. Who is this kinsman?

12. Discuss Amina's dilemma.

13. Refer to the Mob Action chapter. Discuss the possible correlation between mob lynchings in parts of Africa, Latin America, India and the Middle East, and the racist lynchings from America's dark past.

14. Why do you think Anansi approached Isatou?

15. In the Peer Pressure chapter, do you think Yisa shot the peasant?

16. Discuss Oladele's temptation.

17. How many times does the White Witch reveal herself in the story?

18. In the Good Company chapter, refer to the debate between Oluko and the students. Which position (if any) do you agree/disagree with? Discuss.

19. In the No Way Out chapter, why do you think Proditor spared Eteka's life?

20. If you were in Eteka's shoes, would you have believed Oluko? Why or why not?

21. What do you think is next for Eteka?

REFERENCES

Cann, John. *Counterinsurgency in Africa, the Portuguese Way of War*. Greenwood Press, 1997.

Chabal, Patrick. *Amilcar Cabral: Revolutionary Leadership and People's War.* Cambridge University Press, 1983.

Chaliand, Gérard. *Armed Struggle in Africa: With the Guerrillas in "Portuguese" Guinea*. Monthly Review Press, 1969.

Diamond, Jared. *Guns, Germs and Steel: The Fates of Human Societies*. W.W. Norton & Company, 1997.

Gleijeses, Piero. "Moscow's Proxy? Cuba and Africa 1975–1988." *Journal of Cold War Studies* Vol. 8.2 (2006) pp. 3–51.

Jayaprakash, N. D. "India and the Bandung Conference of 1955." *People's Democracy*, 6th ed., March 2005. 3rd ed, June 2010.
http://politicalaffairs.net/article/articleview/1224/1/99.

Nehru, Jawaharlal. Speech to Bandung Conference Political Committee. Bandung Conference. Gedung Merdeka, Bandung, Indonesia. 1955.

Sosrodihardjo, Kusno (Sukarno). Opening Speech at Bandung Conference. Bandung Conference. Gedung Mederka, Bandung, Indonesia. 18th April, 1955.

The University of York. "Race, Faith and UK Policy: A Brief History."
http://www.york.ac.uk/ipup/projects/raceandfaith/discussion/bam-hutchison.html (accessed October 31st, 2012).

Venter, Al J. *War Dog: Fighting Other People's Wars-The Modern Mercenary in Combat*. Casemate Press, 2008.

Westad, Odd Arne. *The Global Cold War.* Cambridge University Press, 2005.

Wright, Richard. *The Color Curtain.* World Publishing Company/Banner Books/University Press of Mississipi, 1956/1995.

Zhukov, Arthur. "In Bandung." *International Affairs*. Associated University Presses: Cranbury, 1955. Page(s): 75–81.

ACKNOWLEDGEMENTS

"I have fought the good fight, I have finished the race, I have kept the faith." – 2 Timothy 4:7

My wonderful wife and my beautiful daughter for all the love, smiles and laughter; my brother Koko for his support over the years; Professor James Cramer for his time, insights, and references (I enjoyed our Hoboken café talks back in 2010); Professor Odd Arne Westad, Professor Jared Diamond and Professor Patrick Chabal (R.I.P.) for sharing your wonderful books with the world and for taking the time to correspond with me; Nick Macharia, my boy Tunde Mendes and his Capoeira family, plus John Kagwa, Kehinde Mendes, Eli, Elvis, and Emma Davis for all the help with translations; Ama Koram for reading through my earlier drafts; Grant Bergland, Sara Barford, and Rebecca McLeod for their professional editorial feedback; my buddy Heather Getzinger for proofreading and priceless feedback; Jonathan Awotwi for our formatting workup session (and the grilled chicken!); DJ Grifta, Shuko, Osunlade, The Geek Squad, CHIMS, Jack Sparrow, C-Sick, Jafu, and Evil Needle—thank you all so much for allowing me to use your amazing music in my promotional videos; Stephen and Jabari for helping me shoot my earlier web promos; Deryl Braun for your amazing artwork, insight, and friendship over the years; every martial arts club and boxing studio I have been affiliated with; every food blogger and musician that has supported my project; every architect/designer that has responded to my queries; the staff of the New York Public Library and the Mid-Manhattan Library at Bryant Park; every Embassy and Consulate that has entertained my queries over the years; all my supporters on social media (shoutout to Ed Tony and Shay Leigh); Mr. Edward Peterson, Jr. for the good strategic conversation when I came down to Texas in 2015; good friends like Chayvonne and Calvin, who have always been there for my family come rain or shine; all the good folks that have and continue to support my work with donations; every reviewer that took a chance with this independent project; every media outlet that has shown me love and given my hustle exposure...

And, of course, you the reader: I thank you for granting me an audience.

About the Author

Ben Hinson is the product of multiple cultures and varied experiences. Born in Nigeria to a Nigerian father and Ghanaian mother, he has also lived in Ghana, England, and numerous locations in the United States. He has worked in the real estate performance analytics, financial prime brokerage, banking, and advertising industries, and has developed out-of-the-box analytical solutions and digital media strategies for many of the world's top brands. His client list has included the likes of JM Smucker's, PNC Bank, Morgan Stanley, Campbell Soup Company, Bank of America, TEVA Pharmaceuticals, DIRECTV, CoverGirl, Heineken, LG Electronics and Mercedes-Benz. In 2010, he founded Musings Press LLC. He is the author/creator of the Eteka series, the GOAT Index, hickamsdictum.com and several collections of lyrical poetry.

WWW.BENHINSON.COM

WWW.FACEBOOK.COM/OFFICIALBENHINSON

PLEASE VISIT BEN'S WEBSITE
AT WWW.BENHINSON.COM, WHERE YOU CAN LEARN
MORE ABOUT ALL THE FEATURED LOCATIONS IN THE
ETEKA UNIVERSE. HISTORICAL OVERVIEWS, RECIPES,
ARCHITECTURAL HIGHLIGHTS, MARTIAL ARTS
TECHNIQUES, AND MORE ARE COVERED, ALL
DESIGNED TO GIVE YOU A TRULY INTERACTIVE
READING EXPERIENCE. ENJOY!

MUSINGS PRESS™

CPSIA information can be obtained
at www.ICGtesting.com
Printed in the USA
LVHW080545310720
661836LV00001B/12